Love Wasn't Enough. . . .

LEITA—She crossed the world yearning for the man she left behind, but there would be others to fire her desire. . . .

BREVE—Love was a luxury he couldn't afford, marriage an unthinkable bond for the man with a secret too dark to share. . . .

STEPHEN—His ambition was as finely chiseled as his face; he and Leita would be the perfect couple. She would be his—no matter what he had to do to win her. . . .

DARCY—She was beautiful, ambitious and cunning—a suitable match for Stephen, who filled her arms but not her thoughts. She had great expectations—and Leita would be her ladder to the top. . . .

JACK—His noble blood could not conceal his ignoble nature. What he couldn't earn he'd steal, who he couldn't love, he'd destroy. . . .

SUSANNA GOOD

BURNING SECRETS

A KANGAROO BOOK
PUBLISHED BY POCKET BOOKS NEW YORK

Distributed in Canada by PaperJacks Ltd., a Licensee
of the trademarks of Simon & Schuster, a division of
Gulf+Western Corporation.

A POCKET BOOKS/RICHARD GALLEN *Original* publication

 POCKET BOOKS, a Simon & Schuster division of
GULF & WESTERN CORPORATION
1230 Avenue of the Americas, New York, N.Y. 10020
In Canada distributed by PaperJacks Ltd.,
330 Steelcase Road, Markham, Ontario.

Copyright © 1979 by Susanna Good

All rights reserved, including the right to reproduce
this book or portions thereof in any form whatsoever
For information address Pocket Books, 1230 Avenue
of the Americas, New York, N.Y. 10020

ISBN: 0-671-83216-6

First Pocket Books printing November, 1979

10 9 8 7 6 5 4 3 2 1

Trademarks registered in the United States and other countries.

Printed in Canada

Chapter 1

GRAY-GREEN LEAVES OF THE TALL CHINESE ELMS HUNG carved in the still heat, high over dragonflies tracing circles in the glassy water of the river. Dr. Jefferson Hardy shortened his stride and looked down at the girl walking beside him. Perspiration dampened the curling wisps of red-gold hair at her temples and ran glistening between the fullness of her breasts. Her pink lips pouted a smile; barely seventeen, Leita Johnston was innocent of her power. Still, the excitement she felt at his closeness was not to be denied. He was, after all, a handsome twenty-nine.

He took her arm and guided her into the shade of the elms. She dropped gracefully onto the grass and had pulled off one slipper when his hand grasped her shoulder.

"I don't want you to leave me . . ." he began, looking into her violet eyes. And before she could recover from her surprise his lips were brushing hers.

1

Moments later her hands crept up the strong, quivering muscles of his back as he crushed her tightly against him. In spite of herself her lips parted and she moaned with delight at his kisses.

Inflamed by his hunger for her, he pressed his mouth over hers and down into the damp crevice between her breasts. Tiny pink buttons rolled into the grass, as her lace camisole tore under his hands.

"Oh, no!" she breathed, as his lips searched and pulled at her flesh, finally fastening on the pinnacle of her breast. In desperation she rolled her head away as his mouth searched again for hers.

"Jeff," she whispered in protest, pushing against his chest. Taking her push for the convention of modesty, he slid his hand into her hair and once more caught her lips with his own. When the warm, exciting tip of his tongue touched hers she arched her back, trying to escape, but the throbbing bulge of his manhood turned her loins to liquid fire.

"I love you Leita—you don't know. . . ." His voice was hoarse, but the drumming in her ears almost drowned it out as his hand, moving under her voluminous petticoats, caressed the flesh between her thighs. "I want you to be my wife. . . ." He groaned, his tongue caressing hers deeper and deeper. She wrenched away, gasping, and rearranged her clothing.

"We can be married any day you choose, my darling." He pressed her face against his chest, and she felt the breath shuddering through his tall frame. "I'll speak to your father this evening."

Leita felt a tremor of alarm run through her. "Good Lord above, Jefferson, I can't marry you."

He drew back. His eyes were brown with glints of gold, like his hair, and they widened for an instant before crinkling at the corners as his smile spread. "Good Lord above, you're joking!" His laughter boomed out, startling a sleepy bluejay from a branch above them.

"I surely am not joking. I'm sorry, truly sorry for what happened just now but . . ."

"Sorry? When I've been waiting for these weeks past to take you in my arms! Sorry? For love? I want to marry you, Leita."

Poor Jefferson, what have I done to you? Leita thought, her heart sinking at the love and anticipation in his eyes. You came home from the war to find your wife dead and buried, and now I do this to you. Contrition for her flirting overcame her, and she pressed her hot cheek against his shoulder.

He kissed her tenderly then. "I was too impetuous. You don't have to be bashful with me, my love."

Then the bewilderment and frustration she had felt for over a year exploded in her and she tore herself from his arms.

"Please try to understand. I'm not in love with you, and I'm not going to marry you or anyone else—not for a long time! Maybe never!"

Her tirade only half-spent, she turned and ran through the copse of trees. Jefferson Hardy stared, then ran after her, catching and pinning her against the slippery trunk of an old elm.

"No young lady kisses a man that way unless she's in love with him. You can't say you don't love me; I know better."

Her cheeks were pink from the heat and her struggle, and tears welled up in her eyes. "Maybe I'm not the nice young lady you think I am. Maybe I'm like those hussies that drive around Manleyville in their buggies!"

His laughter boomed out again. "What could you know about hussies?" He smoothed the tendrils of gleaming hair back from her brow.

"Well, I've just proved it by leadin' you on like that

3

when I'm not in love with you and won't ever be." She tried to clear the hoarseness in her throat. "I couldn't help it, Jefferson. And I almost didn't stop you—*I almost didn't.*"

"That, my precious Leita, is love. Maybe you don't really know what love is. How could you? Barely seventeen and hardly any young men left in the county to court you—which has been my good fortune." He essayed a smile.

Leita sighed with exasperation. "Are you just bein' willfully stupid, Jefferson? Love means that one man is more important to you than anything else, and you want to spend the whole rest of your life with him."

A shade of panic touched his eyes. "Are you telling me that you're in love with someone else?"

"I'm telling you that I'm not in love at all." She looked at him steadily and he glanced down, stricken by the force of her statement. "I think if it had been any other handsome man that kissed me I would have felt exactly the same and done exactly the same." He looked up, and this time it was her eyes that fell. "Another five minutes of wild kissing like that and I would have been down there in the grass with my petticoats pulled up like any common trash."

Jefferson Hardy winced. She went on: "There—you see! What do you think of your 'nice young lady' now?"

Jefferson spoke soothingly. "You just don't know what you're talking about. I'm sorry. It's my fault. I took you by storm and it was all new to you."

"The thing is, Jeff," she said, her voice barely above a whisper, "it wasn't new to me at all." She swallowed hard and gazed back over the fields of white cotton, at the long roofline of the mansion she had been born in. The sky was clear now. Back then it was filled with black smoke as far as the eye could see . . . fields burning, houses burning . . . getting closer and closer to Wisteria Hall . . . and soon Yankee soldiers were galloping up the drive . . . and carrying off the butchered stock and what all . . . and setting fire to the fields. . . .

Her eyes were misty as she turned back to Jefferson. "There was nothing I could do. . . ."

"Leita, what in God's name is gnawing at you?"

"He forced me. . . ." She sank down onto the grass. "I never told a living soul." An alarming comprehension overcame him. He dropped to his knees and took her face in his hands. "It's all right, you can tell me. It will be all right, I promise you." A doctor's reassurance could be consoling.

She nodded, hesitated, took a deep breath. "The night after the Yankees butchered the last calf I went out to walk and be by myself. I was tired and miserable and worried about Daddy and the boys. Most of the soldiers were gone by then. But two stayed behind to finish up, burn down the house."

She paused to quell a quaver in her voice, regained her composure, and went on: "I was walking along close to where we are right now, wrapped up in Mama's carriage coat, when I heard somebody coming up behind me. For a minute I was scared pea-green, but then the moonlight fell on him just right and I saw it was this Lieutenant Nathan. Now all along he had been treating me decently and behaving practically like a gentleman—so I had no fear of him. I even liked him a little. Can you understand that, even though he was a Yankee?"

Jefferson nodded, the muscles in his back rigid with tension.

"I was feeling lonesome and we talked—he talked mostly. But he was acting peculiar." Leita's words were coming faster now and her voice rose slightly.

"Then it happened. Quick as lightning he put his

arms around me and started kissing my face and my neck. I started screaming—I'd never been touched like that before. He put his hand over my mouth. I can still hear him whispering, 'I'm not going to hurt you, sweetheart,' all frantic and breathlesslike. He was big and strong, Jefferson, and I couldn't get out from under his hands or away from him! Pretty soon he was forcing me down onto the ground. . . . Well, I guess you can figure out the rest without me having to tell you."

His fingers bit into her arm. "Are you saying that Mr. Johnston wasn't even told of this?"

Leita sighed heavily. "Tell Daddy, so he could grieve and feel miserable that there was nothing he could do about it? Tell Daddy about a soldier who by then was miles away?"

Jefferson started to speak, but Leita stopped him. "It's over and done with. Anyway, I'm not finished with what I have to tell you," she said sternly. "I knew after that night that falling in love was different from what I'd thought. I knew—"

"My God, Leita! You were raped! No wonder you're afraid of love. Oh, if only I'd known, I would never have pressed my love on you. It will take time, but eventually it will be only a dim memory. I can wait till hell freezes over if need be and—"

Leita threw her arms up in exasperation. "Will you listen to me? You've got to give up any ideas you have about me being in love with you. I kissed you back because of what my body was feeling, and if I can have almost those same feelings with a Yankee soldier who has forced me to give in to him, and caused me pain to boot, I know for certain it isn't because I'm in love." He stared at her in disbelief, and she faced him squarely. She wasn't through.

"Do you understand what I'm trying to say? Lieutenant Nathan was polite, kind, and handsome. I liked him, and maybe I flirted a little bit, not knowing I was playing with fire. But that night I learned something I never would have dreamed of before." Leita's voice dropped. "You see, after I got over being scared by his being so rough, which was mostly because he was scared, I—well, I felt things I'd never imagined. And a little while ago I felt the same with you when you were loving me."

His hold on her arms loosened and he turned his face away. She looked at his profile steadily for several seconds and then drew a deep, shuddering breath. "Jefferson, I've learned that I can be stirred, but at the same time my heart stays my own. I know that when I do fall in love I'll feel much, much more than that, and I won't be fighting it, either."

He sighed, shaking his head in bewilderment. "It seems I know less about ladies than I had thought. You have certainly taught me that. I truly don't understand you, Leita." He put his arm loosely around her shoulders. "But you mustn't feel that I think poorly of you for what you have just confided."

She looked up at him and a little wry smile curved her lips. You may say that, she thought, but it's plain to see you do feel different toward me. She knew full well that the blood that had stained her petticoats that night had been the irreplaceable evidence of highly valued virtue. She reflected for the hundredth time on the unquestioned etiquette that applied to the daughters of wealthy landowners where courtship was concerned— an etiquette that subjected a young woman to intimate scrutiny by at least a servant, if not a member of the family. It was a practice that bespoke not Puritanism, she knew now, but its opposite: the recognition that young blood was hot and that constant vigilance was the only restraint. She had puzzled over the conventional belief that those same daughters were not subject

7

to the passions that stormed within their suitors. Now the wry smile appeared again. It's nothing but a great big lie, she almost said aloud.

Hand in hand, Leita and Jefferson walked silently back to the verandah of Wisteria Hall, the only mansion in that district that had been spared when Sherman's army marched northward to Raleigh.

Chapter 2

LUCY MAE JOHNSTON'S SMILE WAS BRILLIANT AS SHE SAT up in bed and caught Dr. Hardy's hand in hers. "My dear young man, I have had the best of everything all my life. It's hard to kill a lady who has lived easily and well. Now, there's not a glass of port on this whole plantation to offer you, but you are to stay to supper."

"On one condition: that you don't go near the kitchen. You need rest and plenty of it. The worst is over. But I must caution you, Mrs. Johnston, that any undue exertion in your weak condition could make you seriously ill again. Now follow my advice and remember to take the medicine, and I promise you that in two or three weeks from now you'll be fit to dance a jig."

Jefferson glanced at Leita, who was pulling an ivory comb through her mother's heavy auburn hair. "As usual, I'm pleased to be invited, providing I'm not the cause for extra work."

Leita smiled reassuringly. "Fact is, if you will be kind

enough to carry in a little kindling you'll lighten my suppertime chores."

Lucy Mae's laughter was rich. "Leita has a list of accomplishments I never dreamed a daughter of mine would acquire. We have both learned enough about cooking to keep five men fed since Bessie died, as well as other mysterious but necessary tasks we never laid a hand to before."

"My tutor's concerns were Latin and French. Laundry and flatirons never crossed his mind." Leita smiled wryly as her graceful hands plaited Lucy Mae's long hair into a heavy braid.

"We are all good stock and blood tells." Lucy Mae patted Dr. Hardy's shoulder. "Look at you, young man. Half the folk in this county depend on you as they depended on your father before you. The holocaust you survived was a crucible for you. You returned to a changed land," her velvety eyes darkened, "to find yourself bereft, to everyone's sincere sorrow, but I believe life will shine for you again."

Remorse and embarrassment coursed through Leita and she interrupted. "Now mama, since you are feeling so well, Dr. Hardy and I shall put ourselves to some useful labor. The men are due in from the fields in less than an hour and I must fly."

Jefferson's silence was constrained as they walked to the summer kitchen at the north end of the house, but Leita's customary lightheartedness had returned. Prior to their passion of the afternoon she hadn't dreamed of making him the repository of her secret. Memories had haunted her half-sleep, memories of Lieutenant Nathan's passion, at first brutal, then tender. Dreams had awakened her, dreams of desire tinged with the deep need of love, but a love that had not found its focus in the personable, striking lieutenant. Now that Jefferson was privy to her self-discovery she felt a new freedom.

She imagined him to be transformed into a confidante, rather than the bitterly disappointed suitor he actually was.

In the summer kitchen she ran over to the long deal table that stood under the open window. "We're having something special tonight." And she held a big crockery bowl under Jefferson's nose in case he doubted her word. "That's wheat flour, Dr. Hardy, and we're having biscuits—not cornbread, but real-for-sure biscuits!"

"How did you come by that?" he grinned.

"Oh, we have ways," she said with a wink.

He took the heavy crock from her and set it back on the table. "I'll go see to that kindling now, so you'll have a hot oven for your delicacies."

He went outside, looked up at the gathering rain clouds and hurried over to the woodpile.

Leita watched him through the open end of the summer kitchen, open to let the heat escape and any random breeze cool the room. She looked at his broad back, the muscles rippling as he wielded the ax, his feet set wide apart in their highly polished boots. Any other girl would be just delirious with joy if Dr. Jefferson Hardy proposed to her, she mused. Her face flushed and she touched her hot cheek, remembering his hand between her thighs only hours ago.

The men came to the pump at dusk, just as the sky opened and the downpour began. They scooped up dabs of the yellow lye soap and washed and splashed to the squeaking accompaniment of the pump handle.

The lamps cast a soft light on the long table when Samuel Johnston said grace, followed by a short prayer for the soul of Richard Johnston, "our beloved son and dear brother," who died at Gettysburg.

Leita's father was a vital man with a full head of wavy gray hair, and six feet tall. His china blue eyes surveyed his family with open satisfaction and the slight twinkle that usually shone there.

"I understand that this is a somewhat momentous occasion," he smilingly announced as he held up a biscuit.

"And that's not all, Daddy," fifteen-year-old Belle piped up, her black eyes dancing. "I got a whole bucket of raspberries this afternoon for a cobbler."

Her auburn-haired brother Matthew lifted an eyebrow. "I'm glad to hear you spent the afternoon gainfully for a change. Young Tom must have thought you were sick when he missed his shadow."

Belle closed her eyes disdainfully. "You didn't even ask who toted the pail for me. Tom Wentworth wouldn't let me go into the brush alone, not with all those snakes around."

"You must have bribed him good, Belle," Matthew chuckled, spooning gravy over the split open biscuits on his plate.

The cool breeze from off the river floated through the open windows, and the smell of beans and ham blended with the scent of chicory from the boiling coffee pot. Leita turned to Dr. Hardy, her cheeks pink from the heat and the hair on the nape of her neck damp and curling from the cold water she had splashed on at the pump. Dr. Hardy was looking at her moist lips and gave a start when she spoke.

"If you don't take that plate of ham I'm likely to starve to death, Dr. Hardy."

He turned quickly and took the plate from her father who was holding it out to him. Samuel Johnston's wise blue eyes lingered on him. So that's the way the wind blows, he thought. His gaze passed to the daughter he admitted only to himself to be his favorite. She is the spitting image of her mother at seventeen, he thought for the hundredth time—the same shining, red-gold hair and the intelligent, laughing, violet eyes. Just like her, too, cocksure of herself and meeting the world with a kind of recklessness that preys on my mind.

Samuel chewed thoughtfully. "Did your mother eat well, Leita?"

"She ate a biscuit and some rice and broth, Daddy."

He turned to Dr. Hardy. "I'm everlastingly in your debt, Jefferson. I'll make a small payment with half a hog at butchering time, though."

"That is like being paid in pure gold. I'll be more than happy with just a ham. Your daughters showed great presence of mind, driving the hogs out into the swampland before Sherman's men could find them."

Eugene Johnston, twenty-four and dark like his sister Belle, ladled more marrow beans out of the tureen. "Thanks to the breed sow that was saved, we had a good litter last spring. All things considered, we were luckier than most planters around here. At least we weren't burned out. The biscuits are light, Leita. You're improving mightily."

Leita felt she had been delivered from the last subject she wanted to talk about, what with Jefferson seated beside her. "And are *you* improving mightily at picking cotton? If you learned as quickly as I do you would have it all in to the gin by now," she teased.

Eugene shook his finger in mock anger. "You're getting mighty full of yourself, little sister. Maybe you'd like to turn the cooking over to Belle and come out in the fields for a spell, like the Baxter women are having to do. You'd sing a different tune then."

"Two days of Belle's cooking and you'd carry me back from the fields yourself," Leita laughed.

Samuel Johnston stroked his gray sidewhiskers. "We will have a different crop next year, gentlemen, and a different life."

Eugene passed the stone jug of sorghum to his

13

father. "It's strange to think we won't be here a year from now."

"I dream of it!" Leita exclaimed. "I love South Carolina—I love Wisteria Hall, but oh, the journey—those forests and all that strange country—new sights every day—different people!"

Jefferson Hardy looked at her, a dull dismay in his eyes. Her heart is set on it, he thought.

"I received a letter from Robert today." All eyes turned to Samuel. "He continues to sing the praises of Indiana and has completed arrangements for our purchase."

Dr. Hardy shifted in his chair to face Samuel. "I don't quite grasp it yet, Mr. Johnston. Wisteria Hall still stands, you have sons with you to work the land. You could prosper again, after a fashion at least. Why leave South Carolina and trek up there to a semi-wilderness?"

"Jefferson, you're not the first one that has asked that, straight out." Samuel Johnston smiled as he refilled his coffee cup from the granite pot. "This plantation was a sight to behold long before you were born. A hundred or so fieldhands, a dozen house servants and fine sea-cotton stretching as far as you could see. It brought the highest price in the European market because it made the most delicate lace. But now our labor is gone. This ground isn't enough for me and my sons. We landowners are creators, when it comes right down to it. I intend to take a sizable piece of ground and wrest it from the wilderness, just as my great-great grandfather did here in his time. I'm only forty-eight and fortunate to be alive; I'm ready for a new chapter in my life. The fact is that William and his bride-to-be can make a good living from these holdings."

Dr. Hardy's long fingers stroked the edge of his knife

as he pursued the subject. "Can five of you clear enough land to make it pay—pay well?"

"No. Our plans encompass more than that." Samuel took the saucer of berry cobbler that Leita handed him, waited till the cream jug reached him and then drenched the cobbler before he resumed. "I made two fast friends in my regiment. Nathaniel Knox, an indigo planter from down around Charleston and Micah Tillett, who grows tobacco in North Carolina, just outside of Greensboro. We whiled away many a long hour talking about what we wanted to do when that blood-bath ended. It was a way of drowning our fears, you understand, a way of feeling certain for a few moments anyway that we would all get home. Toward the last we all saw that whatever happened, the life we had led before was gone; it was then I began thinking of Robert Bond's adventure. With his help, Micah, Nathaniel, and I have purchased twelve sections of land up there, signed and deeded."

"Twelve sections? That's twelve square miles!"

"Exactly," Samuel responded. "Part of it hardwood forest, which is valuable of course. The rest of it will be tillable when cleared."

"What an undertaking!" Dr. Hardy exclaimed. "I'm only waiting to hear how you plan to go about this Herculean task."

"Happily, we go well-funded. This part I prefer that you look upon as a confidence; it's not a secret in that sense of the word, but a gentleman doesn't usually advertise his financial affairs." Jefferson nodded in agreement. Samuel continued: "My mid-life venture has a very solid base, due in great part to my brother-in-law in Philadelphia. He is well versed in matters of finance, you see, and some years ago helped me undertake a heavy program of investment, most of it in the expanding northern railroad systems. As it turned out, his advice was as good as gold." Samuel paused, pushed his chair away from the table and stretched his long arms as lightning flashed through the window and a crack of thunder rent the air.

"My questions are answered," Jefferson said. "Only my regret remains, regret at your leaving."

Samuel offered Jefferson a cigar and gestured toward the window. "Well, that's something you won't be doing tonight, my friend—not in that deluge."

The rain had stopped, but the sky was still a sheet of gray when Jefferson Hardy mounted his black and white mare and started out for Manleyville early the next morning. Trees lay toppled over in the fields and broken branches were scattered all about, attesting to the fury of the recent storm. The road was pocked with deep puddles, and he kept his horse to a walk. It was a totally dreary day, consistent with the mood he was in.

He was trying hard not to feel dejected when he heard the sound of hoofbeats behind him—and moments later the sound of Leita's voice as her chestnut gelding came cantering up. He looked at her with surprise and alarm, fearful at first that her mother had had a relapse.

But Leita promptly allayed his concern. "I just thought I'd ride along with you a ways—that is, if you don't mind."

He studied her quizzically for a moment. "Not at all."

They rode in silence for a while before she turned to him and said, "I just wanted you to know that I'm mighty sorry if I misled you. I hope you'll forgive me."

"There's nothing to forgive," he responded, then, smiling wistfully, added, "but if you ever change your mind about getting married, I'd appreciate being the first to know."

She smiled. "Some lucky girl will have snared you long before that."

They stopped when they came to the fork where the road to Manleyville veered to the left. "Well, I'd best turn back now," Leita said.

There was something in his eyes that made her turn away quickly, but he grasped her arm. "There's something important you ought to remember. Any man that loves you isn't going to forget it, not right away—nor ever. I would ride away with you right now if you wanted it that way. Remember that—no man is going to love you lightly." The smoldering, longing in his eyes took her off balance and she was so moved that she was wordless. She reached out and touched his fine, brown hair, and the next instant she wheeled the chestnut and cantered off.

A stiff wind had come up from the northwest, and she decided to take a shorter route back, turning off the road and onto a narrow trail through the woods. No more than a few yards along the trail, she suddenly felt the horse shudder—and in that instant she looked down and saw the deadly coral snake, its bright red and yellow and black bands slithering, its fearsome jaws spread wide. Leita tightened her grip on the reins and dug her knees in hard as the horse whinnied and shied, then reared in panic and took off down the road at a furious gallop. "Easy, Bub, easy," she panted, to no avail, as the frightened animal fled on, veering right at the fork and onto a winding road she was not familiar with.

She didn't see the five men riding abreast; her head was bent low when she cleared the curve and her eyes were tearing from the cold wind. But she looked up just before the gelding swerved and saw a vivid green waistcoat in the center of a phalanx of riders hurtling down upon her.

17

"Whoa, whoa!" a voice bellowed. The end rider, a big black-bearded man in a wide-brimmed hat, swung his horse to the left, making an opening for her.

"Whoa Bub!" she heard her own voice rising in a scream as she pulled with all her might at the reins, but the chestnut's unleashed strength opposed her. Bub's heavy withers flexed and he turned sharply, ignoring the narrow opening in the rank ahead of him. His hooves scattered the stones at the side of the road as he gathered his forelegs for the leap and soared high, vaulting a ditch and clearing a four-foot rail fence. Bub tossed his head and snorted with unmistakable arrogance, but when he galloped across the field his reins were dragging. Leita lay in a hollow, her red-gold curls tangled in the chill mud.

"Jesus, she isn't dead, is she?" the man in the green waistcoat called out, wheeling his horse.

Leita's lashes fluttered and her eyes opened wide. A sodden, wide-brimmed hat blotted out the sky and strong, gentle fingers were exploring her neck and arms. She looked up into black eyes and an even blacker brush of beard.

"What are you doing?" she mumbled, still dazed, and struggled to prop herself up on her elbows.

"You just rest easy now." The man's gloved hands pinned her shoulders to the ground. Fright cleared her head suddenly and she rolled to the right, kicking out as she raked her nails down his chest, tearing at his coarse, mud-stained shirt.

He loosened his grip. "It's a God's blessing you're not hurt, little girl!" He stood up and called back over his shoulder: "She's not only alive, she seems to be in fine shape."

"We'll be on our way then, seeing as how we're in a hurry," the green-vested man called back and cantered on with no more delay.

Leita scrambled to her feet, her violet eyes wide with surprise. The stranger's voice had been deep and rich, with the cultivated drawl of a well-bred Southerner. "You're no Yankee!" she cried out accusingly. "What are you doing riding with them?"

She pushed back the hair that was matted to her cheek with mud. The top of her dress had ripped, revealing worn lace, sweat-dampened to her full breasts.

The man's coal-black eyes were narrowed in a puzzled appraisal as they swept over her tangled hair, the tiny amethyst eardrops and the proud set of her shoulders.

"I'm no Yankee, and you're no common hoyden, young lady. So what are you doing riding hell-bent on a mount a good two hands too high for you, and all alone to boot?"

Leita felt her heard pounding under his scrutiny and her fingers fumbled as she pulled her torn dress together. "What I'm doing is none of your affair!" she snapped. She turned and sighted Bub at the far fence line. Picking up her skirts she ran toward the horse, intent on getting away from this disquieting man. Her thin slippers weren't made for treading rough furrows and she slipped, wrenching her ankle.

"Damnation!" she gasped, pulling her skirts higher as she perched on one furrow and jumped to the next. In two strides he caught up with her, grasped her around the waist and set her down firmly.

There was a suggestion of laughter in his deep, rich voice. "I'll thank you kindly to stay here with both your feet on the ground while I fetch that horse."

Leita turned her face away ungraciously, tight-lipped, but she watched his tall figure with curiosity as he strode off. His rough suede jacket was as road-stained as the breeches that tapered down his long legs into high, cordovan leather boots, gleaming with polish.

"Probably stole them," she muttered, then called out as he approached the gelding that was now idling at the fence corner: "You'd better watch out. That horse is unpredictable and full of the devil!"

The wind carried his laughter back to her. "I have an idea that makes two of you."

He mounted the gelding, cantered back across the field and Leita drew in her breath with surprise as the horse, at his urging, leaped the fence and the ditch. He dismounted and tethered him quickly.

"You know horseflesh, anyway," she acknowledged grudgingly as he approached her. "Bub only jumps when he wants to, never when the rider wants him to."

"Horseflesh aside, are you in any kind of trouble?" His dark eyes were stern and the deep voice very serious. "If you're riding for help you had better tell me." His shoulders looked massive to Leita as he towered above her, and her eyes dropped. She looked at the dark hair curling out just above his open shirt front—anything to avoid those searching eyes.

"I'm not on any errand of mercy, Mr. whoever-you-are, and I don't need anybody else nibbing into my business!" she snapped.

A wide, free smile broke through the bushy, black beard. "I hope you're right," he answered nonchalantly and swept her up in his arms. She screamed and pushed hard against his chest and he set her down again so abruptly she lost her balance and started to fall, her arms opening wide as she clutched at him. He caught her, then pulled a surprisingly clean and fragrant handkerchief from the recesses of his jacket and began wiping her mud-caked cheeks.

"Hasn't it occurred to you that I'm going to have to carry you back across that ditch?" His words were sharp and quick. "You'd never make it in those flimsy little slippers and all those petticoats. So why don't you just pretend you're grown-up now, and stop your thrashing and screaming?"

"All right!" she shouted, "go ahead and carry me. Any old way I get back to my horse is fine with me."

His dark brows flew up and in that instant her feet were off the ground, her arms clasped tightly around his neck as his long legs carried them over the fence and down and up the stony bank to the roadside. In one swoop he set her onto the saddle and pressed the reins into her hands.

"Now, Miss, you settle down and get where you're going, and don't be in such a hurry. You'll get there faster."

He mounted his own horse as Leita, mud-stained and irritable, wheeled Bub and cantered off.

"And be careful," he shouted, turning his bay in the opposite direction.

When Leita looked over her shoulder with the intention of calling out a belated thank you, the bulky, black-bearded figure turned in the saddle and doffed his wide-brimmed hat. She stared as a shaft of winter sunlight struck his bared head, illuminating a wide brow and straight, chiseled nose. His curling, jet-black hair gleamed in the brightness. She couldn't see the expression in his eyes, nor hear what he called back to her.

She rode on, wondering all the way home who he could have been.

Samuel Johnston held his crystal goblet high and led the traditional toast to the crop. No lashing thunderstorms had come to sodden the previous bolls, the fields were picked clean and the whole crop was in to the gin. After that the days melted together. A jubilant

Christmas celebration was followed by a ball given by the McBrides to announce the betrothal of their daughter Eleanor to William Johnston. Their March wedding would precede the departure of the Johnstons in late April, giving William and Ellie ample time for a wedding trip to Charleston before assuming their stewardship of Wisteria Hall.

The day after the wedding three specially built conestogas arrived from Charleston. Furniture that had been in the Johnston and Carlisle families for four generations was loaded into their shadowy, cavernous interiors.

A wet, overcast day in April saw Nathaniel Knox, Samuel Johnston's former companion in arms, ride up the lane preceding two wagons loaded full of the Knox possessions. That evening an impromptu party was held that spilled over the verandah and out onto the rolling lawn of Wisteria Hall.

Early the next morning the Johnston-Knox wagon train rolled down the drive. Leita cantered on ahead until she came to the first bend in the road. As she waited for the others to catch up, her eyes swept the familiar countryside and clouded over with mist as they settled for one long last look at the house she was born in.

Chapter 3

They traveled inland along the Fall Line Road, one of the two main roads that led to Philadelphia. The other route, the Coastal Post Road, was shorter, but Samuel and Nathaniel had decided to avoid it because the rains were more frequent and heavier there than in the foothills. An even shorter route, over the mountains and through the Cumberland Gap into Tennessee, would have been possible on horseback, but crossing the Smoky Mountain range with heavily loaded conestogas was too risky. On reaching Philadelphia the wagons would veer directly west onto the Forbes Road to Pittsburgh, a city of over 50,000 people. From Pittsburgh they would head southwest to Wheeling, Virginia, where they would take the old Cumberland Road into Ohio and thence into Indiana. All told, they would cover about thirteen-hundred miles before reaching their destination in northeastern Indiana.

As they headed inland following the Santee River,

the countryside was still riddled with the vestiges of a war now two years ended. And it was this that took much of the savor out of Leita's excitement at first. But at least the company was pleasant. Jerome Knox, who was twenty, had collar-length brown hair and the gentle eyes of his mother. His body was compact and muscular, and he was easy to talk to. Leita liked him, as often as not rode beside him, and the warm friendship they developed made the long days pass more quickly.

The nights took her on a different journey, borne by the dreams that still came to her. But now the old dream—Lieutenant Nathan's strong arms enveloping her, the feel of his hungry mouth on her own, her mounting passion under his caresses—the old dream had given way to a new version. The face above her had metamorphosed into the face of the dark-bearded stranger with the laughing eyes, now shining with tenderness and desire. His hands would cradle her face gently, his kisses tender, inflaming her as she returned them yearningly and passionately while his hands moved over her bared breasts and the weight of his body pressed against her. . . .

She awoke one night in a torment and sat up, rubbing her hot cheeks. She remembered him now—never having thought of him during her waking hours—his image coming back to her through the trickery of a dream. And she wondered why—why him? The dream returned, often, and sometimes she fell asleep waiting for it.

Leita's skin was pinkish-gold from the sun, and she glowed with health from the days spent riding. She ate the potatoes roasted in the campfire. And the boys shot rabbits which, while lean and stringy from the winter, tasted delicious roasted crisp and brown on sharp sticks over the fire. The countryside was lush and green and rolling, and the Smoky Mountains cast a bluish haze on their left as they rode through the foothills. They forded rivers at their spring flood, but the wagons made it through over the stony bottoms and the teams clambered up the banks, seemingly refreshed by the cold, rushing waters. They crossed the River Neuse just south of Greensboro and camped out for the night. They would arrive at the plantation of Micah Tillett by midmorning of the next day.

· That morning Leita pleaded with her father to be allowed to ride on ahead with him and Nathaniel Knox to apprise the Tilletts of their arrival. He consented, warning her that they would keep a fast pace. She tied her wide-brimmed straw hat securely and prepared for a hard gallop. The road wound past orchards and rolling fields, marked off by fencing that had once been white but was silver now from lack of paint. The dirt, recently turned by mule-drawn plows, was blacker here, without the tinge of red iron farther south, and the smell of the rich earth was heavy on the air.

Leita was a little out of breath when the two black horses came pelting around the curve ahead. Startled, her horse shied and reared.

She grasped the reins, pulling and shouting, "Tom—down Tom!" when a hand grasped the bridle and forcefully brought Tom under control.

"You keep your seat well, don't you ma'am?" a voice drawled, and she looked up into two dark eyes.

The man wore a rough, suede jacket open over a sparkling white shirt. Tufts of curling black hair showed above the open collar. Leita looked up from his chest to a strong chin with a slight cleft in it. His hair was a shining black, with crisp waves and thick sideburns reaching down to his jawline. He smiled slowly as Leita's eyes traveled over him, his teeth gleaming white in a face that was tanned and smooth. His eyes were laughing now, and she felt confused as he stared frankly

25

back at her, inspecting her long-lashed violet eyes and her face framed in blowing, red-gold hair.

She finally found her tongue. "I ought to keep my seat well, sir. I've been riding since I was knee-high to a stoat."

He put his head to one side and pursed his lips, as if to keep from laughing.

"I thank you for stopping my horse," she continued, making a desperate effort to fight the confusion those laughing, dark eyes caused her.

His lips, full and almost chiseled, curved into a smile again. "It was my pleasure, ma'am."

Samuel Johnston reined up beside them. "I want to thank you for assisting my daughter, sir." Samuel doffed his wide-brimmed hat. "Samuel Johnston at your service."

The younger man looked at him with pleasant surprise. "I am Breve Pinchon, from Charleston, and this gentleman"—he gestured toward the short, stocky young man behind him—"is Joseph Tillett."

Joseph Tillett extended his hand, a gratified smile on his pudgy face. "We've been riding out every morning for five days to make sure you got a proper welcome." Leita noticed that though his hair was dark, his skin was fair and his eyes were a beautiful, clear blue.

Breve Pinchon had been leaning lazily on the pommel of his saddle during this exchange. He turned toward Leita.

"I don't believe I have had the pleasure, ma'am," he murmured in a soft drawl.

Samuel interposed hastily, introducing Leita to both of the newcomers. The tall, dark man bowed in the saddle. Joseph Tillett did the same, although lacking the grace of his companion.

Leita made a small bow from her seat on the horse and saw in Breve Pinchon's eyes a glint of—what?

Amusement? Admiration? Who is he? she thought uncomfortably. She found herself confused and disturbed in a way she had never known before. Her cheeks were hot. She dug her heels into her horse and went to join the others up the road.

Greensboro, North Carolina, had gone unburned and for the most part unscathed by the Civil War, and the Tillett mansion, which was to remain in the stewardship of two of the sons, shone resplendent at the end of a long avenue—red brick, white doric pillars, a gleaming fanlight over the entrance. The household was in a flurry with a full staff of servants scurrying around the high-ceilinged rooms preparing for the ball to be held that evening.

Mary Jo Tillett, twenty-one years old, dark-haired, with a piquant, dimple-marked face and wide, china-blue eyes, leaned out the window of the bedroom where Leita was dressing.

"My, but your brother is good looking!" she exclaimed. She was watching tall, auburn-haired Matthew Johnston.

Leita came over and followed her gaze. The gravel circle below was full of young men.

"We're going to have plenty of menfolk on this trip, aren't we? You knew Colonel Pinchon was coming with us, didn't you?"

"Why is he coming?" Leita realized too late that her voice was sharp, and Mary Jo turned quickly, her eyes cool and appraising on Leita's face. She paused before answering.

"Because he is on his way to Chicago. He stopped off for a visit and Daddy asked him to come with us. Breve can do anything, you know, and Daddy says we can use an extra man as capable as Breve. He's even going to stay in Indiana with us for a spell, long enough to lend a hand in organizing. Breve's mother was Daddy's second cousin and we've always been real close." She ended with a smug little smile.

Mary Jo had accented the word *close* and Leita remembered the proprietary way she had tucked her hand in Breve's arm earlier. She was conscious of an incipient dislike for this coquettish, rather brittle girl.

Mary Jo, Belle, and Leita came down the stairway together. Leita's pink satin gown cast a glow on her bare shoulders and the bodice fit snugly over her full breasts, outlining the dark shadow of cleavage. The dress flared out from her small waist, and rose-trimmed silk panniers adorned the sides of the full skirt.

Breve Pinchon was holding a conversation with Matthew when he looked up and followed Leita's progress down the stairway, his eyes dark and still on her as Matthew went on talking. He met her with a low bow at the foot of the stairs. Leita looked into his face and felt a tightness in her chest. She drew a deep breath as she stepped forward and he held out his hand to her, the candlelight burnishing the smooth, tan skin of his face.

She felt his fingers curl gently around hers and when he said "Good evening, Miss Leita," in his rich voice she knew it wasn't the tightness of her stays that was causing the constriction in her breast; it was this tall man with his burning black eyes on her. His ruffled shirt gleamed below a determined chin, and his shoulders were broad in the elegantly cut black coat that hung above sharply creased, fawn-colored trousers. The scent of cigar smoke and cologne wafted off him. She dropped her eyes, unable to meet his any longer, hoping he couldn't feel the tremor that ran through her.

Breve placed Leita's hand gently into the crook of his arm. "May I?" he asked gallantly. Leita noticed Mary Jo's lips compressing slightly. Leita nodded and Breve guided her into a long room highlighted by a grand chandelier full of twinkling tallow candles. Long tables covered in white linen lined the sides of the room; at one end were platters of food and a freshly roasted suckling pig. Leita curtseyed her way through what seemed a hundred introductions and then sat down. Breve left her side briefly and returned with two plates piled high with roast pork surrounded by creamed potatoes, peas and watermelon pickle.

They began eating, Breve ravenously and Leita trying to curb her hunger; there simply wasn't room for what she wanted with her stays laced so tightly.

"I understand you are joining us for the trip north, Colonel Pinchon."

"That's right. I'm traveling north anyway and I may as well lend a hand," he replied serenely.

"And what takes you to—Chicago, isn't it?"

He smiled, tossing off a shrug. "A new life. Bigger and better things." His smile faded. "Nothing is left in the South for me. No family—and the business wouldn't be a tenth of what it was in 'sixty."

"What business?"

"Cotton brokerage. The cotton volume will be way down from now on—no labor to tend it. So I'm going to Chicago. The mining business in this country is booming and Chicago is the investment center. Not to mention railroads. I have a fortune to make—and one to redeem." His last words were spoken so softly she almost didn't hear them. "I'll stay in Indiana long enough to help Micah get settled. He has been a good friend and I owe him a great deal."

He folded his arms across his chest, then pushed his chair back from the table and surveyed her thoughtfully. "And what about you? Leaving your home—not knowing what lies ahead of you—the rough life of the road."

"It hasn't bothered me a bit," Leita chuckled. "I love it, and I'm excited about the life ahead of me. I never wanted to get married back home, to live and die in the same place and never see a thing of the world. And I'm going to make a trip to the continent when I'm twenty. This journey isn't the end for me."

"And when will that be?" he asked.

"Two and one-half years. I'm seventeen now."

"You're only seventeen?" His surprise was evident.

"I'll be eighteen in August," Leita added defensively.

He stared at her for a moment, then chuckled softly. "You'll be married before you get to the continent. And what will your future husband think of your gallavanting off to foreign parts?"

"Oh, I won't have a husband for a long time—maybe never," she said emphatically. "I'm not afraid of being an old maid."

He laughed heartily. "I shouldn't think you would be, my dear. It's likely you'll get hoarse from saying no."

"I didn't mean it that way," she blushed. "I only meant that I'm not so worried about gettin' married that I'd marry the first man that came along."

"I would guess that first one has come and gone," he said, taking a sip of his wine and looking at her over the rim of the glass.

"That's neither here nor there," she remarked, looking for a way to change the subject.

The music had been playing continuously for some time. Leita glanced toward the ballroom, then rose abruptly.

"If you'll remember, I have the honor of the first dance with you," Breve Pinchon drawled.

She nodded and he escorted her across the hall and into the ballroom. He slipped his arm around her waist

30

and they glided onto the floor, his hand resting lightly on the small of her back. She was acutely conscious of being in the curve of his arm, so close she could rest her head on his chest. Unable to think of anything to say, she danced silently, breathlessly aware of the nearness of his mouth as he looked down at her. The dance ended very quickly, it seemed to her, and she was swallowed up in a crowd, besieged by new acquaintances, as Breve Pinchon's broad back disappeared across the room.

Eventually, she escaped out onto the verandah. Breathless from dancing, weary of making conversation with one stranger after another, she skimmed down the wide steps and strolled across the damp grass. The evening was overcast, yet mild for April. She strolled idly, lifting her curls off the nape of her neck now and then to feel the cooling breeze. She started to stroll back to the ballroom when a familiar laugh rang out. She looked up and saw Breve Pinchon and an older man conversing on the verandah. Now the same laugh, deeper this time, boomed from Breve's throat. Her brows knitted in reflection, Leita stood watching as he spoke when suddenly the moon escaped from the clouds overhead and shone down brightly into the clearing. It fell on Breve, his broad forehead and finely cut nose, nostrils flaring, but the lower part of his face was in dark shadow from the tree branches. Leita stood immobilized, her breath caught in her throat. His eyes gleamed in the night like black diamonds, his dark, waving hair framing his forehead but his jaw was obscured in deep shadow, as if he were bearded. And then she realized. The dark stranger who had turned in his saddle and lifted his hat—the sunlight had shone down, illuminating his features right down to his black beard. They were one and the same! This suave, sleek Colonel Pinchon with his elegant, drawling speech was the dark hulk of a man who had picked her up out of that field back in North Carolina, the man who had entered her dreams all unbidden. Her heart beat frantically in her breast. He had known all along! What had he called her then, almost a year ago? A hoyden! He had known from the first minute when he had grabbed the bridle of her horse. And he had been laughing at her, all through this day and the evening, when he danced with her, when he pumped her with questions. He had known full well she hadn't recognized him. How could she have? It was as if he were two different men! Anger welled up in her; he had been patronizing her all along. Her cheeks were hot as she thought of the dream where his mouth and hands tasted her body—!

She marched up to him boldly and, hands on hips, stood there glaring. The older man took this as his cue to leave.

"Well, you're quite the man of mystery, aren't you, Colonel Pinchon? You've spent the whole day, ever since this morning, just laughing up your sleeve at me, making a fool of me. I don't want you ever to speak to me again, do you hear?"

He threw back his head and laughter rolled out of him. His hands were on his hips as he faced her. "So you remembered me, did you? I wondered if you would."

"You couldn't behave like a gentleman, could you? And tell me who you were. No, you had to be laughing up your sleeve at me all this time." She was livid with anger.

"Hold on a minute! I did behave like a gentleman. That is exactly why I didn't remind you of our first meeting. If I remember right, you were quite upset at the time, and I didn't think it would be discreet to bring it up. And I haven't been laughing at you—not for one moment. Oh, occasionally I would think of you stomping off across those furrows, as mad as you are now, and—" here he broke out in another chuckle.

Leita turned and stormed off. Reluctantly, she knew that his protest was a reasonable one, but the feeling that he had been patronizing her persisted and fueled her rage.

He was beside her in two strides. "I want to extend my apology to you, Miss Leita. For what, I'm not exactly certain, but apparently I've hurt your feelings, and I would never do that—certainly not willingly."

His voice was low and his hands were on her shoulders. She looked up into his face and melted, her knees went weak and she clasped her hands in front of her to keep from touching his chest. His nearness and the tenderness in his voice sent her heart hammering so she could barely hear her own words. Why, oh why, did this man cast such a spell over her? She wanted nothing more than for him to take her in his arms.

She looked down. "It's all right. I just hadn't thought of it the way you explained it. I felt like such a fool."

He clucked his tongue, his eyes soft on her, and they turned and walked back toward the lighted house, his hand holding hers.

Chapter 4

HER HAIR WAS DAMP WITH DEW WHEN SHE AWOKE AND the smell of the fallen pine needles intense in her nostrils. She pulled the blanket up under her chin and snuggled down.

"Hey, there. It's time to rise and shine." The half-whisper brought her up. Breve was crouched across from her, a granite mug of coffee in his hand.

"Here it is, all sugared and blowed," he grinned. "The sun's near up."

She took the coffee and ran a hand through her tangled curls.

"I suppose you want the rest of your breakfast in bed," he chuckled. He wore a shirt of maroon plaid, and his India-black hair curled damply from his swim in the river. He sipped at his own mug and smiled at her. The dense ash and elm trees towered above them and a luminous, milky light diluted the darkness of the sky.

"I'll bring you your coffee tomorrow morning," she promised.

"You'll never make it. That first bird wakes me up, but he only sings a lullaby for you," he laughed and strode back to the campfire.

She slithered out of her pallet and made for the thicker woods. Pulling up her nightgown she squatted beside a tree and then scampered away from the amber puddle she had made. She pulled the gown over her head then and plunged into the frigid water of the river. Her skin was pink and tingling when she climbed out, and she scrubbed herself dry with the nightgown. Dressing quickly, she joined the group around the fire and ate her fried eggs and grits with gusto.

Spring in the foothills of the Smokies was verdantly beautiful, fragrant, and wild with delicate color. Leita carried a sense of excitement within her from morning till night, and her dreams lulled her to sleep. The days were like movements in a symphony, rich with beauty, compellingly beautiful. And each day, every day, he was there. His skin had changed to an even darker tan, his teeth showing whiter as he smiled his lazy, nonchalant smile. He rode beside her, sitting effortlessly in his saddle, and she gloried in his very presence. She watched him at night, carrying heavy armloads of wood into the clearing, his stride easy and graceful. She observed him covertly in the glow of the fire as he sprawled on the ground, the firelight flickering over his high cheekbones and well-shaped nose, his nostrils flaring slightly above those chiseled lips.

Never had she met a man so sure of himself, so strong and confident in his every moment, so quick to take command of any situation. Her father, with his quick energy and decisiveness, was the acknowledged leader of the group, but Breve commanded equal respect. They conferred frequently, and when a decision was to be made it was one or the other who was consulted. The fording was sometimes difficult, as when the rushing spring waters overran their banks. But Breve invariably found a spot where the bottom was stony and would hold the weight of the wagons without miring them down. He would sit his horse in midstream, shouting directions and urging the teams on—the last to come up the bank, his face flushed and his eyes sparkling from the challenge he had overcome.

The confusion she had felt in his presence was gone. She could talk with him easily now, without a rush of blood to her cheeks and a debilitating attack of shyness. The change had come about when she faced the fact she was in love with him: that this was the one man she could love with all her heart, the man she wanted to marry. And as her awareness of him heightened, she longed to press her cheek against that broad chest and feel his strong arms around her. Time and again her eyes were drawn to his mobile, sensual lips, and she grew weak at the thought of that mouth on hers. She knew in her bones that he had fallen in love with her. But she was puzzled by his attitude. He seemed determined that nothing should pass between them smacking of courtship. Often when he was riding with her he would suddenly leave to join her father or one of the other men. Never a word, never a gesture to show that he loved her. But deep down she knew, and she waited.

Late one afternoon Breve joined her suddenly. "I've been meaning to say something to you," he began, quite seriously. "Sometimes you're riding a good piece ahead of the rest of us. I've noticed how you charge off on your own and I don't think it's safe. These hills are full of hiding places—and cutpurses and thieves aplenty. Some of those bushwhackers could see a lone woman and decide you were an easy mark. There's no sense inviting trouble," he said firmly.

"I wasn't aware that I had been inviting trouble," she said a little stiffly. "Besides, Tom is a very fast horse. If anyone started after me I could turn and be back before they could catch me," she went on confidently.

"Well, you just think you could." His tone was severe. "We're coming to some pretty desolate stretches here in Virginia, and I don't want to have to worry about you riding alone."

"Oh, fiddle!" she exclaimed. "What would a robber want with me? I don't carry any money or other truck. You're making a mountain out of a molehill!"

"They could be looking for something besides money. Do I have to speak plainer than that?"

She looked at him in surprise. He was really angry.

"All right. It's something I hadn't thought of and I'll remember it. You can quit scowling now."

Leita looked to her left at the mountain ranges covered with their thick carpet of evergreens and gave a little shudder at the dark, impenetrability of it all.

"I'll be careful, really I will," she assured him, almost meekly.

"That's good enough," he replied, and dug his heels into the sleek chestnut and cantered ahead to join her father.

They had camped alongside the Shenandoah River that night. The forest around them was still, except for the sounds of the wood animals and the nocturnal chatter of the birds. They had struck camp later than usual and darkness fell quickly. The conversation around the campfire had fallen to a murmur. Some were already asleep in their pallets.

Feeling restless, Leita decided to walk down to the river and picked her way through the fallen tree branches and thick undergrowth toward the sound of the rushing water. She found a space thickly matted with leaves and sank down to gaze at the moonlit water. The trees stirred gently in a soft evening breeze and the swish-swish of the water over the stones soothed her.

When she heard twigs snapping and footsteps approaching, she eased into the shadow of a tree trunk. She peeked out when the footsteps halted and saw Breve's broad shoulders outlined in the moonlight as he stood on the bank of the river. He was smoking one of his thin cigars and looking up at the milky-white sphere of the moon hanging low over the trees on the far shore. His feet were planted wide apart, his long legs tapering down to the dark russet boots he kept highly polished, no matter how many rivers were forded or how dusty the road was.

She drew a deep breath. Watching him stand there alone, she felt the intimacy of their being so close together in the night.

He sighed heavily, then tossed the remnant of his cigar out into the river. At the same time he heard the rustle of leaves on the ground and turned quickly, his eyes searching the darkness.

"It's only me," she called softly, going toward him.

"What are you doing out here at this hour?"

"I came out here to think. I guess I was feeling restless." She leaned back against the tree trunk. Her eyes were dark in the night and her hair caught the moonlight, tumbling over her shoulder in a golden ripple.

He gazed at her thoughtfully. "How could you feel restless after being on a horse all day? You've got real stamina, my dear."

She hated it when he called her "my dear," as if he were an old uncle.

"Oh, there are things to think about," she replied with a slow smile, "and out here in the moonlight is a good place to think."

He looked down for a moment, seemingly at a loss for words—so unlike him, she thought. When he finally spoke, his eyes avoided hers. "Don't you think you had better be getting back? It's getting cold and damp out here and we can't have you catching a chill."

She felt the sting of rejection—he was doing it again! She turned aside and moved off quickly when a sharp briar caught her in the face, grazing the skin down over her bare collarbone where her blouse was open. Her gasp brought Breve to her side.

"What happened? Are you hurt?" As she turned toward him he saw the blood oozing out in droplets down her cheek and throat.

"Damnation! You ran into a thorn bush. Wait a minute, I'll wet this." He pulled a handkerchief from his pocket, dipped it in the cold water and returned to her side. She closed her eyes as he patted the damp cloth on her cheek. She tilted her head back while he cleaned the blood off her throat and collarbone with soft touches. The sound of his breathing and the touch of his hand as he held her by one shoulder sent a tingle up her spine.

She opened her eyes and looked up into his face, soft with tenderness. Her hand crept up his chest and her lips parted. He gazed at her for an instant and dropped the handkerchief. His arms swept around her as his face met hers, his mouth coming to life in the softness of her parted lips. She strained against him, her breasts crushed against his chest, and caressed the hard muscles of his back. He released her mouth briefly, traced the line of her neck with his lips and returned urgently to her mouth. Her lips parted farther, and she moaned as the tip of his tongue darted into her mouth. She met it with her own tongue and felt a shudder go through his body. His hand moved down her back, and as he pressed her hips against his, she felt him swollen

40

and pulsating with desire. She dug her fingers into his back with a frenzy she had never known before, not even in her dreams of him. She ran her fingers through his crisp, dark hair while he covered her throat with kisses. Then he found her mouth again, and she felt his warm breath sigh into her as his hand reached inside her blouse and cradled her breast. He played with her hardened nipple while the tip of his tongue stroked hers. Suddenly he pulled his lips away and uncovered her breast. She rolled her head as he kissed her breast tenderly, and she moaned with pleasure when he pulled her nipple into his mouth. She sank slowly onto the soft bed of leaves, pressing his head tightly to her breast and he came down with her, over her. Running his hand along her hip, he pulled her skirt up, caressing her thighs while his lips and tongue caressed her nipple. She felt a mounting tension low in her belly as she helped him remove her undergarment. His hand moved between her legs, exploring randomly at first, then with purpose. Her hips arched up and when she moaned, he brought his mouth to hers again. She was quivering with a longing she had never imagined when his hand stopped moving, and she sighed gratefully when she felt the warm, turgid fullness of him entering her. He buried his face in her hair and whispered, "Oh, Leita." Her heart was pounding as he sank his flesh into hers, filling her with love and joy and extracting the same. "How I love you," he murmured. She ran her hands down his flanks, clawing at them, urging him on, bobbing in the swell of her own urgency as her legs enveloped him. She was caught up now in the gathering force of the mounting tide. He did not have to wait. He moaned, plunging his tongue into her mouth once more, muffling her cry as the full weight of him came down on her. As her body arched to meet his, she gasped. Waves of incredible pleasure were sweeping over her from every direction, rising and falling and convulsing her until the ecstasy had spread to every fiber of her being. A moment later she fell limp in his arms. His cheek was damp with perspiration as it pressed against hers, and she could feel the thundering of his heart as he rested. The ensuing minutes of silence were broken only by their breathing and the murmur of the river. Then he kissed her gently, tenderly.

"I've been afraid of this—since the first night." His tone was bleak, and in the moonlight he looked so sad that Leita jumped up. Ignoring her disarranged clothing, she seized his arms.

"What a thing to say!" she cried. "I love you. . . . I love you and now you know it! I won't hide it any longer."

He closed his eyes in despair. "It was my fault. You're so young, Leita—so very young."

"I'm almost eighteen. Lots of girls my age have already married and had their first baby!" she cried.

"Oh God. I hadn't even thought of that." He wiped his hand across his face. "I didn't think of anything—I just lost my head. Now listen to me, Leita. There are things you don't understand, things I can't tell you. But—" He faltered, searching for words.

She looked up at him, a block of ice forming in her chest, and waited.

"There can't be anything more between us. Nothing, do you understand? There are reasons I can't tell you, but I will tell you this—you would thank me if you knew. That's all I'll say. I'll have to forget what happened tonight, and you will have to put it out of your mind—now and forever." His voice was harsh and insistent.

"Are you saying you don't love me?"

He looked down into her face. "I'm saying there can't be any love between us, now or ever. Whatever I feel doesn't matter—it's impossible. The sooner you realize that, the better. I'm to blame for what happened. It won't happen again."

"How can you treat me this way?" she implored him, tears streaking down her cheeks.

He looked at her, the little muscle in his jaw jumping and clenching, then looked away. "Believe me when I say it's all for the best. There's nothing more to say. I'm going back to the camp now, but not till you've gone." He continued staring at the water, his face hard as stone.

Her hand came up, and the sound of her slap shattered the stillness. He never flinched, didn't even look at her. She froze for an instant, then turned and ran blindly through the trees.

She lay listening, waiting for the owl to hoot again. It had to be close to dawn, she thought. She had lain in her pallet for hours, turning and tossing, suffering the most anguished humiliation and pain.

For the first time since she had met Breve Pinchon she was experiencing despair, and she writhed in its grip. There were moments when she refused to believe it—he would change his mind. Whatever he thought now, he loved her and he would change. But why? Why his reluctance? Not just reluctance but downright refusal and renunciation! What were the reasons he couldn't tell her? He couldn't be married—Micah Tillett would have known it, and that would be no dark secret, no mysterious cause that he couldn't speak of. Stubborn, stubborn! She gritted her teeth in rage at the quality they shared. She raised up and looked across the campfire, hoping Jerome would be awake, needing someone to talk to whom she could trust. But he was laid out, fast asleep. Everyone was sound asleep. One of the horses stamped the ground and whinnied softly.

In her dismay she had not bothered to change into her nightgown. Now, unable to sleep, she got up quietly and slipped into her boots. At least no one would bother her now. She roamed off through the trees, hugging her shawl around her. The air was cool, and there were little crackling noises made by the nocturnal animals. She had never been afraid of the dark, even as a child, and now she welcomed it.

The river gleamed whitely under a high moon. She reached a small rise and made her way to the top of it, looking downstream to where the water rushed over a small dam. The moonlight struck her full as she stood there, her profile chiseled in light. Finally she came down carefully, picking her way through the trees. She stopped after a few yards; she had left the path back to the clearing and the trees were thicker here. A twig snapped behind her and she hurried along, thinking of bobcats. They were night predators and though they seldom attacked humans, they were vicious if someone unwittingly crossed their path.

Another twig snapped and she gathered her shawl more tightly around her, wishing she hadn't ventured into this unfamiliar territory. She heard a soft crunch behind her just as the hand covered her mouth and the burly arm went around her. Her stifled scream became a gurgle as her neck was jerked backward. She struggled, but the arm held her tighter, and though her breath was almost cut off, the stench was penetrating—the turgid scent of a long unwashed body. Now a beard scraped her bare neck. She kicked hard with her foot and felt her heel strike solid against a shinbone.

"Goddam it!" a voice rasped. "I'll fix you, girlie."

The last thing she felt before she lost consciousness was the heavy fist that came smashing into her jaw.

He bent above her for a moment. "Well, girlie, you're a rare prize, you are," he muttered.

The man knelt then, his jacket showing a tear where one sleeve joined the body, a dirty wool shirt showing through. He drew a strip of grimy cloth from his pocket and shoved it into Leita's mouth before tying the ends in back of her head. Then he drew a knife from a sheath and cut a length of rope from a coil at his belt. He turned her over on her stomach and tied her wrists together tightly, then quickly cut another length and tied her ankles together. He looked around cautiously, sucking on his teeth. His beard, dark and uneven, hung below a face whose eyes were set close together under dark, bushy brows. The broad-brimmed felt hat he wore was grease-stained and crumpled. After tying the last knot securely he picked Leita up, hoisting her over his shoulder almost effortlessly. He gave one last look behind him at the smoke curling up from the campfire beyond the trees and started walking. His feet hit the ground almost noiselessly, and a smile creased his grimed cheeks as he half-loped along with his burden.

He had gone a good mile when he threaded back from the riverbank to a black horse tethered to a tree in a small clearing. The horse whinnied softly.

"Quiet girl," he cautioned, and with Leita slumped over his shoulder, he put his foot in the stirrup and grunted as he hoisted himself up onto the horse. Then he carefully lowered Leita's inert form and placed her in a side-saddle position in front of him. He looked her in her face for a moment, sucking on his teeth again. Then, digging his heels into the horse's sides, he started off. It was another half mile before he guided the horse across a stream. Eventually he came to a barely discernible trail that led up into the hills.

Leita stirred and her eyes fluttered open. His stench

was oppressive, and she stared up in horror at the grimy face. Her wrists burned, chafed by the rough rope, and she struggled for a moment. His arm jerked her roughly and dark little eyes burned down into her face.

"Now you listen here, girlie," he said roughly, "you and me will get along just fine as long as you set quiet. If you've a mind to start cuttin' up I'll just have to belt you again, you hear?"

Leita's jaw ached fiercely. Where was he taking her? They were going uphill, which probably meant he was holed up in the mountains somewhere. Remembering what Breve had said about the difficulty of finding anyone who had been carried off into the hills, her heart sank. The angle of the climb forced her weight against him, and the gag was so tight in her mouth that she had to breathe rhythmically through her nose to keep from stifling. But there was nothing she could do about the terrible smell.

The smelly rider finally reined his horse to a stop and let out a shrill whistle, so sharp it hurt her ears. He whistled again and twice more before he muttered, "Aye, there 'tis."

She turned her head and saw a dim yellow light ahead. It swung back and forth. Somebody was signaling with a lantern.

"Took you long enough to hear me," her smelly captor growled. "Was you asleep?"

"Hell no, we wasn't asleep!"

Suddenly Leita was bathed in the yellow lamplight, and she saw a skinny man with a ragged coat over a filthy leather vest. He wore no shirt that she could see and his brown beard reached down to his collarbone. His hair was long and tangled.

"What in hell you got there? What're you doin' with a woman?"

46

"Just call Pa."

Her captor dismounted, grunting heavily as they both reached the ground awkwardly.

"Christ, my arm's asleep," he complained, shifting her weight to his other arm and swinging the arm that had held her pinioned on the long ride.

"All right now, Jed, what's happened here?" The voice came from a tall man with a grizzled beard and two small black eyes gleaming in the lamplight.

"I got us somethin' better than horses, Pa! Just look at this." And the man called Jed turned Leita around by her shoulders. The older man scanned her briefly. "Better than horses, huh? Well, I ought to horsewhip you! You never had no sense and you sure as hell aren't improvin' none. How'd you get her?"

Smelly Jed said, "I was just creepin' along stealthy like, on my way to them horses and I spied her standin' on a little rise by the river, all by herself. She's a sight for sore eyes, ain't she?" he inquired, a note of pride in his voice.

"You crazy son of a bitch! And what are we going to do with her now?" the old man snarled.

"Hell, Pa, what do you suppose? Ain't had a woman for months, none of us has, and now we got us a young one. You can have her first, Pa." His voice had descended into a whine.

"I ought to kill you and be done with my troubles! Take that gag out of her mouth. There ain't nobody up here to hear her scream. She can scream her head off if she's a mind to. Loosen up her ankles too. If you had any sense you'd a done that miles back, instead of carryin' her so awkward. Anybody but you would have." He turned and spat a huge glob onto the ground.

Jed's fingers fumbled at the knot, and the old man

reached over and undid it quickly. Leita shuddered. His hand rested on her shoulder for an instant. "Just a filly, ain't you?" he said.

There was another man standing behind the brown-bearded one. He was comparatively clean-shaven, with only a dark stubble on his chin and he stood tall and broad. They must be brothers, she thought, as she rubbed her sore lips. She leaned over and spit, to get the taste of the dirty rag out of her mouth.

The old man turned toward the stubble-chinned one. "I just want you to look at this, George. This is what is going to roust us out of the best place we've had yet or keep us holed up for a month of Sundays."

"Pa!" Jed protested. "She ain't going to cause us no trouble—she can cook for us and we can all of us lay with her. You ain't too old for a woman and you don't need to tell me you are!"

Leita flinched and jumped back as the older man's fist struck Jed hard in the stomach. He doubled up with a sickening grunt and his father landed another blow that sent him to his knees.

The older man was breathing hard as he glared down at him. "I sent you down to git us a horse, a horse we needed bad. A whole wagon train down there, six wagons we counted and horses to spare. I sent you alone because it only takes one man to steal a horse, for Christ's sake. And you went down there and kidnapped a girl! A girl that comes from wealth, too, mind you, and from a set of wagons that's just boilin' with young bucks. And what do you think them young bucks is goin' to be doin' as soon as they find out this little filly of theirs is gone?"

The one with the brown beard spoke up. "They'll come lookin' for her, that's what they'll do."

"That's the first sensible thing I've heard tonight," the old man snorted. "They'll come, all right, and they'll come hell-bent for leather. They've probably started already."

"Pa, they was all sleep!"

"Shut up, you idiot! What if one of them gets up to take a piss and sees she's gone? Yessir boy, you've done us in this time."

"They can't find us here, Pa. We're ten miles wound into the hills."

"What the hell difference is that? And you just stay down there, you dumb bastard!" He kicked Jed sharply in the ribs as he started to rise up from all fours. Jed yelped in pain and held his side.

"If it had been a horse, like you was supposed to get, what would they have done? They'd a scouted around for two, three hours at the most and gone on. You think they'll mosey around for a couple of hours lookin' for this girl? How I ever spawned such a sop-head I don't know. They'll scour the woods clean round that river and they'll find that trail, that's what they'll do! They'll follow your tracks in this spring mud and inside of thirty-six hours they'll be tear-assin' up this hill. Thirty-six hours at the most—if we're lucky." He turned to the stubble-chinned man. "George, you load up those horses with grub, grub enough for a week. Come mornin' we're headin back fu'ther into the hills and we're gonna have to last out."

Chapter 5

BREVE AWOKE WITH A START. HE HAD SLEPT RESTLESS-
ly, after long hours of bitter thought. He had said what
he had to say. He could never tell her the real reason.
From now on he would have to keep a wall between
them, as he should have from the beginning. His head
ached and his mouth felt brackish. The campfire had
burned low and he examined the sky overhead. A dim
glow to the east signified that dawn was about forty-five
minutes away. Leita's soft lips against his burned real
again in his mind, and he shook his head and got up
quickly. If ever he had to get a hold of himself, it was
now, he decided.

He refrained from looking across the fire toward her
pallet, and stepped quietly into the trees to relieve
himself. He went to the river to wash up, then gathered
an armful of wood and returned to the clearing. This
time he glanced toward Leita's sleeping place, and
was surprised to see her blankets pushed down and the

pallet empty. She must have gone into the woods, he thought. Funny I didn't hear her. He laid part of the wood carefully onto the fire after forking up the embers and spooned coffee into the three granite coffeepots. He stopped midway and cocked his head. There was no sound from the copse of trees on the other side of the clearing. He set the pots on the grate over the fire. It burned briskly now and he stared at it for a few moments. Then he turned and brushing his hands on his breeches, walked into the trees, careful to step on plenty of twigs to warn her of his coming so she would call out in case she was relieving herself.

The wood was quiet, except for the scattered twittering of the waking birds. Maybe she's seen me and is keeping away—embarrassed after last night. He walked back into the clearing. She wasn't there. He walked quietly over to her pallet. Bending down he rubbed his hand over her pillow. Damp and cold. He rubbed his hand quickly down over the blanket inside the pallet. It was cold and damp with the morning dew.

My God in heaven, he breathed, she hasn't lain on this for hours! His stomach gave a lurch and he walked swiftly to where Samuel slept with Lucy Mae curled up beside him. Samuel opened his eyes as Breve bent over him. Breve beckoned silently, and Samuel got up, pulling on his breeches and grabbing his woolen shirt as he walked away from the sleeping figures.

"What's the matter, Breve?" His eyes were narrowed as they scanned the other man's face.

"It's Leita," Breve whispered. "Her pallet's empty and it's cold and damp and covered with dew. She hasn't been in it for hours."

"Where could she be?" Samuel asked, bewildered.

"That's just the question," Breve answered grimly. "I've about covered the piece of woods on that side and there's not a sign of her."

"We'd better roust the others out and start looking."

Soon Samuel was explaining the situation to the others, and they gazed at one another in dumb surprise.

Calls of "Leita, Leita" spread through the woods and down the river as they loped off. The air was heavy with the promise of rain. Eugene and Matthew had ranged out on either side of Breve, and they were working their way upriver while the others went downriver.

Suddenly Matthew called out: "Breve, come here."

Breve ran and found Matthew hunkered down on the ground, brushing leaves aside.

"Look at this," he pointed. "Not one of us wears a boot like that. Look at the print of that heel."

Breve squatted down. "Those are home-cobbled boots," Breve whispered. "None of us wears home-cobbled boots."

Matthew looked at him with concern. The healthy tan of Breve's face had paled to ivory.

"Somebody's been scouting the place in the night. It's still fresh," Matthew said.

Breve crouched along in a duck waddle, his eyes on the ground, then raised up. "Here's the match for it."

They worked their way silently, following the tracks when Eugene called out: "I've found some of Leita's footprints! She's been in this part of the trees."

"Follow them," Breve called back grimly, his gaze never lifting from the ground.

Matthew stopped. "Breve," he said softly, "his tracks lead to right here."

"I knew it," Breve said. "I just didn't want to look for a minute."

They made a circle and found the singular footprints again, leading back to the river now and sunk very deep in the mud.

"He's carrying her now," Breve said. "Matthew go tell the others we've found the trail."

Minutes later Eugene came up, looking somber.

Breve's eyes narrowed and his heart began to pound when he saw what Eugene was carrying. It was Leita's blue shawl.

The sun had risen but it shone weak and yellow through the heavy gray clouds. The light was uncertain here in the darkness of the trees, and Breve kept his eyes on the ground. Then he saw the hoofprints beside the tree and the pile of cold droppings.

"He had a mount," he said resignedly. "I'll follow the trail if someone will bring me my horse. We're going to be slower than him, I'm afraid, and he's already hours ahead of us."

"If she's been harmed we'll string him up. I'll do it personally," Samuel declared, his shoulders drooping with his anguish.

Breve marched on, scanning both sides of the riverbank. Farther up the winding river he thought he detected a gap in the trees. He turned, impatient to start, and saw the horses approaching single-file along the water's edge.

"He crossed here," Breve called out, "and I think I see what might be a trail up yonder."

He leaped onto the horse that Matthew had brought and waded into the river. On the other side he looked down and saw the hoofprints along the back.

"We'll have to go single file and check to see that we're keeping the trail," he called back.

"You lead the way, Breve," Micah Tillett called out, "and we'll double-check the hoofprints. "You'll be able to go faster that way."

Breve waved one arm in agreement and spurred his horse. Presently he reached the opening in the brush he had seen earlier. He looked down at the mud and smiled in tight-lipped satisfaction. The prints were precise and clear on the ground and they pointed uphill. He wheeled his horse into the faintly marked defile between the thick growth of bushes and trees and began working his way uphill.

Jed's father stood with his hands on his hips. "They can't find the trail till light, and then it's gonna take them a while. Come sun-up one of us takes this girl downstream and turns her loose. Takes her blindfolded, just to be sure. She can make her way somewheres—the main thing is to get shut of her and get shut of her fast. If we was to turn her loose at night worse harm might come to her—parts of these hills she could stumble around in for a coon's age and not find a chimney. Now get off the ground, you no-good son-of-a-bitch, and take care of that horse."

Jed rose slowly. All this time Leita had not uttered a word. Her relief was so great at the prospect of deliverance, that she could scarcely breathe out of fear that the old man would change his mind. He started toward the low shack, outlined in light from the lamp that the brown-bearded George held in one hand. George was staring at Leita, his eyes flat and expressionless. The old man glanced at him, stopped in his tracks and turned.

"You all better understand something right now. This girl's not to be handled! If she was to be handled there's a right good chance that just gettin' her back wouldn't be enough for those young bucks with the wagons. They'd be out for blood then, you bet you, and they'd follow us till they got it. First one of you that goes to lay a hand on her gets an arm broke, and you know I'm not too weak to do it. I'll lay your heads in with a shovel in a minute flat! I haven't lived this long to get myself strung up because of any goddam girl, you hear?"

All three of them nodded dumbly.

He turned toward her. "Well, sister, come on. You can roll up in a blanket in front of the fire and that will have to do you. Just foller me."

She took a step toward him and fell, her ankles still numb from the ropes. He pulled her to her feet.

"Can't walk, can ye? Well, here goes." He scooped her up in his wiry arms almost effortlessly and walked toward the shanty.

"You don't stink," she said in surprise when he set her down at the door.

He threw back his head and emitted a racketing laugh as he slapped his leg. "First words out of your mouth—not surprisin' seein' as how you've been up aginst Jed. Must have stunk you out. Every so often we take him down and dump him in the river. He ain't partial to water, Jed ain't, and he about stinks me out too. I should'a held his head under for half an hour or so the last time we did it. What's your name, sister?"

"Leita Johnston."

"Well, that's a good southern name. Your pappy in the war?"

"Yes, and my four brothers. One was killed."

"Four brothers, eh." A frown creased his brow. "Jesus Christ," he muttered. "Well, come on in, girl. Tomorrow you'll be back with your folks and you can just try to forget gettin' waylaid by a skunk. Scared you some, didn't he?" he said, looking at her sharply. Her face was pale in the light of the fire from the fireplace, and the skin under her eyes was darkened with fatigue and strain.

"He scared me something awful."

"Well, you don't need to be scared of him. He's a coward, that one is, on top of bein' a half-idiot."

"I thought you'd all be like him," she whispered, sinking down onto the blanket he had spread out on the

56

floor. He threw another blanket down and reached into a cupboard for a third one.

"We got plenty blankets—easy to steal off lines when the women airs them in the spring. Jed ain't slept under none of these, so they don't stink." His voice was harsh but his eyes were sober and gentle on her. "So you thought we'd all be like him. You must 'a had some fears, sister. Time was, years back, I was an honest farmer. Poorer'n Job's turkey, but an honest man, as honest men go." He hunkered down in front of the fire, a jug in one hand and a tin cup in the other. "I went off to that war, and when I got back my few little outbuildings and my house was burnt to the ground, and the ground got burnt too—Shuhman's men did everything but salt my patch of land. Even my plow all broke up and not a mule to my name. I had no money, exceptin' Confederate money which weren't no damn good. Only one thing to do and I done it; I took to the hills, my boys along with me. They ain't had no mother since they was knee-high to a pup. She died of the fever. I done a fair job of raisin' them." He stared at the fire and she shivered and wrapped the blanket round her.

"They're not bad—leastways two of them ain't. Jed's a cull, that's all there is to it—a plain cull. Pissed in his bed till he had a beard, he did. Well, he done a poor night's work tonight."

She pulled the blanket more tightly around her shoulders.

"You're chillin', ain't you—what is it—Leita?"

She nodded dumbly, her teeth chattering, and he uncorked the jug and poured an inch of the clear liquid into the cup.

"I'll put on the kettle and make you some tea. I'll put a little of that white lightnin' in it and it'll go down better, laced with molasses anyway."

He rose and placed an ancient kettle on the hob and got down a tin can from a shelf and spooned tea into a brown pot. When the tea was brewed he poured some into the corn liquor in the cup and then stirred thick molasses into it with a bent spoon.

"Now you just drink that down, sister, and you'll sleep like a top. If that don't warm you enough we'll pour you another."

Leita sipped tentatively and then brightened a little.

"I reckon that's hit the spot," the old man said. "I'm goin' outside now to make sure Tom has stowed enough stuff. You rest easy."

She nodded and looked around her. The shanty was larger than it looked from outside. The floor had been rudely laid with lengths of rough pine and there was a bedstead in each of the inner corners; one had three posts, with one broken off. A table stood in the middle, beyond the fieldstone fireplace. A tin cup stood on the table with a few pieces of cutlery standing in it. There was no stove; evidently they used the fireplace for their cooking. It was rough, but not too dirty, all things considered, she thought. The drink warmed her, and she nodded over the cup. She lay down on the floor, snuggling into the scratchy warmth of the blanket, and fell asleep at once.

Later the men filed silently to bed, and the old man got up once and spread an extra blanket over the sleeping girl. He stood looking down on her for a moment, his long-johns rumpled around his bony knees, then shook his head and crawled back into bed. They rose quietly before first light, pulled on their trousers and went outside. All four of them stood back in the trees, making water and rubbing their sleep-dimmed eyes.

The old man was buttoning up when he announced: "Jed, I'm goin' to give you a chance to make some amends for the trouble you brought on us. You're gonna be the one that takes the girl back down the hill and lets her loose. Now, for Christ's sake, don't go so close to that camp that you get caught. Don't go clear to the river, whatever you do. Turn her loose just the other side of that line of brush about two miles up from the river and hightail it back here."

George rested one arm against a leafed-out sycamore and rubbed his chin, yawning. Jed remained silent, staring at the ground as he adjusted his greasy trousers.

"We gonna head for the cave the Davisson brothers used last year. It'd take the devil himself to find that, and we gonna hold up for a good week. Now we better get somethin' in our bellies. You boil up some coffee, Lester, and George, you hot up the rest of those grits and fry the sowbelly. It'll be another hour before the sun is up and we can bolt our vittles and be on our way while them folks is still rubbin' their eyes."

Leita awoke as they came into the shack and sat up in alarm.

"Don't know where you are, do you?" George grunted as he knelt to stir up the fire.

"I do now," she said grimly.

"What you need is a bowl of hot grits to set you to rights."

She threw off the blankets and rubbed her shoulders to relieve the ache from sleeping on the hard floor. She rose then and straightened her skirt.

"I'm just goin' to step outside," she said, making for the door, and they nodded.

She scampered through the trees till she was out of sight of the shanty. After she relieved herself, she was struck by a thought, and reaching down, pulled and tore at a piece of the petticoat edging until she had freed a fairly long strip. She looked around quickly and tied the fluttering white embroidery on a bush.

Lester handed her a steaming bowl of grits when she got back in, and she settled down on a rickety chair beside the table, warming her hands on the bowl.

"Molasses in your coffee?" Lester asked. She nodded and he spooned a heaping spoonful of thick brown molasses into the hot black coffee. The others were squatted round the fireplace. Jed hadn't spoken a word; he stared into his bowl as he ate, and grits slipped into his tangled beard. She looked at him and shuddered.

"Douse that fire, boys!" the old man called, and they did straightaway.

"Now Leita," the old man turned to her, "Jed's goin' to ride you downhill and turn you loose. You gonna be a piece from your camp so's he won't get caught, but he show the way for you, and you just get to the river and follow it. You gonna run into some of your folks out lookin' for you, like as not. Now I hate to do this, but for our own sakes we're goin' to have to blindfold you."

She nodded, understanding the precaution.

"And I'm tellin' you, so you can tell your menfolk, we goin' to other ground, so if they want to find us they have a real piece of work cut out for 'em. I know these hills like the back of my hand and I could hide out for a year without bein' found out, so they be better off just to forget about us and go on their way."

"There's no reason for them to come and get you. You've been kind to me, sir."

"Sir! How 'bout that, Pa!" George guffawed.

"That's just polite speakin'," his father retorted. "We can't take no chances—we be long gone anyways."

Leita nodded and he handed her a worn woolen frock coat that had once been brown.

"This'll help keep the chill off you, Miss."

Jed went outside, then stuck his head back in the doorway and called: "Well, come on if you're comin'."

She hesitated and looked at the old man.

"Go on, Missy," he said kindly. "He learn his lesson by now. You gonna be all right."

She felt a quivering in her bowels but forced herself to the doorway, hugging the old frock coat tightly around her as if it were a suit of armor.

George stood beside Jed's black mare with a strip of cloth in his hand. "I'm just goin' to tie this round your head now, girlie," he said.

She looked at the cloth and noted with relief that it was fairly clean. George blindfolded her, then lifted her onto the saddle, seating her behind Jed who was frowning sulkily.

"You sure got your saddlebags loaded, Jed," George said. "Looks like you cleaned out half the stores."

"Don't aim to starve to death," Jed replied brusquely, wheeling the horse. Leita put her hands gingerly onto his back to brace herself, and the horse galloped off down the trail.

After riding a good thirty minutes they struck fairly level ground. Jed reined up without speaking a word. Thank God, she thought. But Jed turned quickly in the saddle and shoved a gritty cloth into her mouth. She tried to scream and pulled at the cloth with her hands. He grabbed her, clawing her hands away and pulled her down off the horse, twisting one arm behind her.

"You just hush now," he rasped. "I ain't through with you, girlie, not by a long sight."

She almost fainted from the pain in her arm.

"You fight me anymore and I just have to put you to sleep again with my fist," he whispered, grunting as he held her pinned by one arm. "Now, I gonna let go your arm just long enough to tie this gag. One peep out of you and I just might break your jaw this time."

I mustn't panic, she kept repeating to herself in spite of the terror that gnawed at her innards. A drop of rain hit her cheek softly, and then another. He hoisted her back onto the horse and mounted quickly, wheeling off to the right. There was a clap of thunder, and the raindrops came more quickly now.

"Tarnation," he muttered.

Let it come, Leita prayed with renewed hope. Soft ground would make their tracks plain as day. If only Breve would hurry. . . .

There was a slit in the rear wall of the shanty. Breve put his face to the crack, breathing softly while he waited for his eyes to adjust to the dimness within. . . . Empty! He turned to the others. "Empty as a tomb," he breathed. He felt sick with disappointment and made his way to the front of the shanty. Samuel stood against a far tree, his rifle at his shoulder. Breve kicked hard at the door. He raised his own rifle and ducked back against the wall. Nothing.

Samuel and Joseph Tillett came up and followed him inside.

Breve looked at the kettle on the hearth and stuck his finger into the quarter inch of grits on the bottom. "Still warm." He looked at Samuel. "They stayed here the night, anyway. That means we have a better chance of finding them."

Joseph Tillett scratched his head. "In these hills?"

"We'll find them. We'll spread out and cover the ground and run them down," Breve shot back.

Eugene ran into the shanty, holding the lacy petticoat strip.

Samuel took the lacy strip from him and examined it closely, his face haggard from worry.

Breve's impatient outburst jarred them. "Well, we can't stand around here all day. Time is precious. Let's move!"

62

The water was rolling down Leita's neck. Branches caught at her skirt, showering more water onto her and she tried to shrink inside the coat. Jed galloped on, silent and single-minded, threading his way through a narrow trail, at times almost completely overgrown.

On they went, higher and steeper, and her heart sank at the thought of how far they had come on this obscure trail. Animals stirred in the brush, and birds began to flutter and preen their damp feathers. They were approaching a narrow defile between two tall outcroppings of rock. A stunted tree grew out of a crack at a tortured angle. Something moved. She looked up, and the moment she caught a glimpse of the dark shape, a harsh, yowling scream split the air. The horse reared. One hoof caught in a deep hole in the trail, and the mare screamed and whinnied. As the horse reared, a lithe long shape leaped from one side of the jutting rock to the other. Leita slid backward, down over the rump and tail of the rearing horse, and Jed was thrown to the side. The horse fell, landing on top of him, and Jed let out a scream of agony.

Leita sat up, breathing hard. Her eyes searched the top of the rocks for the bobcat. The horse tried frantically to right itself in the narrow space and finally scrambled up, neighing frantically. Limping at first, it started off, then broke into a hobbling canter. The bobcat was nowhere in sight. Leita heard a moan, and she looked over to where Jed lay. His right leg was bent out at an unnatural angle. He tried to move, then let out a shriek. Grimacing with pain, Jed pulled up the leg of his trousers. Leita gasped. The garish white of a blood-soaked bone protruded through a jagged break in the flesh halfway down his shin, and he was moaning terribly.

Leita backed away.

He stared at her with wild eyes. "You ain't goin' to leave me? I'll die! I'll die here alone!" he screamed.

She turned and ran back down the trail. Yes, he was scum, and he deserved to die, she reflected, at the same time wondering where in this wilderness she could go to find help.

The rain had slowed a little, for which Breve was grateful. It had rained just long enough to suit their purpose. A harder rain could have washed out the prints that everything depended on. Still, he was disquieted by the thought of how slowly they were progressing compared with the galloping horse that was carrying their quarry even higher into the hills. Suddenly the clouds parted and the sunlight beamed down through the trees, illuminating every leaf and branch and making the trail that much clearer.

It was then that he froze in his saddle. There had been a sound—a swishing and a light thud, thud. He signaled for the others to halt. Jumping down from his horse, he crouched in the thick cover, his rifle at his shoulder as he sighted at the curve of the overgrown trail.

Leita came running breathlessly around the curve and stopped short at the sight of the horses. Breve's finger froze on the trigger, and Jerome gave a whoop of joy as he hurtled out of the brush.

Leita held a hand to her pounding heart, unable to speak, and Breve reached her first. She looked up at him and threw her arms around him and pressed her face against his wet jacket. They stood like that for what seemed long minutes to Jerome and Nathaniel. Breve swallowed to hide his emotion, looking down on her soft golden hair, darkened by the rain.

"Is he after you?"

"He's a good two miles back. His leg is broken, and

the bone is sticking up through it." She breathed deeply, still clinging to him, and he hugged her tightly, his relief overwhelming all restraint. Then he led her to a fallen tree and squatted on the ground in front of her.

"Are you all right, Leita? Are you hurt—or anything?"

She shook her head and rubbed her hands over her mud-streaked cheeks.

"What were you doing in the woods after everyone thought you were asleep?" Jerome asked.

Leita dropped her eyes. "I couldn't sleep," she answered softly. She was pale with fatigue. Her lip quivered, and tears welled up in her eyes. "I never thought I was in danger so close to the camp. He came to steal a horse—" she choked.

Breve put his arms around her and drew her head down onto his shoulder. Nathaniel and Jerome looked at each other and turned away. Jerome gave a cough of embarrassment and they both peered up the trail.

Leita sobbed, unable to stop, no longer able to contain the pent-up torment she had endured for two days. Breve smoothed her wet hair back from her forehead and groped inside his jacket, producing a handkerchief. He wiped her cheeks tenderly, his face sober.

"We've got to go back and get him," she said.

"You're damned right we're going to get him," Breve replied, helping her to her feet. . . .

But it was to no avail—and perhaps just as well. When the party reached the jutting crag of sandstone some thirty minutes later, the man they had come to get lay dead in a pool of blood that had spilled from the severed artery in his leg.

The nightmare was over. Breve put his arm around Leita's waist. "We're going to get the horses and go back to camp and get some breakfast. Then we'll dump this worthless corpse on the local sheriff and be on our way."

They rode back in silence, Leita still smarting from her aching jaw and chafed wrists, Breve lost in his own disturbing thoughts. It was no good, he reflected bitterly, it could never happen. . . .

Chapter 6

Virginia in the spring was blindingly beautiful, in spite of the rains. The day they approached the city of Washington and sighted the white capitol dome gleaming in the rain-washed sky, Leita stirred with excitement. The rains had abated the night before and the sun shone warm and bright. They passed rolling green fields and beautifully trimmed lawns where sheep grazed and February lambs scampered beside the ewes. Soon the fields were behind them, and the houses drew closer together, and they were rolling down Pennsylvania Avenue, sixteen feet in width and a wonder for its time. The street was muddy and the passing carriages splashed her skirts. It was the first time Leita had seen Negroes dressed like whites, and she stared with curiosity as they ambled down the narrow pedestrian path. At the hotel where they were to stay, she marveled at the sight of the heavy chandeliers and the wine-red carpeting in the lobby. Couches and wing-backed chairs were set about, and black attendants in livery stood at careful attention. It was much larger than the hotel in Charleston.

Leita, Belle and Mary Jo seated themselves in the tall chairs while they awaited the rest of the party. One of the liveried servants presented himself immediately. Leita stared up at him, at the bright green frock coat trimmed with gold frogs and the snowy white jabot beneath his black face. She smiled in delight; he looked as if he were dressed for a ball. They ordered coffee and he smiled, too, amused at the spectacle of these mud-stained girls ensconced in their chairs, looking happily around like a litter of young kittens.

Presently, Lucy Mae swept up, with Anna Tillett and Judith Knox bringing up the rear.

"Well, girls, we'll live like civilized ladies for a night or two now," she said, her eyes twinkling at Leita and Belle, who were staring at the plump nudes and cherubs cavorting on the frescoed ceiling.

The liveried servant returned, wheeling a cart with a silver coffee pot and delicate china. The scent of fresh coffee made Leita sigh, and he suppressed a smile as he poured. He whisked a damask napkin off a plate, and Leita selected a petit-four with pink frosting. She bit into it happily, savoring the rich, yellow cake on her tongue.

"Someone's been staring a hole through you ever since we sat down," Mary Jo whispered, with a coy little grin.

"Who?" Leita asked, and wheeled around. She met the stare of a slender, dark-haired man leaning against one of the ornate pillars of the lobby. He held a gold-headed walking stick, and his frock coat was a dark, Prussian blue, adorned with silver buttons. There was frank admiration in his eyes, and he continued to survey Leita even after she met his eyes. Leita blushed and looked away, conscious of her windblown hair and mud-spattered skirt.

"He's a handsome devil," Mary Jo whispered again. Leita risked another glance. Her admirer was now speaking with an older man whose gold watch chain extended across a very ample paunch. Leita allowed herself a long look at the younger man's well-cut profile. His brows winged gracefully above hazel-green eyes, and his lips curved delicately at the corners.

Just then he glanced her way. Leita blinked as he focused his gaze directly at her, inclined his head in a bow, and smiled. She turned away.

It was not until later that evening that she discovered who he was. She had gone with the others to the theater, and afterwards the whole party trooped off to a place called L'Enfant, where there was food, music and dancing. She had just returned to her table after dancing with Jerome when she was addressed by an unfamiliar voice.

"Good evening, Miss Johnston."

She turned. It was the stranger, resplendent in evening dress.

Jerome interceded. "I don't believe we've met," he said coolly.

"We haven't, but I inquired about your party at the desk. My name is Stephen de Jean and I am from Chicago. I am here for a short stay on business, but I learned that you were journeying to Fort Wayne, Indiana, and since I have a sister living there, I thought I would take the opportunity of introducing myself." His smile and his manner were disarming. Jerome relaxed. Introductions were made, and when the man showed no sign of moving off, Jerome invited him to join them. On being introduced to Samuel he presented him with an engraved card.

"Stephen de Jean, Investments/ 530 N. Lake Street,

Chicago," Samuel read. When Stephen mentioned that he visited Fort Wayne frequently, they fell into conversation easily and it was some time before he spoke to Leita.

When he asked her for the pleasure of a dance she accepted. She noted with some satisfaction that Breve was watching them from the far end of the table, and she smiled fetchingly up at Mr. de Jean. They conversed lightly as they danced. When the music ended, he detained her with a touch on the arm. "I visit Fort Wayne frequently, as I mentioned. Perhaps you would allow me to call on you after you are settled. It would be my great pleasure. I shall, of course, ask permission of your father."

She smiled, flattered, but sensed something of a contradiction about him, as if his manners belied the man he really was.

"I'm sure that would be most kind of you, Mr. de Jean. I shall know so few people. It's very nice to make a new friend." She cocked her head to one side. "I detect a slight accent, Mr. de Jean. That's not a Chicago accent?"

He laughed heartily. "No, my dear, it is far from that. I was born in France—Paris, actually—and came here when I was quite young. Your sharp ears have found me out, though I flatter myself that I speak your language quite well."

"France," she said, intrigued. "It is one of my dreams, to see London and Paris and Rome—and I shall, too, when I am twenty." Her eyes sparkled as she spoke, and de Jean's lips curved in a smile, revealing small, perfect white teeth.

"One of your dreams—and you have others, no doubt." He looked at her thoughtfully.

"Everyone has dreams. Most of them can come true if you're determined to make them."

"And you, my dear, you are determined, I'll wager."

"That I am, Mr. de Jean," she replied, thinking of Breve. "Life is too short to be otherwise, don't you think?"

"I agree, Miss Leita. I, too, have dreams, though they change from time to time. But I feel, as you do, that with determination they can all be accomplished. The trick is in knowing what you want and grasping the opportunity."

"Once I decide on what I want, I am not very easily dissuaded," she replied with a laugh.

"Nor am I," he said. She eyed him speculatively; it had sounded faintly like a challenge.

The hour was late when the party broke up. Stephen bent over her hand and brushed it with his lips. "Until we meet again, Miss Leita, and may you have the most pleasant of journeys."

She smiled her goodnight. Jerome and her father escorted her out on the walk.

"That's a mighty polished young man you've picked off, Leita," Samuel said.

"He's interesting, isn't he?" she replied. She had noticed that though Breve was considerably larger than de Jean, something about de Jean's presence almost put him on a par with the rugged, manly Colonel Pinchon. I think I'll enjoy having him call on me, she thought defiantly. I'm not going to go into hiding just because I'm being so pointedly ignored.

"Frankly, he reminded me of a black panther getting ready to spring," Jerome remarked.

"You have such an imagination, Jerome," Leita laughed.

"I'm just observant. And usually I'm right," Jerome said flatly.

Breve hadn't entered the conversation at all.

Rain poured in torrents the day they left Washington, but the weather had improved considerably by the

71

time they reached the Delaware River and entered the environs of Philadelphia. Samuel had not seen his sister Grace since before the war.

The welcome was festive, and Samuel's sister was bursting with pleasure at this reunion.

Leita went sightseeing with the others, but Breve was not among them. He had vanished the first day, saying he would stay with friends he had promised to visit. It wasn't till the last morning of their stay that Leita saw him, handing a lady down from a carriage, a tall and slender lady with long dark curls brushing the shoulders of her ivory silk dress. Breve saw the sightseers, waved and came over to them.

"It's good to see such a bevy of southerners in this northern city," he said, and then presented the lady. She was a Mrs. Valerie Prescott. The whole group retired to the Meriton Hotel, and over lemonade Leita learned that Mr. Prescott had been killed at Antietam. So the lovely Valerie is a widow, and she's got to be at least twenty-six, Leita thought, trying to keep from staring at her. That Breve and this woman were on terms of intimate friendship was obvious. The lemonade was giving Leita heartburn.

"Valerie was in school with my sister Melody," Breve explained, handing around a plate of cakes. Mrs. Prescott's hands were smooth and elegantly long-fingered, and her complexion was a glowing ivory, with a slight bloom on her cheeks. Leita felt somehow young and gauche in the presence of this tall, willowy woman. Breve hadn't met her eyes once, and Leita's stomach became more unsettled when Valerie's reticule slipped from her lap and Breve handed it back to her, their fingers touching and lingering for a moment.

The rest of the afternoon was a blur to Leita until Fairmount Park. Jerome joined Leita on the riverbank there, away from the others, and they strolled along in silence. She saw them, their arms intertwined, in the shadow of two great oaks. As the man bent to kiss the woman, Jerome chuckled: "We ought to turn around and not disturb them."

Leita smiled wistfully—until a shaft of sunlight pierced the shaded retreat, and Breve's dark curling hair and broad shoulders were unmistakable.

Leita's heart hammered so hard she thought her ears would burst. The fleeting jealousy she had felt at Mary Jo's proprietary airs toward Breve was nothing compared to the sickness that swept through her now. Her breast rose and fell as they hurried away, and she bit her lip to hold back the tears.

Later, on the drive back to the house, her cheeks still flaming with humiliation and a jealousy so deep she hadn't known such a feeling existed, she made a vow. Someday, when he wants me very badly, I'll make him just as miserable as he's made me.

That night after supper she was slinging lingerie into her trunk when Mary Jo entered. "Well, what did you think of her?" she breathed.

"Think of who?" Leita snapped.

"Why, Breve's mistress, of course," Mary Jo retorted.

Leita's breath caught and she leaned over, pretending to adjust the ribbon that threaded through the lace of her camisole. "Who told you Mrs. Prescott is Breve's mistress?"

"Well, at least you know what a mistress is." Mary Jo laughed and curled up like a kitten on the divan. "She is the coolest cucumber I ever laid eyes on. And she's as old as he is, maybe a year or two older. She certainly has kept him busy. We haven't seen hide nor hair of him since we got here."

"*I* don't see how you can tell all that from just drinking lemonade with them," Leita snapped, flinging a petticoat at her trunk.

"Honey, she's been a married lady, and she can take

a lover without all the fuss and pother that goes on around an unmarried girl. She doesn't even have to be chaperoned. Besides, this isn't gossipy old Charleston."

"I can't imagine a lady like that being swept off her feet so quickly," Leita remarked bitterly.

"But don't you see, that's just it! She doesn't have to worry. She knows she's beautiful and that Breve isn't going to be here long enough to get in the way of her other suitors. She knows exactly what she's doing. Breve's not husband material for her—as far as I know he's poor as a churchmouse right now. The war beggared his daddy's business you know."

Leita's lips were thinned as she resolutely went about her packing. She could think of nothing to say without revealing feelings she had no intention of sharing with Mary Jo.

"Anyway, it's just a passing fling, so to speak. Something drives Breve—I'm sure you know that by now."

Leita glanced up surprised. Mary Jo's heart-shaped little face was solemn.

"Oh yes. There's a mystery of some kind about Breve's father's death. His cotton warehouse burned to the ground, and he died in the fire. Breve dragged his body out, but there is more to it than that. He's been different ever since—haunted almost, haunted and driven. He's like a man with blinders on. But I expect you'll be the one he tells eventually." Mary Jo's voice was low and contemplative.

Leita stared at her in astonishment. "What are you talking about, Mary Jo?"

Mary Jo stood up and smoothed her skirts with deliberation. "Some day he'll tell you, Leita. Whatever it is that's bothering him. He'll tell you, because you're in love with each other."

Mary Jo glided out of the room, leaving Leita more bewildered than she had ever been in her life.

Breve Pinchon's horse was never tethered in front of the elegant house on Cherry Street, but was taken around to the back. Valerie Prescott lived alone with a staff of three servants.

He continued visiting her since that first night, when he entered her room, ostensibly for a cup of hot chocolate before leaving and found her stepping out of her dress. . . .

The candlelight cast a golden glow on her ivory skin. She casually asked him to unlace her and he complied, not terribly surprised since he had known her as a precociously passionate young girl. She pulled her camisole open and took his hand, pressing it to her small, full-nippled breast. He kissed her willing mouth, with her tongue flicking between his parted lips. Her nipple hardened under his fingers, and he pulled off his own clothing in haste. Then he plunged into sexual release with Valerie as if it would obliterate the night that haunted him. He found Valerie aggressive in bed, voracious even; her ivory-skinned hips heaved against him and her smooth slender legs wrapped tightly around him, pressing him more deeply into her. Afterward he felt empty. The miasma of yearning tenderness that Leita evoked in him was still there, even as his body was depleted.

As the night wore on he sought to empty the anger of his renunciation into Valerie Prescott, and she was eager and expert in response, sitting astride him, her black hair tumbling over her shoulders, moaning softly while his hands massaged her moving hips. He slept till noon the next day, and spent the remainder of his time in Philadelphia at her house. His determination to exhaust his love for another woman with hours of lovemaking diverted him, occupied him, but changed nothing. The night before he was to leave Philadelphia, he took her on the floor of the drawing room, her dress pushed up around her hips. Later, in bed, while her small, febrile mouth worked over his body, he pressed her head against him and finally thrust into her in an explosion of lust that was almost cleansing.

The next morning, as he resumed his westward journey with the others, he turned in his saddle and his eyes sought Leita's. The blue serge had been cleaned and pressed, and her hat hung on her back below the torrent of hair. She looked at him coolly, then turned away. She knows, he thought, letting his horse out till he led the file. She knows about Valerie, but how little else she knows. Will the day ever come when I can tell her?

They still had over six hundred miles to travel, but their progress improved when they finally reached the Cumberland Road, the main thoroughfare to the midwest. Samuel heaved a sigh of relief at the sight of the wider, smoother roadbed. They crossed the wide and muddy Ohio at Marietta shortly after that and another day's travel through mountainous country brought them in sight of a gently rolling land, heavy with virginal forests. The earth was black, rich loam. Samuel's eyes grew bright at the challenge of this virgin land and the campfire was vibrant at night with talk of plans for clearing acreage.

Leita watched Breve, looking for some kind of softening in his glance, but there was none. He rode ahead, vibrant and virile, and she constrained herself to ignore him as he did her. She envied Belle her contentment in Harvey's attentions. Belle is just like a little broody hen; she will settle down someday and never know any yearning, she thought. Her heartache had subsided some, but it never left her; the warmth of his body and the strength of his arms stayed with her. She slept heavily at night, visited by dreams of his mouth on her lips and the weight of his chest and thighs against her. The dark, curly hair that covered his chest brushing her smooth skin, and the feel of his lips and tongue on her throat and breasts—how real it all seemed, how real it all had been. She would awaken barely rested on these nights, and sponge her body languidly, lost in a rapturous, sensual need.

They were in heavily wooded country for the last days of their long journey. They had passed Indianapolis, where Mrs. Johnston had made an addition to their party. A young girl named Jeannie McNamee, orphaned and working as a harassed little chambermaid in their Indianapolis hotel, had begged to be allowed to come with them to Fort Wayne. She had lived there until she had been parceled off to an aunt after her mother died. Lucy Mae couldn't refuse her.

"Our first servant," Belle had remarked dryly.

There were no large towns between Indianapolis and Fort Wayne. They saw cleared fields where fat, pinkish hogs milled in pens made from split rails and cattle foraged in the sweet spring grass. The houses were mostly of split logs, an occasional brick or frame house marking a settler who had been here longer and prospered accordingly. They ate cold rabbit and cornbread in their saddles, passing the stoneware jugs of buttermilk from hand to hand. Leita's excitement mounted. They were nearing their destination, and her torments were forgotten in this hour.

They had passed another stretch of dark, thick forest when they saw a man turning out of a lane just ahead of them. He was tall, over six feet, and wore a drooping, golden mustache.

She heard her father's voice. "It's Robert, by God!" and the man turned in the saddle, putting one hand up to shade his eyes, then raced toward them. It was Robert Bond, her father's former neighbor and longtime correspondent. Their long journey was truly over.

Chapter 7

THE TILLETTS AND THE JOHNSTONS MOVED IN TO THEIR new homes within a week, but the Knoxes remained at the Bonds' because Judith Knox had fallen ill. It was Jeannie McNamee, the spare little orphan, who had recognized the symptoms.

"That there Miz Knox looks like my ma looked when she took sick. She's got the lung fever, I'd say. Don't appear to me she'll last through winter."

"Oh good Lord, Jeannie!" Leita had exclaimed. "She's just frail and worn out from the trip. You mustn't be morbid."

"Well, that's what took ma," Jeannie had answered stubbornly, emptying Leita's wash water into the slop jar. "And I've seen it real close. Took care of her and all till they put the coppers on her eyes, I did. Her cheeks is all pink, just like when they're took bad."

The old doctor who was summoned had confirmed young Jeannie's forebodings. Judith Knox had consumption, hasty consumption that killed fast, and with care, might last till Christmas.

The rest of the women took charge of readying the Knox house for occupancy. It was Polly Bond who thought of the nurse.

"You know, there's a little half-breed Miami Indian girl that took care of Mrs. Hostetler when she had the same thing. She's about sixteen, and her name is Winona. The Hostetlers couldn't say enough good about her. She seems to have a real touch with the sick. She lives in a shack down by the river with her mother. If it's all right with you, Nathaniel, I could ride down and talk to her about it."

Nathaniel Knox, red-eyed and gaunt with grief already, agreed quickly, and Leita volunteered to accompany Mrs. Bond.

It had rained the night before and the whole world was washed bright. The river road was narrow and overhung with trees, and they rode over three miles before pulling into a clearing where a weatherbeaten shack nestled in a copse of sycamore. The silvery gray boards were covered with fish heads, long since dried in the sun.

A tall woman with blue-black hair in a long braid came around the corner of the shack. A long knife glinted in her hand, and Leita sucked in her breath in a moment's alarm.

"Hello, Little Otter," Polly Bond called out cheerfully.

The woman's lips widened in a spare smile. "Howdy, Mrs. Bond." Her eyes gleamed black under heavy brows and her face was a light, reddish brown with long creases running from her strong nose to the corners of her wide, thin-lipped mouth. The dress she wore was made of hides and hung to her feet, which were shod in moccasins made of hide and sewn with red and blue beads.

"Is Winona here? We've got a sick woman at our house and I came to see if Winona would be willing to come and help with her."

"Winona is on bank, watching her traps. You ask her." Little Otter turned and spat expertly, hitting the trunk of a sycamore.

A truck garden lay to the left of the shack, and a wide frame held a tautly stretched deer skin. Leita and Polly stood at the top of the bank. A young girl was busy below, winding sinew around a woven wooden trap. She looked up, shading her eyes from the sun. She laid the trap down carefully and climbed up the steep bank. The girl stopped shyly at the sight of Leita, who was staring. Polly nudged her. "Don't stare—they consider it insulting."

Leita had expected to see a reproduction of Little Otter, but Winona had bright blue eyes in a smooth, round face, a straight nose and full lips. Her hair was pulled back smoothly from a high forehead and braided into two long, dark braids interwoven with yellow beads. She wore a red and yellow shirt and a black skirt that touched her calves. There was a silver ornament in the shape of a turkey on the shirt and a fresh, piney scent came off the girl's brown skin.

Polly introduced Leita, then explained their mission.

"I will come tomorrow," the girl said laconically.

With the business concluded, Polly and Leita went to their horses and with a final wave rode down the road.

"You know," Polly said, "most of the Indians around here were sent to Kansas way back before the War. Old Richardville stayed and died here, though. He was Winona's father."

"Richardville? That's an odd name for an Indian."

"He was named Jean Baptiste Richardville, actually—he was part French. There are a lot of breeds around these parts, but it's only the low whites that take up with an Indian woman. Winona doesn't have much chance. She's too white for the young bucks to want for a squaw, but she's been raised to be independent. They keep that cabin and trap fish and hunt and ask for nothing from no one. I just hope that some drunken bargeman doesn't take a fancy to her, but she stays out of town for the most part. Her mother knows we'll look after her."

With Judith seen to, the others went about their business, calling at the Knoxes every day and otherwise occupying themselves with settling.

The men spent every day from early dawn till late dusk on the land. Samuel hired crews. At night he and his sons returned weary and hungry.

Leita didn't see Breve from one week to the next. She plunged into the life of the town. There were young people aplenty and parties and afternoon teas, and the days flew by.

Their housekeeper, engaged by Polly Bond, was a big, rawboned "widder-woman" named Esther Ridenour, with huge freckled arms and a knot of auburn hair stuck tight to her head with horn pins. Little Jeannie McNamee flew around like a ball of flame, anxious to prove her worth, happy to be able to see her father and brothers again, but Robert Bond had been leery of the arrangement.

"I know those McNamees. They're river trash. The old man is a drunk and the oldest boy—Tom, I think it is—is a bad piece of work. Why Zollner keeps him on at the tannery I don't know. He's a thief, for one thing. Just be sure that he keeps his distance. You don't want that tribe hanging around."

Leita and Belle had seen him once as they were riding back from a shopping expedition. The man's face had a narrow, pointed chin, with a thin mustache over a curiously tiny mouth. His eyes were gray and close together and his nose was thin and pointed.

"Good afternoon, ladies, and what a fetching pair you are."

"He's drunk!" Belle whispered, and they flicked their horses into a canter.

"I'm going to tell Pa," Belle said.

"Who was it? Did you know him?" Leita asked.

"That's Jeannie's brother. I've seen him stop by the kitchen door for her. He's a piece of scum," Belle declared.

Leita dismissed the incident. Belle gave Samuel a recounting of his insolence. Samuel's eyes narrowed thoughtfully, but he said little.

The Johnstons had barely settled in when they received a message from Stephen de Jean, saying he would be in Fort Wayne the following weekend and requesting permission to call. A large bouquet of hothouse flowers was delivered the day before Stephen arrived on a Saturday afternoon.

There was a birthday ball that evening at the Hotel Tremont and he escorted Leita. When she swept down the stairs, the look of admiration on his face was ample approval for the trouble she had taken in dressing. She had picked the yellow silk because Breve had said once that yellow suited her better than any other color. She knew he would be there tonight. Jerome had mentioned it.

When Stephen bent his head over her hand, the pleasantly male aroma of cigars and the discreet cologne he used wafted up to her, and suddenly she felt altogether pleased with herself and the evening.

"You are a cultivated rose in this raw country, Miss Leita," he said, raising his eyes to her.

"There's nothing very raw about you, Mr. de Jean," she answered, and he burst out laughing.

He took her arm then, and led her to an elegant looking carriage. The night was sparkling with stars and she was stirring with anticipation. She had seen Breve occasionally, riding to the Tilletts after a long day in the fields. And that was all. Tonight he would see her having a lovely time with Stephen de Jean.

Breve was there, all right. He was with Laura Willoughby, a brown-haired, soft-voiced girl that Leita couldn't find it in her heart to dislike. As the evening wore on, he presented himself for a dance. She was stricken with surprise; this was the first time he had approached her directly since her escape from the renegade in Virginia. She placed her hand in his and held her head erect to keep from trembling. He seemed preoccupied and didn't say much at first, even as she tried to engage him in small talk. Finally he came to the point—the reason, she realized later, that he had confronted her at all.

"I see that your Washington friend lost no time in turning up here," he began flatly.

Leita nodded, gratified—at least he had noticed, and obviously without pleasure.

"I want you to be careful—very careful with him, Leita." He looked at her directly then. "I don't trust him. He's suave and he's urbane. And he is also not a man to be taken at face value."

"He is a gentleman, Breve. He has given me no reason to doubt it," Leita replied stiffly.

"Not yet he hasn't, but the time will come, and then it may be too late," Breve said.

"And just what do you know about him that leads you to make such an accusation?" she flared.

"Nothing—not a thing. But I'm a bit older than you,

Leita, and I've been around some. I can smell a rat from a long ways." His mouth was taut.

"You're jealous! Just downright, vindictive jealous."

He looked down at her for a long moment, his eyes dark and mysterious. "That too, Leita. That too."

The music stopped as she gazed up at him. His eyes held hers and in them was the memory of that night. And then he released her, abruptly. They left the floor, and he led her back to Stephen, bestowing a curt nod on both of them before he stalked off. But Stephen's eyes on Breve's back were cool and thoughtful, and he took careful note of Leita's flushed cheeks.

The weeks of summer flew by, and Leita became increasingly caught up in the social whirl of welcome she had received from the Ramseys and Higginbothams and the community. And there was Stephen; never more than two weekends passed before he returned to Fort Wayne to squire Leita to the picnics and dances and Sunday after-church dinners. She seemed always to be getting ready to go somewhere.

She was washing her hair that Friday afternoon. The housekeeper was upstairs taking her afternoon nap. Everyone else had gone out.

Leita wore only a thin petticoat and camisole. The heat was heaviest this hour of the day, and she enjoyed the shiver from the cool rinse pouring over her scalp. She reached blindly for the towel on the chair behind her, wrung out her long hair with one hand and wrapped the towel around her head. She straightened up and let out a little shriek.

Tom McNamee stood no more than four feet away from her, his small eyes staring at her half-bare bosom, then surveying the rest of her figure. He slouched insolently over to the table and set down a small reticule.

"I brung my sister's pursie back. What you screamin'

for? I ain't touched you. Looks to me like you could use some touchin' though." His feral little eyes stroked her again.

"You get out of here! Get out!" Leita screamed, grabbing one of the chairs and swinging it at him.

He ducked away and laughed. "You're full of ginger, ain't you now. Just what I like. Yow-wee! You'd be a hot little armful!"

As he made a dash for the door, she threw the chair at him. He slammed the screen against it, ripping the screen. He stood there grinning for a long moment, then jumped off the big latticed porch and ran across the yard. He leaped on an old horse that stood by the curb and waved an arm high as he rode off.

"If only I'd had a gun—" Leita said aloud, trembling with fury and fear. . . .

"Did he touch you?" Samuel Johnston's voice, usually so heavy and full, was subdued.

"No, I don't know whether he would have or not if I hadn't thrown the chair at him. Those awful eyes just raked over my whole body—and there I stood, half-naked!"

Jeannie McNamee stood in the kitchen, sniveling into a thin little handkerchief. "I know he's my kin, but don't blame me. He's always been mean. Ma used to say he was meaner than cat-shit. Please—it ain't my fault," she moaned, her pinched little face all swollen. "Anyways, he hid my reticule, I know he did. When I was to the house I put it on the one shelf where I always put it and when I went to get it it warn't there. He must'a hid it on purpose to have an excuse to come here."

Samuel glanced at his wife, then walked to the back door.

"Don't wait supper for us. I'm takin' the boys with

me. We'll be back before too long." And he was gone. . . .

The McNamee cottage was a jerry-built hodge-podge set in a group of ramshackle dwellings all much alike, their dirt yards cluttered with debris.

Samuel threw his horse's reins over a post. The others dismounted and followed him to the door, which stood wide open on slack leather hinges. A surprised young face appeared in the doorway, and Samuel peered past it into the gloom of the interior.

"I'm looking for your brother Tom."

"Oh Jesus! What's he done now? You're Mr. Johnston, ain't you?" The boy had a pinched face beneath a shock of tow-colored hair.

"That's right, and it's nothing to do with you, boy. Now, where is he?"

The boy swallowed noisily. "He et, and then he went off agin. You'll stand a good chance of finding him at Klines."

Samuel looked at the despairing green eyes in the frail face and hesitated. His sons had mounted and were waiting impatiently for him.

"Son, you go in town to my house and tell Mrs. Johnston I said for you to sleep in the carriage house tonight. Go on now, boy."

The boy nodded, astonished, and watched from the doorway as the horses went clattering down the street with Samuel in the lead.

They reined up at the third tavern along the Canal. Samuel pushed his way through the smoke-filled stink of unwashed bodies. The sweaty men, hard-muscled from unloading canal barges, looked up with curiosity as Sam and Eugene and Matthew and Paul peered over them.

A heavy-set, dark-haired man with beefy jowls stood behind the bar. He narrowed his eyes at the sight of

Samuel and his sons, then folded his arms and watched them in silence, waiting to see what would happen.

Eugene's eyes had just adjusted to the half-dark of the steaming, smelly tavern when he spied the flat-backed head of Tom McNamee at the end of the room. Tom had paid no attention to the newcomers; his eyes were fastened on the greasy cards in his hand, and the three men with him were likewise occupied. The table held puddles of water and spilled beer and Tom was just wiping the heel of his hand on his leg when Samuel's hand closed over his left arm, jerking him upright and spilling a mug of beer.

"Hey, leggo of me!" Tom yelled, before he recognized the man who had hauled him to his feet. Samuel dragged the wild-eyed Tom McNamee through the crowd. Someone darted forward and grabbed Samuel's free arm. He drew back his fist, but Matthew seized his arm and twisted it quickly.

Samuel stopped, his knuckles whitened with the strength of his grip on Tom's arm. "I want you all to understand who my quarrel is with. This cur McNamee is on his way to a horsewhipping. That's what we do where I come from when a piece of trash like this takes it on himself to frighten and insult an innocent young girl."

The room quieted immediately. A few men shuffled their feet and looked at Tom's contorted face with furtive curiosity. Samuel had done what he intended, forestalled a free-for-all. These were rough-and-tough men, rugged and ragged, who took their Saturday night brawls for granted. But many of them were southerners—some second generation—who still behaved with chivalry where females were concerned.

Samuel could see he had enlisted a touch of sympathy.

"He forced his way uninvited into my home this

afternoon—when there were no men around. He made obscene remarks to my daughter who was half-clothed in the kitchen. He terrified her. Now if you men will just stand back, this piece of scum is going to get a little bit of what's coming to him."

"Ain't nobody goin' to do nothing?" Tom shrieked. "He's told you a pack of lies!"

No one lifted a finger as Samuel forced Tom out the door and stopped at his horse. He pulled the crop out of the side of the saddle. Tom sniveled and flailed wildly.

"Need any help, Pa?" Eugene asked.

"Not with a weak coward like this." The crop fell on Tom's shoulders. "Now, you stay away from my home, you bastard!" Samuel raised his arm high again. "If you so much as peel an eye at any decent young girl I'll do this with your shirt off." The riding crop descended again. Tom made a break for the tavern door but ran into a wall of bodies. Samuel's hand caught his hair and jerked him backward.

Tom screamed. "God, he'll kill me! Ain't anybody goin' to help me?"

A voice spoke up from the crowd. "You got it comin' to you, McNamee."

Passersby had gathered on the dirt path and watched with interest.

"What'd he do?" a woman called. She was dressed in a dirty blue-sprigged cotton, and her red hair was frizzed around her thin, rouge-painted face.

"Went in this man's house and scared his daughter with some bad talk," the bargeman called back, spitting again.

"T'ain't no more'n you've done to me, many's the time," the woman called back.

The men whooped with laughter at this.

Samuel decided Tom had had enough and went to

replace the crop in the saddle. Eugene and Matthew did the rest. They picked Tom up, carried him to the horse trough and dumped him unceremoniously into the cold water.

Tom McNamee scrambled out of the trough and stared Samuel full in the face for the first time, his little gray eyes filled with hatred.

Samuel pointed a finger at him. "Don't ever set foot on my property again. Do you hear?"

Tom's black hair was plastered down over his bony skull. "I hear," he said shortly.

As Samuel led his sons back down the dusty, hard-packed dirt of the street, satisfied that he had taken the only possible action, it was as well that he couldn't foresee the future.

Chapter 8

Breve Pinchon shouldered his way through the crowds in the Chicago train station, came out into a cold, biting wind, and got into a hansom cab. The hotel was only a few blocks away. He claimed his reservation and was seen to his room, where he washed up and changed. In thirty minutes he was out on the street again.

He proceeded north. Unencumbered with baggage now, he carried only the slim leather portfolio that his father's attorney had presented him with at the reading of the will. It was mid-afternoon and the watery winter sunlight streaked the windows and boards of the buildings with cool yellow light.

Well, Pinchon, he mused, your holiday is over. No more frolicking around in the great outdoors, swinging an axe. It was time to get down to serious business. To use what money he had, invest it shrewdly, make more, and, with luck, in two years be able to call his own tune in this town.

He reached Randolph Street, swung left onto it and stopped outside an imposing, whitestone building. Thwaite and Harrington, Attorneys at Law, a bronze plaque read. He made his way up one flight of stairs.

"Mr. Harrington received your wire, sir," the clerk said politely and ushered Breve into the chamber of the eldest of the two partners.

Breve's eyes flickered over the old man who held out his hand to him. Moses Harrington was remarkably spry for his eighty-nine years. A pair of bright brown eyes sparkled above the slow smile that creased his leathery face as he extended a thin hand.

"It's a pleasure to lay eyes on you, son. Your grandfather and my father stayed close all their lives." He indicated a chair.

"I didn't know," Breve said in surprise, lowering himself into a leather armchair.

"Oh yes. My father was a seafaring man. You did know that, didn't you?"

"Yes," Breve nodded, "he was mentioned in my grandfather's journal."

The old attorney eyed him intently. "Then you know the story?"

Breve nodded. He laid the portfolio on the wide mahogany desk and, extracting a key from his waistcoat pocket, opened it and withdrew a heavy envelope. He handed the envelope wordlessly to Moses Harrington.

The stiff pages rustled as the attorney looked them over. Breve clipped the end off the cigar he had been offered, lit it and closed his eyes.

Moses Harrington got up from his desk, drew a cord and the draperies on one section of the wall parted to reveal a large safe. He bent over the lock, murmuring to himself, and the door swung slowly open.

The attorney spoke as he withdrew a slender metal box and brought it to the desk. "My father kept to the sea, you know. He sailed the Caribbean as captain of his own ship until he was in his late seventies. Then he came ashore and festered and grumbled until I agreed to his going out again. He went on his own ships as a sort of elder statesman, and he festered no more. How that man hated dry land!"

Breve noticed that his father's name was embossed on the box, which the old man now unlocked and opened.

"He loved the islands," Harrington continued. "And he went ashore in Charleston regularly to visit with your grandfather. He saw you when you were just a pup." The old attorney withdrew a handful of keys from the box and held them up, looking at them thoughtfully. "And here are you and I, shipmates of a kind."

"Your father saved my grandfather's life, you know, as well as my father's," Breve said with feeling.

"Yes . . . well, I gleaned as much, though he never put it that way. Those were black days in the Caribbean. Black and dangerous days. And the horrors that took place on that island defy telling."

Harrington reached for a heavy overcoat that hung on a clothes tree, donned it and turned to Breve. "Now we're off to the Illinois Bank and Trust to see to your legacy."

"My legacy," Breve mused. "I'll be surprised if there is anything left of it. My father had to borrow right and left before the war ended."

Moses Harrington turned his bright brown eyes to the younger man. "Do you remember the parable of the talents? The story of stewardship?"

Breve blinked. "Yes, pretty well."

"Your father knew it well, and took it seriously." The old man's face wrinkled up in a smile.

They drove in Harrington's carriage, were ushered

through the marble portals of the bank and into the echoing chambers of the vaults. The boxes that the attorney called for were set on a long table, and Harrington bent over them, inserting a key into the lock of the first.

"I've taken a personal interest in this, you know. Due to the special circumstances." Moses' wispy voice echoed in the vault as he went on unlocking each box and throwing the lids back. "Now." He beckoned with a bent finger.

Breve went around the end of the table and looked down into the boxes. Each was stacked three-quarters full. The gilt lettering on the railroad shares, the mining shares, the utility bonds gleamed dully under the gas light.

"Good God!" he breathed. Then he turned and looked into the complacently smiling eyes of the old attorney. "Are these viable? Is this stock in current enterprises?"

Moses Harrington's laughter was surprisingly deep. "Viable! I should say, viable! Union Pacific, Pittsburgh and Allegheny, mines, coal. And all growing about as fast as that bean that Jack planted. Money makes money, you know." He chuckled. "All done through foresighted investment—and a touch of daring at times. You'll pardon a little self-congratulation."

"Pardon it! Mr. Harrington, what you've done—"

"Now hold on, young man, there was plenty there to begin with. That was a sizable amount your father sent up here to me. I was only the steward. Thankfully, your talents grew. You're wealthy again, Mr. Pinchon."

"No . . . not yet," Breve answered pensively.

Moses Harrington's sparse old brows lifted. "You have high standards, don't you? Most people would consider this pretty near a fortune."

"It is, but this is blood money. You know that, if you know the story."

Moses appeared to consider this, clicking his tongue softly against his teeth as he did so.

"It's blood money—and I have to redeem it. When I make this much again, make it through ventures that can stand up under the clear light of day, then I'll be a wealthy man again. I'll use this for my stake. What comes after, and only what comes after, will I consider rightfully mine."

The teller was summoned to replace the boxes. Moses Harrington handed the keys over to Breve and wished him luck.

"And now it's near time for dinner. I dine at the Pantheon Club and I would be honored if you would join me. Afterward you can hightail it around Chicago if you like, but you'll have to do it alone. I don't go in for much high-life anymore." His brown eyes twinkled mightily and the seriousness of their conversation was dispelled.

In the carriage the old man fondled the head of his walking stick, then spoke. "Mr. Pinchon, it doesn't take a whole lot of brains to make money, you know. Unless you're working under a handicap. For instance, a man with an active conscience has to have a *lot* of brains to make a fortune. It takes a lot of brains to find honest ways to enrich yourself when the dishonest ways are so numerous—and so easy." He stared out the window for a moment, then turned to Breve. "My intuition tells me you'll succeed. And my intuition is very good. It improves with age."

Moses Harrington slapped the head of his walking stick and leaning back, bestowed a smile of regard on Breve.

Leita had known he would leave, and came to accept it, but after Breve departed for Chicago she alternated between a lonely longing and hot anger at having been so ignored.

It was December now, and outside the snow lay heavy and white, a milky yellow sun shining down on it. Stephen was to return to Chicago the next day, but this afternoon they played Piquet and the cards still lay in front of them. They were alone in the house and Leita made hot chocolate, knowing that Stephen was fond of it, and cut a heavy fruit cake. Stephen had finished eating and was leaning back watching her as she finished her cake and took a sip of the chocolate.

She set her cup down and reached for a napkin but stopped when she felt Stephen's hands grasp her shoulders and turn her toward him. He looked at her for a second, his hazel eyes smoldering, then he gathered her to him. His face came down on hers and his tongue flicked out, caressing her upper lip with light little touches. The heat of his breath, the subtle scent of his cologne, the sensuous touch of his tongue on her mouth—it was enough to arouse her when she least expected it.

He felt the breath go out of her and the next instant his lips were moving wet and hot on hers. She responded fiercely with a queer little violent tremor, a passion totally free of tenderness or yearning, but strong and burning through her. He withdrew his mouth from hers and caught his breath, only to search for her lips again, and the next instant his tongue was in her mouth. He bore down on her with deep, devouring kisses and she grew weaker and weaker, the blood surging through her body in a tumult. He finally managed to work his hand down the top of her dress and began stroking her breast lightly. She arched her back involuntarily, pressing against his hand for the space of a long, throbbing kiss. When he thrust his hand down inside the camisole, kneading her breast with his palm, she took his hand away.

"You must stop—you must," she whispered while his

mouth was traveling down her throat, plucking at the tender skin.

"No," he whispered, "we're alone . . . finally."

He spoke not a word of love, and it was the furthest thing from her mind as his lips searched the curve of her breast, his tongue moving in quick little strokes that made the blood rush in her ears. She laced her fingers in his smooth black hair, pressing his face closer, her own eyes closed to everything. His hand moved down to her hip and he pressed her back against the sofa, grasping her thighs and insinuating his hand between them. She was breathing faster and he moved his body onto hers, pulling her dress back and burying his face in her breasts. She thought of nothing but the sensations as the throbbing, hard bulk of his manhood pressed against her love-starved body. He strained against her and then suddenly freed one hand and tore at his trousers.

"Oh stop!" she cried. "Stop right now, please!" She wrenched her body sideways and escaped the embrace that her young body desired, desired in spite of her will.

He sat up then and smoothed his hair back. Leita's fingers were moving frantically on the buttons of her bodice. With a smile he reached out and helped her, slipping the loops over the remaining buttons with his quick fingers. He was almost purring and looked up at her with a glance of pleased appraisal.

"You are a woman, you know. I hadn't been certain till now. Being in love with you is going to be an experience."

"I'm embarrassed, Stephen, downright embarrassed. I reckon there's a little harlot lurking in me that has to come out now and then."

His eyes narrowed. "What strange notions you Americans have. Your education has been neglected, my dear—not to say distorted. Harlots feign passion for

97

an end; pure desire is foreign to them. You are simply a desirable and passionate female who should be married as soon as possible. I intend to speak to your father when I return on my next visit," he said serenely, buttoning his coat.

"Has it occurred to you that asking me might have some trifling importance?" She was flush with anger, and he regarded her with amused astonishment.

The housekeeper's heavy footsteps sounded on the stairs just then, and Stephen touched Leita's arm lightly. "I will be back after supper, and we will have a walk and talk about this," he said gently.

Leita shivered in the blast of cold air that came through the doorway when he let himself out.

He returned that evening undaunted as ever, and they went for a stroll. The evening star had come out, shining blue-white in the dark sky. Stephen smiled down at Leita, and she could see the glint of his eyes as he tucked her arm closer to his. The snow crunched beneath their feet and the rattle of horses' bells was the only sound that broke the night. She held her silence, scuffing the snow with her boots, one gloved hand warm in the crook of his arm and the other cozy inside her muff.

Stephen was drawing contemplatively at his cigar when he suddenly said, "Leita, I would never have dreamed of taking such liberties this afternoon if I had not every intention of asking you to be my wife. I even presumed that your acceptance of me was implicit in your acquiescence. I had no thought of taking you for granted."

She waited a moment, putting her thoughts in order. "I wasn't thinking of marriage this afternoon, or anything else. I simply responded, with no thought— and certainly with no modesty. Unfortunately, I have a passionate nature." He sought to interrupt but she continued implacably, determined to get this over with.

"I am not in love with you, Stephen. I like you very much but—"

His eyes were warm on her now, with the tiniest grain of amusement. "You are too young to know much about love. Only your dreams, little one, you know only your dreams. When you are my wife you will learn."

"I'm not ready to marry, Stephen. It's not just that I'm not in love with you. I intend to be free and learn how to live, to be my own woman, before I give myself to anyone else."

"What an independent, unconventional little lady you are! I rather suspect that you are your own woman now, but I am my own man and I will tell you this. I am not patient, though I manage to give the impression of being self-contained. But if something suits me, I can wait till the time is ripe before acquiring it. Remember this—I have every intention of making you my wife. I'll not beseech you, but don't ever think I have forgotten just because I'm not languishing before your eyes. When the time comes you will marry me."

Leita was almost riveted by the forceful certainty of his speech. Then she blinked and shook the spell away. "I am not promising anything, Stephen," she asserted.

"I know you're not. But I am." And leaning down, he kissed her lingeringly.

They walked silently on through the snow.

Eugene Johnston and Breve Pinchon left the Board of Trade building at the corner of Munro and Lasalle. The February snow crunched under their feet. Restive, after a tense afternoon, Breve started off at a trot, scooped up a handful of fresh snow from the base of a lamppost and pelted Eugene squarely on the chest. And the chase began. The two of them raced along the slippery walk, scooping up snow and hurling it at each other until Eugene unleashed a wildly aimed snowball that knocked the derby off a ponderous old gentleman. Breve hung against the lamppost laughing as Eugene hastily and apologetically retrieved the man's hat, all the while trying to keep a straight face.

"Now before you ruin my reputation as a dignified man of business, let's stop off for a glass of Madeira before we change for dinner," Breve said, limp with laughter.

"And I suppose you have something planned for after dinner?" Eugene asked with a smile as they sat over their wine.

"Of course. This is your first visit. I have to make it a lively one if I'm going to prevail on you to join me."

"A year at the most, Breve. Just as soon as the work is far enough advanced to warrant Father hiring a reliable overseer."

Breve raised his glass. "And then it will be Pinchon and Johnston. God knows I need someone I can trust. Just wait until you get your teeth into this town! It's bubbling like a witches' cauldron. Just the changeover in the mining process has made millions for the right men."

"What changeover?"

"Getting away from placer mining. It was damned wasteful; literally tons of gold were lost that way. Now with quartz mining they are extracting the gold with machinery from the deeper veins of quartz. Once your initial investment is returned, you have an efficient, high-profit operation."

"But do you ever stop?" Eugene inquired, half-joking. "You work all day, concentrating every minute, even when you appear to be just chewing the fat with someone—"

"Especially then," Breve injected. "I have to be wise as a serpent and appear to be harmless as a dove. If you intend to stay on top in this race, you keep your thoughts to yourself and spare no effort in finding out what the other man is up to." Breve chuckled, but Eugene, having observed him for the past week, knew that he meant every word.

"And then you're out at night till all hours. Do you realize we haven't gone one evening without attending a gathering of some kind?"

"And that is necessary, too." Breve leaned back and stretched. "See and be seen, my friend, without ever being too available. And we're expected at the Brockmeister's for dinner this evening. They're entertaining a United States Senator whose ear I have to get. So dust off your tail coat."

Eugene dressed with care, all the while mulling over Breve's explosive activity. From the first day, when Breve met him with an elegant carriage, complete with coachman, and took him to his spacious rooms, Eugene had been reeling with surprise. But his surprise lessened on reflection; Breve's energies were not new to him, his quick mind and his background in commerce formed the obvious foundation for his successful foray into the field of finance. His offices were luxurious, the door lettered in gold leaf, BREVE PINCHON, INVESTMENTS. That his business was brisk was evident from the constant stream of callers. And Eugene had witnessed more than one seasoned veteran of the stock exchange asking Breve's opinion of various enterprises. In fact, Eugene's visit had taken a little time to arrange because Breve was out of Chicago so frequently. Their half-formulated plans to go into business together had taken solid shape during this visit, with Breve formally inviting Eugene to join his firm. Eugene had accepted readily. Life on the land was wholesome, but the business of business was exciting.

After the lavish dinner at Brockmeister's and a somewhat turgid hour or two of the musical which followed, Breve flourished them out of the Gold Coast mansion, and they made the rounds of a few of Chicago's more colorful establishments.

When they finally returned to Breve's rooms they were both somewhat the worse for wear. Despite quantities of Port and Madeira, along with the hot brandy and water pressed on them to "ward off the cold," neither felt like going to bed yet. So they built up the fire, took out their studs and sprawled in front of the fireplace.

Breve continued to drink. Eugene had noticed the change in Breve's disposition over the past couple of hours, and now the Port wasn't alleviating his dark mood any.

Eugene began pulling off his boots. Even in his cups he was careful not to mention Leita. He knew full well there was something deep and strong between his sister and this man, but he knew, too, that for some reason it was dangerous ground.

"I hope you can get back for even a short visit soon, Breve. Everyone would be glad to see you, my father and mother particularly," Eugene offered, albeit somewhat drunkenly.

Breve was silent for a moment. "My God, but you're lucky. Both parents alive, and no enmity between them. I have very little family left," Breve ruminated, "all I have is a past. A past that I won't be free of even when I've made my fortune."

Eugene let out a laugh. "*When* you've made your fortune? My God, man, I've seen your books. You have a fortune in working capital alone!"

Again Breve fell silent, and the faraway look in his eyes did not escape Eugene's awareness. Breve's past was none of his business, and even though Breve himself had brought it up, Eugene had discreetly veered away from the subject. He knew only what Micah Tillett had told him—that Breve's father had died in a warehouse fire, that his mother had committed suicide four days later, and that Breve had been living in torment ever since.

Breve took another sip of Port. His eyes were languid, but his mind was alert. "What would you say if I told you that what you call my 'fortune' is smeared with blood and stinks of burnt flesh?"

"Breve, for God's sake! What kind of hell do you carry with you?"

Breve gazed contemplatively at his partner-to-be. There was no question that he trusted Eugene to be his partner. But trust was nothing if it wasn't mutual. Eugene had a right to know—an obligation, even, to share that trust. Breve spoke as if he were reading from a newspaper. His voice was calm, almost chilling.

"My mother had a sizable inheritance. She invested most of it without telling my father, who assumed that her money was coming from interest on her legacy. Eventually, he learned the truth—that for six years she had been investing in a company illegally engaged in slave trading. My father was furious. He appropriated the money, which was considerable—more than double the amount my mother had inherited—and arranged for it to be sent to an attorney in Chicago, the son of an old friend of his, with instructions that the money was to be invested and held in trust for his son. Whom you are now looking at. So much for my 'fortune.'"

Eugene sat transfixed as Breve poured himself another glass of wine and continued:

"The war was fought on many battlefields. My home was one of them. My father hated slavery and all it stood for. My mother, on the other hand, was a conventional southern lady. She fretted over what she called my father's 'near demented sentimentality about niggers.' That was the reason she never told my father about her investments. Up until the time he found out, they'd had a contented, one might even say happy, marriage. It is strange to think that their love endured only as long as neither confided in the other. But once the truth came out, it was all over. You see, my father also had a secret. . . ." Breve squeezed his eyes shut and pinched the bridge of his nose. He blinked several times, then took out his watch and squinted at it. "It's late and you're probably tired. I don't want to keep you up if—"

Eugene shook his head. "It's all right, Breve—if you feel like talking, I'm listening. I think maybe it'll do you good to get it off your chest."

Breve nodded pensively. He got up and went over to a cabinet and after a few moments returned with what looked like a notebook. "This is one of the journals my father kept. The final entry tells it better than I ever could."

Eugene reached over and turned up the gas lamp, then took the journal and started to read at the place Breve was indicating. . . .

I have done it! And what demon led my tongue to speak I know not. And on such slight provocation! She is distraught, wild with anger. I left her in a frenzy, since she would not let me near her. She looked at me with such eyes—as if I had been a ravening beast! What will happen now I do not know. Is it possible that my anger, my revulsion at her despicable enterprise of all those years ago has lain within me, coiled like a serpent to destroy my home, to destroy the love that has endured, however scarred, down these thirty years? It must be, else why would I have told her? The bile rose up in me and my only wish was to inflict the truth on her—to attack her with the truth—that a nigra is a human, to leave her no escape from that fact that she was married to a white man whose blood was half-black. What is to come now? I have no doubt she will leave

104

me. My life ruptured—torn asunder—and it all stemmed from an argument over two servants that she had decided to turn out into the street. Her heartlessness, her dismissal of them as if they were animals, enraged me. I have been exhausted of late, worried about the future, dismayed by the turn of fate that sent the fortunes of the South and my own state crumbling into ashes and ruins. I was ripe for combat, I see it now, and the devil on my shoulder took charge of my words. Thank God Breve returned alive and whole. His presence in the house has been like balm to me. He will have to be told, and soon, I suppose. I was younger than he when my father gave me his journals to read and I well remember the turmoil of my mind when I learned what my father had survived, and of my mother's fate—and, not least of all, my lineage. But I take heart. Breve is made of strong stuff, confident and generous of spirit. He will accustom himself to his history and its implications. My heart aches as I realize anew that she need never have known if not for my outburst of temper, a temper that has always been my curse and my undoing. She said I lied, that my imagination had taken an insane turn. That I was taunting her with a horror that I knew would revolt her beyond words, only because of my terrible, vengeful temper. But the devil led me on. I remember shouting that she could read the truth for herself, that it was all there, in writing, irrefutable, in my father's journals, which I had kept since his death in the safe in my office. She grew quiet then. How I remember that stillness. She well knows that I am not given to extravagant falsehoods, or any other kind for that matter. Her voice was so low when she asked me how long I had known of it—when did my father tell me of this terrible thing? When I answered that I had been twenty-five,

*answered coldly as I recall—her face grew paler than
I have ever seen it. I was certain she was about to
faint and stepped forward to support her with my
arms. The force of her revulsion left me almost
speechless from that moment on. She threw her
arms out, pushing me away while her face contorted
in such a mask of disgust that my heart turned to
stone in my breast. It was at that moment I knew
that I had damaged her irreparably, that my wife
was gone from me and would be forevermore.*

*"Destroy them!" she shouted. "Go at once and
destroy them! No one must ever know that my
children's father is a nigra!" I answered that they
would never be destroyed, they were the record of
my father's life. It was then that she became frenzied
and I feared she would lose her senses, so violent
was she in expression and movement. I could not
soothe her, I could not speak with her, and finally,
in despair, I left. I mourn when I think of the future.
Surely she will leave me now. I cannot imagine life
without her, my fiery, quicksilver, loving Louise.*

Eugene finished reading, rubbed his eyes and sat
staring at the embers smoldering in the fireplace.

Breve managed a weary smile. "Well, at least you
haven't fainted from shock or run for the nearest exit."

Eugene looked up, solemn, reflective. "Can you
think of a reason why I should?"

Breve studied him for a long moment and decided he
would never regret making this man his business
partner. He started to pour another glass of Port, but
changed his mind and put the top back on the bottle. "I
didn't tell you how it ended," Breve said.

Eugene guessed that this was the part Micah had told
him about—what but not why. "I'd like to know,"
Eugene said.

"The rest of the story is unwritten for the simple reason that my father did not live to write it. He often went to his warehouse office to write in his journal. He was there when the fire broke out. The building went up like a tinder box—cotton warehouses always do. I found his charred body the following morning next to the metal box he kept the journals in. Apparently he had tried to save them. He succeeded—even in death. When I brought the body home that morning, my mother became hysterical and for the next few days she was in a state of shock. She didn't speak, she didn't eat. Everyone thought it was grief—which it was in part. But the private hell she had cast herself into was far more tormenting than anyone knew."

Breve took out a handkerchief and blew his nose. "Four days after my father's death she took arsenic. She left a suicide note saying that she could not live with her conscience, that she was to blame for my father's death, that she had paid someone to set the fire. Not a word about the journals. . . . No one believed her for a minute. It didn't make sense. The fire had been an accident, they said. Everyone was certain she had gone mad from grief and shock. I was too stunned at the time to even think about it. . . ." There was a catch in his voice, and Breve stopped to clear his throat. "I believe now that she was telling the truth. . . ."

Eugene shifted uneasily in his chair.

"You see, my mother was a very determined woman. She wanted those journals destroyed, and she would find a way to do it somehow. Whether or not she hired someone to burn down the warehouse was never proved. But I believe she did arrange to have it done, never realizing that my father would be in the warehouse on that evening. She did not want him dead—of that I am certain. . . ."

Breve fell silent. For a long while he sat staring into

the fireplace until his head began to nod and his eyelids fell. . . .

It was almost dawn when Eugene fell into bed, but as tired as he was, sleep proved impossible. He had of course been deeply moved by Breve's tragic and incredible account. And he was flattered that Breve had taken him into his confidence. Better than anyone, he now understood Breve Pinchon, man and mind, and he respected him more than ever. He also understood the reason for Breve's relentless repudiation of Leita's love. And he could only wonder how Leita would feel if she ever learned the truth. . . .

Breve accompanied him to the station the following afternoon. Their conversation was casual along the way, but for one serious moment Breve dispensed with small talk.

"What I told you last night was in confidence, Eugene. I burdened you with my one and only secret. Let it remain a secret."

Eugene responded quickly. "You have nothing to worry about, Breve. And I think you know that I'm a man of my word."

Breve nodded and his smile was warm. "Yes, of course. I don't know why I even mentioned it."

Back in Indiana, Samuel Johnston listened carefully to Eugene's recounting of Breve's business affairs. Samuel approved of his son's acceptance of Breve's offer, even to the extent of urging him to leave sooner. But Eugene demurred at this, well aware that his father would need him for several months more.

These conversations were kept private at Eugene's behest and though Leita hung on his every word, she learned very little of Breve's new life. Eugene was scrupulously careful not to fan the flame that he knew was there.

Chapter 9

JUDITH KNOX, PALE AND THIN, COUGHING IN FITS AND spitting blood, had somehow survived the worst of the winter. Leita called at least every other day and often read to the pink-cheeked, emaciated woman.

Night and day, Judith Knox's needs were tended by Winona Grayhawk. Occasionally, Leita watched Winona brew the potions that miraculously soothed the racking, retching cough that tore at Mrs. Knox. One afternoon Winona stood over a steaming kettle filled with what appeared to be roots. The smell that arose was dank, like the underside of a log.

"What is that, Winona?"

"I went out early and dug up more comfrey root. It's best this time of year when the sap is running."

"Is it to make her sleep?" Leita was intrigued.

"No, it's to keep her chest from filling up," Winona replied quietly.

"Where did you learn all these things, Winona?"

"From Little Otter, some anyway, mostly from old Red Wing. He knew everything about medicines; if he was here now he might be able to save her, but he died before he could teach me all that he knew. Still, anything that helps," Winona ended philosophically, straining the unappetizing brew through a clean tea-cloth.

They ate together then, talking companionably. And then they made what to Leita seemed a longer and longer journey up the stairway.

Judith Knox died on the first day of March. Leita stood by Jerome at the graveside. Jerome flinched as the handful of dirt was thrown on the new wood of the coffin, and Leita never left his side through the rest of the afternoon when the house was full of sympathetic neighbors and friends, all of them laden with enough food to feed a regiment, Leita thought.

She felt disconsolate the next day. The March wind had softened somewhat and she could see swelling buds on the black walnuts, showing tiny slits of yellow-green already. She threw down her embroidery suddenly, and changed into her riding clothes. When she cantered her horse down the street it was with no thought of a destination, only to get out in the early spring wind and leave her sadness behind. Then she made for the river road. She would visit with Winona.

It was a good six miles and she rode hard. The wind brushed her face and her hair flew out behind her with the spring sun striking it to a golden flame. As she came around the next to the last bend before the clearing, she slowed down and saw that the muddy ground was churned up with hoof marks leading off between the trees. It must be Leslie Knox, she thought. He often rode out here with Winona. Towheaded, shy Leslie had found a companion in the soft-spoken Indian girl and even spent Sundays fishing at her mother's cabin.

Leita guided her horse in through the trees and on down to the edge of the bluff. The water below was flowing rapidly now in the spring rush. She looked around, puzzled, and then saw a chestnut mare, its reins looped loosely over its head. The horse wasn't familiar to her, and she shrugged and turned her horse to head back out to the road.

The narrow, muscular figure of Tom McNamee stood hidden behind two close-growing trees. His gray eyes gleamed as he watched her. She reined her horse in when she had cleared the trees and stopped to make sure Leslie and Winona weren't in sight.

Tom McNamee slipped along stealthily till he reached his horse and was in the saddle when Leita started on down the road at a leisurely trot. He guided his own horse quietly through the trees along the bank, intent on staying hidden. Presently he came to the opening he was looking for, a spot where the distance between the river bank and the road was only a few yards wide. Tom spurred his horse suddenly and emerged from the trees directly behind Leita.

Leita heard the sudden clatter of hooves and turned around pleased, thinking it was Leslie. Her heart froze at the sight of Tom McNamee, a ghastly leer on his thin face, spurring the chestnut mare till it was abreast of her in an instant.

She dug her heels into her horse, frantic with fright, but Tom's mare easily kept pace with hers. She crouched down in the saddle, panic turning her thighs to water.

Tom laughed, a sudden, shrieking laugh. "Ride on, girl! Ride hard! You won't get away this time!" His leer was almost in her face, so close was he.

He's mad, she thought—clean out of his head! He knows if he touches me, Daddy will kill him, and he doesn't care!

He was breathing hard, watching Leita's face as his horse galloped beside hers. He reveled in the terror in her eyes. Her mouth was pinched, and he laughed aloud when she took her riding crop and lashed out at his face. He caught her arm and wrested the crop from her hand in one movement, then lashed her horse's flank with it, easily keeping pace with her.

Tom's eyes were sharp on the road ahead now, and he reined his horse exactly abreast of Leita's and so close that their feet almost touched. They rounded the curve and came to the clearing where Little Otter lived. At that moment Tom reached out one arm and jerked Leita from her saddle.

She hadn't been expecting this. He had made no move to touch her or to grab her horse's halter, and she had begun to hope that he simply intended to frighten her to death and then ride off when they reached a house.

But he had no such intention. He knew that Little Otter was gone from the cabin. He had seen her ride off on her pony with her saddlebags bulging. He would have raped Leita in the mud, if necessary, but Little Otter's cabin would be more comfortable.

Leita hung from his arm, kicking vainly, and he reined in quickly and slid down from the saddle, grasping her with both arms now. She struggled wildly, raking at his face with her fingernails. She was astonished by his strength.

He picked her up and kicked the cabin door open and carried her in. She began to scream. He brought his hand across her face in a thundering slap. Then he threw her down in the corner onto a pile of skins— Little Otter's bed. Leita scrambled to her feet, screaming, and he held her with one hand and struck her across the face again and again, stunning her with the force of his blows.

"You be quiet, you high-and-mighty bitch!" he snarled.

She held her hands to her face, giddy and weeping now. He drew his wide leather belt from his trousers and threw it down on the skins.

"That's to use on you if there's so much as one yelp out of you." He unbuttoned his trousers quickly and pulled them off. He grabbed at her and ripped her jacket open; the buttons flew, rolling across the floor. There were tiny beads of sweat on his forehead where the straight black hair hung down, and a little dribble of saliva at the corner of his mouth. He stooped and retrieved his belt, then tore at her clothing. She stood there, weaving weakly and almost numb, aware only of the sound of his breath rasping in his throat and the force of his hands jerking at her blouse, tearing it open to reveal her breasts bulging over her loosely bound stays.

He turned her around roughly, found the buttons of her skirt and ripped it down and threw it to one side. She had her face in her hands. He stopped and gazed at her for another moment before ripping at her under-things and exposing her bare flesh. His hands were trembling now at the prize in front of him, and he raised the belt and brought it down on her buttocks. She screamed again and he laughed as she ran from him. He pursued her, brandishing the belt and bringing it down again and again on her bare flesh. Welts raised and reddened on her back and the tender flesh of her hips. She was hysterical now, convinced he intended to kill her. Little Otter's cooking pot sat on the hearth and she made a wild grab for it and threw it at him, but in doing this she had to face him, and when the whistling belt descended on her breasts she shrieked in an agony of pain.

He ducked the pot easily and lunged for her. Stunned

113

by the pain, she stumbled and fell and he pinned her arms behind her easily.

"I knowed you'd be a wildcat—scratching and screaming, but you're gonna get it all the same!" His face was flushed and swollen now. He stared at her bare breasts.

"You're a right pretty piece, ain't you? Nobody'll have you after I finish with you, though!" he said thickly. "I'm right ready to give you something in spite of you bein' so unfriendly," he panted.

He dragged her again to the pile of skins and threw her onto them, then knelt over her and pulled her legs apart roughly, with one hand clawing at her most private part. He was swollen and his member protruded out of his gray, shabby drawers. He grabbed at it and tried to enter her. Leita clenched her eyes shut, the tears pouring down her cheeks.

He began to curse. Her flesh was unwilling and his efforts to violate her were in vain. Her fear had closed her to his thrusts, and all she felt was the pain. He shoved at her thighs, pushing them farther apart and jerking her against him, to no avail. His fingers were tearing at her delicate flesh when he suddenly let out a racking gasp and fell forward onto her. His body shuddered violently. She could smell the sickening rancid grease he used on his hair. Then she realized he had stopped moving and she opened her eyes.

Little Otter stood behind him silent, her dark eyes bright in the gloom. The long skinning knife in her right hand was dripping with blood. She looked long into Leita's unbelieving eyes, at her swollen, red face where a bruise was beginning to darken her jaw, and then tossed the bone-handled knife to one side. She bent down and took hold of McNamee's shoulder and hip and heaved him over onto his back. She was careful to turn him onto the bare floor so as not to stain her furs with blood.

He lay staring upward, his eyes starting from his head. Little Otter spit full in his face and the spittle ran down his cheek.

The Indian woman put her arm under Leita's shoulder and pulled her to a sitting position. The smell of the buckskin and the sweet, clean fragrance of herbs filled Leita's nostrils and she gave a gasping sob and buried her face in Little Otter's warm shoulder. . . .

The inquest was cut and dried. Justifiable homicide was the verdict, and Little Otter was not only cleared, but became something of a celebrity. But the ordeal wasn't over for Leita.

Samuel Johnston was having a branch bourbon and water with Sheriff Mellinger.

"This town is boilin' with talk, and I'm worried about my daughter. McNamee didn't get his aim accomplished, as you know from what she told you, but it's hurtful for her to have everybody whisperin' behind their hands."

"I understand, Sam. But you know people as well as I do, and they'll believe what they want to believe and they'll keep chewing on it till they wear it out."

"They don't want to believe the truth. That's the awful part of it. It was brought out plain and clear at the inquest—that he didn't succeed in raping her, but these goddam lascivious gossips would rather think otherwise."

"It's a hell of a lot harder to violate an unwilling girl than people realize. But we can't do more than we've done, Sam. She'll just have to ride it out."

Samuel stood at the window of the sheriff's office. The inquest had compounded the injury. The memory of that scene outside the courthouse—the way the faces

115

on the crowded walks had turned toward the buggy as it pulled away from the curb, Leita sitting erect, her face pale, her head high, her shoulders trembling—continued to haunt him like a recurring nightmare.

Something has to be done, he thought.

The mahogany door of the side entrance opened as Leita ran up the flagstones. She hurried past the maid and ascended the stairs, calling out: "Mary Jo, if you're taking a nap I'm going to waken you anyway."

Mary Jo's trilling laughter issued from the opening double doors on the left and she ran out, her silk afternoon robe trailing behind her.

"Honey, I wasn't asleep. I'm ever so glad you came. I've been looking at the spring lady's book." Mary Jo hugged Leita briefly, then called over the railing. "Martha, will you bring us up some fresh coffee and a little plate of angel-food? Now, how did you get away from that party?" She pattered up to Leita who had thrown herself on the chaise longue.

"I just up and left, that's how. They were all tryin' so hard not to look at me, bein' so polite and all, and then that fat Mrs. Raymond said how worried they had all been about me, and that sheep-faced Mrs. Hoagland—oh, can't you just imagine what they were like, all of them fairly slaverin' to hear the details over again and not believing for a minute that that beast didn't ruin me for life!" Leita pulled at her curls in an exaggeration of frenzy.

Mary Jo threw her arms up and shrieked. Then she magically pulled her vibrant face into a lugubriously lengthened grimace. "We're just *so* glad, my dear, that you weren't really harmed," she intoned.

Leita chortled with delight. The imitation of Mrs. Hoagland was almost perfection. Mary Jo chuckled with pleasure at her own performance and flopped into an arm chair. "I feel just like a little worm for crawlin' out of that party this afternoon. I didn't really have a sick headache at all, and bein' as selfish as I am, I didn't think much about you. I just wasn't in the right mood to listen to any banter about us Southern girls bein' so particular that we can't make up our minds who to marry and such clap-trap as that. Well, never mind, by the middle of summer they will have mostly forgotten about you."

"Sometimes I think they won't ever stop staring at me. One of the loafers downtown even spoke up loud enough for me to hear, something about 'That Frenchie ain't with her.' Meaning, of course, that Stephen de Jean has abandoned me because my virtue has been destroyed. I tore the buggy past him and laid mud all over the two of them."

"That was the last thing you should have done! You simply have to pretend you don't hear things like that and sail right past them. How could you give trash like that the satisfaction of even knowing that you notice them?" Mary Jo exclaimed heatedly.

"I was near to suffocating with fury, that's how," Leita retorted hotly. "Trash or quality, it seems to me they're all thinkin' about the same thing."

"That temper of yours is always your undoing, Leita. A little mud wouldn't bother that scum."

"Well, then next time I'll lay my whip to the first one that speaks a piece of insolence I'm meant to hear!"

"Oh, mercy!" Mary Jo groaned.

She answered the maid's knock, took the tray from her, and banged the door shut with her slippered foot.

With a silver pot in each hand, Mary Jo poured steaming milk and fragrant coffee into two porcelain cups while Leita unbuttoned her coat and flung it onto the lace coverlet of the canopied bed.

Without lifting her eyes from the cups, Mary Jo

117

asked quietly, "Has Breve Pinchon even written you a note since it happened?"

Leita walked to the window alcove and smoothed the lace around her throat. "I have not had one scrap of correspondence from Colonel Pinchon, nor do I expect to. He neither knows nor cares about what befalls me, and my sentiments toward him are identical. Wealth and more wealth—that is what he lives for. I'll be happy never to lay eyes on him again."

Mary Jo controlled the corners of her mouth, suppressing her amusement at the indignation in Leita's tone. "In that case, you're going to have to endure a little unhappiness, honey." Her smile escaped as Leita's eyes widened for an instant in surprise. "You and I are going to Chicago for a visit, and I'll be most mightily surprised if you don't have to lay eyes on Colonel Pinchon a time or two."

"I'm not going to Chicago. I wouldn't set foot there and have that conceited brute think I came chasin' after him."

"My, this angel food looks good," Mary Jo murmured nonchalantly. "Now drink some coffee and I'll tell you why and how we are going to Chicago." She pushed the plate toward Leita and continued, her little pussycat smile deepening her one dimple.

"Daddy has a cousin in Chicago. I know you've heard it mentioned. A letter came this morning, inviting me especially, for a nice, long visit, since Daddy had told them he wouldn't leave here now, because he's so wrapped up in clearing all this land. I'm just dyin' to go, particularly since Daddy and Mama won't be goin' along." Her china blue eyes twinkled. "And they were considerate enough to include in the invitation any friend I might care to bring along. Now that was real thoughtful, since they are strangers to me, even though we're kin. I knew right away that you just

118

had to come." She took a sip of her coffee, ignoring Leita's gesture of refusal. "Now you do too have to come. In the first place, it will be the best thing in the world for you to take a little trip and get away from this gossipy town. Why, everywhere you turn somebody's whisperin' behind their hand! You can't deny it, and you know how it's aggravatin' you. By the time we get back, there'll have been at least two other scandals and you'll be old hat. And in the second place," she went on, disregarding Leita's obdurate expression, "I couldn't have nearly so much fun if I went by myself. Daddy's cousin and his wife are even older than he is and they have an old-maid daughter in her thirties! She probably wraps herself up in a shawl every afternoon for a nice long nap. Now wouldn't that be a lark for me? Not knowin' a soul in that big exciting city and bein' cooped up with an old-maid cousin? I declare, I don't know what I'll do if you just downright refuse me!"

Leita sighed. She'll hound me every minute till I agree, she thought, but I don't want to—tempting as it is to get away from this. What if I would see him? He has a power over me and he knows it; he turns my insides to fire even when I'm hating him for it.

"I'd rather go to Philadelphia. We could go visit my aunt and uncle there," Leita offered.

"But we've *been* there, honey! And here we are just a few hours from a city bigger than Charleston even, a city just teeming with theaters and parties and exciting people."

Too many exciting people, Leita almost murmured aloud.

"And that's another thing," Mary Jo bubbled on. "You've got a dashing beau who lives there. I know Stephen has invited you time and again and you've refused."

119

"Three times," Leita interrupted, "and I've been too busy."

"Too busy, my foot! Too stubborn is more like it. Are you really going to let Breve Pinchon cheat you out of living your life? Think of the good times we could have. And you know Stephen would be so delighted at you comin' that he might, he just might, know some handsome gentleman who would consent to keep poor little me from bein' a wallflower."

Leita burst out laughing at this. Mary Jo adjusted the pink silk folds of her robe and fluttered her eyelashes in mock coquettishness.

"You know it's almost true, Leita. The Rankins probably have some fusty old stick of a third cousin they're plannin' to fob off on me, and I'd just die of boredom. With Stephen to show us around it would be different. And he's so mad about you he would round up all kinds of exciting escorts for me, just to get me off his hands."

Leita felt herself weakening. It was true; Stephen would outdo himself to show them a glorious time. And she felt a little contrite at Mary Jo's graphic description of what her visit would be like otherwise, thinking it might not be an exaggeration. A middle-aged spinster wouldn't be the sprightliest companion for a visit. And Mary Joe was, after all, her friend.

"I just can't believe that a girl that's as proud as you would let just one man control her life to the point where she wouldn't take a wonderful trip just because she might bump into him. Now I know Breve Pinchon is awful conceited, but he's not stupid enough to think you would go all the way to Chicago just to see him. And he also knows that a girl as beautiful as you can take your pick of suitors, and just because you two got a little close months and months ago doesn't mean that you haven't forgotten him completely and forevermore. Anyway, he writes to Jerome Knox you know, and Jerome says that Breve is dashing around over the country half the time, out in San Francisco and back to New York and I don't know where-all, looking after his mines and railroad stock and all that truck. So you probably don't have to be afraid of seeing him at all." Mary Jo had been picking at her cake nonchalantly during her speech, while watching Leita narrowly.

Leita flared. "I'm not the least bit afraid of seeing him! What a ridiculous thing to say. He's less than nothing to me."

"Well, I'm certainly glad to hear that!" Mary Jo exclaimed and rose to preen herself in front of the gilt-trimmed standing mirror. "Then there isn't a reason in the world why we can't go and have a perfectly elegant time together. Not a reason in the world!" she concluded, turning to face Leita, her blue eyes sparkling with delight and triumph.

Chapter 10

HIGH OVERHEAD THE METAL ARCHES WOVE IN AND OUT and Leita tilted her head further back as she looked in wonder at the lofty roof of the LaSalle St. train station. The steam escaping from the locomotives was cascading and whooshing round the tracks. Mary Jo pattered along beside her like an angry mouse, but Leita was enthralled as she strolled down the platform oblivious to Mary Jo's indignance.

Mary Jo continued her tirade. "We made a dreadful mistake in not allowing Stephen to meet us. Here we are, good as stranded in this awful barn of a place."

"Oh, hush! We're not stranded at all. We can just hire a carriage if your uncle doesn't turn up. We're not children, Jo."

"But it's so downright inconsiderate not to be there when we stepped off the train. Cousin Caleb must be a dreadful boor, to leave us to traipse around like this."

Leita's eyes shone with anticipation and interest as they surveyed the bustling crowds.

"Mary Jo, in the first place the train was early, rather than late, and you know we were told that was a rare occurrence. In the second place," Leita went on, irritated by Mary Jo's petulance, "any number of things could have happened to delay Mr. Rankin. You had better quit gnashing your teeth and watch for anyone who looks like him."

"Oh, Lordy, I thought I would know him right away, I studied his picture enough. But there must be a hundred old men with muttonchop whiskers hurryin' along in this station," Mary Jo fretted. "At any rate, we'll soon be at the entrance and you can just take charge of hiring us a carriage. I'm worn to a frazzle, jolting around on that train for hours and hours."

"The porter will get us a carriage. Please don't faint with exhaustion until you're seated, Mary Jo." Leita's acerbic reply was robbed of some dignity by the breeze that gusted through the entrance, forcing her to grab for her bonnet, which was almost blown off.

"Tilt it a little more to the right," Mary Jo advised as Leita adjusted the bonnet. "It does beat all how you can put on any old thing and look like a beauty. I feel as if I'm leavin' a funeral, all muffled up in dark blue, like a crow, and there you are, shining and glowing. Half the gentlemen we pass turn on their heel just to look at you!" Mary Jo exclaimed.

"Navy blue is not a becoming color at all, but if we weren't wearing these traveling costumes we would look like chimney sweeps, what with all this soot flyin' around. They do look a little as if we were in mourning. Maybe the gentlemen are turnin' around in amazement at such a poor little homely creature as you," Leita laughed.

"You know I look fit for the grave. You needn't torment me with it." Mary Jo looked again at Leita whose red-gold curls fell gleaming over one shoulder of the navy blue faille coat, trimmed luxuriantly in loops of soutache braid. Her pink and ivory skin was luminous and the big violet eyes were accented by the blue highlights in the silk bow tied under her chin. "There's a smudge of soot on your nose," she remarked, and taking the lacy handkerchief that Leita proferred she dabbed at the spot. The porter behind them who was in charge of their two trunks and mountain of hatboxes took the opportunity to light a coarse black cigar.

"I do believe you must be cousin Mary Jo." The rich musical voice issued from a slender, statuesque woman in pearl gray silk. She extended a gloved hand. Leita studied her with interest. Her oval face was framed in two glossy black coils of hair covering her ears, from which hung long pearl teardrops. The face broke into a smile. "I'm Darcy Rankin, and it seems I owe you an apology. I was delayed, and that abysmal train was early. I feel so remiss in not welcoming you, but we will make up for such a seemingly inhospitable beginning."

Leita almost laughed aloud at Mary Jo's amazed expression. Her friend recovered her poise in an instant and held out her arms for an embrace, receiving a feathery touch on both shoulders in return.

"I'm just so astonished, and you don't need to apologize one little bit. You couldn't help it if that train was ahead of time, and I'm just delighted to meet you, cousin Darcy. And I'd like to present my very dearest friend, Miss Leita Johnston."

"It's a pleasure, and we're so happy you accepted our invitation, Miss Johnston," the musical voice intoned. The lips that curved over small white teeth were red, a very vivid red, Leita observed as she offered her hand and made the polite rejoinders.

"Now, the carriage is waiting and we will soon be in much more comfortable surroundings. If you will just follow me." Darcy Rankin swept ahead of them, holding the gray silk skirt banded in violet velvet high above her gleaming narrow boots. Mary Jo turned a look of such droll surprise toward Leita that she was obliged to cover her mouth and bite on the finger of her white kid glove to hold down her laughter.

Seated in the carriage, Darcy graciously inquired about their journey and the state of health of everyone in the Tillett family. Leita paid no more attention than was required for the sake of courtesy; she was looking out the carriage window, her eyes wide with attention as they rolled down the broad width of LaSalle Street. The four- and five-story buildings, red brick and gray stone with their scores of windows throwing back beams of light from the late afternoon sun, the boardwalks filled with men, some strolling, some waddling, all of them with a protective hand ready at the brim of their derbies and stovepipes, the high-stepping teams drawing the multitude of carriages and barouches—the panoply fascinated her. This is Breve's milieu, she thought. He walks these streets, and his carriage delivers him to the door of one of these buildings.

"The loop is not the most beautiful section of the city, Miss Johnston. I'm glad you find it interesting. You are looking at the men and monuments that turn our wheels of commerce, but you will see prettier sights." Darcy Rankin's words held a touch of amusement.

"The wheels of commerce hold a certain fascination, too," Leita replied thoughtfully.

"Commerce is an unusual taste for a young girl," Darcy Rankin observed serenely.

"Oh, Leita is just made up of unusual tastes. It's her daddy's fault. She had her nose stuck in too many books for too long. It gave her strange ideas." Mary Jo's tone was teasing, and Leita wrinkled her nose at her in reply. The newly met cousin reclined languidly against the maroon velour upholstery, her hazel eyes, long and slightly downsloping, rested speculatively on Leita's face, and Leita suddenly, inexplicably, had a moment of unease.

She turned her attention to the blue-brown waters of the Chicago River as the carriage clattered across the Michigan Avenue bridge. The high-masted ships, some docked, and others plying serenely in the gusty wind, their sails billowing, entranced her. Slower-moving barges, laden with coal from Pennsylvania and grain from the plains states, drifted along, manned by mysterious, gutteral crews.

North of the river the change was dramatic and Leita leaned forward in her seat. The massively built stone and brick mansions of Chicago's Gold Coast loomed austerely among the elm and maple and fir trees lining the avenues that led to them. Leita knew that Stephen maintained one of these imitation baronial halls, "for the sake of making it plain that I am a man to be reckoned with," he had explained with an ironic smile, his French accent, so faint usually, slurring the "reckoned." His letter had expressed his gratified surprise at her impending visit. "I will be at your pleasure every moment. At last I can show you the manner in which you should live, and all the delights (however aboriginal) of this burgeoning metropolis."

The fact that he was acquainted with her hosts would smooth his path considerably, Leita thought, not without a touch of wryness, at Stephen's seemingly limitless sphere of influence. "Happily, I am on a basis of some friendship with the Rankins, and so won't be regarded as an unknown, importunate suitor of their houseguest. I spoke with Mr. Rankin only this afternoon, expressing my pleasure at my newfound knowledge of his relatives, whom I consider to be my friends. He declared most hospitably that he should consider me a welcome caller, providing of course that I was not *persona non grata* at your home in Fort Wayne. This last was one of Caleb Rankin's heavy-handed pleasantries. To the end of reassuring him in this respect, I have taken the liberty of addressing a letter to Mr. Johnston, asking if he would be so good as to apprise Mr. Rankin that I met with his approval as a suitor of his very highly regarded daughter. Voila, I shall spare no effort to impress you with my city." Stephen's characteristic humility, Leita thought.

The carriage turned, gates were opened, and eventually they alighted in an oval drive before a broad stone terrace. A woman with dun-colored hair and sharp little bones in her face stood awaiting them. Mary Jo and Leita were presented by Darcy Rankin to her mother and ushered into a vast and rather gloomy hall, oppressed rather than decorated by several reproductions of Roman statues. Darcy Rankin's slim, cool, elegance seemed totally unrelated to the hesitant, meager little woman who was her mother. Richly dressed in dark green watered silk, Mrs. Rankin's tiny hands fluttered at the lace fichu that decorated the space below her corded neck.

"You must be in need of refreshment. If you like, I will ask Arthur to bring trays to your room. Your baths will be ready quite soon, that is of course if you would like to bathe." Mrs. Rankin fluttered, her eyes darting here and there.

Leita took pity on her shyness and hugged her quickly. "I can't thank you enough for inviting me, too, when I'm not even kin, and a bath sounds absolutely lovely."

"Oh, my dear, it will be such a joy to have you young people here." Mrs. Rankin's pale brown eyes filled, and her hands fluttered faster than ever.

Darcy Rankin smiled graciously and led the way up one side of the double stairway. The mahogany balustrades seemed to reach to heaven where the light poured down through a stained glass dome three stories above the first floor. Mrs. Rankin trailed behind, arm in arm with Mary Jo, but it was Cousin Darcy who did the honors, showing them their chambers, separated by a sitting room that looked out over a formally sculptured garden.

After their hostesses had left them with the information that the dinner guests were due to arrive at eight, Leita tossed her bonnet onto the window seat and collapsed beside it, choking with laughter.

"Now what is so funny?" Mary Jo inquired, unbuttoning her long, dark coat and looking at it with distaste before throwing it over the back of a chair.

"Your old-maid cousin, who 'wraps herself up in a shawl every afternoon for a nice long nap.'"

"I was never so astonished—just never! Isn't she the most elegant, gorgeous creature? I was just bowled over! Did I show it?" Mary Jo's eyes were wide with a dismay that was only partly exaggerated.

"Your surprise was very apparent, and you needn't fret about it. I'm sure she took it as a compliment."

"What I simply do not understand, Leita, is why in the world a beauty, an absolute beauty like that, is still an old maid. Whatever happened, do you suppose? Maybe she has had a tragedy, maybe her fiancés were all killed, or shot in duels. Perhaps she's a man-hater and just turns down proposals right and left. I won't rest till I find out," Mary Jo stated emphatically.

"Somehow I don't think that could be true, Jo. I would swear she isn't a man-hater, but there is something about her, something subterranean, really." Leita tapped her chin with a forefinger, pensively.

Mary Jo stood in front of a pair of tall windows, festooned with royal blue velvet and gold tassels. "You're right. It must have been a tragedy. If she had been homely as a mud fence there would have been lots of beaux for her, considering the size her dowry must be."

"Oh, you are crass, Jo! Maybe she's like you, and would rather flirt than breathe, and won't make up her mind to settle down with just one." Leita was disrobing and Mary Jo began to unlace her stays.

"You're a fine one to talk—you're as stubborn as a Missouri mule and slip right through the fingers of every man who falls in love with you. Maybe she was just like you, with her head set on seeing the world and painting or something—too independent to even consider her proposals."

Leita cast the whalebone stays aside with a voluptuous sigh of pleasure. "And maybe she's very happy that she never made herself subject to a man she didn't love," she retorted.

"Or she might have been too proud to be subject to the man she did love," Mary Jo said pointedly, then nonchalantly began stepping out of her own crinolines.

"This is in the nature of a small, but welcoming gathering for my niece, Miss Tillett, and her friend, Miss Johnston," Caleb Rankin declaimed with an avuncular arm around Mary Jo's shoulders. His florid rectangular face, adorned with gray, mutton-chop whiskers, beamed above the starched wings of his collar. Caleb Rankin was himself almost a composite portrait of a successful entrepreneur, Leita decided, looking at the somber oil portrait of her host hanging above the bronze and marble fireplace. The chandelier in the mahogany-paneled drawing room illuminated the satins and discreet sprinkle of diamond lavaliers and eardrops adorning the arriving guests, discreet since a dinner party in a private home called for a less brilliant display than a ball or an evening at the opera. Even Mrs. Rankin glittered a little, the light glancing

130

off her diamond and ruby brooch, too large in scale for her and undoubtedly a gift from her hearty but, Leita suspected, unperceptive husband.

She stood in the reception line, being presented to and welcomed by each of the guests. Flushed with pleasure, she reflected that she had been wise to override her resentment of Breve's cold indifference—she might have cheated herself of what promised to be an interesting and exciting visit. Her flush deepened as she looked to the left and saw Stephen de Jean in the foyer handing his hat and cane to the waiting butler. Shiningly impeccable as always, his silk ascot pierced by a milky-white opal stickpin, she was struck again by how handsome he was. The next moment he was bowing over Mrs. Rankin's outstretched little claw, and Caleb Rankin was shaking hands with him boisterously.

Caleb Rankin chuckled, giving Leita a roguish smile. "You didn't know your best beau was going to show up tonight, did you? Mrs. Rankin and I thought we'd surprise you."

It seemed to Leita that everyone in the room had turned to look as Stephen bowed low over her hand. When he raised his head, an impish gleam shone in his eyes.

"How very nice to see you, and how thoughtful of my host and hostess to insure that there would be more than one familiar face on my first night here," Leita murmured, dropping a little curtsy toward the Rankins, hoping that the interest of the bystanders would be dispelled by her formality.

The impish gleam in Stephen's eyes was heightened, if anything, and he moved on, greeting Mary Jo and Cousin Darcy with a courtly compliment apiece.

After the reception line disbanded, Leita found herself in a group where Cousin Darcy seemed to be holding court, looking regal in ecru satin banded with

131

vermillion, which set off the gleaming dark coils at either side of the almost perfect oval of her face. Stephen materialized at Leita's side and a tall, barrel-chested man with ginger-colored hair and sideburns smiled benignly at them both. "And now we have the pleasure of meeting your nice friend, Stephen," he boomed genially. "And what does a southern lady think of our little town?" A slight accent sharpened his words and Leita was framing a reply when Stephen spoke. "Hugo, that is an unfair question when you know that I haven't had the opportunity of showing it to her yet. You have my permission to ask her again two weeks from now and I may be held responsible for her reply. My partner is not a happy traveler, Miss Johnston. That is why any journeying that arises in the course of our business is undertaken by me."

"Ah, but one journey you made had very felicitous results," Hugo Wenzler added, with an archness that was ludicrous in so big a man. His ginger-colored mustache, waxed stiffly, spread upward in unison with his smile, which exposed large, slightly yellowish teeth.

Darcy Rankin laid her long, beringed fingers gently on Hugo Wenzler's arm. It was an almost proprietary touch, Leita noticed.

"Miss Johnston showed a keen interest in the loop district, Mr. Wenzler. I believe that Mr. de Jean is going to have a very receptive audience to his guided tour. She doesn't even find commerce dull."

"But commerce is never dull, Miss Rankin. That is a rumor perpetrated by some who wish to discourage those who might enter it if they fully realized the rewards of it."

"You sound as if you are bantering, but I know you are deadly serious," Leita said. "There are many things I look forward to seeing and one of them is Mr. McCormick's works. He was from Virginia, you know, and I have heard so much of how he has revolutionized the harvesting of grain. His reaper is of considerable importance to the area where I live now."

"That should be very easy to arrange. The gentleman you speak of is standing over there and I will request his permission." Stephen nodded in the direction of a slender, gray-haired man who stood in an attitude of listening to a voluble, heavy woman in black silk.

Leita looked at him with interest. "I hadn't realized it was *that* Mr. McCormick when we were introduced." Her interest was artless, as artless as her unawareness of the admiring appraisals of the guests. She was wearing an apple-green silk, the deep flounces of the skirt caught up with golden bows and a finely pleated, golden bow decorated the front where the apple-green silk rose to a demure decolletage. Her hair, shining like polished bronze, had tiny golden beads woven through the waves, which fell into a swept-back cascade of curls.

The butler announced dinner and Stephen offered Leita his arm. "I am to have the honor of taking you in, I believe. You are going to find it so difficult to elude me that it will not be worth your while, Leita, my dear," he murmured, out of hearing of the others.

"I have no intention of eluding you, Mr. de Jean. I am highly complimented by your attentions," Leita whispered back in mock formality. He laughed appreciatively.

The pair directly across the table began questioning her about her journey from the South and she soon was conversing animatedly. The wax tapers glowed brightly over the white damask covering of the long table, and reflections from their orange flames shimmered across the heavy silver serving dishes. Stephen sipped the mellow burgundy, his eyes roaming over the arch of Leita's throat and the opulence of her gleaming shoulders rising from the delicate folds of silk. His narrow

133

nostrils flared slightly and suddenly as he thought of the heaving passion he intended to elicit from this fiery girl. Mine to mold, he thought, and six months from now those vibrant charms will grace my table. His faint smile was complacent.

"Pinchon is an independent customer—a shade too independent. He will consider no partnerships. 'My enterprises are my own, my responsibilities my own, and the gains belong to me.' I have it on his own word. He may come a cropper, but I see no sign of it yet."

"He impressed Jay Gould, all right, and then he refused to join him."

Leita took a sip of her suddenly tasteless wine. The volume of laughter and soft ringing clatter of silverware seemed to rise perversely as she strained to hear.

"But a charming guest, you must admit; if one disregards his habit of canceling engagements at the last minute to go roaming off like a gypsy."

"Colonel Pinchon is far more predatory than even a gypsy, my dear, though in some respects your comparison does have merit."

"He roams as a wolf roams, with a keen eye intent for his prey. He snaps up controlling shares as if they were so many jack rabbits—and he hunts alone."

"Well, he has returned from the hunt again. He was at the Davises' last Sunday and I did manage to elicit from him that he plans to attend the reception for the Morgans."

"If he doesn't scent the trail of a potentially lucrative mine or a foundering railroad between now and then."

"Then he will disappear again, I suppose. Such an elusive man, but such a fascinating one!"

Stephen had to repeat his question before Leita, lost in reverie, realized he was speaking to her.

The dining room of the Mays Hotel echoed with the

pleasant hum of voices of those affluent enough to bask in its luxury. White-coated waiters lifted the heavy silver covers of the serving dishes to display fresh-caught lake salmon and potatoes Lyonnaise. Leita fingered the delicate crystal stem of her wine glass. They were awaiting the arrival of Mary Jo Tillett and Luton Parker and Stephen's partner, Hugo Wenzler, who was calling for Darcy. After lunch they were to go sightseeing. Leita's eyes had swept the room when she stood at the entrance. She had looked for Breve's broad shoulders and jet black hair, thinking that just possibly he might be lunching here. Her relief was mixed with a stab of disappointment, and she carefully kept her eyes on Stephen after they were seated, resisting the temptation to search the room more carefully.

Stephen leaned forward and traced his finger contemplatively on the tablecloth. "I do visit France regularly, as I have told you. I was fourteen when my father brought us here for what was to have been an edifying six-month visit—a Grand Tour in reverse. Then Louis Napoleon, the pretender, the object of ridicule, managed to get himself elected President of the Republic. King Louis Phillippe was exiled in England, and Papa refused to return to France. He would not live under any member of the Bonaparte family; he was an obdurate royalist. In consequence my sister and I are, for the great part, Americans. But we are definitely French, too."

"And what do you think of Emperor Napoleon now? He is certainly not an object of ridicule any longer."

"It is not so much what I think of our Emperor as what I hope for him," Stephen replied enigmatically.

Leita's interest was piqued. Stephen's self-possessed charm mitigated against any exposure of his private convictions. His veneer was so disarming that the fact

135

that he was essentially self-contained usually escaped notice. "And what do you hope for him that he doesn't have?"

"Awareness, Leita, awareness that the smoke is still curling from Prussian gun bores. It has been a scant two years since Prussia defeated Austria."

"But Prussia got what it wanted, surely—the states between its eastern and western halves?"

"Ah, but that was only a beginning: the remaining German states still lie outside its maw. Night and day he should remember that war against France would be a most compelling common cause—one that Otto von Bismarck would welcome with open cannon as a means of welding the other German states to Prussia. He is salivating for it. Furthermore, he is preparing for it; not tomorrow or the next day, but in some year to come."

"Oh what a horror to think about, Stephen! To try and find an excuse to go to war! When I do go abroad, and at times I can hardly wait till my twentieth birthday, I want all to be serene."

"It is my second fondest wish that your sailing will be a most joyous occasion. The guns shall not blaze and the cannon shall not boom, but spring shall flourish when you sail. You will note that is my second fondest wish. The first you are well aware of, since it is only in your power to grant."

Leita smiled at him, keeping her smile noncommital with difficulty. His unflagging devotion, his airy disregard of any obstacles in his determination to make her his bride, along with his sensitivity in not pressing her when she had made her sentiments clear, all these things enlarged him in her eyes. His warm, good humor never failed—she had never known him to bait her or to behave domineeringly, despite the fact that he was obviously a powerful man, moving with ease and sharp-eyed certainty in a world where fortunes were made and lost overnight. Perhaps someday, she thought, perhaps you will be the man I marry. I might even weaken sooner than I think. Her harsh experiences in Fort Wayne, the shade of Tom McNamee advancing on her in the dusky light of the little cabin, the stares and whispers of the town seemed far away now as she sat across from this man with the handsome features and almost serpentine grace.

"Of course," he continued, returning her smile, "it is my opinion that you should sail to France and stay in Paris before you visit England. Since your plans are for the summer of your twentieth birthday, you have ample time to decide, but, from the summit of my wide experience"—here his smile flashed—"I would say France and then Italy, stopping in Switzerland, of course—then tour England. You will find the contrast even more marked. Florence you must give time to. Not only is it the capital now, but the city itself is a vibrant museum of palazzos and statues. Of course Paris—what can one say? You will have to see for yourself "

"And that is exactly what I want to do. Imagine how fluent my French will be by that time. Reneé is angelic, suffering my terrible accent and correcting me so gently, and you, Stephen, you deserve a medal for your tutoring."

"You are surprisingly fluent now, and your accent is indescribably charming."

"Simply indescribable would be a more accurate description," she laughed.

"And here comes the dependable Hugo with your hostess." Stephen gestured and Leita turned to see Darcy gliding between the tables with Hugo's majestic height lumbering docilely along behind her.

"Stephen, you never say, but do you think those two will ever marry?" Leita whispered.

Stephen pursed his lips and offered only a Gallic shrug in reply before he rose.

Darcy bent and greeted Leita with a swift brush of her lips across Leita's cheek while Hugo clapped Stephen on the shoulder and bowed with a heel-click to Leita. "Have you not eaten? Such patience must be rewarded. Where are Miss Tillett and her swain? Ah, yes, I will have sherry, and you, Miss Rankin?" Hugo Wenzler seated himself, smiled at all of them and proceeded to pour a diminutive amount of sherry into Darcy's glass. Leita was accustomed by now to his genial flow of questions and exhortations. Hugo reminded her a little of a rust-colored setter, his expression always one of simple affability. "A very astute businessman, a little ponderous and heavy-handed, but when it comes to investment, his wits move like mercury," Stephen had described Hugo.

"And where are you guiding Miss Johnston this afternoon? Not to more factories, I hope. Such grimy places for a fresh young lady."

"Cyrus McCormick's establishment wasn't wasted on her," Stephen replied.

"I was astounded. I have never seen so many men at work under one roof. And twelve hours a day! Our slaves wouldn't have been able to stand up to such a life. And the hovels they live in!" Leita exclaimed.

"*Mein Gott*, Stephen, you did not take her through those shanties and tumble-down cottages?" Hugo's German accent was intensified by his astonishment.

"I saw it, mud and filth and all!" Leita affirmed. "And you mustn't blame Stephen. I insisted and he knows that I mean what I say. If they can survive living like that, I most certainly can survive driving through, even with a handkerchief at my nose."

"She was determined, Hugo, and Leita isn't given to vapors. She is genuinely interested. I explained that these people in all probability lived in much worse hovels before they came here to be gainfully employed. On the positive side, Leita was much impressed by the speed at which the machinery is turned out."

"Oh, yes," Leita declared. "My father says that the scythe will be a thing of the past when every farmer is able to cut his wheat with the machinery—Mr. McCormick's invention is surely a marvelous thing. The factory was grimy, of course," and she nodded at Hugo, "but I was fascinated by it, and Mr. McCormick couldn't have been more hospitable. Did Stephen tell you we dined with him?"

"No, I only knew that Stephen arranged with Mr. McCormick for you to see part of the works. And how did you find Cyrus, my dear Miss Johnston? Did you tax him with the living quarters of his employees?"

"Of course not. I simply asked him why someone didn't build decent little houses for those people to live in."

"Oh ho ho!" Hugo laughed as he and Darcy exchanged glances. "And what did Cyrus reply to that?"

"It was his opinion that they lived as they chose. I believe he said that soap and water cost very little and was not in short supply. I became tactful for once and let the subject drop, or rather Stephen changed it."

Mary Jo and Luton Parker arrived then.

"I told Luton we would be the last here and keep you all waitin', but he just insisted on a quick drive along the lake." Mary Jo's blue eyes were bright as she fluttered into the chair that Luton held for her. "Now see, he is too much of a gentleman to tell you what a fibber I am. I was the one who wanted to take the drive and I thought surely we wouldn't be this late. There now, I've made my apology."

"And a very contrite one, too. I hope you don't feel so guilty that your lunch is spoiled," Stephen chuckled.

"She is barely able to hold back her tears," Luton remarked.

"Never mind their teasing, Jo. The time flew; Stephen was telling me about Emperor Napoleon and making out the itinerary for my trip to Europe."

This started a discussion which bounced from one topic to another through the sumptuous meal.

When they left the hotel the group parted; Darcy accompanied Hugo in his carriage and Stephen assisted Leita into his open barouche. Luton Parker handed Mary Jo up while Leita looped her long gauze scarf more securely under her chin and tucked her hand into the crook of Stephen's elbow. She had grown more content by the hour. Breve's dark presence, which had occupied her thoughts almost exclusively since her acceptance of Mary Jo's invitation, had begun to recede. Stephen hadn't once pressed her with passion or proposals of marriage during these past days. He had allayed her restive loneliness with the tenderness of his attentions, diverted her with his carefree presence and enthusiastically arranged for her to see every aspect of this huge, bustling city. At least he never patronizes me, she thought, feeling a tingling rush of warmth at the gentle pressure of his body against her.

"After we visit the Stock Exchange Leita would like to drive along Water Street, along the riverfront. I hope you two are agreeable to that," Stephen announced.

"What on earth for?" Mary Jo asked with dismay.

"Wouldn't you like to see all those ships and barges loading and unloading? Why, they carry cargo clear down to the port of New Orleans. It's bound to be fascinating!" Leita explained eagerly. Luton Parker caught Stephen's eye and suppressed a smile.

"Leita, honey, they're just dirty old boats and dirty

140

old barges and a lot of dirtier ruffians working on them. Do you think that will be fascinating?" Mary Jo addressed her question to Luton.

"Your description is accurate in some respects, but it is an impressive sight." Luton adroitly managed to agree with both of them.

Mary Jo threw up her hands in dismay. "I don't know what I was thinking of when I coaxed you to come, Leita." Her smile belied her words. "I suppose next you'll be wanting to set up your easel on the docks while they're rolling hogsheads around you!"

"I'll have to see first how picturesque it is, and then you can come with me and read to me while I work," Leita rejoined.

"It's just as well that we've reached our first port of call before you young ladies can carry on with your arrangements." Luton's smile curved sardonically as it so often did, contrasting with the boyish ringlets that no amount of brushing could straighten out.

Leita looked up at the looming edifice of the Chicago Stock Exchange and a few minutes later was looking down from the wide gallery onto the floor below where frock-coated men clustered in groups like so many swallows, conferring, persuading, and gesturing. The hubbub, a muted roar, wafted up to the high gallery.

"Voilà, before your eyes." Stephen gestured toward the huge floor scattered with high desks and walls lined with boards where the results of the day's trading were scrawled. "This is the arena where those of us who invest our funds create and support the companies that buy and sell and manufacture. Of course, the real decisions are made in the private rooms of clubs and over after-dinner cigars and brandy," he concluded.

"Then the scurrying around that's going on below is only the tip of the iceberg," Leita observed as she leaned over the railing, watching a young messenger boy run weaving through the clusters of men, brandishing a fistful of papers.

"Very succinctly put, Miss Johnston. You could compare this activity to the flopping of a beheaded chicken—the deed is done but the last steps still have to be taken."

"Good heavens, Luton, what a gory turn of mind you have!" Mary Jo shuddered as Leita laughed, thinking that the scurrying messenger boy bore some resemblance to Luton's analogy. He was lost in the crowd and she looked again, then sighted him running down beside the wall. Just as he reached a doorway he drew up short and removed his cap. Leita's breath stopped and the next moment a tremor ran through her. She could just see his features, the chiseled mouth, firm above the strong chin and the heavy brows shading those black eyes. His curling hair, dead black in the soft afternoon light coming through the tall windows, was swept back from his forehead. She watched as he reached in his pocket and tendered a coin to the boy, then walked along slowly as he scanned the sheaf of papers.

Breve stood tall, half a head above the man who joined him, as he reached into his waistcoat pocket and drew out a cigar, apparently listening intently to the other man's words. She felt paralyzed, unable to take her eyes off him until he looked up and seemed to be absently scanning the galleries while the other man continued to speak rapidly. Suddenly she heard her own voice saying, "Let's go to the riverfront now and get out of this stuffy building."

Stephen's voice seemed to come from miles away, and she barely felt his touch as he guided her to the stairway to the accompaniment of Mary Jo's expressions of relief at their departure from such a dull spectacle.

She didn't notice Mary Jo's piercing glance at her when they reached the street. The drive along the waterfront seemed interminable but she kept up a steady flow of questions and comments as the barouche threaded its way through the laden wagons and past the moored ships where winches swung overhead with barrels of beef and pork and lengths of lumber locked in their iron jaws. Stephen and Luton Parker were discussing the cost of water shipment of iron ore when Mary Jo leaned over and under the guise of tucking one of Leita's stray curls back under the gauze scarf, whispered in her ear. "I saw him too, and he saw you—I know it." Leita felt her face grow hot and her eyes fell. Mary Jo gave her cheek a quick pat and the next moment, to Luton's surprise, was exclaiming over the gigantic size of a bargeload of logs. She was, in her quick way, giving Leita time to compose herself.

The grounds of the Davis mansion glowed with the pastel lights of Japanese lanterns strung between every tree and festooning the bushes around the pool with its huge fountain. On the broad terrace that faced the fountain tall Chinese urns were filled with pussy willows and lilac. Two long damask covered tables held bowls of punch and raspberry shrub and champagne and the waiters hired for the occasion swerved through the crush of guests, managing their laden trays skillfully. Some of the guests were invited for the reception only with an even more select list of one hundred who had received invitations for the dinner to be held for the young banker, J. Pierpont Morgan, son of the Connecticut merchant who had taken his expertise to England and established the banking house of J. S. Morgan &

Co. in London while his compatriots were embroiled in the Civil War. As a tribute to the influence of his father and his position in Eastern seaboard society, as well as the judgment of acquaintances that the thirty-year-old John P. Morgan's piercing eyes were the outward sign of an even more piercing intelligence, the Davises had sent out engraved invitations to over two hundred members of Chicago's elite to honor their visiting friend.

"And why is he so terribly important?" Leita asked Stephen, after having curtseyed her way through the reception line and exchanging a few words with the massively built man who was the guest of honor.

Darcy Rankin coolly interrupted. "He is so terribly important because he is so terribly rich, Leita."

Hugo Wenzler guffawed and Stephen nodded at Leita in amused affirmation. Leita shrugged and unfurled her fan. Her dress was a sapphire bengaline, with a huge overskirt of silvery silk gauze. Her creamy shoulders rose out of the folds, and a cluster of fresh violets was fastened at her bosom. They moved from one group to another where Stephen was greeted with a warmth that was often flirtatious by the richly jeweled women and a comradely respect by their husbands.

Leita had refused to discuss Breve the night before, though Mary Jo had launched into an unwelcome monologue about why he hadn't even sent a note, since she was certain that he knew full well they were in Chicago. "Jerome would have written him, I just know it, and I think it's downright rude of him not to at least pay his respects."

"It's entirely possible, Jo, that Jerome didn't give him the full particulars of whom we were staying with. I imagine Jerome finds things to write about besides our activities, even if he did happen to mention that you and I were coming to Chicago." Leita had tried desperately to keep the conversation relevant to what Mary Jo seemed to consider Breve's default in etiquette.

"Oh, fiddlesticks! I know that Jerome went rushin' straight for pen and paper after you told him we were comin' up here for a visit. If you want the truth, and it's about time you got a taste of it—Jerome thinks you're too stiff and proud to realize that Breve Pinchon is really in love with you."

Leita buffed her nails, trying to remain calm under Mary Jo's observant eyes. "It just happens that Jerome Knox is a real for sure romantic. When it comes to falling in love he sees nothing but stars and moonlight. We've been gone from South Carolina almost a year now and I can tell that Jerome hasn't forgotten that silly minx that turned him down back in Charleston. Now he would deny it, but he's only waiting till their holdings are parceled out and his share comes to him in his own right before he tears back down there to throw himself at her feet again. I'm sure of that, and it just breaks my heart for him. He is such a good-hearted, sweet boy, and he hasn't been serious about one other girl in all these months, and they're flirtin' themselves blind, just dyin' to say yes to him. He's the blind one, and he's too nice to be able to see that Breve Pinchon is a money-hungry conceited devil of a man, for all his good looks and his charming manners." She plied the nail buffer furiously. "He only uses those charming manners when he is in the mood to. He can be a brute and a bully just as easy, and a haughty one, too."

"Now that's exciting. When was he ever a brute to you?" Mary Jo questioned lightly and easily.

"Enough times for me to know what he really is! He'll never wrap me around his little finger again, I can tell you that. Now I don't want to talk about him anymore." Leita flung the buffer and it struck the

145

pedestal of a table before it went skidding across the floor.

"Is that why your face went as pale as death when you saw him this afternoon, because he'll never wrap you round his little finger again?"

Leita turned her head to hide the tears of rage that started up in her eyes. "If I turned pale it was because I got a little dizzy," she countered, grabbing a hairbrush from her dressing table. "That gallery was up so high and it was stuffy in there," she added lamely.

"Oh, so that was it," Mary Jo agreed smoothly. "Well, Stephen saw it and he saw what was makin' you dizzy, but he is too quick and clever to let on. He just pretends that Colonel Pinchon doesn't exist. But I'll tell you this, he's mighty watchful and I'm just positive he will see to it that you're kept as far away from Breve as he can keep you." Mary Jo spoke softly as she toyed with the ribbons of her nightgown.

"Stephen wouldn't waste his thoughts on something so foolish. I don't think he has any regard for Breve at all and certainly no cause to be jealous. How could he be jealous of a man who avoids me as if I had the smallpox—and not only that, when we are thrown together we fight like two cur dogs?" Leita exclaimed.

"Jerome says that you underestimate Stephen de Jean."

"Oh, I know, and Stephen reminds him of a 'black panther just waitin' to spring,'" Leita deprecated. "Well, Stephen de Jean is a gentleman, too much of a gentleman to behave the way Breve Pinchon behaves."

"Well, I personally think that Stephen de Jean is the answer to a maiden's prayer, and it's obvious that I'm not the only one that thinks so. He has to have every attribute that a woman glories in. He's gallant, good-looking enough to blind you, thoughtful, attentive, and

146

absolutely dripping with money. But Jerome is serious about not trusting him."

"Now I dearly love Jerome, and you know it, Jo, but he is like an old mother-hen sometimes. If a body doesn't come from South Carolina and Jerome doesn't know who his granddaddy was, then he's an outlander to Jerome. Stephen has never given me any cause to distrust him, and until he does I'll just rely on my own opinion."

Mary Jo stood by the table and removed a jonquil from the vase. She twirled the stem in her fingers as she spoke. "Remember, I told you once that there was a mystery about Breve? That something was driving him, something he hadn't told anybody about? Jerome agrees with me; he says that he thinks Breve is a man with a mission, that something is goading him and he'll be running like a horse with blinders on till he gets whatever he's after."

"You and Jerome are sure busy making excuses for a self-centered adventurer. Well, I'm not! I was just a girl when I got taken in by him, but he'll never while away the time playing with my feelings again!" Leita broke off her expostulation as a knock sounded at the door to her bedroom. Mary Jo giggled at her scowl as Leita padded across the floor. She threw open the door to find Darcy Rankin, still coolly elegant, even with her dark hair covering the shoulders of a loosely sashed silk wrapper. A maid stood behind her bearing a tray with a pot of hot chocolate and three cups.

"What a lovely surprise! I'm glad we hadn't gone to sleep yet," Leita said graciously, her exasperation turning to relief at the interruption.

Two hours later, when sleep still hadn't come, she stood on the small balcony outside the sitting-room french doors, and looked up at the dark, blue-black sky where thick clouds obscured the stars. A rushing breeze blew her thin gown back over her ankles and she shivered, but didn't go in. The planes of Breve's face, highlighted in a shaft of sunlight as he scanned the gallery, seemed to be engraved behind her eyes. The bulky width of his shoulders and his hand reaching into his waistcoat pocket for a cigar in that oh-so-familiar movement—she had felt as if she were touching him, feeling the rock-hardness of his arms around her. Stephen could arouse desire in her and she welcomed his presence. Perhaps that was love, she thought—or perhaps that is what it is becoming. Perhaps real love comes slowly. But the other—what was it? When just the sound of his name and the sight of him turned her heart into a thumping millstone in her breast—and that it should be a man who repudiated her at every opportunity, who despised her for her vulnerability to him and who freely took his pleasure with any beautiful woman he encountered. I must have been bereft of my senses to let anyone see me affected by that cocky, vain—she couldn't think of anything hideous enough to call him and returned to her bed where she finally fell asleep.

Now she walked through the high-ceilinged rooms of the Davis mansion, her hand on Stephen's arm, as they joined one group and then another. She fought an occasional bout of embarrassment at the frank admiration with which she was surveyed.

They had moved out onto the terrace when Stephen suddenly begged to be excused. He would return in a few moments. Leita watched his progress through the crowd which had begun to thin rapidly as the reception guests departed, leaving those who were exalted enough to have received dinner invitations.

Leita looked around. Stephen was locked in an

animated conversation with the thin-faced Mr. Rockefeller. Unaccompanied for the first time in days she looked around, her fingers playing softly with the violets on her dress. Out of the corner of her eye she saw a tall young man approaching her purposefully and she sped quickly and gracefully down the bank of steps from the terrace to the lawn. She fled past the fountain with its marble mermaids and cherubs jetting streams of water into high arcs. Brilliantly colored Japanese lanterns were strung even through the maze, which was one of the Davises' importations from European gardens. She entered it now, taking a delight in being hidden. Cries of laughter and the hum of voices carried clearly through the soft evening air as she wandered happily down the short avenues of the maze.

The distant crunch of footsteps on gravel reached her ears; they were approaching her little lair of solitude, but she couldn't tell from which direction they were coming. With a sigh, she half rose. There was no point in staying if she was going to be interrupted. Then she froze.

"Now that you have compromised yourself—and me, I might add—by coming out here in full view of a great many interested parties, tell me what is so important that it couldn't wait until tomorrow afternoon."

"Oh, now you're angry again! Breve, my love, I'm sure that no one thought a thing about us strolling around the fountain. They are all drinking like cossacks anyway. And it's precisely because of tomorrow afternoon that I simply had to see you now."

The woman's tone was plaintively seductive and so soft that Leita could barely hear the words. The blood was drumming in her ears, and her head felt light. It had been so long since she had heard that deep, rich voice. She clasped her hands tightly in her lap, locking her fingers together to still their trembling.

149

"Yes I am angry. There are quite a few of my acquaintances back there who are *not* drinking like cossacks, and I don't relish gaining the reputation of a man who pursues a married woman in full view of her husband. The fact that you are married in name only, as you so blandly put it, doesn't justify your flaunting your affairs publicly. I don't intend to be tarred with the brush of an empty-headed dandy or a feckless fool either."

"I assure you, no one could ever think of you as either!" Her voice came more distinctly now, sharpened by anger. "I had to tell you that I received a letter this afternoon from Bertie's sister and I must leave tomorrow morning for New York. It's a totally inconvenient family crisis and since Bertie can't go I must, and that means I can't see you tomorrow—I am so crushed and disappointed."

I have heard that voice before, Leita thought, searching her mind for the face of its owner.

"And I am leaving for San Francisco next week, so I will see you when I return—that is, if you have returned by then." Breve's voice was crisp.

"Darling, I most definitely will have returned. Wild horses couldn't keep me there longer than a week. Please don't glare so. I will idle my way back to the party unattended and no one will suspect—oh I do loathe leaving you. Could you possibly meet me in Saratoga?"

"Not unless Saratoga has removed itself west of Chicago. I will be gone the better part of a month—longer perhaps, depending on what crops up when I get out there."

"Do you ever think of anything but investigating god-forsaken mines?"

"Yes, you know I do." His chuckle was husky. The rustle of silk and a little gasp were suddenly smothered in silence—a silence that palpated in waves encircling Leita as she sat trapped on the other side of the box elder, a palpitating silence that seemed to strangle her till it was suddenly broken.

"Damn Bertie's sister! We've only had one evening since you returned, and now I have to wait for weeks." Her voice fell to a murmur and then a moaning sigh, cut short by another silence, an interval in which Leita twisted her fingers convulsively. What can I do? If I get up I run the risk of meeting them at any one of the turns before I can get out of the maze. But to sit here like a spy, while that beast is making love to someone just a few feet away—I can't bear it another minute!

The woman's voice came again, low and rasping with desire. "Oh, I don't want to go back—I don't want to leave your arms. Can't you delay your trip to San Francisco and come east to meet me? I can't bear to be parted from you."

"You will bear it beautifully, my dear." Breve's voice was low, with a sardonic note. "You will find a paramour in New York and enjoy yourself thoroughly. And as far as my delaying my trip, I will be meeting with Collis P. Huntington, and that is far too important an engagement to delay. I trust you to be astute enough not to mention that fact to anyone. My interest in the Western Pacific railroad is far too important to subordinate to the pleasures of your bed, however superb they are. You have an acute perception of business, which is one of the things that make you such an exemplary lover, aside from your glorious body." Breve's last statement was accompanied by another husky chuckle and the woman laughed softly.

"Now, I am going back first, and you are to wait here for a suitable interval before going back with some very good reason for having come out here. As a pillar of society, you will manage it perfectly, I am sure.

Anyway, the night is falling fast now, and it's entirely possible you won't be seen until you choose to be. Goodbye, my dear."

The gravel crunched under his feet and Leita stood up, bracing herself with one trembling hand against the insensible marble Apollo. I'm glad, she thought defiantly, I'm glad that I was here to be shown again what he is. He has an animal power that he uses when he likes and I am never going to be affected by it again—never!

Her breath was coming fast and she resigned herself to wait until the unknown woman on the other side of the shrubbery would leave to rejoin the party. Once I was certain I was in love with him! What a fool I was!

Hoping desperately that Stephen would not come looking for her in the maze, she stood in the darkening twilight, her eyes glistening with unshed tears, tears that she couldn't explain.

Leita stood at the edge of the ballroom floor, her foot tapping to the music as Mr. and Mrs. Davis led off the quadrille that officially opened the ball. The waiters were already circling with glasses of vintage champagne as she and Stephen took their places. I am going to have a perfectly wonderful time, she told herself, gazing at Stephen's handsome face. She curtsied to the measure, laying her hand on Stephen's outstretched arm. Once during the promenade she looked up to see Breve standing on the sidelines, looking at her with an expression of astonished surprise. The lady beside him who was endeavoring to capture his attention followed his gaze to Leita, who inclined her head toward him with a smile.

The quadrille ended and they were met by Luton Parker. "Now you two come along over here. I have already picked off two glasses of champagne for you and there is just time to drink them before the waltzing begins."

Mary Jo was glittering in white silk with a scarlet tulle overskirt. Her gloved hand was resting on Breve's arm and, despite the protestations Leita had made to herself, she felt her knees grow weak. The black cravat gracing the neck of his sparkling white ruffled shirt was no darker than his eyes as they rested on her. He stepped toward her, taking her one hand in both of his and she looked up into his face. There were more lines there than had been a year ago. This glistening man towering over her was different in some respects from the man who had held her in his arms beside the river in Virginia. There was even a small, black mustache over the finely chiseled lips. He looks worried, she thought with a sense of astonishment. Then the next moment—well, no wonder. Working night and day to make more money than anyone could ever want or spend, not to mention his pastimes.

He had held her hand wordlessly for a moment and now, when he spoke, his voice was low, even tentative.

"Are you feeling well, Leita?"

"Oh, I'm very well," she replied, "and it's kind of you to ask." The edge of bitterness in her voice was like the sharp side of a thin, gleaming blade. She was peripherally aware of the elegant woman at his left, who was taking her measure with a supercilious curiosity. Another female languishing after him, she thought scornfully.

"And you, Colonel Pinchon, how have you been faring since I saw you last? Are you making your two fortunes fast enough?" Leita's voice was brittle. Mary Jo warily moved Luton Parker off with her to the outskirts of another group, leaving Leita and Stephen facing Breve and his partner.

Breve's eyes glittered dangerously for a second. "No

man who had made two fortunes would work as hard as I do, Miss Johnston. It's only by chance that I am here tonight, and thereby have the undoubted pleasure of greeting you, since I am off on business again next week. You will give my best to all your family, won't you?"

His lovely companion eyed him with a questioning little pout and tucked her arm through his in a proprietary gesture that inflamed Leita further.

Casting all caution to the winds, Leita snapped, "I most assuredly will, and they will be happy to know that while you lead such an arduous life, you do find diversions to lighten your burdens." This last was accompanied by a raking glance over the lady at Breve's side. Leita dropped an abrupt little curtsey and turned on her heel. Stephen bowed and spoke a polite word or two before he followed Leita. There was a smug little smile on his face.

Breve looked after them, a muscle in his jaw clenching and unclenching.

"And who might that rude little thing be?" the woman beside him inquired coolly. "I hear that Stephen de Jean is quite besotted with her."

"That rude little thing is a headstrong brat, and I wish him well of her," Breve replied, his voice icy. "She will make life hell for any man she deigns to choose."

"My, such enmity!" his companion observed laughingly.

Breve's left brow lifted sardonically. "No enmity at all," he denied smoothly, "simply an assessment of character." He broke off then as they were joined by two other couples, but she noticed that he remained preoccupied for some time, casting quick, knife-like glances around the room now and again till his eyes found the girl in sapphire blue.

Leita was dancing with the guest of honor. J. Pierpont Morgan was a lighthearted partner, surprisingly graceful for so big a man. He whirled Leita dexterously through the measures of the cotillion; the silvery gauze of her skirt flowed and swayed around her, and Leita's amethyst and silver filigree eardrops swayed and her eyes shone. When the music stopped, Morgan led her from the floor, resuming the anecdote he had begun earlier about his school days in Germany.

She saw Breve again later, just before the midnight supper. He was sequestered in deep conversation with Mr. Rockefeller. They had commandeered a small bibelot table, which they had placed between them, and were comparing the figures they were jotting on a napkin.

Why should I be perturbed that he doesn't give me a second thought? Leita mused. I'm obviously the furthest thing from his mind. She was swept into a waltz by Ronald Grosse and afterward, her hair glistening in sweat-dampened tendrils, she sank onto an ottoman and fanned herself energetically while she watched Stephen move with his assured grace to the buffet table.

She didn't see Breve standing by an open window. The breeze made the tip of his cigar glow red. He seemed to be looking at her intently, yet he had the glazed look of someone whose thoughts had drifted to another time and place.

Half-asleep, Leita rubbed her cheek across the lace on the pillowslip. She knew it was a dream but her eyelids felt leaden, and her arms clutched the pillow while Breve rode away from her, taunting her as she spurred her horse to follow, laughing at her as she cried out to him, only to wheel his horse suddenly and come riding at her, his face a mask of fury as the hoofbeats thundered toward her. Then the hoofbeats stopped, and a hand was running through her tousled hair. . . .

"I've been knockin' and knockin' on that door! It's high noon and you must be sleepin' like the dead, Leita."

Leita rolled over and struggled out of the dream. "It was you, then, that was the thudding sound," she murmured dazedly.

"I should say it was," Mary Jo replied, a smile wreathing her heart-shaped face. "And I've brought a tray with coffee and hot milk and a whole pile of cinnamon buns. Not that you deserve them," she added with a frown of vexation.

Leita threw back the coverlet and sighed, then stepped out and padded over to the washstand. Mary Jo poured water from the ewer into the porcelain bowl and stood watching, as Leita splashed her face and rubbed it briskly with the towel. Mary Jo handed her a pale pink wrapper and began pouring the coffee while Leita pulled a brush through the tangled mane of red-gold hair that reached down almost to her waist.

"Now, what do you mean about my not deserving them?" she asked, throwing the brush aside and settling herself on the chaise longue. "I'm awake now and I can deal with your mysteries." And she lifted the cup to her lips, inhaling the scent.

"Whatever possessed you last night? I haven't had a minute alone with you till now. You went running up the stairs when we got back from the party, and you were undressed and in bed with the lamps out before I could turn around."

"I was tired," Leita answered, taking another sip of her coffee. "I just wanted to curl up and go to sleep. I'm sorry if I was mean, Jo, I didn't intend to be."

"Oh, it wasn't that you were mean to me," Mary Jo protested. "I didn't think that for a minute. I knew you just didn't want to talk about what happened, but I do and I'm going to." She buttered a cinnamon bun lavishly. "Whatever got into you to be so nasty to Breve last night, right off like that, when he hadn't done a thing to throw you into a fit except to ask you how you were feelin'?"

Leita cradled her cup in her hands and looked out the window. Bright sunlight streamed in across the scarlet and blue pattern of the Persian carpet. She was still trying to clear her head of Breve's face, cold and frightening in its anger as he rode toward her in the dream.

"Am I supposed to fall all over him, grateful and happy that he asked me how I was feeling, as if I were a sick child with the measles?" she retorted indignantly and set her cup down so hard that little droplets of coffee splashed out onto the embroidered linen tray cover.

"Well, you silly goose! He's been worried about you. That's obviously why he asked you that, first thing. You know he heard what happened and—"

"Worried about me, my foot!" Leita answered hotly and picking up a knife began sawing viciously at one of the sticky buns. "If he was so almighty worried about me he could have put pen to paper to write to me, which he did not. If he thinks I am going to stand and be patronized by him, he has another think coming." Having succeeded in dividing the bun, she picked up one of the pieces and took a bite, her teeth almost snapping together.

"Don't you realize he asked you that way because he couldn't say much else in front of the others? People here don't know you were nearly raped and had a man killed right over you. He couldn't say any of the things he was thinking, and I think you were downright hateful to him!"

Leita leaped up from the chaise and paced round the floor, wiping at her fingers with a napkin. "There are a few things you don't seem to realize, Mary Jo, and one of them is that Breve Pinchon is only interested in making love to the pretty women who throw themselves at his feet. And I'm not one of them, and I never will be again!"

"So you're admitting you were once," Mary Jo retorted calmly. "Well, at least you've come to that. And I don't think Breve is all that interested in the others. My Lord, honey, he's a man. You don't expect him to live like a monk, do you?"

"I don't expect him to do anything—he does what he pleases and so do I, and our lives have nothing to do with each other. If you think that I'm going to be mealy-mouthed and sweet to him just because he decides to be polite for a minute at a party, you're wrong. I don't owe him anything—and he can buy up every railroad in the country and make love to every silly woman that comes along for all I care. I see no reason to hide my contempt for him."

"Well, you sure didn't. I suppose you know it set Stephen up like nothing else would. He looked like a pussycat that had been in the cream when you turned your back on Breve like that."

"Stephen is thoughtful and gallant and kind. It's an example of Breve's taste that he had a nasty thing or two to say about Stephen at one time." Leita sank back onto the chaise and poured more coffee for both of them.

"So Breve doesn't trust him either. You never told me that before," Mary Jo said, alert with interest.

"I never told you, because his opinion doesn't mean a thing to me."

"Well, we'll see who comes out ahead in the long run, honey. All our people think the world of Breve,"

158

she went on contemplatively, "the way he gave up his time to help my father and came on that long trip up here just so we'd have another man to look after things. He was a good friend to me, I know, when everybody around was just chortling with delight over me getting disgraced like I did." Mary Jo's face was pensive and a little wistful, both expressions uncharacteristic of her.

This was the first time Mary Jo had ever referred to her abandonment by the man she had fallen in love with as a swept-away sixteen-year-old, and Leita was instantly mollified. "Oh Jo," she pleaded, "I wasn't thinking about him being your friend. My tongue just got away from me, as usual. I know how you must feel about him for standing by you through that awful ordeal." Mary Jo's blue eyes looked steadily into hers. "Yes, I know," Leita said softly. "Daddy told me about it, mostly because he thought I was jealous of you and Breve, which I was, I'll have to admit. I respected him for it, and I respect you for being so brave about it and so loyal to him. I'll give the devil his due," she went on wryly, "he has his strong points, but I feel sorry for any woman who falls in love with him or any man who gets in his way," she concluded with one arm around her friend's shoulders.

"You don't have to feel sorry, particularly for me," Mary Jo smiled impishly. "I learned more about men the year I was sixteen than most girls do in their whole lifetime." Leita's gaze traveled to the window again. This wasn't the first time she had been tempted to tell Mary Jo about Lieutenant Nathan. She bit her lip and resisted the impulse. It's all in the past, she thought, just like my wild, crazy love for Breve. I'm not going to remember any of it—it's the future that counts.

"As for Breve, I don't pretend to understand him," Mary Jo spoke clearly, "I don't think anyone does. I only know him in some ways, but—"

159

Leita interrupted. "But his hardness and coldness and that God-awful ambition of his will keep anyone from knowing him and, truth to tell, I'm afraid of him, on top of hating him."

"Maybe you're right to be," Mary Jo said seriously. "He's not a skim-milk man."

"And I'm glad that he probably won't even speak to me again," Leita said, reaching for her cup. She didn't notice Mary Jo's keen glance, which was graced with the suggestion of a smile.

Chapter 11

THE MAY DUSK WAS WARM AND STRAINS OF MELODY CAME wafting down on the balmy air. Leita gasped with delight as the carriage pulled up at the dock. The waves of Lake Michigan flashed fire at the crests, reflections of the lights festooning the lacy white galleries of the privately owned paddle-wheeled steamer that lay moored there.

She had been looking forward to this for days. The prospect of a ball on board a ship enchanted her, and she informed her host of this when Stephen presented her.

"It's a floating vulgarity, but it isn't dull," Stephen murmured as they entered the ballroom where the walls were lined with satin covered couches fronted by individual tables where iced champagne stood in silver buckets.

"Vulgar or not, it's gorgeous," Leita whispered back.

One saloon on the second deck was comparatively quiet as the ship moved through the waves, though it was brightly lit and luxuriously fitted with red plush and gilt.

Breve Pinchon sat at one of the poker tables. He had taken his place there immediately after boarding. Now he pushed a pile of gold pieces into the center of the table and took a long swallow from the glass of bourbon and soda at his elbow.

One deck below, in the great saloon, Leita was perched on the arm of a couch, fanning herself and catching her breath after a lively quadrille.

Ronald Grosse presented himself, calf-eyed and adoring, pointing with voiceless eloquence to the dance card hanging from her wrist. They traversed one length of the floor. Less than a minute into the dance, Ronald halted at a tap on his shoulder and relinquished her regretfully. And there stood Breve! There was a hard glitter in his eyes, and the smooth tan of his face was flushed. He swept her a low, mocking bow and encircled her with his arm. The hand that he took was suddenly limp and nerveless.

"Now you don't regret my claiming at least part of a dance with you, do you, Leita? After all, even I deserve to bask in the light of the southern belle who has taken Chicago by storm." A sardonic smile curved his lips.

"How in the world did you get here?" she stammered. "I haven't seen you all evening."

"I stowed away," was his short answer. He swept her in circles so dizzying that it seemed that only his hand pressing hard on the small of her back was holding her up. When their progress was impeded for a moment by the press of the other dancers, he spoke again. "And now, Leita, tell me: when is Chicago's elite going to be presented with the spectacle of you and the wily Stephen de Jean being joined in holy wedlock?" The stone-hard mockery in his voice rendered her speechless for the moment. Then she tingled with anger.

"The very first engraved invitation will go to you, Colonel Pinchon! When and if I choose to marry, that is. The very fact that you insult Stephen raises him in my estimation, since I happen to know how questionable your taste is."

He stared at her, then threw back his head and laughed, his laughter loud enough to turn a few heads curiously in their direction. Why, he's drunk, Leita thought, looking at the dull red flush on his cheekbones and his bloodshot eyes.

"I made a mistake back in Virginia," he said harshly and inexplicably.

"You made more than one mistake," Leita shot back, "but which one are you talking about?"

"I should have left you to the not-so-tender mercies of those bushwhackers that kidnapped you. You would have escaped—in fact, you already had before I found you, if you remember. It would have done you good if you had been forced to forage in the hills for a few weeks. It would have taught you what life is all about—that there are some things that have to be faced without the support of a rich family and the slavish admiration of every man around you. As it is, you'll never find out—you simply point a pretty finger and expect to get what you want when you choose to want it—and you don't even know what you want!"

"I'll know when I find it," Leita hissed, aware only of her fury at his brutal and contemptuous tone. "But I know what I don't want, and that is to be insulted by a ruffian in evening clothes, a pirate in the disguise of a gentleman!" They were at the edge of the floor, near a door that opened out onto the deck. She dropped her hand from his shoulder and, giving him a forceful push, gathered up her skirt and ran through the doorway out into the cool night air. Directly ahead of her was the stairway to the second deck and she ascended it quickly, then ran around the ellipse of that deck and took the next stairway, arriving at the topmost gallery. Panting, she leaned against the rail, slippery with the nighttime dew. The breeze was strong and chilly—thus the deck was free of meandering couples. The noise of conversation and strolling footsteps from the deck below, and the music coming clear from the ballroom mingled with the sound of rushing water from the paddle wheel and the waves slapping against the hull. But she was alone here, thank heaven! Leita patted the droplets of dew onto her hot cheeks. How dare he! If Stephen heard him he would call him out! That image was a doubtful one, she reflected, since Breve was a crack shot and cold-blooded enough to dispatch anyone without a second thought. She looked up at the clouds streaking across a hazy, white moon, and wished the ship would turn around and deposit her at the dock. Suddenly a weight dropped on her shoulders and she jumped, giving a shriek of alarm as strong hands gripped her arms from behind.

"I saw no point in your giving yourself pneumonia just because you can't hear a few words of truth without running away." The weight that had fallen on her was a man's coat. Now the hands turned her roughly. The shadows from the lacy fretwork of the gallery played across Breve's face, highlighting its strong bones.

"I came up here to get away from you—to keep from making a scene in front of everyone!" Leita blazed. "I don't want your coat or your conversation or anything about you! I want only never to see you again!"

"And I suppose you're going to tell me you want that treacherous fop de Jean? That scheming rake you've come so far to see."

"I'm beginning to think I couldn't make a better choice!"

"I thought once that you had spirit enough to
164

investigate life—to grow up into a woman of judgment before you gave yourself away. I really didn't think you were going to let that wily coxcomb make you his ornament." His fingers dug deeper into her arms when she tried to pull away. "So you want to run again, eh? You've changed. You didn't used to be frightened by honesty. What happened to the girl who told me that she knew love would have to be like a picture—the drawing underneath had to be honest and true, and no amount of pretty color would disguise a weak foundation?"

"You, of all men, to talk to me about love! You know nothing about it and you care nothing about it!" she cried, and pushed her palms hard against his starched shirt front.

His eyes glittered like black diamonds. "I almost wish I didn't," he said angrily. Suddenly his arms swept around her and held her in a vise. She struggled as his head bent low and his mouth pressed hard against hers. She kicked at his leg hard with one slippered foot, and he withdrew his mouth and chuckled.

"You are drunk!" she raged at him.

"Just drunk enough to take you to San Francisco with me. Drunk enough to give you a taste of the world." He drew her head to his shoulder, nuzzling his lips into the curve of her throat and moving his mouth up to the tender flesh behind her ear.

"And drunk enough to give us something we will both remember," he whispered, his mouth moving softly over her ear. His lips caught hers fiercely then, and she hung limp in his arms, surrendering to the magic fire that swept through her as his mouth softened over hers, devouring its curves, as his hand traveled down her back and moved caressingly over her hips. Then his lips were on her closed eyelids, and her own hands moved with a will of their own, creeping up his chest till one slipped around his back and the other fondled his strong neck.

"You are coming with me," he murmured, his mouth lingering across her cheek. When he reached her half-parted lips, the sigh that escaped her was smothered as he pressed her tightly against him, bruising her mouth with hungry passion. A shudder went through her as his tongue pressed its way gently into her mouth, touching the tip of her own, then caressing it urgently. His hands moved swiftly over her body, now grasping her waist tightly, now in her hair, moving her head slowly as his warm tongue sought every recess of her mouth. His breathing was harsh, an accompaniment to the wild thudding of Leita's heart. He pulled his mouth away suddenly, and, lifting her in his arms, carried her into the shadows, where he laid her on one of the long Empire lounges that lined the inner wall of the deck. He stood above her for a moment, his white shirt gleaming in the faint light. The next instant he lowered himself beside her. She threw both arms around his neck in an ecstatic embrace as he pressed the full length of his body against her. . . . The boisterous melody of a polka filled the air, and the ship began its slow, lumbering turn. But Leita was insensible to everything but the weight of his body and the moist heat of his mouth as he traced a pattern of lingering, exploring kisses over her throat and shoulders, returning to her eager lips again and again. His strong hands moved over her silk-covered breasts, down over her hips, and he clasped their soft roundness and gripped her thighs through the layers of silk and crinoline. She strained against the long, hard length of him. He drew the shoulder of her dress down, exposing one of her breasts. His mouth enveloped her swollen lips and he drew in his breath sharply as her tongue flicked over his like little touches of flame. She lay gasping, twisting her fingers through the crisp waves of his hair while his lips and tongue consumed the throbbing mound of her breast. The frenzy that possessed him mounted, and she shared in it, blind with desire, until the moment when the flashing fire in her loins blotted out everything but his face above her as he moved fiercely inside her and she met his every thrust with a wild, abandoned passion, a passion that peaked into an eruption that welded his body to hers as he surged into her. It was a moment that had its own eternity. She lay gasping, dispossessed of the frenzy, but filled with a sweet liquid warmth. His face was buried in her hair, and the moist rush of his heaving breath was warm on the skin of her neck. "I will go anywhere with you, anywhere," she whispered, burrowing her face into his shoulder.

"Oh God in heaven!" he groaned, and his hold on her loosened as he raised himself slowly, achingly. He placed his palm on her damp forehead for a moment, smoothing her hair back tenderly. Then, turning his face away quickly, he got up. All she could see of him in the gloom was his silhouette etched out by the high-rising moon. A cold fluttering premonition stabbed her in the throat and she raised up, pulling at the welter of her skirts. Still he made no move. She adjusted her dress, thankful that it wasn't torn. The cold premonition that had been stabbing her in the throat had spread throughout her whole body. Still he made no move, simply stood there, a tall looming figure as ominous as a brooding Jove.

"You can't go to San Francisco with me. You would be ruined." His voice was flat and hard. "I was drunk, drunk as a lord, and when you're drunk you forget."

"And what did you forget?" Leita whispered softly, a whisper of dismay and rising horror.

"I forgot everything of importance," he answered flatly.

167

"Meaning that what just happened was of no importance?" Aching to go near him, to see his face when he spoke this travesty, she nevertheless stood her ground.

"It was of no importance in the long run." Now his voice was iron-hard. "I have no intention of divesting you of your good name for the temporary pleasure of your company." He moved then, and retrieved his coat.

"So it would be a temporary pleasure?" She bit off the word temporary as if it were something sour and unspeakable.

"Yes, my dear, it would only be—could only be temporary." A bitter irony laced his tone.

He knows now that I am in love with him, and still he can stand there coolly, tying his cravat, insensitive and cruel and completely self-serving.

"I suppose you had to prove to yourself that you could best Stephen de Jean, no matter what the circumstances," she sneered, trembling with humiliation.

He stared at her for a moment and finally spoke. "Think what you like. It's barely possible that I might tell you the real reason someday," he said shortly. "Meanwhile, I have a feeling that the eager Stephen is searching for you." His glance ran over her and, stepping forward, he adjusted the straps around her shoulders. Her breath caught in her throat at his touch, and she felt the sting of tears. She jerked away.

"You are *never* to touch me again. Never!" The contempt in her tone covered the choking sob that threatened to break forth. "Whatever happened between us has nothing to do with how I intend to live my life! You were right when you said once that I was nothing but a 'girl-child,' but now I know you for what you are. Nothing more than a pirate!" She fled past him to the narrow stairway, descended to the next deck and ran into a small, deserted room where she repaired her appearance, carefully destroying the traces of a time that had seemed to encompass eternity, but now stung like bitter gall in her heart.

She fabricated a little tale about having become suddenly ill from the motion of the boat, too suddenly to enlist anyone's aid. The tale gained credence from her pallor. Stephen had seen Breve interrupt her dance with Ronald Grosse, but then lost sight of them on the crowded floor. He found Breve a few moments later, solely to ascertain that Leita was nowhere near him. He had no intention of allowing Breve to monopolize Leita for any longer than a dance. Pinchon was a dark horse to be watched, but as long as his insolent detachment held, Stephen reassured himself that the tall southerner was no real threat to him.

Leita was silent during the carriage ride back to Rush Street. Stephen hoped that his carefully laid plans for the next afternoon wouldn't go awry because of her indisposition. He had prepared the setting too well.

The luncheon table was set on the terrace. Robins fluttered down from their nests, pecking at the soft dark soil in the flower beds where peony bushes, heavy with pink and white bloom, offset the delicacy of the mass of spring flowers. Leita stood at the doors of the terrace, having been escorted through the grandeur of the high-ceilinged rooms by their owner.

"After lunch I want you to see the second floor. I have a pair of exquisitely carved doors from a chateau in France that you will find a pleasure to behold," Stephen said.

"You have gone to a surprising amount of effort, Stephen. Importing whole rooms of furniture for such a large house. Do you really get so much pleasure out of it?" Leita asked thoughtfully.

169

"I do, and I intend to get a great deal more. I could, of course, exist much more simply, but I see no reason to. My grounds give me pleasure, my staff is so well-trained that I have to do little more than conduct a once-a-week conference with my chief butler and voila, I am master of all I survey, in surroundings that I have tailored to my own taste."

Leita smiled. She realized he had looked forward with pride to showing her this baroque, many-roomed mansion. The gray stone edifice, elongated by two well-proportioned wings, had surprised her with a magnificence that bordered on pomp. She knew he had been gratified by her pleasure as she surveyed the rooms where the grace of gilt, ivory, and brocade lightened what could have been an overpowering opulence.

Stephen suggested they take a stroll to the site of the summer house that was being constructed on the other side of the lake, and Leita docilely unfurled her parasol and took his arm. They meandered off down graveled paths between brilliant flower beds, stood beside the rippling blue-green waters of the artificial lake and watched a pair of swans circling.

"This is to be your own private retreat. You know of course that this is all your domain. There is no need for you to remain in Indiana for longer than it takes to plan and accomplish our wedding. I ask you to be my wife, Leita, and take your proper place in this world." The pupils of Stephen's hazel eyes were large and she looked into them with a feeling of trapped dismay. She felt paralyzed as he tilted her chin back and kissed her mouth softly and sensuously. Then his arms went around her and his mouth bore deeper. His hand curved around her throat, and his fingers traced its arch, but her lips were lifeless under his. When he drew his head back, his eyes were amused.

170

"It seems I have surprised you. Didn't you know I wouldn't allow you to return to that town to be plagued indefinitely by its gossiping tongues? We can be married within a month, I should think. Don't concern yourself that it isn't sufficient time for a trousseau. Whatever you desire can be gotten here, and you will need some empty space in your trunks for the multitude of gowns that I am sure you will want to purchase in France."

Leita shuddered and raised her hands helplessly. "Stephen, I never dreamed—I told you months ago that I wasn't ready to marry. You have been so thoughtful, so kind—" she fumbled for words—"so wonderful, Stephen, but I thought you realized that nothing had changed." Her voice trailed off in the face of his disbelieving smile.

"But of course it has changed. It has been one year since I saw you enter the lobby of the hotel in Washington, and over six months since I told you you were going to be my wife. I have made no demands on you, nor insisted that you be my prisoner. You have been courted by others, have pursued your interests and taken the measure of your surroundings. I know full well that you are not destined to be a spinster, not with your passionate nature. I haven't been superseded in your regard by any other and now, after your terrifying experience this spring, it is time you shook the dust of that place from your heels and live life as splendidly as you were meant to."

He seated himself complacently in the depths of a long couch placed to look out on the lake, and patted the cushion beside him. Leita obediently sat down. Her mind had been a riot of images while he spoke. Breve's voice sounding in her ears: "just drunk enough to take you to San Francisco with me," as she envisioned his face in the moonlight as he stood over her. Her gaze swept over the tranquil vista of the lake and the overpowering solidity of the gray stone edifice with its turrets and cupolas. It is such a temptation, a temptation to put myself into a prison and risk nothing, not ever again. I might grow to love him, really love him, but I know I don't now. I have only been deluding myself. Suddenly her listlessness fell away, and at that moment she knew what she would do.

"Stephen, I have decided to leave now."

His eyebrows raised. "Now? But you were to stay at least a month. What kind of whim is this?"

"I don't mean leave Chicago. I mean leave now for Europe."

A momentary perplexity distorted the almost faultless perfection of his features. "But we will go to Europe, my dear. Our wedding trip will be an extended one."

"I don't mean for a wedding trip. I can't marry you now, Stephen." She touched his shoulder in a gesture of contrition. "I can't give you any answer at all except to say that it may well be that someday, if you still want me, I will be able to accept the undoubted honor of your offer. Oh Stephen, I am not playing with you or being coy! I simply can't marry now! And you are right about my not staying in Fort Wayne—at least not until the gossip has died down. I need to get away now, for a long time, so that I can forget—" she had almost blurted out his name—"so I can forget what I need to forget."

Stephen's composure left him. Two deep lines appeared around his mouth, and he struck one fist into the palm of his hand. He stood up, paced the length of the little veranda, and spoke with his back to her.

"It is a whim. With you it is one whim after another. You gave me no reason at all to think you had this wild plan in mind!" He turned and faced her, his lips forming each word as if he were carving it with a knife. "You are making me a laughingstock. A certain amount of coquetry is to be expected, charming even, but this mercurial temperament of yours carries coquetry far beyond the bounds of charm! Tell me, are you still enamored of that Byronic Colonel Pinchon? That *parvenu* who comes and goes like a shadow taking every Chicago drawing room by storm? If you are playing cat and mouse with me because of that blackguard . . . !"

"I am not enamored, as you so romantically put it, of Colonel Pinchon. For your information I wouldn't spit on him! I have every right to do what I choose with my life and I intend to do just that!" she cried. "I am not playing cat and mouse with you simply because I don't choose to rush into marriage to escape a lot of fool's gossip! You may call it coquetry, but I call it self-respect!"

His eyes narrowed slightly during her denial of feeling for Breve. Now he reflected for a moment, drawing on his cloak of suavity as if it had never fallen from him.

"Perhaps you are right. In which case I apologize, and I can only beg you to accept it. My disappointment took control of my feelings and I am afraid I lashed out at you unjustly. You must understand that a man in love cannot always be held accountable for his outbursts."

She bowed her head, feeling wretched at the tenderness in his voice, and he kissed her cheek softly. "I'm the one to be forgiven, Stephen. I . . . perhaps I am in love with you and . . . it's just that I'm not completely certain yet. I need time."

"And time you shall have, my love." He enfolded her, but his eyes were thoughtful as he gazed over her head. "This trip could well be just what is needed. I will ask Reneé to write to cousin Annette. The Hidels will take you under their wing with pleasure. Annette's English is excellent—she is married to a baronet, by the way—and you will like both of them. Then there are other friends. Your own French is very understandable and will carry you through with ease. Not perfect, my love, but charmingly understandable." He smiled at her, and she chastised herself inwardly for underestimating the generosity of his love for her.

Chapter 12

Leita had telegraphed ahead, and they were met at the station by Anna Tillett and Mary Jo's brother Joseph. Arriving at the Johnston house, Leita and Mary Jo were hugged and spun around and welcomed with a score or more of questions about the reason for their early return. Leita put them off, saying she had a very good reason but right now it was a secret, and asked where her sister Belle was. Mrs. Johnston said she had been expected for over an hour. It was decided not to delay dinner for her any longer, and the two families were seated at the dining room table when Paul, always the most intrepidly outspoken of the Johnston brothers, raised his voice. "Leita has a secret, and I'll bet my new mare that it's got something to do with Mr. Fancy-Stephen de Jean."

Leita laughed. "I don't see why it should be any secret," she began. Eugene grasped Paul's hand and held it up in a gesture of victory. "You see, Paul was right," he declared to the group.

"No, he wasn't right at all. I cut my visit short

because I decided I wanted to go to Europe now, instead of waiting."

The ladle in Samuel Johnston's hand halted briefly above the tureen, and his eyes caught those of his wife.

"What brought you to that decision, Leita?"

Leita drew a deep breath. Every face turned in her direction. I've started it and now I've got to finish it, she thought. "More than one thing, really. The McNamee business had made me an object of curiosity around town, you all know that. I don't expect the whispering to let up for a while, either. I was having a marvelous time in Chicago, and it occurred to me all in a flash that there wasn't a reason in the world for me to wait till next year for my tour. So I came back right away to ask Daddy's permission."

Leita was bright-eyed and pink-cheeked in a lilac striped dress with a white pique collar and her father seemed to be assessing her countenance, then, apparently reassured, he nodded. "I don't see why not. I see no reason for you to stay around here while the talk still runs high." He had carefully kept his face expressionless, but now broke into chuckles as Leita jumped up joyfully and clasped her arms around his neck.

Mary Jo turned to Micah Tillett. "I hope you approve of my going, too. I would just perish if I had to rust away here by myself."

"I was anticipating that," Micah responded. "I gather you two have it all settled between you. I wouldn't have a moment's peace if I said no."

"I should think a trustworthy chaperone would be the next requirement," Samuel interjected.

Leita and Mary Jo exchanged glances and grinned. "Go ahead, you tell them," Leita said.

"We already have a chaperone! My cousin Darcy is going to France this summer, and she would be simply delighted to have us accompany her."

Samuel looked over at Micah. "Seems like a suitable choice to me. I shall look forward to meeting her soon."

Leita crossed her fingers. He's going to be mightily surprised when he does, she thought.

The Tillets relayed Darcy Rankin's invitation and it was accepted in an afternoon. The passages were booked, and Leita spent her days selecting fabric and standing for fittings.

Her plans were embellished and detailed by Reneé McElheny's enthusiastic participation. Reneé wrote letters of introduction—drew up lists of places that must be visited, and wrote to relatives in Paris apprising them of her friend's coming visit. Leita's trunks were partially packed when Reneé arrived one day, breathless with pleasure, and waving a letter.

"Ma chère Leita, I have the most glorious news! I have here in my hand an invitation. Ma cousine Annette has responded to the news that my friend comes to Paris by inviting—no, by insisting—that the three of you make their hotel your home. She is most pleased at the prospect of a visit from three American ladies! Voila, she will sponsor you!" Reneé plumped down onto a chair, handed Leita the letter and fanned herself exuberantly.

Leita read the flowing script with intense concentration. "I can translate most of it," she announced.

"Ah, your hard work over those terrible verbs comes to fruition, you see," Reneé said proudly, having spent a good many afternoons with Leita and Mary Jo in a tutorial of her native language. "You will adore Annette," she bubbled. "She is the cousin of my mother and she has a heart that is so warm. And you will have such an *entreé* to the court! She was for a time a member of the Empress's household but she resigned her post. Her husband likes to spend a good part of the year in England, and this made her position something of a burden, you understand. She has the responsibility of two large households—the manor in England and their hotel in Paris. Also, they have a small villa in Biarritz. She was excused by the Empress, but she and Sir Charles are still very much a part of court life."

"It seems such an imposition," Leita mused. "After all, there are three of us and we are perfect strangers to them, to insist that we be their guests for the whole of our visit is really quite overwhelming."

"Cherie, the hôtel de Bourait is so large that your host and hostess will scarcely know you are there. It has been the Paris residence of the de Bouraits since the first days of Louis XIV, and that is over two hundred years. It is lavishly beautiful, the frescoed ceilings alone are breathtaking. And as for it being an imposition, there is a staff of at least twenty servants. Besides, Annette and Charles always have guests. Their only child died years ago and their grief was terrible. Since then they surround themselves with friends and diversion of every kind. And now, the lady cousin who is to be your mentor and chaperone arrives tomorrow. She will be pleased, will she not?"

"We're meeting the evening train," Leita replied, "and I think she will."

Darcy Rankin hummed as she stroked her shoulders with the powder puff. It was Saturday evening and she knew Stephen de Jean had arrived a few hours ago, in time to escort Leita to the bon voyage party the McElhenys were giving. A smile played across her face as she sprayed perfume liberally over her frilled corset cover and her firm conical breasts which were jutting out over the stays. The smile had to do with Eugene

Johnston, who had struck her very favorably when they met the night before. I'll wager he is a rather pent-up young man, living in this goldfish-bowl town with everyone's eyes on him. And handsome—good lord he is handsome, she thought, recalling her first sight of the tall, broad-shouldered Eugene with his striking blue eyes and dark hair. She propped her elbows on the dressing table and examined her face in the mirror. She pursed her lips and applied a touch of vermilion pomade, then thrust the tiny jar into her beaded reticule. The problem would be the time and the place, she mused. He is very much the gentleman and it will take a little artistry to loosen his restraint. She smiled again. Stephen is going to have a very chaste weekend, but I see no reason why I should, if I can manage otherwise. Dear Stephen is certainly besotted with that girl, as besotted as he is capable of being. She thought of Leita's proud carriage and the glow of her hair around her face. Well, he has taste, she decided, but that is no surprise. She took the pale gold taffeta gown the maid had spread out on the bed earlier, stepped into it and, using the button hook from the dressing table, fastened the tiny crystal buttons that closed the bodice over her breasts but left her shoulders and a large amount of ivory skin exposed. "There," she said aloud, "surely that is discreet enough for a chaperone." She touched the wine-colored velvet of a jewel box and removed a brilliant emerald pendant. She fastened the clasp around her neck and then touched the stone where it lay just above the cleavage of her firm breasts. And Mother thinks it is only glass—the smile played over her lips again. She was remembering when Stephen had presented it to her after their three days at Saratoga Springs; three days of welcome lovemaking, free of the restrictions of the society where they both

179

moved. Not that adultery wasn't a commonplace in that society, but it had to be accomplished with such infinite discretion. There was more need for concealment if you were unmarried than if you had a husband and a houseful of children, Darcy had often reflected bitterly. Once you had made a good marriage you were in safe harbor—until then you must be like Caesar's wife, above reproach. But whom to marry? That had been the question for some little time. Darcy required more than good family connections and a little money. She admired the exercise of power, though she didn't necessarily covet it for herself. She was content to achieve her own ends quietly—in fact enjoyed subterfuge. She was an actress, and if the stage hadn't been considered an unsavory calling, she would have undoubtedly gravitated to it and won acclaim. Her elder brother had nicknamed her "Spider" and had been reprimanded severely for it, but it was a fitting sobriquet.

The afternoon following Leita's precipitous departure from Chicago Darcy had told Stephen of the "Spider" nickname as they lay among the pillows, and he had chuckled richly. "I think I will tell Hugo that story."

She had turned on him quickly, her eyes blazing. "You tell Hugo nothing! Do you understand me?"

He sat up in bed, one eyebrow raised quizzically. "My dear, you do not order me, ever, and never do you speak to me in that tone. Do *you* understand *me?*" He was amused to note that she was far from intimidated.

"I will not be played with," she blazed. "I am not a mouse for you to sink your sharp teeth into."

He leaned back on his elbows. His well-formed but rather narrow chest was covered with curling dark hair and he stroked it with his palm. "I was playing with you, I admit. I'm surprised to have struck a nerve."

"Of course—you have your power and your position. Your hands have never been tied like mine. I could do what you do easily, if I were a man. Then I would be secure enough to lie back like a sated tomcat and unsheath my claws. You don't know what it is to have your whole future rest on a marriage that you must wait and plot for! You have not the smallest comprehension of what it means to be an unmarried woman in society."

She jumped up, rummaged at the dressing table, and took up the hairbrush backed with mother-of-pearl. She drew her long dark hair over one shoulder and brushed vigorously. Stephen got up. The afternoon sunlight fell on his naked body as he poured two glasses of Madeira. He held one up to her lips. She took a sip and smiled.

"You judge me poorly if you think I have no idea of your predicament. If you were a Frenchwoman of means and intelligence you would have a salon, entertain yourself with whom you please, as long as you did it with grace and discretion, and live a stimulating life until you chose to marry. Here, as we both know, it is a vastly different story." He adjusted a pillow and leaned back slightly, taking a sip of his wine. "Ahh, the shibboleth of chastity in America. The simpering, skim-milk ideal woman of the average man. And when he marries her, what does he do? He runs straight to the arms of a high-class whore. You cannot change this, so you must circumvent it as best you can. I am in complete sympathy with you." He leaned over and kissed her lips, still wet with the wine.

"How do you think Hugo is coming along?" she asked intently.

"You are making rapid progress. You cosset him and generally ingratiate yourself, and you do it beautifully. He began romanticizing Lucille as soon as she was in

181

her coffin, but that is almost two years ago. I think you have nothing to worry about except the cultivation of even more patience."

She sighed and took another sip of the Madeira. "I will be gone for at least two months. You will keep an eye on him, as you promised?"

"Most assuredly. Of course the covey of marriageable girls will descend, but by playing on his hardheaded suspicious nature I can deflect them easily. He will of course correspond with you while you are in Europe with my intended." Here he smiled. "You can reply with nicely restrained affection and sweet concern for his state of mind. There is nothing a basically provincial man responds to more quickly than concern for his well-being and happiness."

"In some ways Hugo is quite sophisticated really," Darcy reflected for a moment. "Though he certainly wasn't in the choice of a wife, I'll grant you. What a mewling, mealy-mouthed wisp she was!"

"She was all of that, my dear. I am only saying that he is an infant where women are concerned, not in the other ways of the world that are important to you both. I couldn't have chosen a better business partner. My instincts are always right."

Darcy eyed him with a glimmer of amusement. "And your instinct for women? Is that always right?"

He raised one eyebrow and the corners of his mouth lifted in a small smile. "If you mean my future wife, my instincts are serving me well there. Leita is a young combination of Athena and Venus."

"War and love! What a prospect!"

"I have no wish to spend the best years of my life with a mindless ninny. Winsome charm is not Leita's forte. Miraculously, there is a flower of the South who looks you directly in the eye. A mind of her own, one of fine quality at that, a temper to match, and a store of untapped passion."

"What a paragon! And only eighteen, too. You chose a very young girl, Stephen. Why? Does it give you a sense of power?"

Stephen pondered this. "Perhaps. I do feel quite in command. I admit I *might* feel at a disadvantage if she looked at me with eyes of experience, in addition to her other qualities. She can be somewhat daunting, even now."

Darcy lay down on her stomach and cupped her chin in one hand. "I can tell you someone else who is daunting. Colonel Breve Pinchon. He is nobody's fool, Stephen, and he is not going to take it lightly when this scheme of yours proves to be a success."

"Ah, but it will be too late then, won't it? His are the hands that will be tied after Leita becomes my wife."

"Perhaps—but what if she finds out that you tricked her? What then? She might very well leave you, wedlock notwithstanding."

"How can she find out? Who will know except you and I?" Stephen threw up his hands. His laughter rang with self-assurance. "You will pen the letter from an imaginary friend, describing the runaway wedding of Colonel Pinchon and a local debutante. I will send it to you at the proper time and then follow—to console Leita and have our nuptials performed in France. It will be comparatively simple for me to be out of town at the time of the supposed elopement of the dashing Breve, so that I can't be expected to know it is a false rumor, repeated quite innocently by your friend. Only you and I will know, *ma chère* Darcy, and, knowing what you have at stake, you will never breathe a word of the means I have used to gain such an important end."

Darcy recoiled a little at the faint menace in his voice. "You know quite well that the plan is safe with me. A year from now I expect to be Mrs. Hugo Wenzler, with your help. Our agreement stands." She drained her wineglass and continued. "I do wonder though. She might turn the other way and be so heartbroken she would refuse to look at another man, much less marry immediately."

Stephen clasped his hands behind his head. "No," he said decisively. "She is a fiery female. Her pride is enormous, and that pride will be so stung that she will accept me on the spot, finally."

"If she is attracted enough to you to accept you in those circumstances, couldn't you win her without them?"

"I have no doubt I can, but it might be a long process. She still has to grow up you know, and there is the possibility that her puppy love might propel her right into Pinchon's clutches at a propitious moment. He is a man to watch. I hear rumblings and speculation about the interests he is amassing. If only half of them are to be believed, he is astute and daring—perhaps reckless is the word—far beyond my first estimation of him. What is the point of gambling by waiting? He and she are too much alike in many ways. Their pride subverts them. Pride is a valuable quality, but it must be combined with foresight. Her attraction for him amounts to a small obsession. I intend to dispel that obsession."

"He is exciting you know. Exciting where women are concerned." Darcy laughed softly, turning over onto her back and stretching her arms luxuriously. Her broad nipples were the palest brownish-red, and Stephen traced a finger around them and then cupped one white breast in his hands while he stroked the flatness of her abdomen down and over the dark mounded triangle. Sun glinted through the drapes and bathed the columns of her thighs as his hand traveled along their soft inner reaches.

"I know a great deal about excitement," he whispered against her breast.

184

She shivered at the light touch of his tongue as his mouth moved across her belly. His hand traveled deeper between her thighs, tantalizing her with light caresses.

"Yes, you do," she breathed hoarsely. His hand parted her thighs with maddening slowness. Her nails pressed little half-moon arcs into the skin of his back, and she gasped with pleasure when his tantalizing lips finally found their target. She moaned, turning her head from side to side, her long dark hair falling over her face. Her fingers traveled from his back up over his lean flanks and grasped the hot, swollen shaft of his maleness. He groaned then, and his mouth caressed her deeper and more fiercely. Suddenly her body arched, she bent her head to his member and her hair fell over his belly, shrouding his thrusting hips in a soft mantle of darkness.

Neither of them knew that the dressing room door was ajar, nor did they know that the austere butler had his pale eye pressed to the opening. His face wore a wine-colored flush and later, when Darcy's pale limbs wrapped convulsively around Stephen's back and her hips swung up, meeting his every thrust, the beads of sweat ran over the man's forehead. He looked forward to these assignations and wouldn't have considered taking another post, even at double the salary.

The gathering that the McElhenys were hosting was a large one, comprised of the moneyed elite of the city and the surrounding area. The local industrialists were there, mostly men from the East who had scented the possibilities of almost unlimited expansion of their capital when the canal system in conjunction with the railroads opened up the fertile, rolling but previously landlocked plains of Indiana and Ohio, opened them for the unimpeded flow of shipping to the port of

Chicago and all major points southward to New Orleans.

Darcy moved from one group to another, had an animated chat with Reneé McElheny in her fluent French and succeeded in charming one and all. Her gaze rested for a moment on Leita, who sat on a divan with Stephen leaning attentively toward her. Leita's blue satin dress caught the flat, white light refracted by the hundreds of crystal prisms in the chandeliers. Leita was smiling as she pushed back her shining red-gold curls. Little wonder that he is so taken, Darcy thought. She intrigues me—I suspect she has a capacity for stubbornness that he hasn't taken into his calculations. He might not be able to effect this as easily as he thinks.

She stood now sequestered in the shadow of one of the marble pillars that ornamented the ballroom, and thought of ponderous Hugo Wenzler, pictured the high-ceilinged drawing room of his Rush Street mansion. A year from now I will be greeting my own guests. I will be established in a fortress of my own, well protected by the bastions of matrimony. A bitter little smile played over her features, but she sighed, her throat tight with a cold fear that her plans might come undone.

"Well, Lucy Mae, what is your opinion?" Samuel Johnston and his wife sat side by side, having seized a moment alone. Mrs. Johnston's auburn hair was piled high on her head and interlaced with a gold velvet ribbon that matched her gown.

"I'm more curious about your opinion," she answered softly. Both knew they were referring to the same question.

"I think that is a very sophisticated woman." Samuel leaned back and spoke with deliberation. "And from that standpoint she is well fitted to accompany our two young women. In fact, I judge that she is rather a woman of the world."

"Woman of the world seems an apt description, but an odd one for a spinster."

"There are spinsters, and there are spinsters," Samuel said meaningfully.

Lucy Mae unfurled her fan and spoke behind it. "You think she isn't virtuous?"

Samuel lowered his voice even more. "In the accepted sense of chastity outside of marriage? No, I don't think she is chaste. Miss Rankin is no stranger to a man's bed, I would swear to that."

"And what do you think that bodes for her conduct over this long absence? She has accepted the responsibility for supervising two young ladies."

"I don't see that they will come to any harm from it. She is self-possessed, neither flighty nor foolish. I would expect that if she took a lover, or lovers, while they are on the Continent that she would conduct her liaisons with discretion."

Lucy Mae Johnston frowned slightly. "I feel disturbed nevertheless. And Anna and Micah barely managed to conceal their astonishment when they met her yesterday." She paused. "Samuel, it is entirely possible I am imagining things, but I fancy there is something a little cruel about that woman. Does that sound foolish to you?"

Samuel's gaze rested on Darcy Rankin for a moment before he answered. "No, a touch exaggerated maybe. She is not a creature of sentiment," he chuckled. "But remember old Bessie saying 'You don't want no lamb guarding a flock of sheep. You want a dog with teeth.'"

"Let us hope that Miss Rankin uses her teeth in Leita's behalf," Lucy Mae said firmly.

Chapter 13

THE HOURS AND DAYS PASSED IN A SMOOTH SEQUENCE. There was no shortage of shipboard acquaintances, but the proffered friendships were turned delicately aside by Leita. She would stroll the decks and lean over the rail to watch the white foam flecking the hull as the ship coursed through the heavy seas of the Atlantic and gaze far off into the distance where line after line of cold, gray waves swept. She chose her own company for the most part, but as day followed day and the ship plied through the eastward curve of the Gulf Currents, her taste for solitude began to diminish. She had slept for hours on end, and yesterday was an ocean away. Her skin glowed, her eyes were clear and shining, and her optimism was restored. A totally different country lay before her, a different language, different customs. And nothing in this strange new world would remind her of what she had left behind.

The hackney cab hurtled over the cobblestones and deposited them at the hotel where they were to stay overnight before entraining for Paris the next day. The hotel was a monstrous old building of gray Normandy stone with a striped orange and green canopy extending over the walk. The lobby was dim and encumbered with heavy pieces of furniture.

"But this is not one of our trunks." Leita looked at the array of baggage piled on the floor. "And my trunk—the gray one—isn't here."

The driver was voluble in his protests and spoke so rapidly that Leita couldn't follow him. The desk clerk attempted a translation. "He says these are the baggages he was directed to bring. He knows not at all of a gray trunk." The scene in the lobby had gained momentum as Darcy got into an argument with the driver.

"If you will excuse me, I may be able to prevail upon this man to return for your luggage." The voice was thin, and rather high, with a pronounced English accent. The man had appeared from the recesses of one of the deep chairs that festooned the lobby.

"We would be most grateful if you could bring this man to reason," Darcy said crisply.

"My trunk is probably standing where it was left, just outside the customs shed. It is gray with a darker gray trim and my name is on it quite clearly. I am Miss Leita Johnston."

"I am honored to make your acquaintance, Miss Johnston. If I may introduce myself. I am Mr. Jack Hidel. I will return to the docks and see that the proper trunk is loaded and brought here."

"I am very grateful for your help. I hope we aren't inconveniencing you too much. This whole thing is a dreadful imposition," Leita answered quickly.

"Not an imposition at all, I assure you." With a sweep of his hand and a stiff little bow Mr. Hidel left them, after nodding severely to the truculent hackney driver.

"Well, that was a piece of luck," Mary Jo said.

"What a predicament—to have my trunk abandoned. I would have nothing to wear but my hats!" Leita laughed.

"We will have time to see our chambers before he returns," Darcy said. They were led up the stairway, viewed their rooms, and returned to the lobby. Leita ordered tea and they were served as they sat on a couch by the tall windows overlooking the street.

"Something just struck me—the name of that gentleman, the one who is, I hope, rescuing my trunk—he said Hidel, didn't he? A Mr. Jack Hidel?" Leita questioned as she poured the clear China tea into a cup.

"Yes. It is probably a coincidence. It's not a terribly uncommon name," Darcy answered.

"And here he is now. And look—they have it!" Mary Jo said. The cab had pulled up in view of the window and the driver dismounted from his box and hauled the trunk down onto the walk. The tall Englishman took a handful of coins from his pocket, paid the driver, and came through the door a moment later. Leita jumped up and ran to him.

"I am so relieved," she exclaimed. "I can't thank you enough, Mr. Hidel. Won't you please take tea with us now?"

His smile was not a broad one, it barely revealed his teeth. But he accepted her invitation. He sat down with the group and deposited his silk hat on an unoccupied chair.

"Did you have any difficulty at the dock? Had the trunk been moved?" Darcy asked.

"None at all. Fortunately it hadn't been claimed by anyone else. One must be careful in France; thievery is very common on the Continent," he said, nodding severely.

"Well, all's well that ends well," Leita observed, and inquired if he cared for cream and sugar.

"Only cream, if you will," he replied, and fell into a tortured silence, which he broke with a constrained "thank you" when Leita handed him his cup. She passed a plate of macaroons but he declined with a quick shake of his long head.

"Our ship only just docked, as you know, Mr. Hidel, and we are bound for Paris tomorrow on the morning train. Are you a frequent visitor to France?" Darcy's beautiful hazel eyes gazed at him directly. She was trying to put him at ease, but the pale flush that circled his slightly protuberant eyes didn't diminish. He swallowed and then set his cup down deliberately before answering.

"As a matter of fact, I do come over frequently. I have an apartment in Paris on La Rue Monceau, near the park."

Darcy smiled. "I imagine you and Mrs. Hidel must enjoy that greatly."

Jack Hidel's protuberant blue eyes widened for an instant. "Oh, I have no wife. But my mother does enjoy the time we spend abroad." His long, slender fingers were busy in a rhythmic tapping pattern.

"That is very thoughtful of you, Mr. Hidel, to see to your mother's comfort and pleasure." Mary Jo's smile was bland, and then her cheeks contracted as she suppressed a yawn.

Leita could restrain herself no longer. "How do you spell your last name, Mr. Hidel?"

"H-I-D-E-L, Miss Johnston."

"That's exactly the same!" she cried. "We are to be the guests of a Sir Charles Hidel. Isn't that a coincidence? Are you related at all?"

"Sir Charles is my uncle, my paternal uncle," the Englishman replied, a flash of interest crossing his face.

"Well, isn't that delightful!" Darcy exclaimed. "We haven't met Sir Charles or Lady Hidel, but she is related to a very close friend of Miss Johnston's in

America. They were kind enough to invite us to spend time with them in Paris."

"Well, well," Jack Hidel was saying pontifically. "So you are going to be staying at Uncle Charles's. You will find it very lively." He jutted his head forward and took a sip from his cup, then put a macaroon into his mouth whole.

Mary Jo's restiveness overcame her. "I'm not the least bit tired. I would like to hire a cab and be driven around. Are you in favor of that, Leita?"

"Completely. But I would like to change first," Leita responded.

"Perhaps—if I'm not being presumptuous—perhaps—it would be rather nice if you ladies would care to dine with me this evening."

"How kind of you to invite us," Leita replied graciously, hoping that he hadn't seen Mary Jo wince.

"That would be very nice. Thank you, Mr. Hidel." Darcy smiled.

"The dining room at seven, then?" He stood up, and his napkin dropped to the carpet.

"At seven, Mr. Hidel."

The train sped through the rolling green valley of the Seine. Leita was enthralled by the tall poplars with their shimmering leaves, the orchards and dark fields with yellow-green shoots surrounding the villages.

Leita and Mary Jo sat side by side with Darcy seated opposite. Jack Hidel sat next to Darcy. Leita and Darcy had felt it was incumbent on them to invite him to join them in their compartment, and he had been shyly pleased. He was listening now to Darcy make conversation. Leita had concluded that the only means of eliciting any conversation from him was to ask questions, but his monosyllabic replies had finally discouraged her. He seemed happy to listen, but one couldn't be certain he was doing that; his china-blue eyes were prone to wear a glazed look now and then, as if he were listening to some internal debate. The night before Mary Jo had pronounced him a strange, dull stick of a man, but Darcy had argued that he simply had the typical reserve of an Englishman and that longer acquaintance would change his manner. Whatever his inward thoughts, it was apparant that he admired Darcy and just as apparent that she was enjoying his attentions, however muted they might be.

"Actually, he's not bad-looking," Mary Jo said. She and Leita had left the compartment to walk through the second-class carriage by way of investigating their surroundings and now they stood on the rear platform of one of the cars while the train stopped at a small village station, watching a woman with two small children and two farmers dressed in tunics and clogs board the train. The air was fresh and fragrant and the chatter of another tongue fascinated Leita. "It's just that he has such a drowned-fish expression," Mary Jo giggled. "I wonder if he resembles his uncle—I certainly hope not."

"I don't think Reneé McElheny would have been so admiring of Sir Charles if he had been as peculiar as his nephew," Leita answered.

"But you'll notice that Darcy doesn't think he is peculiar. Lord above, she is quite charmed by him! She's prattling away as if he were the most entertaining companion in the world," Mary Jo laughed.

"Perhaps she understands him. She's been abroad before; Darcy is a lot more worldly-wise than we are. And too, he is closer to her age. He must be at least forty. He isn't scintillating, I admit. But he seems very nice. He is so soft-spoken and shy."

The train started up then and they rejoined the pair in the compartment.

The winding course of the River Seine made a loop to the southwest as it entered Paris, and the tracks crossed it and carried the train into the Gare St. Lazare. It was high noon and the bustling crowds filled the station where hawkers were selling baskets of cherries, the first of the crop from the south. They descended into an uproar. Mr. Hidel had kindly volunteered to see to all of their baggage, and Leita stood gazing around her. I can't believe I'm here, she thought.

"I hope I am not accosting the wrong ladies. Are you, by any chance, the Misses Rankin, Tillett, and Johnston?" a cheerful voice asked.

"You must be Sir Charles!" Leita exclaimed. The genial, gray-haired man facing them swept them a courtly bow. His dark blue frock coat fell into impeccably tailored folds over his cream-colored trousers and his ascot matched his coat. A smile of welcome creased his ruddy cheeks which were decorated with a short gray beard and the smile was duplicated in his eyes. She knew immediately that she was going to like him.

"I plead guilty to that name. And I am most delighted to make your acquaintance. I found you so quickly because of Reneé's very accurate description of Miss Johnston, 'hair like a Titian painting,' were her words, I believe, and lo, not another lady in the station had such tresses." He thumped his walking-stick for emphasis and kissed each of their hands in turn. "The carriage is waiting, and so is Lady Hidel. She regrets she couldn't be here to meet you but other duties called. Now, I will see to your baggage—" He stopped and his eyes widened with an expression of surprise, colored unmistakably with irritation. "This is most unexpected, Jack."

Jack Hidel had returned with three porters in tow. He halted and made one of his stiff bows. "I'm sorry I didn't wire ahead, Uncle Charles. Spur of the moment, you know. Good to see you. Is Aunt keeping well?"

"Annette is quite well, thank you. I might have

195

known you couldn't resist the lure of Longchamps." A curtain of politeness covered Sir Charles's countenance now.

"We were most fortunate to have met Mr. Hidel in Le Havre, Sir Charles," Darcy's low, musical voice cut in. Sir Charles turned a look of surprise in her direction, and she explained the circumstances.

"I'm glad to hear it," Sir Charles boomed cheerfully. "Ladies are at a disadvantage when it comes to forcing some blighter to right a wrong. I'm delighted that Jack could be of service to you. And now, the footman will see that your baggage is taken care of, and we will be on our way. What a journey you have had! What a long journey!" Muttering amiably, Sir Charles directed the footman and shook hands with his nephew. "I take it that Dora didn't accompany you?"

"No sir, Mother will arrive in a few days," Jack replied.

"Well, would you care to have dinner with us?" Sir Charles asked, rather diffidently, Leita thought.

"Kind of you, sir, very kind of you, but I do have an engagement. Give my best to Aunt."

"I will do that, of course. And we will be seeing you at Longchamps, of course."

"Definitely. Until tomorrow then."

Leita thanked Jack Hidel again and he loped off through the crowd. Darcy cast a thoughtful glance at his retreating back.

The carriage, a footman standing at either side of the coachman, swept through the gate of the mansion on the Rue St. Honore and into the square courtyard where it drew up under a portico. They alighted, and the heavy double doors with their massive bronze knockers opened to an expanse of black and white marble broken by onyx columns with fluted capitals. A lady came skimming toward them, past the butler and a maid who was arranging flowers on an ormolu-trimmed mahogany table.

"Bienvenue, bienvenue—welcome, a thousand welcomes!" she cried and the next moment Leita was enfolded in an embrace so fragrant it was like having her nose pressed in a bed of spring flowers. She received a kiss on each cheek and another hug before her hostess drew back and surveyed the others.

"And you are Miss Tillett—there is no mistaking you, the blue eyes and the dimple. And the lovely and thoughtful Miss Rankin." Lady Hidel embraced each of them and then gestured exuberantly toward the ceiling. "You must be simply and utterly exhausted. Come, we will go to your suites now and there will be some refreshments and you must tell me about your voyage. Come, Charles, you are going to join us, aren't you?"

"In a moment—in a moment, my dear." Sir Charles handed his stick to the butler.

The lady who preceded them so energetically up the broad carpeted stairway and showed them the three large suites was dressed in mauve silk, trimmed with delicate braid of the same color. Darker mauve tassels swung from the panniers of her skirt and the yoke was a fine Alencons lace. Her figure was supple and plumply rounded. Her chestnut hair was dressed with the faultless swirls and wavy tendrils that only a fine hairdresser can accomplish. Her face, though the nose was a touch too long for perfection, was the softened picture of a woman who had been in her youth an incredible beauty and would always be appealingly lovely. There was nothing fragile about her; the lips were mobile and the tiny lines beside her mouth and eyes had all come in the wake of a thousand smiles. The eyes were oblong, still heavily lashed and a dancing, gold-flecked green. Her hands flew in a multiplicity of gestures, hands that were weighted with concoctions of diamonds and emeralds.

"Such a nice little sitting room. I hope you will be so comfortable—so comfortable here."

Leita looked around at the "nice little sitting room," the walls of sea-green brocade, the ivory satin curtains trimmed with gold fringe hanging from windows that stretched from ceiling to floor, the Aubusson carpet that glowed, deeply colorful and the ivory and gilt and inlaid tables with their bibelots and sprays of flowers in crystal and silver vases.

They had gathered in the sitting room adjoining Leita's bedchamber and Lady Hidel poured coffee from a silver pot, mixing it with hot milk that had been sprinkled with nutmeg. "And you three are going to grace and delight us with your presence for a long time. Isn't it marvelous, Charles? It has seemed so empty here."

Sir Charles stood by one of the open windows, looking down into the broad Rue de St. Honore. "Marvelous indeed," he agreed benignly, and raised his brandy glass in a benevolent toast.

"Tonight we are having such a small little dinner. There are quite a few people in town now you know, because of the Grand Prix at Longchamps. And tomorrow—tomorrow will be such a day! Half of Paris is down on its knees praying for a clear sky."

"And the other half is laying bets," Sir Charles laughed.

"Ah oui, myself included, of course. Armand has given me a piece of very inside information—and he said not to take it seriously! Imagine! Not take it seriously when I can place a small bet and have the satisfaction of seeing the Countess Walewska's face fall when I tell her of my winnings?"

"As long as you don't pawn one of your tiaras," Sir

Charles answered equably. "By the way, Jack is in town. He made the acquaintance of these ladies in Le Havre. They had barely set foot ashore, I believe."

Leita had been silent, listening to the crossfire of conversation, but now she related the circumstances of their meeting with Jack Hidel. Lady Hidel listened, her head on one side.

"How maddening! To lose a trunkful of dresses. What a blessing that Jack was there to step in. Did you invite him to dinner, Charles?"

"Of course, but he had a prior engagement," Sir Charles said. "However, we can expect to see him in the box tomorrow."

"And Dora?"

"She stayed behind."

"We are being very rude, carrying on these family conversations when you are weary and longing for baths," Annette addressed Darcy.

"But you will grow accustomed to it," Sir Charles chuckled. "L'Hotel Bourait is not a ceremonious household."

"*Mon dieu*, no! Nor was it ever, I am certain. *Mes chères*, you have time now for the bathing and the naps." Annette gave a tug at the velvet bell-pull hanging beside the mantel. "The servants are on the way." She blew them a kiss and she and her husband left the room.

"You are wearing the Empress's favorite flowers. And so becoming. I had no idea that America produced such beauty—I had thought it primitive and fierce." The Duc de Rastignet gestured toward the cluster of Parma violets at Leita's bosom. She was decked in pale violet gauze, yard after yard of it floated over the darker violet silk underskirt and was arranged in frothy folds around her shoulders.

"It is primitive and fierce. Ordinarily I wear a

199

bearskin, for warmth, you know, but I pin violets on that too." Leita's eyes laughed up at him.

"Ah, but it should be the skin of a tigress that adorns you. It couldn't possibly match the glow of your hair, though."

"You are being charming to my guest! How courteous of you, Sir. And how generous, since you always choose the plainest lady to pay your attentions to, in order that she won't feel cast aside." Lady Hidel flashed a smile at the man whose chest was covered with decorations, including the gold cross of the Legion d'Honneur.

"My lady, I am only attempting to fix myself in her mind before the inevitable onslaught of the cavalry and the more dashing members of the court sweep her from my field of vision. One shudders to think how quickly she would be captured if his Majesty were the man he was ten years ago, nay—five years ago."

"Hush, you naughty man. One can't expect any Emperor to be celibate," Annette rejoined.

"One cannot expect our Emperor to be celibate— unless one has the turn of mind to expect the Seine to flow backward." The Duc smiled.

"Mary Jo Tillett joined the group and the Duc bent over her hand. "How perfectly delightful you all are. You in particular, Sir," Mary Jo laughed, her little white teeth sparkling. "Lady Hidel, if this is a 'small little dinner,' in your words, we are due for some very gay times."

Leita's glance swept over the long room. The carved plaster ceiling, painted with glowing-limbed nymphs and gods and goddesses, the chandeliers with their tall tapers, the ornate carrera marble mantel, the huge gilt-framed mirrors reflected the sparkling jewels and sheen of white ruffled shirtfronts and voluminous crinolines in every color of the rainbow.

"Ah, but this is not a large gathering. It is intimate, in fact. You will see—when we attend the Empress's 'Mondays' there will be at least five hundred. We are gay here—it is what life is for—and it delights me that you are anticipating pleasure."

"Wait until tomorrow. This is a wake compared to the field at Longchamps and the fetes following it." The Duc nodded, his eyes resting appreciatively on the fulsome curves of Mary Jo's décolleté.

"Come, I am going to steal you from M. le Duc to present Octave to you. No, I see he is on his way to us." Lady Hidel nodded to the tall, slim man approaching them.

Later that night, when the last carriage had gone clattering out of the courtyard, Lady Hidel flounced down onto a sofa. "An evening *charmant,* and now it is finished. Not one quarrel, even banker Bischoffsheim didn't restrict his conversation to gold. You enjoyed your conversation with Octave, didn't you, Leita?"

"He is fascinating—such gentle manners," Leita replied. She had been distracted the evening long, interested in this glittering society.

"Tomorrow you will meet them all." Annette's green eyes sparkled with anticipation.

Sir Charles poured a final toast of the pale gold champagne. His sharp featured face was wreathed in a smile. "A hearty welcome to our charming guests." He raised his glass to Leita, Mary Jo, and Darcy. "May your stay here give you as much pleasure as your presence gives us."

Leita felt a tear sting her eye. I am truly going to be happy here, she thought. Once this evening her breath had quickened when a tall, broad-shouldered man with a head of crisply waving black hair had risen from a chair at the other end of the room. Her heart had seemed to stop, but then he turned. Small eyes, set close together, and a receding chin—her heart had resumed its normal beating. I have thought of him once—only once tonight. Life will be joyous for me here—and I will forget.

"Oh, aren't you ready yet?" Mary Jo wailed. Leita stood in her petticoats, the high bed covered with gowns she had cast aside.

"I can't decide. I am so excited! The blue makes me look sallow and the pink washes me out and—I simply don't know what to wear!"

"In the first place your stays aren't tight enough. These are the most stylish women in the world—you can't make your appearance with a waist like—oh, never mind. You are so tiny there that you needn't bother. You don't appreciate your luck."

"If I measured twenty-two inches, I still wouldn't have myself laced in till I couldn't draw breath. What about the green—sprigged muslin?"

"No, no, no. Far too demure." Mary Jo put her hands on her hips and surveyed the heap of flounces and ruffles and ribbons, then turned to the armoire. "It must be dramatic. You should take advantage of your looks and not be modest. Here." She held up a gold silk, trimmed in bright apple-green taffeta. The overskirt was caught up all around with yellow silk roses tied with apple-green taffeta ribbons.

"I adore it. But it is cut too low for daytime." Leita pursed her lips.

"But not for the Grand Prix!" Lady Hidel had come in through the connecting door. "Just the right amount of décolleté for the great day. And there are yellow roses in the hothouse—perfect to adorn your hair."

Leita was fastened into the dress and her sprightly hostess arranged the silk around her shoulders. "Now, the coiffure." She motioned to the maid who scurried into the hall and returned a few minutes later with a gentleman in white silk stockings and knee breeches.

"This is Monsieur Parmais—one of Monsieur Felix's most talented assistants. Now, Parmais—here is an opportunity."

She indicated Leita's luxuriant tresses. "Madame, I agree it is an opportunity," M. Parmais agreed, and opened the leather satchel he had carried in with him.

"M. Felix dresses the Empress's hair and you are in the hands of an expert, my dear." Lady Hidel stood aside and watched as the slightly built man brushed and swirled and pinned, ending with three barely-opened yellow roses which the maid presented to him on a silver platter.

"Parfait," Lady Hidel cried when the last rose was pinned in place, making a fragrant band around the one long curl that fell from Leita's gleaming waves.

"You look like an Irish princess," Darcy observed as she entered. Her dress of scarlet and white set off her pale skin and dark hair.

"A touch or two for Mademoiselle Tillett," Lady Hidel directed, obviously enjoying herself thoroughly, and Mary Jo's glistening black curls were brushed to a higher gloss and drawn back in a cluster behind each ear.

Sir Charles waited in the hallway, his slender frame set off by his faultlessly tailored jacket over the cream colored drainpipe trousers and black boots which gleamed as bright as his top hat.

"You look like a Winterhalter portrait," he called as the group descended the stairway—and they did.

In the Place d'Etoile, the circular plaza where the Arc de Triomphe stood, five broad avenues and four boulevards radiated out, like beams from a stylized sun. The real sun shone down benignly on the horde of carriages that circled the plaza and funneled into the wide Avenue de l'Imperatrice. Elegant landaus with silver-spoked wheels flashing, horses with plumes and silver-trimmed bridles high-stepped, drawing the sea of carriages that carried the Marquis, the Ducs, the Comtes; the aristocracy of the Continent and the British Isles converged on the Avenue de l'Imperatrice this bright June morning. Along with the nobility, the bankers, the financiers, the moneyed, though untitled aristocracy rode resplendent in their carriages. The avenue led into the Bois de Boulogne. What had been a ruined forest twenty-five years before, the abandoned hunting ground of the Valois kings, Prefect Hauffman had carved and cleared and landscaped with flowers and waterfalls and winding streams. The racecourse, the now famous Longchamps, had been inaugurated a scant ten years before and the Grand Prix was now one of Europe's leading races. Cavalry officers in flashing scarlet and gold displayed their mounts as they cantered through the traffic.

Leita quickened with excitement as she stood in the box and surveyed the stands, packed with elegantly dressed women and men. "There is the Duc de Morny, Leita. It was he who inaugurated Longchamps." Lady Hidel beckoned with her fan, and the Duc, his face lined above a chest full of decorations, stopped by the box. His pale, jaded eyes scanned Leita quickly as he raised his head after brushing her lips with his hand.

"Women and racehorses, they will have been the death of him," Lady Hidel remarked after he had moved on.

"He looks ghastly," Mary Jo whispered.

"It is the arsenic," Lady Hidel whispered back.

"Is he poisoning himself?" Leita inquired.

"Entirely voluntarily," Sir Charles entered the conversation. "He cannot bear the thought of age, there-

fore he uses arsenic for its supposed powers of transforming the complexion and rejuvenating one. It is
obvious he is multiplying the dosage. He is as gray as a
November sky."

"I fear he is going to attain his desire very soon—he
will never see old age at this rate," Lady Hidel said.

The box was filling with friends and suddenly there
was the blare of trumpets and everyone in the stands
stood up. The beat of drums and the flourishing tricolor
heralded the entry of Napoleon III, Emperor of
France, and his Empress Eugenie. The Cent-Gardes,
their tunics as blue as the sky above, golden cuirasses
swinging at their sides, preceded the carriage drawn by
six horses white as foam. Leita bent forward, eager to
see. The carriage had drawn up in front of the royal
box, two footmen in powdered, towering wigs let down
the steps and opened the gold trimmed doors. The man
who stepped out paused and waved his gloved hand in a
seigneural gesture, acknowledging the roar that went up
from the crowd. He is certainly not a majestic figure,
Leita thought. His rather large head, nodding to left
and right, sported a tuft of beard trimmed to the shape
of a narrow spade. Above that his mouth was barricad-
ed by a heavy mustache which was twirled into two
long, stiffly waxed prongs that extended the width of his
face. His face was pale and lined, and the eyelids hung
long and sleepy, obscuring the pupils. The woman he
handed down—could that be the Empress? Leita
remembered hearing that she was much younger than
her husband. How striking the contrast was. Vigorously
beautiful, she seemed to give off waves of vitality. Mary
Jo nudged Leita and whispered, "You are wearing the
Empress's colors." Eugenie's dress was a shimmering
apple-green, flounced with white lace and touches of
white satin, matching the ostrich plumes that set off the
red highlights of her hair. A rivière of emeralds

cascaded over that famous bosom. She bowed regally and the cry of "Queen Crinoline" could be heard from the very end of the stands where a place to stand cost five francs. Their majesties, preceded by footmen, took their seats in the royal box and the crowd subsided finally.

"That applause was due to my entrance, you know. Our Emperor has such *vaniteux* he presumed it was for him."

"Armand—you are reprehensible, but my darling, you are finally here," Lady Hidel cried and embraced the newcomer.

He was of medium height, with blond hair that fell over his ears, and large brown eyes. His forehead was broad and intensified the thoughtful quality of his eyes. He removed his yellow gloves before grasping Sir Charles's extended hand.

"You were sorely missed last night, but I'm delighted you made it this morning."

The man shrugged. "I regret I wasn't able to join you last night. I am always such a scintillating addition." His mouth curved in a smile that would have been sardonic in a less gentle countenance.

"You are just barely forgiven. But I musn't hector you—though you know how I worry about you." Lady Hidel stroked his arm.

"Are these the visitors from an ocean away?" he inquired, smiling on Leita.

"They are—and you are all going to enjoy one another thoroughly." With her white-gloved hand still on his arm she presented him. "May I introduce M. le Comte Armand de la Penseans du Favre. He is charming, kind, and almost without a fault."

"Due to the fact that I am Lady Hidel's godson and she is one of the most charitable, as well as most gracious, women in the world," he finished her introduction.

"I am never charitable when I praise you, Armand dear. I am charitable when I praise some others I could mention, but never you." Lady Hidel's smile held a tender affection.

"Miss Darcy Rankin of Chicago." Darcy's extended hand received a light brush of the Comte's lips, also Mary Jo in turn. "And this is the lady your cousin described as having 'fiery tresses and a spirit to match, I believe,'" the Comte said as he took Leita's hand.

"I shall have to use more chamomile on my hair to rid myself of the reputation it brings me," Leita said.

"You musn't," Armand smiled kindly. "This would be a cold world indeed without a little fire."

"Good morning, Aunt." Jack Hidel stood in the entry to the box. The severity of his gray frock coat and matching gray trousers was relieved by a bright blue ascot.

"Jack, you would have surprised us completely had not Charles met you yesterday. A good morning to you, and how was your crossing?"

"As usual. Nothing worthy of note." He raised his head from her hand and his glance flickered over the group.

"I suppose your bets are all laid?" Sir Charles inquired of his nephew who had seated himself beside Darcy Rankin.

"I have committed myself to Black Star," Jack replied with a nervous little nod. His ginger-colored hair held a few streaks of gray which trailed down into the long sideburns decorating his long, flat jaws.

He reminds me of a turtle, Leita thought. He blinks around, yet his eyes hardly ever meet anyone's squarely.

The Duc de Rastignet appeared, resplendent in his scarlet and gold uniform and black shako decorated with a bronze eagle. It was obvious that the cavalry officer had made a point of joining them because of Leita's presence. He was a sophisticated man, too restive to remain on his family estates. He had served in Mexico with Marshall Bazaine, as a daring member of the illustrious cavalry regiment of the Garde Imperiale, the Guides, "Intrepid horsemen, above reproach and without fear . . ." Effortlessly charming, he pursued women, danger, and excitement, never failing to find all three. As a second son, his inheritance would be slight compared to his elder brother, a fact that concerned him not at all. The wealth of the Rastignets was immense, quite sufficient for a man with no responsibilities who, when he married, would marry wealth at least as great as his own.

Lady Hidel cast a benign eye on his presence, making a mental note to apprise Leita of the Comte's well-known nonchalance where females were concerned. She would warn Leita that he burned high, like a Roman candle, but guttered just as quickly. On his part, the Comte had vowed to devote some time to this intriguing girl with the violet eyes and provocative air of independence. She excited his curiosity as well as his admiration.

Now he raised Leita's parasol for her and they sat together, he attentively explaining the finer points of the horseflesh that was to take part in this event and she listening just as attentively.

"Your responsibility is a great one," Jack Hidel observed.

"Responsibility?" Darcy said questioningly. The race was over. Jack Hidel's horse had won, happily the same horse that Lady Hidel had wagered on. Jack, however, had only placed his substantial bet after an

208

exhaustive study of the field, each horse's running record and its bloodlines. Now Jack and Darcy were strolling through the grass outside the huge, striped tent where chilled wine and pressed duck and other elaborately prepared cold dishes were being served.

"Yes. The responsibility of chaperoning two such," he hesitated, "lively young women." He glanced meaningfully toward Leita who sat surrounded by young men, some in well-cut frock coats and polished top hats and others in the brilliant uniforms of the cavalry.

"They are lively, I agree. But I don't find it a burden, Mr. Hidel. They are both well-bred young ladies, young and beautiful, of course, and I expect them to be sociable."

"Nevertheless, it is obvious that you are a woman of judgment and discretion. It is only to be hoped that they learn to emulate you."

Darcy substituted a smile for the laughter she repressed. He is really so terribly correct, she thought, and wondered if he had ever ventured on a love affair.

"But I suppose they come naturally by their rather independent ways. In America the customs are different, I believe," he ended timorously.

"Firstly I thank you for the compliment, Mr. Hidel. But you must keep in mind that you and I are both older, also it is likely that we are rather reserved by nature. I am a spinster and it is notoriously assumed that spinsters have a somewhat different outlook on life."

He drew himself up. He was barrel-chested and now he thrust his chest forward. His words rang with indignation. "You are obviously a woman of taste. I recognized that immediately. Women of taste don't give their hand to the first brash fellow who comes along and asks them. That is for silly girls." He directed

209

a hooded glare at Leita's group. "That de Rastignet for instance—the fellow is a boor. A woman of your delicacy would have nothing to do with a man like that, though you can be sure he recognizes your beauty."

A faint flush crept over Darcy's cheeks. She had been touched by Jack Hidel's shyness, had decided already that he was a very sensitive man. Now she was warmed by his obviously sincere admiration. She ventured a bit of personal history. "I was engaged, when I was very young"—she paused, her eyes downcast—"he was killed, killed in battle."

Chapter 14

PARIS WAS STILL ENVELOPED IN ITS LONG TWILIGHT WHEN the closed carriage rolled to a stop and Jack Hidel paid the driver before alighting. He always used a hired carriage for these expeditions. He passed through the door of the well-kept townhouse and handed his walking stick and silk hat to the young maid.

"Mr. Hidel, what a joy to see you!" The woman bearing down on him was plump enough to be maternal looking but her gown of polished cherry-red satin cut low over an effulgent bosom invalidated the comparison.

"You have been neglecting us recently. It has been almost two weeks." She kissed him familiarly on the cheek and taking his arm drew him through a doorway into a room walled and curtained in the same cherry-red. Crystal lamps sparkled and the tables were draped to the floor. Jack settled himself into a chair with a voluptuous sigh and took the glass of brandy she poured for him.

"I have been occupied—too occupied. No time to relax at all," he said.

"I know. I have seen you several times with the ravishing lady."

He smirked. "She is an American."

"Ah, these Americans. They do manage to monopolize the attractive men." Her smile was just short of being fatuous, and there was the suggestion of a twinkle in her eye when her caller smirked again.

"One must show them around, if they are ladylike, which she is. She has an onerous responsibility though. She is chaperoning two girls." He sipped at the brandy reflectively and then downed the glass. "One of them is a terribly forward creature. Conceited and self-centered. She obviously thinks that because she is a beauty she can do anything she likes. Spoiled—disgracefully spoiled, Madame Charbonnel."

"It is sad, the way these young girls are coddled and flattered," Madame Charbonnel commiserated as she refilled his glass.

"It is disgusting. She shows no respect at all for her elders." Jack glowered and emptied the glass again. "A sound spanking is what she needs. She has never been disciplined."

Madame Charbonnel's highly colored lips twitched but she controlled them in the same second. "I take it you speak of the one with flaming hair."

"My word, you see and know everyone, don't you?" Jack Hidel looked taken aback.

"I only chanced to see you taking coffee one afternoon on the Boulevard des Italiens with three ladies. I noticed one as being especially vivacious. A trifle old for spanking, though," she smiled innocently, and then rose to answer a quiet knock at the door.

Returning, she opened a filigreed case and extracted

a cigarette. Jack leaned over and lit it for her. "I really feel that I must return to Cairo soon, Mr. Hidel. The gentleman I just spoke with is returning there. He tells me that the canal is proceeding inexorably to completion, the town is alive with visitors and investors from all over the globe, and the new opera house alone is a sight worth the trip."

"I share your interest. The Orient holds a definite attraction, but what a crowded mess it will be—the flotsam and jetsam of the world!"

"Crowded yes, but I intend to see it again before I die. I am going to ride on a camel to view the pyramids," Madame Charbonnel declared.

Jack viewed her corpulent body and the white hands that looked as if they belonged to a large, plump baby.

"Are you serious? Have you really determined to go?"

"I have not taken so much as a week away for five years. If I had been foresighted enough I would have transferred this establishment to Cairo three years ago when it became apparent that the canal was going to be completed in spite of every obstacle. I would have made enough to retire to my little piece of land in Gras by now. As it is, I richly deserve a holiday and I have made Ilse my assistant with that end in mind. I shall probably be robbed blind while I am gone—but there, I have made up my mind."

Jack pondered this and Madame Charbonnel decided that now was the time to bring their conversation to a tactful close. She was wanted in one of the other rooms. She filled Jack's glass and then gave a gentle tug to the bell rope. Jack had taken the first sip when the door opened to admit a girl of about fifteen. Her hair was dark and fastened behind with a bow of bright orange. The flimsy gauze dress she wore was gathered over large breasts whose nipples cast two round dark shadows. Her eyes, a light hazel, were impudent and knowing and she stood in front of Jack, one hand on her hip and her shoulders thrown back. Insolence emanated from her as strongly as the scent of patchouli.

"Mr. Hidel, this is Constanzia. She comes from Turin and when she arrived last week I thought of you immediately. Constanzia, this is one of our most important clients and it is a mark of favor that you are presented to him."

Constanzia curtseyed low and the gauze gaped, exposing her breasts. Jack Hidel inclined his head. A dull red flush had crept over his flat cheekbones and washed his forehead.

"Madame Charbonnel has given me a most delightful chamber. Will you come and see it?" The courtesy of the speech was belied by the arrogant expression on the girl's face. Jack nodded and Constanzia took his brandy glass and tucked her other hand in the crook of his arm, pressing against him as she did it. His flush deepened and he gave her a sidelong look, a look of conspiratorial lust, and she giggled and rubbed his arm. Madame Charbonnel waddled to the door, opened it and swept through with Jack and Constanzia behind her. She was joined in the hallway by a blond woman dressed in Prussian blue hung with beads of jet. Both women watched the pair who disappeared when they reached the top of the stairway.

It was a charming chamber that Constanzia took him to, pink and gilded as a gigantic peach. Constanzia's pale brown, long-fingered hands moved to his cravat and untied it. His hands touched her waist lightly, hesitantly, and she moved sinuously against him. The flush on his face deepened and he gave a sidelong glance at the windows, open to the sounds of the boulevard below. She laughed. "M'sieu likes it in

214

the dark?" Her abdomen had already encountered the hard bulge in his trousers.

He swallowed audibly and nodded and she sauntered to the windows, deliberately exaggerating the motion of her hips. She was wearing nothing at all under the thin gauze which was flounced and gathered so that her skin and the darkness of her pubic triangle was visible in a certain light. She drew the curtains and turning saw that he had dropped his velour jacket on a chair and was jerkily unbuttoning his shirt.

"You must let me do that," she exclaimed and proceeded to finish the unbuttoning, humming a little tune while her fingers flew. As he awkwardly drew his arm out of one sleeve she thrust her hand inside the belt of his trousers and flicked her nails over his groin.

"Don't! I don't like to be tickled," he said pettishly.

"Not even there?" Her laughter was coarse.

He shook his head and seemed not to know what to do next. Bare, his chest was white with a few, scattered, ginger-colored hairs and the muscles of his arms were flaccid.

"Sit down. I will take off your boots." Constanzia bent over rather than kneeling and Jack Hidel sunk his long chin into his breastbone as he stared at her almost completely exposed breasts. They were immense and his breath was rasping in his throat by the time she had bared his feet.

"Now M'sieu, it is time to show me what you have for me." She pitched her low voice lower still and looked at the space below his belt meaningfully.

He stood up and hastily struggled out of the tightly fitting drainpipe trousers. He stood awkwardly on one leg and then the other in order to discard his drawers.

"Oh, M'sieu!" Constanzia breathed admiration. "You are like a stallion."

A surprisingly sweet half-smile crossed Jack's face as

215

he gazed down at his swollen member. Constanzia's long fingers stroked him lightly. Jack groaned, still staring down.

"Meraviglioso!" she murmured. This one is truly in love with himself, she thought. He wishes only for someone to join him in admiration of this phallus of his. Look at him—she almost let her inward sneer become visible. Standing there—he hasn't even touched me—just staring like an ass at himself.

True enough, Jack's hands were caressing a semicircular pattern on his abdomen, moving in widening arcs as he stared down at Constanzia's teasing fingers.

"What does that mean?" he whispered, "What you just said, mera-something?"

"Oh, M'sieu, it means wonderful!" She put as much avidity into the word as she could. Enough of this, she thought, and ran her hands down the inside of his thighs, then removed them abruptly and pulled down the shoulders of her dress, at the same time untying the ribbon which held the gathered waist against her body. The dress fell to the floor in a heap around her feet. Jack stared; his eyelids were fully raised as they seldom were and the pupils of his china-blue eyes were darkly dilated circles.

Constanzia's fleshy breasts pointed into wide, dark purple nipples. Her waist was rather thick and merged quickly into somewhat straight-sided hips. There was a line of dark hair from her navel to her pubic mound which was so lavishly haired that its tendrils spread over into her groin. Madame Charbonnel on inspecting her had deliberated over whether or not the girl's thighs at least should be depilated free of hairs, but decided that this faintly animalistic trait might appeal very strongly to some tastes. Her intuition had been right.

Constanzia gave a gleeful laugh and ran to the bed, threw herself on it and beckoned for Jack to join her. He lay down beside her, but on his abdomen, with his

216

face buried in his arms. Releasing one hand he touched her arm, then groped until he found the nipple and rolled it between his fingers. When he raised his head it was to look at the erect, purplish nipple, then he turned over quickly and lay spread-eagled, never releasing the nipple. His member spiked up, heavily engorged and she grasped it.

"That feels wonderful," he sighed, almost as if she were binding a wound. Obediently she stroked him, pulling on the redness of the shaft and stroking the area behind it. His breath was coming faster and she waited, expecting him to leap on her and enter her at any moment. The long flat planes of his cheeks were puffy with lust and he stared at her hand rhythmically working the distended length of his organ. Suddenly he turned on his side toward her, curving his body into an arc. Her hands slipped away as he raised onto his knees and, putting his hands under her arms lifted her into a sitting position against the piled-up pillows. How does he expect to get into me like this? she thought but the next moment it was apparent that was not his intent. He straddled her and with a knee on either side of her he thrust his hips forward, pressing the pulsating tip of his organ into her nipple. He moved his hips rhythmically, his eyes narrowed into slits as he buried the hard end in the rubbery cushion of her breast, drawing it out, thrusting again. His face grew redder and his breathing harsher, his hand left her shoulder and squeezed her breast into a more resistant mound. He showed no sign of altering his position to a more conventional one and Constanzia watched fascinated as his face contorted into a grimace that she could only connect with pain when he thrust his member deep into her breast and held it there. He was convulsed and shuddering when she felt the jet of fluid drown her nipple and flow down, covering her breast in warm stickiness.

"You have ended?" Her voice rose in astonishment.

He hung his head, his face still marked by the painful grimace.

She stifled her laughter. She couldn't afford to offend her first customer.

He fell over beside her and flung one arm over his face. She lay there for a few minutes and then, overcome with curiosity, she whispered in his ear. "Is it that you are afraid of the sickness? I am clean, you know—very clean."

After a long minute he shook his head, his face still shielded by his arm. "No, I am not afraid of the sickness. Madame Charbonnel would not have anyone who wasn't clean. It's only . . ." his voice died out.

Constanzia, puzzled beyond discretion, prodded him gently.

"What then?"

He sighed. "I just like it . . . that's all." And he would say no more.

Constanzia, who had been slapped, beaten, sodomized, and had already borne one child, lay back and sighed. So this is Paris, and the house of the famous Madame Charbonnel. She laughed uproariously then and when Jack, alarmed for fear he was being ridiculed, asked her why, she told him frankly that it was because she might never have to douche again.

One woman stepping off the train from Le Havre was close to seventy. She was dressed in mauve silk trimmed with darker mauve braid and a bonnet that, though it matched the expensive dress, was devoid of any style. Her smile was beatific as she laughingly exchanged parting words with the woman who had shared her compartment.

She looked up and smiled complacently as Jack Hidel approached her. She patted his arm once or twice and he gave her shoulder an awkward pat by way of greeting before they moved toward the doors.

"Well, and how have you been?" Jack inquired.

"Oh, well enough, and how have you been keeping?"

"About the same."

This was the length and breadth of their conversation until they reached the apartments on the Avenue Bosquet.

Dora Hidel settled into a chair with a gratified sigh. "And now for a nice cup of tea." Dora's eyes were small, small and dark as shoebuttons. They took her son's measure quickly and piercingly while he filled his pipe, then veiled themselves in their customary blandness when he sat down across from her.

Jack leaned back and watched as his mother poured milk into a cup, filled it with strong, steaming tea and presented it to him.

"Well, how is Aunt Laura doing?"

"She's getting deaf as a post these days. And I prophesied true, that granddaughter of hers is heading for a bad end." She picked up a small frosted cake and evaluated it. "Very nice, cream-filled, too."

"Well, we knew what Betty would come to."

"What she would *have* to come to, the way she was spoiled!" Dora Hidel added triumphantly.

"What has she been up to?" Jack asked, pouring milk into both their cups and refilling them.

"Why she's slipping out and meeting a young officer, that's what she's up to," Dora replied.

"Did you tell Aunt?"

"No, I wouldn't like to say anything. They'll find out soon enough," she said, with an air of virtuous forbearance.

"She'll get herself pregnant, that's what she'll do." Jack nodded solemnly.

"And then the young rascal won't marry her. They'll have a time hushing that up!" Dora said emphatically. "And the money that is spent on her! She thinks pound notes grow on trees. Seven guineas for a bonnet! Now, I ask you! They've always given her every little thing she wanted."

Jack put one of the small cakes into his mouth whole.

"I suppose Annette's guests are still with her. Does she appreciate the time you have taken to entertain them?"

"Oh, you know Annette, flighty and thoughtless. Childish too, you should see the way she dotes on those two young girls. She will never act her age."

"And spending money like water, as usual, I suppose."

"Worse than ever. They went off to Compiegne yesterday and if the boxes I saw delivered are to be believed Annette spent as much money as the Empress just for a three-day visit."

"Charles should have put his foot down years ago, Jack. That woman will spend him into the grave and leave nothing for you, I fear. I've been economical all my life, but then I wasn't raised to have all of Annette's highfalutin notions and snobberies." Dora was, in fact, the daughter of a successful draper. She had married into the Hidel family as the result of ingratiating herself with one of her father's titled customers to the extent of being taken as her companion. Young Horace Hidel, a peevish and antisocial young man with a nasty temper, had been an easy mark. She had inflamed his ire at the rest of his family, fanned his jealousy of his brother Charles, who by law of entail would inherit the title, egged him on in his hostile outbursts against whoever crossed his path and soothingly supported his weaknesses. So soothingly that when she confided to him that she was going to bear a child he married her immediately, delighted to confront his thunderstruck family with this evidence of his independent action. The child had been a girl, now married and presiding over a modest country estate in Norfolk. Horace Hidel had died three years later of blood poisoning, just a few months before Jack's birth. Dora, with her condemning tongue and readiness to deliver a blow at the first sign of defiance had reduced her son to a tongue-tied, resentful boy-child very early. Jack had remained docilely in her control and when he grew into young manhood she adopted the placating, soothing manner that marked all of her relations with males. Unendingly ingratiating, Dora had raised deviousness to an art form; her sharply envious nature she concealed with the ease of a gifted actress. Smugly complacent in her role as paragon, she poured another cup of tea for the forty-one-year-old man in whom she had successfully nurtured a searing mistrust of any other female.

"He'll never put his foot down. Charles has always been a silly fool about Annette," Jack remarked dourly.

"A woman can ruin a man, but some men never learn it. She has been pulling the wool over his eyes for years, carrying on with one man after another."

Jack protested mildly at this. "That is your imagination, Mother. Annette is dramatic about everything she does, but I have never seen her behave with any impropriety with another man."

"That is because you are gullible, Jack. She has never fooled me, not for a minute. You don't realize the things a woman can get up to. Now, tell me . . . you mentioned this chaperone . . . Miss Rankin, isn't it? You said she seemed to be a sensible sort."

"She is sensible. She is a mature woman. American, of course, but not brash and forward."

"Is she in the employ of these girls' parents?"

"Oh Lord no. Her father is a financier in Chicago. She is an heiress, quite wealthy in her own right. One of the girls, a Miss Tillett, is related to her, a second cousin I believe. Miss Rankin invited her and her friend to accompany her. It was a very gracious gesture and I'm sure she didn't know what she was letting herself in for."

"Troublesome, are they?" Dora Hidel inquired with a glint of interest.

"Wild and badly behaved, Miss Johnston in particular. She cavorts around with no discretion whatsoever. The girl is only nineteen and she has more swains than I have had hot dinners."

"Typical spoiled young girls that people have always made a fuss of," Dora affirmed.

"Given everything she wants—says and does what she pleases. Miss Tillett at least is capable of polite conversation, but the other one—simply tosses her head with a 'how do you do' and then ignores your presence as if you weren't there."

"I will no doubt meet them on Sunday. Miss Rankin in particular."

"Yes." Jack's reply was brief and at the mention of Darcy's name a concealing mask of indifference swept over his long face, a change of expression which his mother marked with interest.

Comte du Favre returned early from Compiegne and Leita found that she was pleased to have his quiet company in the almost deserted house. Darcy had sent a note to Jack Hidel the evening of their return and Jack called the next morning and took her off for a drive. She was in high spirits when she returned and surprised Leita. Darcy wasn't usually so communicative.

"Mr. Hidel's mother arrived while we were gone and

I met her. Jack took me to his apartment for lunch. What a dear, sweet little old lady she is."

"Is she really?" Leita's lack of interest was marked but Darcy continued.

"He is so good to her. She told me when we were alone that she doesn't know what she would have done without him all these years while she was widowed. I think that says a great deal about his character, don't you?"

Leita made a noncommittal sound of agreement and Darcy swept on in her enthusiasm. In truth Darcy felt it boded well that Jack had presented her to his parent alone without waiting for a group occasion. Tortoise-like he may be, but things were moving inexorably in the right direction.

The afternoon before Sir Charles and Lady Hidel were due to return from Compiegne Darcy sat alone in the drawing room working at her needlepoint frame. Leita was out with Comte du Favre. He had suggested that they picnic in the Bois de Boulogne and Leita had fallen in with his suggestion with enthusiasm. The cook had packed a hamper with paté and little rolls and cold fowl and Leita, armed with her sketchbook, had set off happily with Armand. They had politely inquired if Darcy would care to join them but she had declined with a smile. Leita realized she was waiting for Jack to drop in and was relieved that there was no necessity to press her further.

When the footman brought mail in on the silver salver Darcy put down her needle and flipped through it idly. Her winging black brows drew together in a frown as she saw the letter addressed to Miss Leita Johnston, in a bold, firm hand that was unfamiliar to Darcy. She turned the envelope over and drew in her breath in surprise. B. F. Pinchon, Esq., the script was flowing but starkly legible.

Darcy pushed the needlepoint frame aside and rose. She stood by a window and tapped the corner of the envelope with a fingernail while she reflected. This was unexpected. She hadn't once heard Leita mention Pinchon. She glanced at her tiny sewing scissors. It would only take a moment to slit open the envelope and satisfy her curiosity. She decided against this, not out of scruple but from a reluctance to know the contents, to be even more involved than she was. She debated for a moment as to whether or not it would be wise simply to leave the letter for Leita. After all, Stephen de Jean couldn't hold her responsible for the delivery of the mail. But he would, she knew full well. For her part she cared not a penny whether Leita married Stephen or Breve or a hottentot for that matter. Something within her said that her anticipation of Jack Hidel's proposal was going to be fulfilled, and Hugo Wenzler was a distant figure now. Her selection of Hugo Wenzler as a future husband and protector had been conceived in cold blood. Jack Hidel was a different matter. His timidity, his diffidence appealed to her. Stiff and cold though he was, her instinct told her that he was a very vulnerable man. She felt a tenderness for him, arising partly perhaps from her childless state and partly from the pity that the strong occasionally feel for the weak, but her emotions were aroused and her whole being was occupied with her determined dream of becoming his wife. *And* I am something of a snob, she conceded to herself with a smile. It will be very pleasant to visit Chicago as the wife of the heir to an English title.

But she frowned again at the remembrance of Stephen's icy anger the night of the party in Fort Wayne. She well knew his capacity for malevolence and Stephen would not take it kindly if this letter from Breve contained something that prejudiced his own plans—in any way. He was quite capable of some underhanded trick, a piece of discrediting gossip perhaps, that would alienate Jack, or at any rate put an end to her hopes. She tapped the letter again, and then moved swiftly, out the door and up the stairway to her suite. Undecided, she looked around her boudoir. Not the jewel box—too small. Then she opened the carved doors of the armoire, pulled down one of the many hatboxes resting on the shelf, opened it and thrust the letter down between the layered tissue paper and the side of the box. She replaced the lid, tied the cord and thrust it back onto the shelf. There was a tap at the door to which she called out a cool "come in." The maid informed her that Mr. Hidel was awaiting her pleasure in the drawing room. Darcy restrained her smile of pleasure, thanked the girl, and going to the mirror pinched her cheeks severely and applied pomade to her lips before she descended to greet the man she was certain would change her life.

Chapter 15

"MY DEAR, I KNOW IT WAS SHE. ONE COULDN'T MISTAKE those eyes," the Duchess de Versigny shrilled.

"But she never goes out, simply never. It has been years since anyone but her servants glimpsed her," Lady Hidel maintained.

"I tell you, it was she. She came out through the front doors, mind you there was a servant on either side of her, and down the steps and into the carriage. She was draped, nearly suffocated really, in a black lace mantilla, but those eyes and the line of her profile were unmistakable. It was the Countess de Castiglioni."

"But why a servant on either side, as if she were infirm? She's not that old, though she must be very close to fifty now," the Princess Metternich questioned.

"Still, she might be in poor health, living as she does. It isn't wholesome, never to see the light of day or take any exercise in the fresh air," the Duchess de Versigny offered.

"Who in the world are you speaking of?" the Princess Clothilde asked peevishly.

The little cluster of ladies were part of a crowd of two hundred massed in a long gallery that ran into the Imperial dining room. The gallery was furnished with straight-legged pier tables and square armchairs, all of which were occupied as their guests awaited the entry of the Emperor and Empress.

It was the Princess Metternich who responded to Princess Clothilde's question. "We are speaking of the Countess de Castiglioni, my dear. A lady whom you have never seen and in all probability never will. She caused quite a stir here shortly after your husband's cousin became Emperor. She was without doubt the most beautiful woman I have ever seen."

"And you were the only woman in the court who didn't detest her on sight," Lady Hidel injected.

"Beauty never disturbs me, Annette. It is an advantage to have the face of a merry little monkey, one can't be envious of something that one could never aspire to. No, I didn't detest her but I found her extremely irritating. A more stupid woman couldn't be found and she was completely mute in the company of females."

"Why was that?" Leita inquired, interested in this little history.

"She disliked them, if one can attribute enough intelligence to her to support the emotion of dislike, which I doubt. It was probably the case that she saw no opportunity of gain from any female and she ignored all of us with an empty stare that would have done credit to a cow."

"The only spark of interest she ever betrayed was when she found a mirror. She would quite literally gaze at her reflection for minutes on, until someone came between her and the glass and then she made no attempt to conceal her vexation," the Duchess de Versigny added.

"You forgot the interest she displayed where the Emperor was concerned," Lady Hidel laughed.

"But of course, she was sent here for precisely that purpose, but Cavour was a fool. The Emperor has always been notoriously susceptible to even a pretty face, let alone a beauty, but none of his petite amours could ever have the slightest political influence on him. As far as Napoleon is concerned, women are for one thing only." Princess Metternich wrinkled her flat little nose.

"Except for the Empress," Lady Hidel murmured.

"Oh, granted, but then Eugenie was and is a different cup of tea altogether," Princess Metternich agreed.

"The Countess de Castiglioni's star might not have waned so quickly if she hadn't deliberately antagonized Eugenie," the Duchess de Versigny offered.

"You mean the affair of the coiffure, of course," Lady Hidel amended.

"That and the Aphrodite costume."

Leita was puzzled. "How did she antagonize the Empress with a coiffure?" she inquired.

"Oh, my dear," the Duchess began with relish, "it was a very important ball and the Countess harangued and threatened and cajoled poor Felix, the Empress's hairdresser, to coiffe her tresses in the same style the Empress was to wear."

"An example of her stupidity," Princess Metternich said with a grimace of disgust.

"Finally he did, because at that time the Emperor's carriage was often seen outside her hotel, waiting the whole night through and Felix didn't care to offend the current favorite. Her arrogance was beyond belief. I am sure she thought of herself as another Pompadour, ensconced in the protection of the Emperor from thenceforth, and there she made a ridiculous mistake. Constancy in such things is no part of his makeup. He simply took what she made so readily available and was just as quickly bored as he was inflamed."

"She would have bored a fence-post, let alone Napoleon." It was the Princess Metternich again.

"Quite right," the Duchess laughed, "and when the Countess made her entrance into the ballroom, flaunting the coiffure and no doubt expecting that the party would be amused at Eugenie's expense, she found her conceited little plot was the final die cast against her in the Empress's esteem—though she had never esteemed her, she had simply tolerated her. Do you remember that evening?" she turned to Lady Hidel who replied, "To this day."

"The Emperor ignored her completely," the Duchess chuckled.

"And no one but that wretched little gossip, Viel-Castel, even approached her," Lady Hidel added.

"She finally left, in utter disfavor."

"It was worse than the costume debacle."

"And that was a riveting scandal," the Duchess continued. "She came as Aphrodite. It was shortly after she arrived in Paris and her measure hadn't yet been taken. And oh, my dears, you should have seen her! Absolutely nude under the sheerest gauze—and there were hearts appliqued on the gauze. One on each nipple, if you can credit that, and another in an even more intimate spot. Everyone was aghast, simply aghast! She might as well have come straight from her bath. Of course the men were all stupefied, staring at her like so many oxen. There was this beautiful creature with every line of her body exposed, and as blasé about it as if she were bundled up in sackcloth."

"The Empress you know is quite religious and has strong feelings about modesty, and there was this creature in a costume that not even a Variétés actress would have appeared in at the time," Lady Hidel explained to Leita.

"She was asked to leave, and received a sharp note the next day from the Empress which didn't seem to discompose her in the least, although she never appeared in the nude again."

"She had accomplished her purpose. Every man in the court was salivating after her."

"But why will I never see her?" Princess Clothilde's harsh little voice was querulous.

"Because she is in hiding, Clothilde. She went into hiding with her first wrinkle. It is said that there are no mirrors in her chambers, none at all. She simply cannot bear the loss of her beauty and she never comes out—has no contact with anyone. She has imprisoned herself out of vanity."

"How dreadful," Leita murmured.

"How merciful really. She has spared us all her onerous presence. And this was a woman who had her huge bed made up with black satin sheets."

"Black sheets? What on earth for?" Princess Clothilde was truly bewildered now.

"Because she thought the black satin made her skin appear all the whiter. She was her own obsession."

Leita was occupied with the image of a nude woman reclining on black satin sheets when she noticed that silence had fallen in the long gallery. Two palace officials were moving from one group to another and the guests began to file toward a door, the gentlemen separating from the ladies with each forming a separate line. Even the whispering ceased as they waited. Then the double doors swung open and the Emperor entered, the grand ribbon making a bold red diagonal across his chest. The Chamberlain Adjutant, M. de Combelot, minced along behind him. The Emperor halted at the head of the line and fingered his long moustaches as he spoke a few words to the Count de Morny. Then he moved on down the line, speaking a few words softly to each one. Bankers, financiers, an author or two, the famous artists Meissonier and Cabanal, Cabinet ministers, all the members of the

"Interior Court" which comprised the twenty or so individuals with permanent apartments at St. Cloud, stood in line to be greeted by this stooped little man with gray skin and secretive eyes.

Meanwhile the Empress had entered with Madame de Llorentz in attendance. Ever the leader in fashion, Eugenie was dressed in nile-green silk, overlaid with paler silk gauze. Four strands of pears so large they were globelike rested on Eugenie's powdered white bosom. She progressed with short steps down the file of the ladies, two or three of whom were presented by Mme. de Llorentz. The loudest sound to be heard was the swish and rustle of the billowing crinolines as their owners curtseyed deeply, each in her turn.

Leita marveled for a moment at the ease of her timing. She reached the end of the file at the same moment as the Emperor and each crossed over to the opposite row, where the same procedure was repeated. It was a very long time to stand in hushed silence and Leita felt like breaking into a run when the ceremony finally ended in a rush of resumed conversations and laughter. The Palace Adjutant General announced that dinner was served and two footmen in brown velvet surcoats and black knee breeches opened the gilded doors of the dining room.

Louis Napoleon and Eugenie put an end to the milling disorder by taking up a position, side by side, and a procession formed behind them. Armand appeared at Leita's side and offered his arm with a smile. The procession was a grand one and took no little time. The couples were widely spaced, with each allowing room for the lengthy, flowing train of the lady ahead. These avalanches of lace and satin trailed over the deep, turkey red carpeting and the scent of patchouli and essence of violet filled the air. As they entered the dining room a military band concealed in an adjoining gallery commenced a fanfare of trumpets. The gentlemen wore the formal knee breeches and white silk stockings required for a court-dinner and the procession was such a majestic one that Leita felt a glow of excitement and wonder.

The white cloth was punctuated with silver discs, polished so highly that they glared in the light of the six chandeliers that overhung the table. Silver epergnes, mounded with hothouse peaches and grapes, were interspersed with vases of flowers and smaller epergnes piled with preserves. The Empress released her husband's arm and took her place in the center of the table. Napoleon ambled around and seated himself directly across from her. Then the others broke ranks and chose their seats. Leita found herself beside the elegantly mustachioed Duc de Gramont-Caderousse. His longtime mistress, though she was not stingy with her attentions to others, Madame de Persigny seated herself a little further down. At least I won't be bored, Leita thought. The Duc was a famous boulevardier, witty in conversation, and ever ready with a gallant gesture. She foresaw correctly. All through the courses—thick asparagus soup, Rhine carp a la Chambord, guinea hen in jelly, right down to the brandied fruit and soft, ripe cheese—she was kept entertained, laughing and marveling at his tales of his sojourn in Mexico and his artfully innocent questions about life in that "tiny little country" she called home. She looked up several times to see Jack Hidel's eyes fixed on her in a fishy gaze, no doubt disapproving, she thought. Darcy had remained at home, unable to attend because of a severe headache.

When the dinner finally ended, the ushers and footmen were ranged against the walls and the procession formed again with the military band playing full force as the not-too-sober group promenaded out of the dining room. Then a very gay fluttering about began as the ladies scurried upstairs to change into their costumes for the ball. The chambers were crowded with harassed maidservants, brought along for the evening, and their mistresses, stepping out of crinolines and casting them aside, searching for this ribbon, that bow, requesting a hairbrush in peremptory tones. Finally the last domino was in place and the doors in the upstairs hall banged opened and shut amid squeals of laughter as the Minervas and Athenas, the fairy princesses and shepherdesses thronged toward the grand ballroom where the music had begun and footmen in gold and green livery glided around with trays of punch and champagne.

It was just after midnight when Leita sat down abruptly. "I simply must rest for a moment," she laughed, and accepted a proffered handkerchief and dabbed at her sweat-glistened forehead. She had been dancing forever, it seemed, and she quenched her thirst with another glass of champagne. She had lost count of them as the evening wore on and it seemed that the trays of lemonade were never near when she stopped dancing for a moment. The champagne prickled pleasingly on her palate and Georges Rivet, a young grenadier in the Imperial Guard, plucked a dish of burnt almonds from a passing tray and placed it in her lap. Leita nibbled at a handful of them and looked up at the long gallery. Though the ballroom was crowded the gallery was alive with onlookers who had taken seats there for a better view of the colorful crowd below. The bare shoulders and backs of the women, their flowing hair and chignons decked with rosebuds and diamonds, and the colorful costumes of those who had chosen to dress made a glorious, shimmering display. Leita had been apprehensive about her costume but now looked down at her flowing, pleated dress with satisfaction.

Trying it on at Felix Worth's she had declared she could not, would not, appear in public wearing only this, but Felix had assured her that it was not only gorgeously suited to her, but she would find herself dressed as modestly as anyone there.

"Diana the huntress, chaste and fair," he had declaimed and adjusted the drape of gleaming white silk, banded in gold thread woven into a Greek key design. She had been persuaded.

Descending the stairway to the ballroom she had felt bereft and nude without her crinoline. The sweeping draperies of the classic toga Felix Worth had designed for her molded the flowing lines of her hips, clinging softly to them and falling to the floor in a multitude of pleats. Her breasts were covered, but the sleek material outlined them so faithfully that their generous curves were even more enticing. The material, draped in a cross over her breasts, slid over either shoulder and fell to a low pointed V in back, bordered on its outer and inner edge with the Greek key design. Her hair was swept back and caught in a gold net and the bow she carried in emulation of the goddess was heavily gilded. It is marvelously comfortable, she thought, looking down at the outline of her thighs which had always been covered with the bell-like crinolines and layer upon layer of petticoats. Comfortable wasn't precisely the adjective her partners would have applied to the graceful, flowing draperies. With the lush outlines of her body revealed and yet concealed, she had been the object of many a lustful stare.

Jack Hidel stood a few feet away and slightly behind the chair where Leita sat. Fond of brandy, he was sipping at yet another glass, rolling the sweet, burning liquid around in his mouth as he stared at the line of Leita's throat while she laughed and bantered with the grenadier. Jack was swaying slightly, his cheeks were flushed and his fingers felt stumpy and thick. He had been indulging his taste for the brandy since the beginning of the evening and the blood was pounding in his temples as he supported himself with the back of a chair. His eyes never left Leita and they grew more fixed when she stood up. The heat had cleaved the silk to her buttocks and they were outlined in all their firm, yielding fullness. The phlegm rose in his throat and his fingers gripped the glass tightly. He downed the rest of the brandy at one swallow and took another from a hovering footman. The skin of Leita's bare back shone pink and white and there was a mole just above the slight dip that curved into the small of her back. She was laughing again. Doesn't she ever stop laughing, he thought. The bile of envy coursed along in his racing blood. But never laughing up at me like that. Shallow, silly bitch! She leaned over to gather up another handful of almonds and one drape fell aside, exposing the white heaviness of one breast. He swallowed, the turgid weight in his groin grew heavier as it passed down into his throbbing organ. So that empty-headed little slut is going to waltz with the Emperor! Louis Napoleon had presented himself with a bow and Leita stretched out one bare arm in a gesture of happy acquiescence. She felt warmly toward the whole world tonight and shyly pleased that the Emperor had sought her out. Jack's brows drew together and a cynical little laugh passed his long, narrow lips. That disgusting old devil will have her skirts over her head before the night is over, he thought. Streams of light flowed over Leita's bare arms and Jack treated himself to another brandy as he pictured Louis Napoleon astride a recumbent panting Leita.

After the dance with the Emperor Leita felt parched. Georges had wandered off to fulfill her request for lemonade and she drank two more glasses of the deliciously cool, iced champagne while she waited for him. The burnt almonds, which she adored, had intensified her thirst. She was feeling gloriously giddy and in a mood to embrace the whole world when a touch on her arm made her turn.

"I am a very awkward dancer, but I would appreciate the honor." Jack, rendered almost spontaneous by the brandy, bowed a trifle unsteadily.

Leita, who felt incapable of disliking anyone this evening, offered her hand and they had covered half the length of the floor when she stopped and almost laid her head on Hidel's arm.

"I am so dreadfully dizzy," she giggled. "I am sure it's all the champagne I've drunk. It's the heat, you know." .

Jack smiled tolerantly. "I know what you need. The fruit punch. Nothing like fruit juice when champagne has affected you. Now you just sit down right here and I'll return in a moment."

He commandeered a footman and received the punch, but moved into a window embrasure for a moment before returning to Leita.

She drank it thirstily, savoring its tart sweetness and smiled gratefully at him.

"Better?" he inquired, his tone kindly.

"Marvelously better. Let's see if I'm still dizzy." She felt remiss at having disliked him so much. He was almost human this evening, so talkative and bright-eyed. His eyes, always hooded except when staring, were brilliant, and dancing with light. Leita noticed it and attributed it to the effect of pleasure. She had no way of knowing that this fleeting brilliance was due to his use of ether as a narcotic. The habit was not unknown to her but she would never have attributed it to this dry and correct man. Its effects became doubly potent in conjunction with alcohol and was a pleasure

237

that Jack often availed himself of. He was usually equipped with two or three tiny silver vials, one containing ether, and he had not come unarmed tonight.

Leita was chattering away, asking him questions about England, when she suddenly felt more than dizzy. The room was whirling and her ears rang. She felt as if her head was going to fall off her shoulders.

"Oh dear," she murmured. "I feel ill, ill and very sleepy all of a sudden. Oh why did I drink all that?"

"Simply because you were thirsty. It can happen very easily," he said cheerfully and led her off the floor. She sagged against him for a moment and he held her upright. The other figures were blurred and hazy, and she went unresisting, supported by his arm, as he led her down a gallery. The noise of the ballroom faded away when he closed the door of the small anteroom and still clinging to him, she saw the couch which seemed to be floating somewhere against the wall. She groped toward it, sleep—to lie down was all she wanted, and she sank into the downy cushions, completely overcome by the three drops of laudanum that Jack had added to the punch she had drunk so gratefully.

He hadn't formulated a plan. In fact, his imagination had always drawn Leita vividly, aggressively awake. Leita nude, and groveling before him—Leita panting with passion, begging him to take her—Leita, gasping with lust as she clutched at him, imploring him to grant the basest, lewdest desires.

Now the blood was pounding in his temples. She lay on the couch, breathing heavily and deeply, her eyes closed and one arm dangling limply to the floor. He stalked back and forth in front of the couch and then stopped. One hand reached out and very tentatively touched the silk over her thigh. The heat of her flesh seemed to surge into his palm and he crouched beside her. The dress had been cut so that it was split from the waist to the floor, with two panels covering the split for ease of movement. Suddenly his hands were groping feverishly in the folds and he flung the panels open, exposing her hips and legs which were covered only by a lacy chemise. He glanced quickly at her face; it was still and pale. Then his eyes darted to the door, and all around the room, as if he expected to find someone seated in the shadows, and his hands moved over her bare thighs and up over her hips, all the while his eyes, brilliant and staring, rested on the lace covered mound below her abdomen. The phlegm in his throat was almost choking him as his hand pulled at the drape over her breast. There, one white breast, marked with faint blue veins, emerged. The nipple, pink as a flower, puckered under his fingers and his hand became rough as he stroked and clutched at the soft, creamy mound. His face lunged into her breast and his mouth engulfed the nipple, pulling and sucking on it while his other hand fumbled at her opposite breast. Uncovering it finally, he raised his hand. One nipple was puckered and shone damp with his saliva. The other was smooth and soft and he moved his head, extending his tongue, licking at the deep cleft and then moving over the white skin, sucking at the soft flesh, tracing the course of every vein until he reached the nipple. He licked at it, panting, until it peaked, and then he fell to gnawing on it, all the while his free hand grasped the huge bulge between his own legs. He suddenly straightened out and clutched at the top of his breeches, tearing them open. He stared down, breathing heavily, at the long, swollen shaft that arced out from his body. He thrust his hips forward, stroking himself tenderly, then grasped Leita's limp hand and curled her small fingers around the veined redness of his organ. His mouth was

239

open, his tongue flat and protruding slightly as he held her hand tightly moving it back and forth. He pressed her fingers hard against the base of his shaft, then cupped her unresisting hand over the throbbing, em-purpled end. Dropping her hand suddenly he leaped astride her and his hips lunged as he pressed his member into her nipple. The sound of music, dim and faint, pulsed in the air but the drumming in his ears drowned out everything else as he stood up quickly and, crouching at her feet, began to tear at the lace of her chemise. It was delicate and gave easily and his fingers worked convulsively through the soft red-gold hairs between her legs. He had no thought but to violate her most private parts, to degrade her for arousing his lust and then ignoring him. His brows were drawn together and he was smiling as he pressed her thighs, spreading them wide apart as he stared at her. Good, he thought, without the brandy I would have been finished by now. This is what should happen to all shallow little flirts. He pressed into her. Even with the brandy and Leita unconscious and unresisting he was frightened. Only once before in his life had he entered a female in the conventional way and it had been disastrous. A young servant had lain with him in order to make her way in the world and had covered him with scorn for his inept fearfulness. But now he managed to penetrate the opening and gasped as the soft wetness enfolded him. He began to whimper and his buttocks twitched as he pressed deeper, his features grimacing as if he were in pain. It was only a second until his whimpering reached a shrill crescendo as he lunged into her and then fell back. His head was clearing when he finally rose and he exhaled deeply, the breath puffing out his cheeks. The light in his eyes was one of malicious triumph and his mouth twisted in a smile that was almost gleeful. He took out a handkerchief and dabbed at himself, then scrubbed vigorously and examined the handkerchief. The smile had become a sneer.

"Not one drop of blood!" he whispered. "Not so much as a tinge of pink. I knew she was a slut." Leita gave a soft little moan in her sleep and he looked down at her and the sneer broadened. He had had her! And he had known all along what she was. He was in a trance of conceit and tossed the handkerchief onto the couch as he began to close his breeches. He hadn't heard the door open.

Sir Charles Hidel was standing in the doorway. The light was dim in the small anteroom and he narrowed his eyes, as they swept over Leita's recumbent body, her naked breasts, her bare legs gaping wide apart, the torn lace which exposed the mound of Venus, the dress pulled aside and sweeping the floor, with one drape fallen over her dangling arm. Jack stood in profile, his eyes glazed in a trance of conceit and a sneer contorting his face as he dabbed at his member dangling out of his gaping breeches. Sir Charles was stupefied for the moment and then his face paled to an icy white and the few little wrinkles around his mouth deepened as the enormity of what he was witnessing came home to him. His dress sword clanked against the door when he stepped forward crying "Sir!" in a loud, firm tone.

Jack started wildly and the glaze disappeared from his eyes when he saw his uncle. He turned, running toward a window, then wheeled and ran to the left. The relief he felt when the knob turned freely in his hand ran in a shivering wave of weakness through his whole body and he bounded through the door and slammed it behind him.

Sir Charles stopped and ran to Leita. "Oh, dear God, what has taken place here!" he cried aloud. He put his hand on her throat and another on her wrist.

The pulses were pounding sluggishly. He released a quivering sigh. The fear that she was dead, an unreasoning one, but borne of her supine posture and pale cheeks, left him and his jaw set with one muscle quivering as he covered her legs and drew the folds of her drapery over her breasts quickly. He looked around frantically for something to cover her with; nothing in sight but small cushions. He ran then to the doorway and back down the long gallery to the ballroom. Where oh where was Annette? Then he sighted her. She was talking with Princess Mathilde and Prince Napoleon. He tried to control his haste and put his arm on her shoulders as he reached her.

"Would you excuse me please. I would like to monopolize my wife for a moment," he spoke smilingly and hoped that the trembling in his arm wasn't apparent.

"I've always thought you an unusual man, Sir Charles, and now my opinion is verified. Imagine a man who seeks to monopolize his wife! You are in a class with the unicorns," Princess Mathilde laughed.

"Run along with her, you lunatic," Prince Napoleon rumbled. 'His dark hair had fallen down over his forehead and his eyes were bloodshot. "We were just arranging an assignation but I can take it up later." He laughed uproariously at his own joke and the ghost of a smile creased Sir Charles's face as he led Annette away.

"What has happened, Charles?" Lady Hidel asked quietly, nodding to one and another of the guests as he propelled her across the room. At the sight of his face she had known at once that something was wrong.

"In a moment," he said, waving affably at the Duc de Persigny who was beckoning to them. Earlier Sir Charles had been seated in the gallery watching the colorful crowd below. He had noticed Leita and Jack dancing, and had just glanced back at them when Leita

242

sagged against Jack. He had watched, faintly puzzled as Jack helped her through the open door of the gallery and then disappeared. Every few moments his gaze had traveled back to the doorway and when the couple didn't emerge he became faintly uneasy. Finally he excused himself. Perhaps she is ill, he thought. That fool wouldn't know what to do if she were. He had walked down the gallery. The doors of two rooms along its length were ajar, but empty. The third door was closed and he had opened it without knocking, something he wouldn't ordinarily have done but his disquiet had increased in the silence of the gallery. The scene that met his eyes then had stricken him with astonishment long enough for Jack to make his escape. Now his only thought was of Leita. He propelled Annette down the gallery, describing in a whisper the scene he had come upon a few minutes earlier. She quickened her footsteps and they were both breathless with haste when they entered the room. Sir Charles closed and bolted the door firmly behind them.

"Oh mon Dieu, mon Dieu!" she gasped. Leita lay unmoving and pale in the same position Sir Charles had left her.

"Not as bad as it was when I saw her, Annette. Her legs were spread, and bared, her breast bared, as I told you. She looked as if she had been tossed from a cliff."

Annette was bending over Leita, stroking her cheek. She sniffed at the warm breath coming from her mouth, stopped, closed her eyes, and sniffed again.

"Charles, she has been drugged! Come here! Smell this!"

He did as she commanded. It was a heavy, slightly sweet scent that mingled with the ranker scent of champagne.

"It was poppy juice! Don't you remember, when the babies were small? The nurse gave it to them for teething and I caught her at it because they slept so soundly and their breath had that fetid, sweetish odor."

Sir Charles searched his mind for a moment. He had been watching Jack on his trip to get the punch and had seen him step into the window embrasure, which had seemed a little odd at the time. He was well aware that his nephew was addicted to both ether and laudanum.

"He gave it to her, and I know when he did it." His jaw clenched again.

"Now we must get her out of here, and that without stirring up any talk," Annette said decisively. Run and get Giselle, she will be upstairs with the other maids. Ask her to come—no, that will not do! Ask her for my cloak. Tell her she is to come home with Mary Jo, but we are leaving now. We will have to carry her. There is a terrace outside. Can we carry her to the carriage from here?"

Sir Charles was gently lifting Leita's eyelids. Her pupils were dilated and there was not a flicker to show she might be close to awakening.

"It will be awkward, but we can do it. Those windows open onto the terrace you know. I will have the coachman bring the carriage to the back of the drive. We'll manage."

He had almost reached the doorway when Annette called. "But what about Armand? What is he to be told?"

Sir Charles hesitated a moment and his fingers stroked his slightly receding chin. "He can help. Tell him that someone must have slipped the laudanum into Leita's champagne for a joke. We don't know who. He needn't be told the rest."

She nodded in agreement and he sped on his way, more composed now that Annette's decisive strength was there to support his.

244

Sir Charles retrieved Leita's cloak as well as Annette's, pried the Comte du Favre away from his game of Piquet and carried him along to the anteroom, all the while giving him an abridged version of what had happened.

Armand's gentle features had contracted with apprehension and distaste during Sir Charles' recital and when he saw Leita's limp figure he clucked his tongue sorrowfully.

"I suppose one of the debauchees that surround this court thought it a very funny joke to drug this naive young visitor," he said, his features creased with pity.

Sir Charles was opening one of the windows which almost reached the floor, and he glanced quickly at Annette who caught his eye.

"Whoever did it is not going to get the satisfaction of knowing the outcome—they will not see her carried out of here an ignominious little heap," Annette declared sharply. Armand helped her wrap Leita in the cloak.

"The night is chill, and will be cooler still as we travel through the Bois," he said simply, gathering the cloak closely around Leita. Sir Charles moved to help him as he lifted the inert figure but he shook his head. "I have her very securely," he averred, her cheek resting comfortably against the soft velour of his shoulder.

The coachman who held the carriage door open took great pains to conceal his curiosity as Armand bent over and laid Leita across the seat, then stepped in and raised her shoulders to rest against his chest. The ride took place in almost complete silence. Annette and Charles, constrained by their concealment of the real events, could think of no comment unrelated to their nephew and Armand was pensive, holding Leita who was still in deep slumber wrapped warmly in the velvet cloak.

Annette took charge of Leita as soon as Armand set

her on the bed of her boudoir, removing the costume and dressing her in a dimity gown. Sir Charles ordered coffee from the footman who had stayed up until their return and he and Armand drank it in the sitting room of Leita's suite. Armand finally took his leave and Sir Charles repaired to his own suite. When he emerged a few moments later he was dressed in a dark frock coat and trousers and a light cape swung over his arm.

"But you have changed! Where are you off to?" Annette inquired in alarm. She had sent the footman for the doctor and Leita had begun to stir now and then.

The bridge of Sir Charles's narrow, slightly curving nose shone white and his cheeks were mottled with red patches.

"I am going after him, and you are not to be fearful or concern yourself with anything but this poor young girl," Sir Charles said steadily.

"But my dear, how can I be anything but fearful?" Annette's eyes rested anxiously on her husband's face, the pallor behind the splotches of red and the sharp, knifelike brilliance of his gray eyes.

"I don't think I have ever seen you so angry," she said softly.

"I know that you haven't, and I doubt that you ever will again. I'm not going to kill him, but at this moment I would like nothing better."

"But what can you do? We cannot bring charges of any sort against him. This young girl would be disgraced."

"I know what must be done to end this charade once and for all. I will tell you when I get back." He looked at the floor for a moment, then embraced her quickly and left.

Chapter 16

A FINE SHARP RAIN WAS FALLING ·WHEN SIR CHARLES
stepped into the carriage and gave the coachman an
address in Montmartre. The coachman pulled up his
collar and flicked the horses and gave a low whistle
through his teeth. He had never before taken his
master to a brothel! He and Madame must have had a
splendid quarrel, an unprecedented one, for Sir Charles
to go bowling off to a brothel at two o'clock in the
morning—with fire in his eye, too. He chuckled softly.
What a choice morsel for Giselle. She would be aghast;
she fairly worshipped the man. He pursed his lips as the
carriage took a corner. She might well not believe it,
but what a pleasure to tell her that Sir Charles was only
flesh and blood, as other men. Her tirade of abuse and
scorn when she had found him thrusting his hand up the
skirt of that plump little parlor maid might seem a little
foolish to her now.

He opened the carriage door, prepared for a cozy
glass in a hospitable kitchen while he awaited his

master's pleasure. But his expectation of leisure was short-lived.

"Francois, you are quite a strong fellow, aren't you?" Sir Charles was giving him a level look and Francois, taken aback, could only answer, "I can take care of myself, I fancy, Sir."

"Good. Now what I want you to do is very simple. There is a back entrance, as there is to all such establishments. I want you to station yourself there and if, while I am inside, a gentleman should attempt to leave by that entrance, I want you to detain him—forcibly."

"A gentleman, Sir?" Francois was fighting confusion.

"One gentleman in particular, Francois. You are acquainted with my nephew, Mr. Hidel, are you not?"

"I am, of course, Sir."

"That is the gentleman I wish you to detain. We are out on a bad business, Francois. Now I will wait here a moment while you station yourself at the point I spoke of."

Francois took himself down the narrow alley between the outer wall of the building and a high fence. Yellow light cut narrow streaks between the curtains of the windows above him and the sound of music and laughter, muted by the heavy draperies and glass, wafted softly out. Tiens, what a night! he thought, and pulled the wide brim of his hat down as protection from the gust of rain-filled wind that hurtled round the corner of the house. He stood obediently by the back entrance. What kind of bad business? Perplexity wrinkled his every feature. That long-legged milksop of a nephew was surely old enough to visit a whore without his uncle searching him out. The fellow was forty if he was a day. He was acquainted with Jack's coachman and one of their standing jokes was Jack's transparent little ruse of using a hired hack when he visited the

248

bordellos. The coachman was well acquainted with the hack drivers and the cafes they frequented resounded to many a hearty laugh over the peccadilloes of those who rode behind them on plush seats.

Francois hadn't long to wait. Sir Charles beckoned to him from the corner of the house and jumped into the carriage without waiting.

"Not there, Francois," and he gave another address in the same district.

Three more times Francois was deployed to a back entrance, only to become wetter and more curious, if that were possible.

The cobblestones glistened, dark gray and shining in the yellow beams from the carriage lights and the sky was beginning to turn a leaden color just at the rooftops. They passed the La Rochefoucald Market where draymen swore and called out to one another as they backed their carts to be unloaded. The smell of cabbages and onions and the dank rich odor of fresh earth filled the night air. La Rochefoucald Market was patronized by all the prostitutes in the area and tomorrow at eleven would be aswarm with tired, sleepy-eyed women, haggling over the vegetables for a *pot-au-feu*.

From the time Jack reached his majority, as well as before, Sir Charles had kept himself informed of his pastimes, and the manner in which he satisfied his appetites. Due to this surveillance, he knew for a fact that Jack patronized the houses he had just visited and was confident of finding him. He was equally certain that he wouldn't have returned to his apartment. Just why he couldn't have said; it was an intuitive assumption. When he entered Madame Charbonnel's she swept into the hall and greeted him with both hands extended. She knew him, of course, it was her business to know everyone, also her business never to show surprise, though she certainly felt it now. He had never even kept a mistress, she knew, never dallied with an actress or one of the elegant courtesans that adorned the boulevards. Ah, well, sooner or later—.

"Good evening, Madame. I have a request to make in confidence." His speech was terse. The search had not cooled his anger, quite the opposite. It had built to an inferno. The man was in a sizzling rage and she saw it immediately.

"Of course, my Lord," she answered, and gestured to the door on her left. They entered the room and she closed the door carefully behind her.

"And now? You may repose your confidence in me, my Lord. It is my stock-in-trade." She smiled composedly. What in God's name is wrong? The man looks close to murder!

"I am searching for my nephew, a Mr. Jack Hidel, Madame. It is imperative that I find him—immediately. It is also imperative that he not elude me, if you follow my meaning. He is most assuredly not searching for *me*. Is he in this house? And if so, in which room?"

Jesus Christ and all the Saints! she thought, while her face remained smooth and unmoved. A pretty pickle this is!

"When I said you could repose your confidence in me, my Lord, I meant it most sincerely. In all justice I must add that others repose confidence in me, also knowing that it is unbreachable." Her voice was as smooth as vanilla cream and she was prepared to draw this out—she needed time to think—if she could get him back into the hall she could signal to someone.

"Madame, I seek a man who has just committed a ime! A heinous crime!" Sir Charles' lips whitened as e spoke and the muscles in his jaw were twitching so violently that Madame Charbonnel took a short step backward. "I am sure that you will direct me to the man I spoke of, but if you do not—" he paused and his eyes bore into hers, "if you do not I will see the Emperor in the morning, no later, and your place of business will be shuttered and closed by tomorrow afternoon!"

"My Lord, I do not question you or seek to obstruct you. You speak of a crime. I will take you at your word. I do not maintain a sanctuary to harbor criminals." She had raised her hands palm forward and her plump shoulders moved in a shrug. So be it—whatever was afoot here, it was plain she had best comply with this man and see that his errand was completed quietly without upsetting the whole house. Notoriety she feared above all—it could empty her house of clients who would never return. "I will go with you."

They left the room and ascended the stairway, passed down a hall and turned left into another.

"Don't tell me she's taking them on herself now." A perky brunette in an open robe of yellow silk giggled to her companion.

Madame Charbonnel stopped and inclined her head slightly toward the closed door facing them. Sir Charles withdrew his hand from his pocket and pressed three gold Louis into her hand.

"No, M'sieur," she said quietly, handing them back. And walked away.

Jack lay with his face buried in Constanzia's breasts. She had fed him hot soup, undressed him, and held him. He had said nothing, simply writhed now and then as if at some thought too unbearable to contain. What to do? was the refrain that ran through his head. Definitely he would cross the channel tomorrow. Take the morning train to Le Havre. He would go without baggage. The thought of encountering Sir Charles waiting at his apartment ran prickles of terror through him. He would stay in England, perhaps take a trip down to Egypt, and wait for his uncle's anger to cool. No one else would be told what happened, he was certain. He could and would say that Leita had been drunk, had tempted and seduced him with perfect willingness. He had been drunk too. He turned the story over and over in his mind. Perhaps after three months or so, and he could easily stay away that long, his uncle's tolerance would overcome his contempt. Time would dull the whole thing. He burrowed his head deeper into Constanzia's soft breasts. When the door opened he thought it was a servant.

"This room is occupied, M'sieur," Constanzia called out with a giggle. The bed curtains were open and Sir Charles walked with deliberation toward the pair. When Jack raised his head Sir Charles spoke.

"You are to dress immediately. I will stand here while you do it."

Jack leaped up and then made a belated clutch for the sheet. Constanzia sat up, her black curls tumbling over her shoulders and her eyes wide with interest.

"Are you a policeman?" she inquired, more inquisitive than alarmed.

Sir Charles ignored her question and reiterated his command. "Immediately, I said!"

Jack's face froze then into its habitual mask of imperturbability. He drew on his trousers, buttoned his shirt, pulled on his boots, all without a word, and walked to the door.

Sir Charles was shorter than his nephew by perhaps three inches. He had a slender but very agile body, always impeccably dressed. Now he snapped his fingers against the wall of the passageway, staring straight ahead. Jack didn't speak. Sir Charles turned right into the hall leading to the stairway and Jack made an abrupt turn to the left, hunched his shoulders together and ran—ran toward the back of the hall and turned sharply into the stairwell that the servants used. Narrow and poorly lighted, it wound into the hallway beside the kitchen. Sir Charles stood watching after him as he bolted, then followed at a quick trot. The clatter of Jack's boots on the uncarpeted stairs was followed by the sound of a door being thrown open and Jack catapulted into the night. Barrels of refuse and garbage, decorated with a marauding cat hungry enough to endure the rain, rose directly in front of him and he swerved to the side, preparing to scale the fence and drop over to the other side. He shrieked in surprise when a strong arm covered with scratchy wool lashed around his neck, pressing against it hard enough to stop his breath. He kicked wildly backward and flailed with his arms, his jacket falling into the mire.

"Here now, Sir. No point in struggling." Francois was breathless with the effort of holding this lunging, struggling man. "Just you calm down, Sir," he grunted. Francois' youth in the alleys and gutters of Paris had led him to the boxing ring for a short time, and though it was touch and go for a minute, his corded muscles held firm.

Sir Charles' voice, as cold as steel, pierced the darkness. "I will summon the Commissioner of the Paris police without the slightest compunction if you do not come with me—and without another sound." Jack sagged. All right, he would go with the old bastard and let him have his say. He signaled his assent and Francois reluctantly loosened his armlock.

"Where to now, Sir? Back to the house?" Francois inquired in a whisper when they reached the carriage.

Sir Charles paused a moment and seemed to study the cobblestones of the street. "To the Bois, Francois. To the lake in the Bois."

Francois stared. To the Bois? In the rain and dead of night? What an evening this was! Giselle would never believe half of it—for that matter he didn't himself.

"Oh, and thank you, Francois. You rendered good service, just now," Sir Charles added unsmilingly.

Francois nodded, acknowledging it proudly. He had well and truly been taken by surprise. Off in a daydream, he had been, standing there under the needlepoints of the rain, not really expecting anyone to hurtle out that back door. I certainly could use a good bottle of wine about now, he thought, flicking the whip over the horses' backs and setting them off for the long drive to the Bois de Boulogne.

The splat of drops on the carriage roof slowed and then ceased as the carriage bowled along the deserted, dark streets. Sir Charles sat silent and erect, his gloved hand clenched tightly around the gold head of his walking stick. Disgust flooded every pore of his body. The vision of Leita sprawled unconscious on that gilded couch, molested and ravaged by this excrescence sitting across from him glared in his mind's eye. His blood seemed to run chill in his veins, but he kept silent. This interview must be conducted out of the coachman's hearing. What he had to relate had been kept the darkest secret until now and the course he intended to take must be kept in strictest confidence by those involved.

They reached the Bois and the carriage rolled along the chestnut-lined avenue to the Lac Inferieur. The dark cumulus clouds, swept now by an east wind, uncovered a sickly, white half-moon. The waters of the lake riffled and sucked at the reed-lined shore and the leaves of the trees were black-green in the eerie light. Sir Charles bade the coachman wait in the drive and strode purposefully through the wet grass with Jack following languidly behind.

Sir Charles pulled at his upper lip with his teeth and prepared to phrase his message. Jack stood facing him, hands in his pockets, looking at the water. He had not once looked Sir Charles in the face.

When Sir Charles finally spoke, his voice was firm and cool. "To begin with, you are to meet me in London two weeks from now, in the offices of my solicitor, Mr. Hovington-Smythe. You yourself are to leave this day for England and stay there until the meeting."

Jack felt a tinge of relief. At least he would be gone. In two weeks the old fool would be over this maniacal anger.

"I will direct Mr. Hovington-Smythe to have the necessary documents prepared. One of them will concern your surname. From henceforth you are not to use the name of Hidel."

Jack's head came up quickly.

"The second document will state categorically that my title—and all of its accoutrements—will terminate at my death—not to be handed on. I will sign this document and you will sign it as an informed witness."

Jack's voice rose high and derisive. "You know full well you cannot do that! I am legal heir, by right of entail!"

"There is no entail! There is no legal heir and I will sign a deposition to that fact."

"You crazy old fool. You seem to forget you are speaking to your brother's son. My having a toss with that silly girl has sent you demented. Have me arrested if you like. We were both drunk! I didn't even take advantage of her; she offered it! If you think I am going to sign my birthright away because you're soft about a silly young girl—"

Sir Charles' face had gone from ashen white to a mottled, purplish-red. "You foul the very air I breathe. If you were my brother's son I would simply cut you off without a penny. But you are not! You are the spawn of incest, my lad. The slimy spawn of your mother's coupling with her own brother! You are tainted, rotten!"

"How dare you speak such filth of my mother? You're insane." Jack's eyes bulged with the force of his hatred.

"Watch your tongue, you silly fool. The filth was committed long ago. I have kept watch over you since, just as I have kept the secret, hoping fearfully that your vile heritage would not come out."

Jack stood almost crouched, his feet planted wide apart. "Gossip!" he shrieked. "Vile gossip about my mother. Because she wasn't one of the nobility. How dare you defile her name!"

"After all these years you are going to have to untie the apron strings, my lad." Sir Charles' voice was icy with contempt. "As for defiling, it is my name that was defiled, mine and my brother's. You howl for proof, I take it. My own eyes and ears constitute the proof. I myself stood outside the door of Dora's chamber as she entertained Hugh while my brother lay ill. Hugh, your uncle that was always underfoot, who lived on the largesse she meted out to him. The same Hugh who died raving in an asylum. God knows how much other bad blood is in your maternal line, but I tell you this—if you had ever shown inclination to marry I would have dissuaded you. Failing that you would have learned the truth from my lips. I could not prevent your birth, but it *is* in my power to prevent your siring any idiots and imbeciles to cloud the name of Hidel. Bad blood, Sir! Bad blood is what you carry and I intend to see that it stops with you!"

Jack's brain was reeling in a tortuous fog. Hugh, Uncle Hugh! He had hated him as a child, hated and envied him for his mother's slavish devotion to him, her constant praise of him. He was always there—lounging in the drawing room, taking tea with her in her private sitting room. Dark little mean eyes and a swaggering gait and frequent outbursts of temper when young Jack interrupted or managed to gain his mother's attention. He felt dizzy now, images of Dora and Hugh laughing together, fuzzy memories of Uncle Hugh's arm about his mother, and one burning memory—he had been folded in the long curtain of his mother's sitting room, hiding, in wait for her. He had seen them kiss; he had been so young, so very young, but how he remembered the sick envious rage he had felt as he peeked out and witnessed that embrace! Nausea gripped him suddenly and his face contorted.

"Heretofore you have confined yourself to whores. But now, tonight, the flaw in you has come even more to the fore. When you drug and assault a young woman of good family, a guest in my house, the time has come to sever all connection between us. I will accept financial responsibility for you—only because you could not possibly support yourself. After the necessary papers are signed and in the hands of my solicitor you are to remove yourself to Italy. Never again are you to set foot in England or in France, never to contact me again. Turin or Florence will suit very well. However, it matters not—that is one choice that is yours. I will see that a semi-annual check is sent to you."

Jack barely heard. The nausea clutched his entrails and his mind was in a haze of horror. That he was to lose everything he enjoyed, everything he had anticipated from the position of nobility. He would be alone, nameless, with a stipend in some foul Italian town. And his mother, never to see her again! He walked unsteadily toward his uncle, his hand raised.

"I won't sign your lying documents. You wouldn't—you couldn't do this. Your mouth is full of filthy lies! You have always hated me and my mother because I lived and your son didn't!" He shouted and there was a crazed gleam in his eyes.

At the mention of his dead son a spasm of rage swept over Sir Charles. "You rotten swine! You're very good when it comes to overpowering a helpless female but a drooling coward when it comes to facing the truth. You are the bastard son of a lunatic, conceived in a vile, incestuous embrace!"

Jack's raised hand swept inside his coat and the next moment his hand held a revolver. The hand was trembling and the muzzle of the revolver lurched wildly.

"It is the only fitting solution," Sir Charles spoke in a whisper and he drew a revolver from inside his frock coat and there was a sharp, metallic click as he released the safety with deliberation, seeming not at all discomposed by the gun in his nephew's shaking hand.

Jack's eyes fastened on the revolver as he heard his uncle's words and with an almost soundless cry of terror he turned and ran stumbling between the trees, his eyes wide with a frantic dread.

Sir Charles looked at him, watched the stumbling run, the arm still flailing the revolver in the air. Repugnance overcame his features and he raised his pistol, steadying his arm with his other hand as he fired. The shot whistled through the dripping tree branches and felled a narrow limb. He had aimed carefully above his nephew's head.

At the sound of the shot Jack threw himself to the ground, burying his face in the grass and groveling frantically. Hysterical with fear, he didn't hear his uncle's footsteps and rolled over with a cry of pain when the toe of Sir Charles's boot struck him in the side.

"You craven bastard. Get up! Go home and make your preparations to depart."

The sky above the trees was luminous with a smoky light when Sir Charles ordered Francois to drive home. Jack lay cowering on the wet grass and, jaws clenched, tore at it with his fingers. Tiny circles appeared on the water of the lake and grew ever wider as the needle-pointed rain drops began to fall again and a dawn breeze ruffled the dripping leaves.

Chapter 17

PAIN RIPPED THROUGH LEITA'S HEAD AS SHE RAISED IT from the pillow and she sank back. Her throat felt as dry as the desert and thirst consumed her. She opened her eyes and was surprised to see Lady Hidel bent over her.

"I am so very thirsty," she whispered.

"Of course you are," Lady Hidel replied, and filled a glass from the crystal water jug. Leita raised her head again and moaned.

"I have such a dreadful, dreadful headache."

"This should make it better. And I have a powder for you that will help the headache."

Leita drank the water thirstily and beckoned for more. Lady Hidel refilled the glass and Leita emptied it again. Now nausea roiled through her.

"What on earth can be the matter with me?" she asked.

"The champagne made you ill, my dear. It happens sometimes."

Leita's mind reached back hazily to the night before

and she sighed, remembering glass after glass drunk in the heat of the ballroom.

"I remember now. It was so hot, and I danced forever, it seemed, and oh, I drank so much," she groaned.

Lady Hidel smiled as relief flooded her. She remembers nothing of what happened with Jack.

"We brought you home when you became ill, and I really think you should stay abed today."

"I don't want to stay anywhere else." Leita drew a hand over her forehead. It was damp with perspiration and she sat up quickly, gritting her teeth at the stab of pain in her head.

"I'm going to need a basin—right away," she gasped.

Lady Hidel went to the dresser and trotted back with the silver hand basin. She held it while Leita retched convulsively over it and smoothed the girl's damp hair back from her forehead.

"There—that is all to the good," she pronounced as Leita fell back among the pillows.

"Did I make a spectacle of myself at the ball?" Leita asked with some alarm when the maid had come for the basin.

"Not at all." Lady Hidel laughed her tinkling laugh but the memory of Leita's still figure sprawled unconscious cast a quick shadow across her eyes. "You simply became ill and sleepy and we brought you home to bed. You don't remember it, do you?"

"No, I don't. But I do remember feeling very ill and dizzy when I was dancing. I was dancing with Jack Hidel," she said in surprise.

"Yes, it was shortly after that when we left," Lady Hidel said guardedly, casting a quick glance at Leita's face. There was no sign that she was recollecting further.

"As soon as you get over feeling ill I will give you the

powder for your headache. I am also making a special tisane for you." She smiled and nodded her head toward a small gas burner where a kettle of hot water was heating. She had had the burner brought to Leita's room after sending her own personal maid on a mission to an apothecary's shop. Dried roots of mountain hollyhock and a few juniper berries lay at the bottom of a hand-painted china pot, in readiness for the hot water.

"And what is a tisane?" Leita inquired, touched by Lady Hidel's motherly care.

"Tisanes are teas made of herbs. A child in France learns early that one cannot survive without tisanes. They are dosed regularly with the brews—if one is healthy tisanes are drunk to maintain health, and at the first sign of an indisposition a tisane is brewed to restore the victim. Some are nasty, but the ones you shall drink are sweet and good. You have escaped my ministrations thus far, but no more," Lady Hidel laughed.

Her maid Giselle had purchased the roots, wondering philosophically whom they were intended for. Hollyhock root and juniper berries had but one use— that of terminating an unwanted pregnancy. Giselle's customary stoic expression hadn't altered when she observed her mistress take the little, paper-wrapped bundles into Mlle. Johnston's suite. So that's how the wind blows, is it? she thought, and offered up a Gallic shrug to the vagaries and predicaments of beautiful young women.

Lady Hidel, in her practical way, had determined on this course while the doctor examined Leita. Convenient that the girl was still in a deep drugged sleep. The inspection of her private parts had been conducted gently and expeditiously after Lady Hidel explained the circumstances to the man who had tended her and her family for many years and whose discretion she trusted.

261

"At this point I can say that the deed was done completely," Doctor Veaubain said quietly as he washed his hands. He looked up into Lady Hidel's anxious eyes. "The canal is full of coital fluid."

She sighed heavily. "I had hoped perhaps that he was surprised before it took place."

Doctor Veaubain shook his head. "I am afraid not. And his face wasn't seen, you say?"

"No," she replied steadily. "He hadn't removed his mask. And he ran from the room. Naturally my husband's only thought was for our guest."

The doctor clicked his tongue. "He must have been an animal." He took the towel she offered him. "Do you know when her last moonsickness took place?"

"I remember it happening. She told me she wasn't feeling too well one day, said that was the reason for her not riding in the afternoon. At this moment I can't remember the day, but perhaps it will come to me."

"Probably not a reason in the world to fret. Highly unlikely that she would conceive over this once." He smiled. "Fate is not always unkind, you know, and your fears will probably prove to be unfounded."

"It would be absurd, wouldn't it?" Lady Hidel laughed, happy that the ghost was exorcised for the moment.

"It would be the height of absurdity," he declared cheerfully.

Just the same, she was taking no chances. There was enough hollyhock root for a month of tisanes and she would see that Leita drank it every day—without fail!

The scarf that Leita knotted round her waist fell to the hem of her skirt. Made of the finest silk, it was actually seven narrow scarves, each a color of the rainbow, handstitched together. Her hair was pulled back into a wide chignon and she pinned blue forget-me-nots into the gleaming coils. It had been over three weeks since the masked ball at St. Cloud. She had sworn never to drink champagne again and held to her vow. She had kept to her bed for almost a full week, ill and weak, and even now her digestion was delicate. She smiled ruefully over this, remembering how Breve had teased her around the campfires when she had filled her plate twice over, devouring her food with a hearty relish. Since the champagne had made her ill she seemed to have developed an intolerance for the thick, hot chocolate the maid brought her in the morning. Heretofore she had loved its frothy sweetness and invariably emptied the whole pot but now at the first sip her stomach churned. She considered the penalty for her over-indulgence a bit too high and wondered how others managed to drink such quantities of the sweet, fuzzy wine without any ill effects. Lady Hidel assured her that the tisanes which she dutifully downed every day would eventually soothe her touchy digestion. Aside from this minor inconvenience she felt wonderfully well. She had seen the Duc de Rastignet but once, a chance encounter on the Boulevard des Italiens. He had greeted her warmly and joined her group for a sherbet in one of the open-air cafes. He seemed to have aged inexplicably. There were fine lines at the corners of his eyes and his manner had been subdued, faintly paternal even. Somehow she hadn't been surprised not to hear from him after that and was told by the Comte de Marnegge, who had eagerly stepped into the breach, that Gustave was working very hard with his regiment, had not been seen at the Imperial Club for weeks, and was spending his free time at his sister's estate near Chartre. This occasioned no little banter among his acquaintances, since it was a marked reversal of his usual habits. The Comte de Marnegge remarked jestingly that he wouldn't be surprised if Gustave took the cloth, so reformed was he.

Leita swept down the stairway in high spirits. Armand was in the drawing room, in evening dress, and taking his walking stick and black cape and silk hat from the butler they entered his carriage and rolled along in the clear, starlit night.

Great yellow globes of flaring gas lit up the front of the Theatre Varieties and the walk and the street were milling with an elegantly dressed crowd; white shirt fronts blazed and bare shoulders gleamed beneath plume bedecked coiffures and the glitter of diamonds lit up almost every ear lobe and bosom. Tonight was the opening night of a new revue starring Hortense Schneider. Leita had never seen this famous actress and looked forward to the evening with excited curiosity. Only the year before Hortense's voluptuous beauty had been greatly admired by the visiting Prince of Wales. Prince Edward had spent a part of every evening in her dressing room, red-faced and jovial and obviously very much smitten. Hortense had taken it as her due, in fact had blossomed out with a diamond and ruby riviere that almost outshone her other jewels and had acquired another villa near Biarritz and an even more sumptuous carriage and four. Gossips chuckled over the Biarritz villa, contending it still might not be far enough from Buckingham Palace to elude the long arm and famous frown of Edward's mother, Queen Victoria.

It was now nine-thirty and the footlights were only just lit. Mary Jo and the blithe Etienne Rocquart hailed them in the lobby.

"You did get a stage box, didn't you, Armand?" Mary Jo inquired breathlessly.

"It was impossible. We shall have to stand in the stalls," Armand answered apologetically.

"The stalls!" Mary Jo repeated increduously and

then manufactured one of her adorable pouts when Armand laughed. She was dressed in gray silk, trimmed all over with scarlet puffs and bows and looked demurely charming.

"He never tires of teasing you," Leita remarked. And they entered the body of the house. It was, for the most part, done in soft green tones, airily and richly accented with white and gold and was filling quickly now with a continuous hub-bub of voices as the attendants piloted the groups to the various seats where they viewed the crowd and exchanged whispered comments. A great glass chandelier hung suspended from the ceiling and bright orange flames danced and threw vivid daggers of light over the cardinal velour of the seats and threw shadows on the draped purple velvet of the closed curtains.

Leita looked at the ceiling, painted with a crowd of rosy-bottomed cherubs and floating, full-thighed Venuses. The gilding shimmered in the light and she thought it was entrancing.

"I'm surprised at Darcy missing this evening," Mary Jo whispered. Her breath was sweet with attar of roses. "She could have come with M'sieur Valbelle—I heard him invite her."

"She is puzzling sometimes," Leita agreed. "She has been mooning around like a lost lamb since Jack Hidel had to leave so suddenly for England."

"No puzzle at all," Mary Jo giggled. "My cool and independent cousin is madly, absolutely in love. And what a choice! It makes me shudder. Just shows you what an end old maids come to." She flicked a satisfied, proprietary glance at Etienne. "It's a great lesson to me," and she grinned wickedly at Leita, who smiled behind her fan. It was just faintly possible that Mary Jo was serious in her vow to marry before another year was out.

The thin strains of the violins tuning up amid the tentative cheeps of the flutes hushed suddenly and the gas in the mammoth chandelier wavered and then fell into short flames. The rollicking strains of one of Offenbach's waltzes filled the air and, swept away on the gaiety of the sound, the crowd hushed as the curtains parted.

Hortense Schneider's statuesque, rounded beauty and her imperious carriage drew thunderous applause when she swept out of the wings. Creamy chiffon, heavily embroidered with gold roses, outlined her body and set off her chestnut curls. Her voice was throaty and rich. The songs were ribald, but the questionable meanings were lost on Leita and Mary Jo, who were unfamiliar with the French idioms. It was a thrilling riotous spectacle and at the entr'acte they made their way through the crowded, gesticulating mass in the foyer and captured seats in the Cafe de Madrid, just next door to the theatre. Armand tucked Leita's lace mantle more closely around her shoulders and she spooned up a chestnut sorbet, while he and Etienne discussed the afternoon's dealings on the Bourse. They made their way back through the crowd and to their seats in good time for the second act.

The ingenue was declared to be enchanting. A dark-haired young woman, she portrayed a wanton shepherdess. The girl had a flair for comedy and received a thunderous round of applause after her first song. As the action continued, the amorous shepherd pursued the ingenue and then burst into a song of frustrated love when she disappeared from the stage. Leita's thoughts raced forward for a moment to the Maison d'Or where they were to take supper after the theatre. The shepherd had disconcerted her for a moment. Tall and dark, with magnificently broad shoulders and a head of curly black hair, she felt swept back down the corridors of time as she gazed at him. In the glare of the flaring, sulphurous footlights his high cheekbones glistened and dark curls of hair sprouted out from the laced ties of his half-opened shirt. I wonder what Breve is doing now, right this minute. The poignant melody sung by the actor, the theme of his fruitless love, struck her to the heart and she swallowed a small lump of grief. If life were only like a play, she thought, when the young shepherdess whirled back onto the stage. Dancing in simulated evasion of the shepherd's passionate pursuit she leaped in the air, her white stockinged legs flashing above the pink, ribbon-wrapped slippers. She tossed her head, darting and pirouetting out of his reach, her gauzy, ruffled skirt spinning out from her thighs. Offenbach's lifting, plangent melody had swept the crowd into his fantasy when the sulphur flare of the footlight exploded and a sword-shaped arc of orange flame, bordered in vibrant blue, struck and forked through the floating skirt of the dancing girl. Leita gasped and the audience sat in rigid horror as the flame devoured the diaphanous material. The dancer's ear-piercing screams reverberated through the theatre and the actor, the only other person on the stage, stood transfixed for a second, then rushed toward her tearing off his shirt, evidently intending to attempt to smother the flames with it. But the girl was a diminutive pillar of fire, running, twisting, in her agony, thereby fanning the tongues of flame which had spread to her lacquered curls. In that moment the stage became a melee; a bucket of water was thrown by a man who came tearing out of the wings but the girl, running frantically, missed its arc. The audience was on its feet, bellowing, roaring, and shrieks from the crowd mingled with the heartrending screams of the young actress, and as the second bucket of water hit her prostrate figure she reeled and fell. The acid-sweetish odor of charred flesh rolled out in a sickening wave over the crowd. Armand was half-pulling, half-carrying Leita up the aisle, forcing his way through the sudden stream of black dress-coats and the crush of crinolines, fighting through the throng that was pressing toward the stage, the better to view the tragedy. When they reached the foyer he had one arm around her shoulders and the position served him well because she fainted then, sagging against him and slipping almost to the floor before he could pull her up.

"It was natural that Leita should faint. That was a scene of horror." Sir Charles sniffed at his brandy and patted his wife's arm reassuringly as she flurried past him.

"Charles, it is not the first time!" she protested. "Armand tells me that Leita grew quite faint in the Champ de Mars only last week. They were watching the Zouaves and Cuirassiers review for the Emperor and Leita suddenly became pale and was near fainting dead away. Armand is more than a touch concerned, but not nearly as concerned as I. Though he does feel that what happened last night was not unusual, considering what they had witnessed. But now I must tell you something that I have not spoken of."

Sir Charles raised his eyes. He stood by the open window and the breeze ruffled the pale brown hairs of his head. Sir Charles was slightly bald and his sculptured lips pursed as he waited for her to continue.

"I ascertained the dates and I am positive that the time for Leita's *mauvaise semaine* has passed. She has missed her flow, Charles. Now what are we to do?"

268

Chapter 18

IT WAS A BRIGHT AND SUNNY HIGH NOON IN CHICAGO. Stephen de Jean lingered a moment on the church steps and gazed at the crystalline blueness of the sky, dotted with clouds like puffs of white cotton. His slender fingers fondled the cigar he was on the verge of unwrapping and he smiled benignly at the crowds on the walk, the panoply of varnished carriages, at no one in particular. High mass, then a pleasant stroll to the Mays Hotel for a drawn-out Sunday dinner, then a drive with whichever lady he had chosen to accompany him; this was his invariable Sunday program, usually followed by a reception or dinner later. But today was special. The day before he had mailed the letter containing the misinformation of Breve's elopement and had carried it to the post office himself. On Tuesday he was to depart for New York and would take ship for France early Saturday morning. Darcy's letters had kept him informed; most useful, the woman was. That Breve had written to Leita had come as a disquieting surprise, but Darcy's interception of the letter had been fortunate in the extreme. Stephen had watched him searchingly after that, but never a word passed between them concerning Miss Johnston; even when Stephen casually brought her name into the conversation Breve's expression hadn't altered. Probably only a gracious little note, Stephen thought, but just as well not to stir up that pot! The rest of it had gone well. No serious suitors. Leita's tastes had undoubtedly broadened by now, even during this short sojourn abroad. A highly suitable, and highly desirable wife she would make. Stephen tapped his walking stick in a discreet little rhythm as he strolled along. He would show her Paris—he would spread it at her feet! But now, he halted a second. There were a few little items in his office he could clear up. If he took care of them today, that would leave Monday free for any last minute preparations. He thought of the dining room at the Mays Hotel, but no one awaited him there and hunger hadn't assailed him yet. He would just stop in and take advantage of the Sunday quiet to clear his desk completely.

The tall, gray stone building with its protruding bays of windows loomed quiet and empty on Madison Street. Stephen ran quickly up the first flight of stairs to the second floor front and unlocked the gold-lettered door. Wenzler and de Jean, the lettering read, Investments. Stephen stepped lightly along the carpeted hallway, then stopped, a bemused expression on his handsome face. The door to Hugo's office was slightly ajar and a trapezoid of yellow light streaked the hall carpet. Stephen stepped in, prepared to extinguish the lamp that someone had carelessly left lit, then stopped in surprise. Hugo Wenzler was ensconced in the depths of a heavy armchair. The lighted lamp glowing on the small table beside him traced sharp little prisms in the crystal brandy decanter and the half-full brandy glass. The floor was decorated with a helter-skelter array of open ledgers and loose sheets of paper. Stephen stooped and picked up one of the sheets to avoid stepping on it.

"Hugo, I've heard of burning the midnight oil, but the Sunday oil? Such industry!"

Hugo's look of surprise was so intense that Stephen laughed.

"I haven't come back from the dead. But I've certainly managed to startle you. It's not like you to abandon your Sunday sauerkraut and dumplings for work." Hugo's German cook and her offerings were a standing joke with Stephen.

Hugo's deep voice seemed to come from the depths of his chair. "And what of you? I have never known you to sully a Sunday with business."

Stephen smiled and glanced down at the ledger sheet in his hands. The next moment his eyes narrowed in perplexity as he reread the sheet. A receipt was attached to it and he read the receipt carefully, then stooped down and retrieved another paper from the floor. His lips were parted as he scanned it, then looked up at Hugo, disbelief in every line of his face.

"This is a communication from General Roon—signed by him?"

"Very true," Hugo said, a slight smile twitching the corners of his fleshy lips. He rose and procured another glass from the sideboard against the wall. It was then that Stephen's eye fell on something that he had observed peripherally as he entered the room. There was a safe in the wall above the sideboard. An open safe, with one ledger remaining in its recesses. The picture of Bismarck that customarily hung above the sideboard was on the floor, propped against the wall. Stephen swallowed.

271

"When did you have that safe installed, Hugo?"

"Last year," Hugo answered briefly, splashing brandy into the glass. Stephen stared at the red and cream silk cravat that Hugo wore. When he spoke his voice was soft.

"General Roon thanks us for an investment of thirty-eight thousand dollars in gold. The head of the Prussian Staff thanks us for gold. Perhaps you would care to explain why?"

Hugo's lips twitched again and he held out the glass to his partner. Stephen shook his head slowly, in refusal.

Hugo shrugged his heavy shoulders. "I have been investing for us, Stephen, investing wisely and well."

"And secretly." Stephen's voice was even lower now.

"And secretly," Hugo agreed. "I am aware of your prejudices and I saw no reason for them to jeopardize a twelve-percent return for us. Twelve percent, Stephen, which I negotiated with ease."

"I don't doubt. And when did this begin?"

"Last year."

"Last year when I was abroad," Stephen stated flatly.

"Correct again," Hugo chuckled.

"And it was also with ease that you falsified my records, falsified the balance sheet of our funds?"

"Now, now," Hugo said soothingly. "A touch of discretion was necessary, my dear Stephen, only because of the prejudices I alluded to a moment ago."

Hugo's imperturbability hadn't wavered and Stephen gave him a long, measuring look, then stooped and swept up a handful of the papers and perused them leisurely before he laid them on the sideboard.

"Thirty-eight thousand is not nearly the extent of it, am I right, Hugo?"

"That was the first loan only." Hugo sipped his brandy.

"You have sent a small fortune in gold to finance the manufacture of Prussian cannon, the completion of Prussian rail systems, all to aid them in what they think of as their secret plan to invade my country." Stephen's tone was still soft but menace hissed and darted in each word.

"Your country? This is your country, young man." Hugo's head was drawn back and he looked down the length of his fleshy nose.

Stephen's voice trembled with emotion. "Two years ago Prussia was victorious over Austria. In a few short weeks the heavy-handed men of the Rhine gathered hundreds of miles of new territory to their gluttonous stomachs. And now you use my money to aid them in their dream of conquering the only civilized country in Europe." Stephen's hand shook. "I will set about recalling the loans this afternoon. Tomorrow I will see that Sagarsee draws up the necessary papers to abrogate our partnership."

"You will do nothing of the kind. It is not within your power to call those loans, not without my signature. I made them and I will tend to them." Hugo's voice boomed and he thrust his thumbs into the slits of his waistcoat. He laughed contemptuously then. "The only civilized country you say? I take it you speak of France? You are laughable, my boy. A debauched race would be more accurate. A nation of effete, decadent, undisciplined dandies, led by a bandy-legged fool who would still be skulking in England in exile if it weren't for the cunning, treacherous Duke de Morny. A man led by the hand to the throne simply by the force of his uncle's name and the conniving of his bastard half-brother."

Stephen looked at the carpet, the flush on his

cheekbones fiery red against his ashen skin. His hand fondled the head of his walking stick and then he looked up.

"Prussian to the core, aren't you? You must know I intend to and will call those loans immediately. That filthy Krupp will not have the use of my money to build cannon to kill Frenchmen!"

"I repeat, you will not—you cannot without my signature. You are being tiresome, Stephen. I am surprised at your loyalties, however misguided. They contradict your credo—always be on the winning side; that is how it goes, isn't it? Quiet yourself, young man. This time you are on the winning side. Prussia will take France in three weeks, and you know it."

Stephen's eyes blazed and then he averted his face. His sources of information were reliable. He well knew that the Prussian General Staff was deep in the most detailed plans, plans involving the deployment of troops at two hours' notice over an improved railroad system. The foundries were humming and the breech-loading rifle was being turned out by the hundreds. He pictured von Moltke, the heavy-chested Prussian general, sending his divisions through the orchards and rolling green valleys of the country he had left as a child, pictured Bismarck in a gutted Paris, and the bile rose in his throat as he looked at Hugo's florid countenance, wreathed in a smile that displayed now the contempt he had obviously felt for him all these years.

Hugo was gathering up the ledgers from the floor when Stephen took a few quiet steps toward him.

"Well, let's see the extent of this venture of yours, my friend."

Hugo looked up and his smile regained some of its old benignity.

"Now you are being sensible. You were never one to fly in the face of gain," and he swept up another handful of sheets.

The walking stick had belonged to Stephen's father. Its gold head was chased with an engraving of fleur-de-lis and now it opened on minute hinges and the hilt of a four-inch dagger slid out soundlessly from the hollow recess in the ebony stick. The velour of Hugo's frock coat was heavy, but presented no serious obstacle to the finely honed blade. Hugo was bent over and remained strangely immobile for an instant when Stephen thrust the blade deep into the area between his shoulder blade and his backbone, then pulled it downward. The ripping sound of the knife in Hugo's back coincided with a deep grunt. One fleshy hand remained splayed outward, barely touching the ledger sheet he had been reaching for when Stephen struck, and then his body slowly unbent. When he hit the floor his body was straight, both arms flailing upward for a few seconds as his initial grunt turned to a gurgle deep in his throat. Stephen stood above him, the hilt of the dagger still buried deep in Hugo's back, watching as he writhed first, then twitched, the toes of his heavy boots striking the floor in a macabre tatoo. Stephen gripped the shaft of the stick as a man grips a barge pole. The red flush on his cheeks had spread to cover his neck above the shirt collar and now he threw his weight into a final, deep thrust, then withdrew the blade slowly. It dripped blood onto Hugo's back. He stood holding the shining, scarlet blade above his partner's back as one would hold a dripping cloth, then withdrew a handkerchief from his pocket and wiped the blade carefully. The small, recessed lever in the handle worked soundlessly and there was a slight click when the blade slid back into the body of the stick.

Hugo lay motionless, his face pressed against the ledger sheet he had been reaching for in the moment before he died.

Stephen's expression was stringently purposeful for the next fifteen minutes. He gathered every sheet of paper, stacked them carefully with the ledgers, and emptied the second brandy glass that Hugo had offered him, rinsing it out and drying it before he replaced it in the sideboard. When he surveyed the room, standing at the doorway with the ledgers under one arm, his gaze rested on the now empty safe, and the ghost of a smile curled his mouth. "The last person I would have suspected of such cleverness," he said aloud, and bestowed a passing glance of appreciation on the blood-spattered body on the floor. Then he walked quickly and lightly down the hall and left the building by the alley entrance.

The Cook County courthouse had an entrance that stretched three stories high. Its general shape was round, in actuality it was decagonal, composed of ten wings and topped by two turrets, one of them very high. Once, in winter, Stephen had climbed the narrow wooden stairway to the taller of the two turrets and looked out over the snow-covered panorama of Chicago. He thought of that today as he climbed the steps with Sagarsee beside him. Samuel Sagarsee, attorney at law, had accompanied him today not in any professional capacity, but simply in friendship. The inquest was necessary, since Hugo Wenzler had been the victim of foul play. Stephen made a small adjustment to the black mourning band on his sleeve and passed into the courtroom in his habitual posture, head high and chin thrust slightly forward.

The courtroom, not surprisingly, was full to bursting. Hugo Wenzler had been a prominent man in Chicago circles, social as well as financial, and the meticulously detailed circumstances of his gory murder had sold thousands of newspapers. Stephen seated himself in a hard wooden chair in the second row of spectators and attempted to settle his vagrant emotions. His father's gold-headed ebony walking stick was laid carelessly across his lap until it prodded Mr. Sagarsee's leg. Then Stephen propped it between his legs and stroked the fleur-de-lis carving while the bailiff called the court into session.

The clerk, Leonard Grosschmidt, perspiring and pale, was called first and recounted in halting sentences his tale of the Monday morning ten days ago. First to enter the offices he, like Stephen, had noticed the light in Mr. Wenzler's office.

Leonard Grosschmidt was a well-nourished man of about forty-five and obviously still in the clutch of the horror he had experienced that morning, in addition to being highly impressed by the prominence of his testimony. His tone was so muted, and his words followed one another in such an unintelligible rush that the judge was forced to ask him to repeat his whole testimony. Stephen moved restively. He couldn't help it. The man was a tedious bore at best and the thought crossed his mind that perhaps Hugo had employed him in some way in his furtive undertaking. Grosschmidt was a native of Ems in Prussia and had been hired by Hugo. What if he had known of the safe? What if he had been privy to its contents? Stephen's tongue felt dry and he looked steadfastly at the shining, dandruff-flaked scalp of the man in front of him.

"Did I understand you to say the safe was completely empty that morning?" The judge's tone was fretful. The hot summer day and the crowded room made the atmosphere dense with the odor of stale cigars and perspiration.

"Yes, sir. I mean yes, your honor. Nothing was in it. It was empty."

"What did Mr. Wenzler usually keep in the safe?" the judge inquired, and as an afterthought ran his index finger around the collar of his robe.

Stephen felt the muscles in his neck quiver and stroked his fingers surreptitiously over his black cravat.

"I don't know. I never saw the safe before, your honor. I didn't know there was another safe in the chambers, beside the large safe in the main room of the office, sir."

Stephen exhaled and realized that he had been holding his breath. The fellow didn't know. He wasn't part of it.

When Leonard Grosschmidt finally stepped down Stephen felt almost weightless with relief. It was going to be all right. The caretaker of the building testified then. He had been on duty Sunday, had fallen asleep in the small anteroom after a heavy dinner. More likely a heavy drink or two, Stephen thought, and almost chuckled aloud. The caretaker had seen no one, heard no one enter. No one ever did on Sunday, for that matter. Of course Mr. Wenzler had come in about eleven. He did that occasionally. No, he thought nothing about not seeing him leave, not seeing as how he'd been sound asleep and all. Anyway, his being there on Sunday was just a lot of foolishness. He had been a churchgoing man until he took this job and the seven-day week was just a way to sweat a man, in his opinion. He was dismissed without further questions, and Stephen rose smoothly as his name was called.

Breve Pinchon entered the courtroom by a side door. He spied one vacant chair and took it. Attending the inquest had been a spur of the moment decision and he still wasn't quite sure what had brought him here. Robbery and murder were facts of existence in this raw metropolis, but he knew that Stephen de Jean would be called upon to testify and he had decided it might be interesting to see what was brought to light by the hearing. The newspaper accounts, lurid in their descriptions and fanciful in their conjecture, were definitely not to be relied on. Breve tilted his chair backward to give his long legs more room and watched Stephen as he seated himself on the stand. I don't like an inch of him, he thought, not for the first time. Good God, but it's hot in here! He swept one hand back over his crisply waving hair and tiny beads of perspiration welled out on his brow. His waistcoat was a canary yellow silk with a design of dark gray leaves. He had gained a little weight since his days in the saddle and the line of his jaw was a touch fuller. His frock coat was elegantly cut, and lay smoothly over the heavy muscles of his shoulders, and the woman next to him cast an appraising look at his roughly-cut, handsome features. He caught a scent of Lily of the Valley and breathed it in. Why hadn't she answered his letter? The explanation of course was that she was hurt and angry. But he had told her that he would explain, and was not finally ready to explain. His hand made a fist as he thought of those clear, violet eyes. She had always looked straight at him, always met his gaze, with that direct pride of hers. Well, that direct pride isn't going to keep us apart, he thought. What will keep us apart is the truth. If she recoils from that then I will have to put the memory of her behind me—I will have no choice. I've loved her from the day I saw her stumbling and fighting her way over those furrows, hotheaded and stubborn. A spasm of desire flickered in his loins as he remembered the softness of her body in his arms that night on the lake. The tender heat of her mouth and the taste of her flesh were memories that struck him at the most inappropriate moments. No other woman could replace

279

her. In moments of coupling, when his lust should have driven everything else from his mind, he would experience a poignant longing for Leita's supple sweetness and a sadness would clutch at his throat along with the shadow of fear, fear that he would never hold her again.

Stephen's expression as he took the witness stand was composed and properly lugubrious, as befitted a man whose partner and close friend had recently met an untimely death.

"Was Mr. Wenzler in the habit of visiting his offices on a Sunday, Mr. de Jean?"

"Not often, but occasionally. Mr. Wenzler was a highly conscientious man of business and when he felt the occasion warranted it he would spend extra time on our affairs. He was an industrious man."

The judge coughed and gave a desultory swat at a bluebottle fly which had been tormenting him these few minutes past.

"The open safe, Mr. de Jean. Can you give us any information about what it might have contained?"

Breve frowned and sat forward, attentive to Stephen's testimony.

"The safe was one of Mr. Wenzler's idiosyncrasies, I'm afraid. He was in the habit of keeping a fair amount of gold coin in it. He had it installed a year or so ago. It was his private keep, you might say."

"He kept gold in this safe?" the judge inquired.

"Yes. As a matter of fact I remonstrated with him when he had it installed. I felt it was much safer to keep such sums in a bank, but as I say, it was one of his idiosyncrasies. He assured me that since no one knew of it, it was perfectly safe and he liked to have a fair amount of money at hand. I am doing him no disservice by saying that Mr. Wenzler was a touch frugal. He would have been the first to admit it. In fact he said more than once that his hoard was an indulgence, that a miser likes to count his money. This was said jokingly, of course, but nevertheless held a grain of truth. I fear that it was his undoing and now my conscience pricks me that I was not more insistent with him."

"You think then that he had opened the safe on that Sunday, thinking himself alone."

"I have no doubt of it," Stephen answered with perfect truth.

"It would certainly appear to have been his undoing," the judge mused. "Yet no one else knew of it?"

"To my knowledge, no," Stephen answered. His tone throughout the questioning had been subdued.

That wily bastard is lying! Breve leaned back again, his black eyes dark and speculative as he watched every nuance of expression in Stephen's face. He is too damned bland and too damned grief-stricken. But why would he lie? What earthly reason would de Jean have for concealing any knowledge about his partner's murder? De Jean wasn't hurting for money, that he knew. His firm did a large and profitable business and for that matter, he had always been a wealthy man. Christ—he wouldn't have killed the fellow for a pile of gold! He was sitting on money enough to keep him in luxury for his lifetime. Breve had made a careful and complete investigation of Stephen de Jean shortly after he arrived in Chicago, due to his distrust of him and a determination to inform himself about the man who obviously sought to marry Leita. Breve rubbed his eyes as he pondered this unexpected knowledge. Possibly it was just greed, rampant greed. Hugo Wenzler had no family that he knew of; his wife had died leaving him childless. Was de Jean his heir? Not impossible. He watched Stephen walk back to his chair. The fellow is a consummate actor, Breve thought, his testimony thoughtful, the manner just right. Well, I'll see what I can ascertain about this business. Breve sat through the verdict: robbery and murder by a person or persons unknown. He left the courtroom, lingered a moment in the corridor, then headed for the street and strode off purposefully.

Breve handed his hat to the cloakroom attendant and glanced into the lounge before striding up the wide carpeted steps to the second floor where the quiet buzz of late luncheon conversation could be heard over the muted click of silver. The Pantheon Club boasted a membership that comprised most of the moneyed men in Chicago. Very little old money, since Chicago had become a thriving commercial center so comparatively recently. Not like New York, where the great-grandsons of Dutch settlers and fur traders carefully assessed a man's family tree before casting their vote for his entry into their private masculine domains. Breve had been sponsored by the Chicago attorney who saw to his trust in the years before he even suspected its existence and now he was greeted by a raised hand from this or that table as he surveyed the dining room. Having determined that de Jean hadn't arrived before him he sauntered into the opulently decorated interior of the bar where immense gilt-framed mirrors threw back the reflection of hand-rubbed mahogany and cream-tinted skin of the por-traits that decorated the silk-covered walls. Breve stationed himself at the end of the massive bar in a position where he could observe those who entered and his vigil wasn't long. Stephen entered in company with his attorney and was immediately surrounded. The murmur of repeated condolences finally ended and Stephen answered the questions about the inquest. He was most forthcoming, Breve thought as he eaves-dropped, but he was unable to see his face through the press of shoulders and taller heads. Stephen finally repaired to a table in an alcove, leaving Sagarsee to expedite their order at the bar. Breve slid from his stool and joined him. Stephen's surprise was unaffected when he looked up to see Breve's tall figure.

"May I sit down?"

"Certainly—certainly." Stephen indicated the chair beside him. What in hell does he want? he thought. He and Breve spoke, occasionally passed a few words about the weather or the market at the stock exchange, but that was invariably the extent of their social congress. And where in hell is my drink! Stephen awaited the brandy and soda anxiously.

"I wasn't in town when it happened and I haven't seen you since, but I wanted to tell you how sorry I am about the tragedy."

Stephen bowed his head for a moment. "And tragedy it was. For a man to be cut down in the prime of life, by some vagrant scum. I realize nothing can be done about the criminal element in this town but we ought to see more hangings. They set an example."

Breve privately thought there were quite enough hangings. Theft drew down a horrendous punishment while robbery committed in the name of commerce was only characterized as "sharp practice." He nodded his head. "I'm in complete agreement. I'm sure Mr. Wenzler would have preferred that whoever it was simply take the gold and leave him with his life."

A sad, wry smile curved Stephen's lips, and he sighed. "If Hugo had foreseen the final outcome I'm sure he would have made that choice, but the sad truth is I can visualize Hugo—" He looked up gratefully as Martin Sagarsee set a full glass in front of him, and deposited a siphon of soda water and a bottle of brandy on the table.

Stephen took a quick sip, Breve noted the eagerness, and then nodded in Sagarsee's direction. "You and Mr. Pinchon are acquainted, are you not?" Martin smiled at Breve. "We see one another fairly often. How are you Pinchon? Hear you had a profitable meeting with Collis Huntington a while back."

Now how in blazes did he know about that? Breve thought.

"We had a meeting. I was out West on other business at the time," he answered smoothly. "It was interesting. Whether it was profitable or not remains to be seen." These lawyers have a grapevine all their own, he thought. He also noted that Stephen had taken the opportunity to drink deeply, almost emptying his glass. The fellow is definitely wobbly on his moorings, Breve observed to himself. Well, on to the business at hand.

"Did Mr. Wenzler have any other relatives in this country?" Breve usually found pointblank to be the best approach. It suited his nature.

"Relatives?" Stephen repeated. "Yes, though I never met them. He has two nephews in New York, his sister's sons. He visited them at least twice a year. He was childless, of course, and he set great store by those two boys. His sister is something of an invalid, I believe, and that was the reason for their not visiting him here. In fact, he looked forward to the time when they would be old enough to make the journey alone. The younger of the two is his namesake." I'm rattling on, Stephen thought. Too much relief, better watch my tongue.

"They are two wealthy young boys now. Their future is assured," Sagarsee said pontifically. He was a narrow, stringy man and slitted his eyes often due to being very nearsighted.

Breve pursed his lips. Well, that takes care of that.

Wenzler had heirs so de Jean doesn't benefit that way from his death. He was turning over the possibility of a quarrel between them when his attention was suddenly arrested by Martin Sagarsee's monotone.

"With the boys' father arriving soon you will stay in this country until the will is settled and his brother-in-law goes back to New York, won't you?"

"Of course, I will have to remain here until the formalities are taken care of."

"Have you made your reservations?"

Stephen had emptied his second brandy and soda and begun on his third. "I am booked for next Tuesday morning. Three days will be quite sufficient for the part I am to play."

Breve smiled his most charming smile. "I'm sure you need to get away. This has been a very bad experience for you."

"A month or two abroad is just what he needs," Martin Sagarsee said, nodding sagaciously.

Abroad is it? Breve thought. So that is what's up his sleeve.

"A blessing that I hadn't gone when it happened. I was due to leave the Tuesday after his death." Stephen sighed. Depend on Sagarsee to bring up his departure. The man was so damned officious. He had kept his plans carefully to himself, only informing Hugo and his butler. But no matter. The brandy had smoothed him out and his hands no longer trembled. It was over. There hadn't been a chance in the world that anyone had seen him enter that building but he had still lain awake the night before, preparing a tale in the event that someone had sighted him, either in the alley or in front of the office building, someone who planned to come forth at the inquest and gather a little limelight with the submission of sensational, last-minute evidence. Mercifully, such a witness had not materialized and now he felt certain none would. Publicity about the murder had saturated the newspapers in the preceding ten days and if he had been observed on the scene it would have come out by now. Bless that drunken caretaker—he would see that he had a substantial remembrance at Christmas time.

"Do you go to Europe every year?" Breve inquired amiably.

"I make every effort to," Stephen replied. "I relax completely there, and I have family friends I make a point of visiting. I forget completely about business."

"I envy you," Breve replied, and carelessly changed the subject by expressing an interest in the Suez Canal, now nearing completion despite the years of mishap and travail.

Later Breve sat lost in thought in the dining room. He had little appetite but simply sat down out of habit, accustomed to taking lunch there. He was joined by two other men and the conversation was casual. So Stephen was sailing for France next week. Damned disquieting. He was anticipating Leita's return in November, had prepared two or three speeches, and the possibility of Stephen's meeting her in Paris hadn't occurred to him. I should have thought of it, he mused angrily. Quite touching, when a man journeys across an ocean to call on you. He leaves no stone unturned. Breve took a swallow of burgundy and picked up his knife prepared to cut into the steaming slice of roast beef which had been set before him several minutes ago. He had no appetite for it. He was thinking how satisfying it would be to thrust his fist into the smug, smiling face that de Jean presented to the world. And then he lay down his knife. A random thought had presented itself and for a few moments there was a faraway look in his dark eyes. When he picked up the knife again it was to attack the cooling beef with relish. He had come to a decision.

The following Tuesday an ocean liner sailed out of New York harbor and Stephen de Jean stood at the rail. The sky was gloomy and dark thunderheads were building in the west but he paid this scant attention. The fact that his voyage commenced under inauspicious, threatening skies cast no pall over his spirits. A forged power-of-attorney rested in a locked portmanteau in his stateroom, along with the notes, correspondence, and ledgers relevant to the late Hugo Wenzler's investment in Prussian armaments. The ship was a new one, had come down the runways a scant two years before. It was called "The Bismarck" and its final port was not England or France but Bremen. Since that eventful Sunday Leita had scarcely entered Stephen's thoughts. He had one mission, that of extricating his gold from Prussian hands. Leita, intriguing though she might be, desirable as she definitely was, had rec ed into a position no more and no less important in his life than the paintings that graced his mansion. She   an acquisition, or would be one, to enhance his life, just as those paintings did, just as an exquisitely prepared dinner gratified him by its excellence. His mind was not on the gloom-dimmed skyline of New York, nor on the welcome he had anticipated in Paris. His mind was in Essen, the lair of Krupp, the Cannon-King who had been the major recipient of his partner's largesse. Stephen had two hundred thousand dollars in gold to retrieve and he was determined to have it in hand before he left Prussia.

Chapter 19

THE AFTERNOON WAS GLORIOUS. THE THREAT OF A thunderstorm merely heightened Leita's anticipation as the carriage rolled along the cypress-lined coolness of the road to Sceaux. Leita wore yellow organdy splashed with pink roses and the fringe of her sunshade bobbled in rhythm with the cantering team. Mary Jo, charming in white studded with blue polka dots, was interrogating a sheepish Etienne about his gambling losses the night before.

Etienne Rocquart, son of a deputy in the Chamber, had proposed, and Leita had been up half the night while Mary Jo fretted and paced, thrown completely off balance by the foreseeable, even sought-after event. Sworn to secrecy, Leita was resisting the temptation to confide this news to Armand, now sitting across from her in the carriage. Matthew Johnston's name had risen once in Mary Jo's wailing indecision, and Leita suspected that down deep in her friend's coquettish little soul was the germ of a steadfast love for her amiable and charming brother Matthew. Matthew, who treated

Mary Jo with the offhand affection of a member of the family, squiring her to parties, racing down the road on Sunday afternoon rides and observing her flirtations with seeming indifference, had never mentioned marriage. Matthew, Leita knew, was single-mindedly intent on carving out his future holdings in the rich, black soil of Indiana. Matthew was very like his father, Samuel, tall, and blue-eyed, vigorous and decisive. Perhaps he has only been waiting for a sign from Mary Jo, Leita thought—a sign that she truly cares for him. She determined to write to him and broach the subject. He could at least write something of his intention to Mary Jo, if he truly had intentions. That would solve it and remove Mary Jo from the horns of the dilemma that impaled her now. Not that there was anything wrong with Etienne Rocquart. But Leita felt very loathe to leave this sprightly girl behind her. Her initial antipathy to Mary Jo, born partly of jealousy of her obvious intimacy with Breve Pinchon, had dwindled, and over the months they had become fast friends. If Matthew loves her he won't stand back while she marries someone else simply because of her sudden fear of spinsterhood. Having solved this to her satisfaction, Leita felt comforted, with a mind free for pleasure.

Leita looked around with curiosity as the carriage turned into a narrow, graveled drive. The inn was charming, its old gray stone walls overgrown with ivy and clematis and climbing geranium. The two couples alighted and strolled past outdoor tables around to the back of the L-shaped building. There was a massive and ancient chestnut tree on the riverbank spreading its huge, green-leafed branches over the purling water below.

"I didn't believe it really. Not till now. Imagine dining in a tree!" Mary Jo exclaimed. The green lawn that swept down to the river was dotted with strolling couples and families, and waiters bearing heavily loaded trays stalked between the inn and the tree. Leita watched fascinated as a slightly built waiter trotted lightly up the wooden steps beside the tree trunk with a tray held high, and disappeared in the welter of leafy branches high above the ground.

"This is delightful," she smiled. Armand clasped her hand in his and preceding her, led her up the steep, narrow wooden stairway beside the gnarled trunk. Sounds of laughter and conversation came from the upper reaches of the giant tree.

Leita's head rose above the edge of the broad platform and the smell of roast chicken and hot bread perfumed the air. The waiter who showed them to their table was a ham-handed country lad, crammed uncomfortably into his starched white coat. Their table was very near the edge of the platform. Leita looked down as the hors d'oeuvres were being served. The green, shimmering water was thirty feet below, and her gloved hand gripped the table edge as a sudden wave of dizziness overcame her. She had felt hungry but now the familiar thickness of nausea rose in her throat and she turned away from the plate of thinly sliced paté. Armand was engaged in a spirited exchange with Mary Jo and didn't notice Leita's blanched lips. She took a sip of her wine and resolutely looked at the forest of green leaves above her head, but this only intensified her feeling of being suspended over a chasm. When the platter of pink, fat-rimmed ham was placed ceremoniously on the table in front of Armand, the hot scent of sizzling fat enveloped her. She turned her head quickly but with no relief. The platform was weaving, undulating beneath her, and shadows of the breeze-stirred leaves seemed to move in rhythm with the planks beneath her feet.

"Whatever in the world is the matter?" Mary Jo exclaimed. Leita was rising shakily, one hand pressed to her cheek.

"I have to get down from here, somehow. I can't stay up here," Leita quavered.

"But you should have told me immediately. Do you feel ill?" Armand was instantly solicitous.

"Yes, looking down makes me giddy. I'm so terribly sorry to be spoiling things like this."

"You're not spoiling things at all," Armand said soothingly. He had picked up her sunshade and was guiding her toward the steps. "We will simply enjoy our repast on solid ground. I'll go first," and he started down the steps.

The lawn looked so very far below and the stairway so precipitous and narrow that vertigo overcame her. The steps blurred before her eyes. He turned and held out his hand to Leita just as she swayed. When she fell, it was with her full weight on Armand. As he fell backwards, his hand shot out and grasped the narrow balustrade. Leita's yellow sunshade went plummeting to the ground below. Mary Jo shrieked and Etienne Rocquart darted past her and caught Leita around the waist from behind, allowing Armand to regain his balance. The diners had flocked to the edge of the platform and were staring with startled eyes at the little group.

Armand braced himself against the balustrade and with difficulty managed to gather Leita's limp body into his arms. He then descended haltingly until he reached the ground. Mary Jo, ready with smelling salts in hand, dashed to Armand's side and when Leita inhaled the harsh ammonia fumes she coughed and choked.

"She's coming around," Etienne observed. Leita's eyes opened then. Armand carried her to a chair and set her down carefully.

"Now don't try to get up."

"I won't. Did I faint again?" Leita looked around puzzled at the ring of anxious faces.

"You just toppled down those steps like a sack of flour," Mary Jo informed her. "If Armand hadn't started down first, like the gentleman he is, you would have fallen all the way down."

"I can't understand it." Leita took the glass of lemonade Armand offered her and sipped at it. "I've never gotten dizzy before just from being up high. Lordy, think of all the trees I've climbed!"

"Well, you're just gettin' on in years," Mary Jo giggled.

But the anxious look hadn't left Armand's eyes. "Are you sure there is nothing else wrong, Leita? Are you sleeping well at night? Do you feel ill in any other way?"

"It's absurd, really. I sleep like a marble angel and I feel marvelous. In fact I feel quite well this minute. The dizziness is completely gone." She paused and then laughed. "And I feel ravenously hungry."

Mary Jo lifted her hands in a gesture of helplessness, and Etienne dissolved into laughter. They were served at a linen-covered table in the courtyard and Leita ate with relish, finishing her meal with a creamy chocolate éclair. Armand sat thoughtfully watching her and never left her side.

The following day the largest reception room at the Hidel's was full. Lady Hidel was holding a luncheon in honor of some visitors from Switzerland. The doors were open out onto the balcony, and the flower-filled room glowed in the summer sunshine.

Darcy sat by the immense marble hearth in conversation with one of the Swiss guests. Darcy, Leita, and Mary Jo were to leave for Florence in two more weeks, and Darcy was being persuaded to stop for a visit at Lake Como on their way. The beauties of the area close to the Italian border were being discussed, and Darcy was quite interested. She heard regularly from Jack Hidel. His departure had been so sudden, but it was an emergency, he said. Oddly enough, his letters to her were sent sealed within envelopes addressed to his mother. He had given no explanation for this. She had received a note from Mrs. Hidel asking her to call and when she did, Dora had handed her a letter, saying in her mild way that Jack had sent it. Darcy hadn't questioned this peculiar arrangement, she simply called regularly on Mrs. Hidel and just as regularly received a letter from Jack, hinting around that she might like to visit England—and telling how much he missed her. Hardly romantic, she thought, and speculated that her absence when she journeyed to Italy might shake him from his complacency. She might have made the mistake of being too acquiescent, too readily available, and now he took her for granted.

She called Leita over to join the conversation about the charms of Lake Como. Mary Jo trailed after her. Armand was comfortably seated in a winged armchair, enjoying an aperitif while he entertained another of his godmother's guests. Mary Jo had sighted a footman with a salver stacked with letters. He placed it inconspicuously on the boule chest just as the Swiss baroness trotted off to buttonhole the Princess Metternich. Mary Jo, always eager for a letter, saw the mail and pattered over and leafed through it. Leita watched with interest—perhaps Jerome had written to her again. Mary Jo returned with an envelope which she laid in Darcy's lap.

Darcy glanced down at the handwriting on the mauve envelope, and suppressed a start. Stephen had kept to his course; this was the letter they had prepared those long weeks ago. And now, how was she to manage this? Fortunately Leita was at hand. While she was deliberating Mary Jo solved it for her.

"Do read it. Unless it's confidential, of course."

"It's only from an acquaintance in Chicago. I can't imagine that it would be confidential, but you would find it tedious, I'm sure. She is probably relating all the latest gossip. She is a great one to keep abreast of things."

"But you know how I adore hearing anything from home! Even gossip about people I don't know," Mary Jo pleaded.

Darcy had carefully established a precedent by reading her letters aloud, sharing the gossip and the news from Chicago with lighthearted amusement. "Do stop me if you find it boring." She smiled and slit the envelope. I'll get this over with right now, she thought. "Annie says it has been very hot—she is using quantities of cucumbers. The sun is so bright that she finds freckles popping out by the hundreds." Darcy smiled. "Annie has red hair and fights a never-ending battle with freckles. Consequently, the cucumbers. It's the same every summer."

"Buttermilk is even better than cucumbers," Leita remarked. "If you mash the cucumbers in buttermilk and leave it on for at least an hour every morning it fades them like nothing else."

"I must write and tell her that," Darcy said, her eyes traveling down the letter. "Oh, they are having a party to celebrate her brother's engagement. He is to marry at Christmastime. Why, here she mentions someone that you knew. An elopement, for goodness sake!"

"Who eloped that we would know?" Mary Jo asked, all ears.

"Colonel Pinchon—Colonel Breve Pinchon. He is a friend of your family, isn't he, Mary Jo?"

"Breve? Breve has eloped?" Mary Jo cried.

Leita sat forward in her chair, her hands trembling, the quivering threads of shock running through her body. She rose—it couldn't be. There must be another Breve Pinchon! She walked to the hearth and looked over Darcy's shoulder as she read aloud. "That dashing Colonel Pinchon has made off with Marceline Summers. No one even knew that he was courting her, but they have eloped. Probably afraid of her father since Colonel Pinchon's family connections are unknown, and she is the apple of her father's eye. However, he will never disinherit her, and he really is quite a catch—so terribly handsome in a forbidding sort of way. They were married in New York, I understand. So much excitement for a hot summer."

Leita's head swam. How could he? Despite everything, she had thought that he loved her. Though she had denied it to herself, she had still been waiting, waiting till her return, waiting till he completed whatever it was that obsessed him, drove him. She had known that he would come to her eventually, would take her in those strong arms and hold her close for all time to come. But now! Now he held someone else— whispered tender words of love to this wretched girl. She thought of his body surging into her, his hungry, passionate kisses and pictured him bare-chested and driven with passion, embracing—it was too terrible! Her legs felt weak, and her upper lip broke out in tiny beads of moisture.

Just then the sound of trumpets rent the air, rising up from the boulevard below. The buzzing guests who had been knotted in groups around the room raised their heads and moved in a body toward the open doors that led out onto the balcony. The clatter of hooves on the cobblestones and the peal of trumpets signaled the passage of a member of the Imperial family. In this case it was Eugenie, resplendent in her gold-trimmed carriage drawn by six sparkling white horses and escorted by the Empress's Guard. Sabers rattled and scarves fluttered from the other balconies in a spontaneous salute to Napoleon's Empress. Darcy and Mary Jo had risen at the first peal of the trumpets and were making their way through the others who thronged to see the spectacle.

Leita, submerged in a torrent of jealous grief, was impervious to the rush. How could he have done this? How could he have taken her that night in seeming love, only to turn his back on her? The droplets of perspiration dampened her forehead as her head spun. She reached for the back of the chair too late. When she fell, she barely felt the blow. Her head had struck the solid marble edge of the hearth.

The blood was running freely from her temple, soaking the soft, golden hairs when Armand picked her up in his arms. Lady Hidel, who had been the last to move toward the open doors, had looked back just in time to see Leita crumple. Armand had barely begun to rise and had moved quickly, but not in time to break her fall.

His face was white now as he carried Leita out of the room and up the great horseshoe stairway. Lady Hidel ran distractedly ahead of him. She flung open the door of Leita's suite, and they entered her boudoir. She rang for a servant as Armand set Leita onto her bed. Lady Hidel quickly loosened and removed the silk band around Leita's throat and began chafing her wrists as Armand stood aside.

"Something is definitely wrong here." He spoke softly.

"I will send a servant for the doctor immediately," Lady Hidel said.

"She is definitely ill. There is no question about it. I remember well when she first came. There was no fainting, no indisposition then." Armand sat down in the small slipper chair by the bedside.

"What was she doing when this happened?" Lady Hidel asked, more to divert Armand than out of curiosity.

She well knew the reason for Leita's fainting and had been growing more distraught by the day. Sir Charles was unable to think of anything more that could be done. She had doubled and redoubled the strength of the abortive tisanes, but they had had no effect at all. Leita simply assumed that she missed her flow because of the changes in her life. Lady Hidel had questioned her circumspectly, and Leita had said airily that such a thing was not unusual for her.

The girl had no idea—no suspicion. To effect a surgical abortion, she would have to be told. Also, Lady Hidel would never consent to this. It was fraught with terrible danger. Unthinkable.

The servant came, was dispatched to fetch the doctor and Lady Hidel paced the floor of the boudoir.

Armand retired to Leita's sitting room during the doctor's examination, rang for a servant and ordered a tray with coffee. He rose and spoke briefly with the doctor when he emerged from Leita's boudoir.

"She has a concussion, I am afraid, but it is a light one to all appearances. She mustn't move around, at least until I see her again tomorrow morning." With a deferential bow, the doctor took his leave and Lady Hidel sank onto a divan and pressed her fingers to her temples.

"Did he give any explanation for these sudden fainting spells?" Armand asked.

Lady Hidel hesitated. She was exhausted emotionally by her concern over Leita. Sir Charles was still in England, seeing to that dreadful business with Jack. What was she to do? For that matter, what could be done?

Armand spoke up firmly when she paused. "Some-

298

thing is amiss. I have sensed your preoccupation for some time now. You are concerned, as I am, about this girl, and I feel that there is something you are not telling me. Whatever is oppressing you will be lightened if you confide it to me."

"Leita is pregnant." The words burst out and Lady Hidel covered her face with her ringed fingers.

Armand was astounded. "Pregnant? How do you know?"

"The doctor is aware of it. It is the most dreadful calamity, Armand. Utterly dreadful! And I am helpless as to what to do!"

"But it is inconceivable. She doesn't seem concerned about anything! She has been as gay and lighthearted—".

"She doesn't know, Armand."

He dropped his hands at his side and rose. "How can that be? You mean she is pregnant and she does not suspect it? There are certain signs—"

"All the signs are there," Lady Hidel answered dryly.

"Then how is it? I am utterly bewildered. And who is the father?" Armand rose and began pacing back and forth.

Lady Hidel sighed. "In actuality she has done nothing—nothing that she knows of—that would be related to her having a child. That is why she is so lighthearted and dismisses these symptoms."

"Then it must be a mistake. There is such a thing as a false pregnancy, I believe, when all the symptoms are manifest, but it is a trick of nature. I have heard of it."

"Not in this case, I regret to say. If it only were the case." Lady Hidel felt a vast sense of relief at having spoken. Armand was right; it had lightened her burden. She poured a cup of the coffee and laced it liberally with hot milk and three cubes of sugar.

"Do you remember the night of the ball at St. Cloud, when Leita was taken ill and we brought her home unconscious?" There was no reason not to speak of it now. If Armand knew one fact he may as well know the rest.

"Of course I remember. She had been drugged," Armand replied.

"That was the night she conceived, and that is why she has no memory of it. We didn't tell you the whole story. It was too dreadful."

Armand stood speechless and Lady Hidel poured a cup of coffee, sugared it and handed it to him.

"Charles arrived on the scene just a few minutes too late. Whoever the villain was who drugged her, he did it with a purpose. Charles saw her from the gallery leaving the ballroom on the arm of a man, and when she didn't reappear he went searching for her. He opened the door of one of the small rooms off the gallery in time to witness her attacker. He was adjusting his trousers at that moment, Charles told me."

"Who in God's name was it?" Armand's brown eyes were blazing.

Lady Hidel sighed. This was the point where candor must cease. She could not reveal to anyone, even Armand, that her husband's nephew had committed this deed. "He was in costume, Armand, and masked. We don't know who he was. He fled through another door when he saw Charles. Naturally Charles's first thought was for Leita. The poor child was lying there unconscious, her clothing in complete disarray. She knew nothing of what had taken place."

"But are you certain she was violated?"

"Very certain. We had the doctor that night. He examined her—she was still asleep—and there was full evidence of sexual congress."

"God in heaven!" Armand exclaimed. He set down

his cup and strode through the doorway into Leita's boudoir. She lay there, her breast rising and falling, quietly, serenely asleep.

"The doctor gave her something to keep her quiet—a very mild sleeping draught." Lady Hidel had followed and stood at his elbow.

Armand reached down and smoothed the hair back from Leita's forehead. A square of white gauze covered her left temple and a patch of scalp shone pink around it where the doctor had shaved the hair away before dressing the wound.

"I will sit with her," Armand said soberly. "You have guests to see to."

"Oh dear, yes," Lady Hidel said distractedly. "I do wish Charles would return soon."

"When will he be back in Paris?"

"Not until next week, I fear. There has been some—some sort of emergency to be taken care of."

"Is it serious?"

"Oh, no. Something to do with the estate and his solicitors. Some dry business that couldn't wait," Lady Hidel said offhandedly. "Do call Giselle, Armand, when you grow weary. She is quite trustworthy and will stay with Leita until I am free."

Armand nodded. "Run along, Godmother." He smiled gently. "All problems have a solution." Armand returned to the boudoir when Lady Hidel left and sat down in the small chair at Leita's bedside. He looked in her face, at the lashes resting on her cheeks and her slightly parted lips. One arm lay outside the coverlet, and he reached out and stroked it tentatively, gently, then sat back and folded his hands in his lap. He seemed unaware of the time, and his eyes were pensive as he sat quietly, lost in thought, till the carriage of the last guest rolled over the cobblestones of the courtyard below and Leita's lashes fluttered.

He rose and leaned over her. "Don't raise up. Just lie still. You struck your head a nasty blow and the doctor has said that you are to rest quietly."

Leita's eyes were wide open now and she gazed up into his face, bewildered.

"You fainted, and you must lie quietly for a while. Would you like some hot tea—or perhaps some lemonade?"

She was very thirsty. "Lemonade, please."

He rang for the servant and came back to her bedside. Leita's hand reached up, and she touched the bandage at her forehead.

"I'm afraid you have lost a lock or two. The doctor found it necessary to shave a small patch around your wound, but it will grow quickly."

Armand's gentle voice soothed her and then she remembered the dream. Darcy—it had been Darcy—who said that Breve had eloped, had married. She shuddered and a tiny smile curved her lips. "I have had such a bad dream. It must have been from my head—it hurts."

"And well it might. A marble hearth is not a good thing to fall on. If you insist on fainting you must be a little selective as to where you fall," he teased gently.

"But why did I faint? I don't remember—"

"Some slight indisposition. Perhaps the room was too close. There were a great many people down there—all running pell-mell to see the Empress's entourage. She must have been en route to St. Cloud."

Leita frowned, still bewildered. "There were trumpets in my dream. I must have heard them."

"That was just before you fainted. I had been talking with Herr Grooten and I remember glancing at you as you got up. Miss Rankin was reading some kind of letter aloud, I believe. Then the whole group jumped up and went flocking to the balcony."

The servant entered and Armand went into the

302

sitting room for a moment to request a tray with both hot tea and Leita's lemonade.

Leita listened to the murmur of his voice and frowned. He had said Miss Rankin had been reading some kind of letter, aloud. That had been in her dream—Darcy's voice, saying that a friend of theirs had eloped. Surely it had been a dream—it couldn't have really happened.

"What was in the letter, Armand?" Leita asked hesitantly.

"The letter—oh, you mean the letter Miss Rankin was reading. Good heavens, I don't know. I recall Mary Jo urged her to read it—something about gossip from home."

Leita felt her heart pounding in her breast. "But you must have heard something!" she insisted. "Did Darcy say anything about an elopement?" She was breathless now and attempted to rise.

"My dear, my dear, you mustn't agitate yourself like this! If the letter was so important to you I will have Miss Rankin come in to tell you. I heard nothing, really. Now you must lie down!"

Leita sank back on the pillows. She felt lifeless—her mind a blur of images. The letter in Darcy's hand. Mary Jo's shrill exclamation. "Breve has eloped!" It must have been true. She remembered looking over Darcy's shoulder at the flowing handwriting, unable to believe the words she had just heard. Now tears welled up in her eyes and spilled over onto her cheeks. She remembered his tall figure that morning outside of Greensboro when he had grabbed her horse's bridle and she had looked up into those eyes, admiring, quizzical. She remembered the sweet, rushing relief she had felt when he found her on that wooded hillside in Virginia, when he held her tightly and she had burrowed her tear-stained face into the hardness of his chest, the tenderness of his lips on her face. His eyes had been hard as black diamonds when he faced her abductor. Then the sound of his laughter filled her ears, his laughter as he sat beside the campfire at night, the firelight dancing on his face and the gleaming, crisp waves of his jet-black hair. He would be laughing as he spun tales with her brothers, reminiscing about his cavalry days. That dark hallway in the inn in Ohio, his arms around her in the middle of the night, the heat of his bare chest warming her breasts through her thin gown. The aching, yearning, tenderness of his kisses, the heat of passion that enveloped them both. The certainty of his love had been deep within her, had defied his apparent indifference, his rejections, his cruelty, because her heart had known that she was destined to belong to this man. But he had never loved her! It was so hard to believe. And now he had abandoned her, abandoned her with finality and without a backward glance. She felt a soft pressure on her cheeks and opened her eyes. Armand was dabbing at her face with his scented handkerchief.

"There is no need for tears, little one. Everything is going to be all right."

A sob clutched at her throat. Nothing would ever be all right again—nothing! How could she ever bear it?

Doctor Veaubain took up his satchel. It was late afternoon of the day after Leita's fall, and this was the fourth time he had called.

"She is in blooming health. The concussion was a light one and she is all but recovered. There is no sign of any other—upset to her system."

"You may speak freely, Doctor. Comte du Favre is my godson, as you know; and he is privy to our predicament." Annette sat beside a small table. Her flowing afternoon dress of blue bengaline swept the carpet and, except for the dark shadows beneath her eyes, she glowed with a mellow, if slightly faded, beauty.

The doctor sighed. "Well, I had anticipated that the concussion would be a shock to her system that might very well precipitate—might effect a solution to the predicament just alluded to. But that is not the case. Such an outcome would not have been delayed for over twenty-four hours. It would have begun within an hour or two of the event. As I said before, she is in blooming health. A very strong young woman. There has not been the slightest sign of a hemorrhage. Most unfortunate—most unfortunate."

Armand glanced at Lady Hidel, who had sat up the night before at Leita's bedside, hoping vainly that something of this kind would happen.

"She is not to be rescued so easily—nor are we," Lady Hidel murmured.

"Too bad, too bad." The doctor had a habit of repeating himself. "If the culprit had been identified, a marriage of convenience could be arranged. What a bizarre occurrence!"

"Bizarre, indeed," Lady Hidel agreed wryly. The doctor took his leave and Armand poured a glass of absinthe and sipped it reflectively.

His godmother glanced at his thoughtful face. "I feel a touch of guilt, my dear, for burdening you with this."

He reached over and pressed her hand. "No need of that between us. I'm very glad that you did. I have reached a conclusion, after deliberating through the night. As so often happens, my first thought proved to be the right one. If we are to have a few moments alone, I will tell you now what must be done."

"*Mon Dieu!* You have arrived at some way out of this? Whatever can have occurred to you? I have been lying awake for nights on end without a gleam of light."

"It is quite simple, really. May I?" He had pulled a cigar from his waistcoat pocket and Lady Hidel nodded a quick assent to his request.

"To begin with," he puffed until the end of the cigar was alight. "To begin with, Leita must be told exactly what transpired that night. And I will tell her."

Lady Hidel spread her hands wide. "I might have expected your wish to relieve me of that dreadful task, but I—we, as her hosts, are responsible. I will not foist that on you, dear."

Armand shook his head and there was an air of finality in the movement. "I will tell her, and then I will ask her to be my wife."

Lady Hidel gasped. "Armand, you are joking!"

"Oh, far from that. I am very serious."

Lady Hidel stood up and paced the carpet in her agitation. "I cannot allow you to sacrifice yourself in this manner. Granted, it is a dreadful affair—a fitting aftermath to a bestial incident. But it is not your responsibility. Charles has even considered a voyage to America with the sole purpose of informing her family before Leita is told."

Armand smiled—almost laughed. "I cannot agree with you that I would be sacrificing myself. I doubt if any man would consider marriage to that lovely girl to be in the category of a sacrifice."

"But you are not in love with her, Armand. That I know. You have spent much time with her, but it has been in the spirit of friendship, of companionship. *Mon Dieu!* You are still a man in the grip of grief."

Armand's eyes clouded. "I grant you that, God-mother. But I have done as you insisted. I have sojourned here in Paris. I have persevered and found that your concern was well founded. Being forced to rejoin the world again lessened my despair."

Lady Hidel looked at him tenderly. "For you, of all people, to suffer through such tragedy—the fates dealt an unreasoning blow. My prayers for you were tinged with a bitter disbelief—a refusal to accept such an unjust God. Now, when I see you smile again my heart soars. There is much of life left to you, my dear, faithful Armand."

Armand embraced her and kissed her forehead gently. "All the more reason to use it well. Now think, Godmother. This young girl finds herself with child by a father unknown. What is she to do? First of all, she must marry. I have no one to care for. The rooms of my townhouse ring hollow as a drum. My chateau lies unused, I have no companion. Furthermore, I have grown to respect her, as well as to feel affection for her. I find her company interesting, as well as diverting. She has character, that young one has, character and strength. My lineage is long, my name ancient, and I feel I could not do better than offer it to her as a shield against the conventions of this world, conventions that will ruin her name before she is twenty unless someone steps in to protect her. I can give love to Leita, if she wishes to take it, and it will make me happy, I believe, to have her by my side and to give my name to the child she will bear."

The tears were coursing down Lady Hidel's cheeks and her shoulders trembled. "I am so touched, so very touched, by your goodness—your generosity." She patted his back and laid her head on his shoulder.

"You have driven yourself frantic over Leita's plight, haven't you?"

"I have, because it seemed I could do nothing. My poor efforts to effect an abortion were without success and oh, I so dreaded telling her—telling her that her whole life was to be changed—her prospects of marriage utterly destroyed, as you know they would be if she bore an illegitimate child."

Armand nodded. "All very true, but now we can procure a husband for her. First things first. And I will tell her myself."

Leita lay awake, staring at the canopy over her bed when Armand knocked and entered.

"You may go now, Giselle. I will sit with Mademoiselle Johnston." When the maid left, Armand pulled up a chair. He felt strangely nervous. He hadn't foreseen that he would feel shy. His temperament was a quiet one, but he had never been afflicted with timidity; his demeanor always emanated poise and composure but now, suddenly he felt timorous. The eyes that Leita turned on him held an infinite sadness, an expression he had never seen in them before, and his surprised solicitude overcame his embarrassment.

"My dear girl, whatever in the world has saddened you so? The doctor tells us you are in blooming health, there is no reason for such sadness!"

Leita gave him a wavering smile. She liked this quiet, considerate man. She saw that his eyes were shadowed, as if he had gone without sleep, and she held her hand out, touching his wrist where little golden hairs gleamed in the shaft of late afternoon sunlight.

"I've been thinking of something that happened long ago, and it made me sad. It will pass."

"It does, it always does," Armand agreed. "And now, are you hungry yet? You have had nothing but broth, and very little of that, I understand. I can ring for something—some cold chicken perhaps?"

"I don't feel at all hungry."

"In that case, I want to tell you something. If you feel strong enough to talk."

"Of course I do. It was only a bump on the head." Leita smiled.

Armand's nervousness returned in full force. "To begin with—I am asking for your hand in marriage." Leita's eyes opened wide. It had been the last thing she expected him to say.

"I know you are surprised," he hastened on. "But I
308

have strong reasons for this—the foremost being my great regard for you, Leita."

Leita raised her head and Armand adjusted the pillows behind her, assisting her into an upright position. Why in the world would Comte du Favre ask her hand in marriage? He isn't in love with me—he is still mourning his wife and child, she thought. Does he know about Breve? Is it pity? Pity and loneliness that inspired this proposal?

"Armand, I am so astonished. I know you are not in love with me and I never expected this. Has Mary Jo told you something that made you think—?" She stopped, at a complete loss. She could not bring herself to say Breve's name, or to speak of this heartbreak that was tearing her apart.

"Mary Jo has told me nothing. What could she tell me? Is something troubling you, Leita?" Perhaps the girl does know, and has confided in her friend, he thought with relief. What a hope, to make my task easier!

Leita saw that he was genuinely puzzled and dismissed her sudden suspicion. She shook her head. His words began to tumble out, without giving her time for further thought.

"You know of my bereavement, and my loneliness. My whole life was centered around my wife and child. Life held nothing for me but grief. But now I know that there is still hope. Your company, your thoughtful charm, the friendship you offered have been like a balm to me, and I will be everlastingly grateful to you for it. And now I find that I can do something to repay you."

Leita smiled. The absurdity of the situation overrode her own despair, and she folded her hand in his. "A proposal of marriage is an overwhelming repayment for a friendship that was so gladly and freely given. I do like you so, Armand, and every hour spent in your company has been an hour of pleasure for me. One must not think of repaying a debt, when no debt was incurred. And I cannot marry—I cannot even think of it, for a reason that I can't bear to speak of as yet. Perhaps someday I will tell you. Someday when my heart is free again."

These words were spoken quietly and firmly. "Are you promised?" Armand asked, surprised. Perhaps there was someone waiting in America. Someone who should be informed of Leita's condition—given the opportunity to do what he was offering to do.

Leita's sigh seemed to come from her very depths. "No, Armand, I am not promised. There is no one—no one."

She is telling the truth, he thought. Very well, whatever burdens her can be dealt with later. For now we must do something about her situation.

"There is more to my proposal than my very great regard and affection for you. I find it very difficult to tell you of this, but it must be told. You must know everything before you can come to a decision." He drew a deep breath. "Do you remember the masked ball at St. Cloud?"

"The night when I got so ill? Of course I remember. You know I have never touched champagne since then."

"What is the last thing you remember of that evening?"

"The last thing?" Leita searched her mind. Why had he diverted his conversation to that night? How strange this was! "Oh, I know. I was dancing with Sir Charles' nephew, and I was very hot and dizzy. I remember nothing after that. I had drunk so much champagne. The rest of the night is a complete blank until the next morning when I awakened here in my bed, feeling very ill, I might add. If I behaved disgracefully no one has told me of it."

Armand smiled dryly. "You didn't behave disgracefully, but something did happen, something you know nothing of. Lady Hidel and Sir Charles have been distraught with worry in these weeks since that night." He paused. She looked so fragile, sitting up against the pillows, her violet eyes wide and puzzled now.

"You were drugged that night, drugged with laudanum. A doctor was summoned when we brought you home."

"Drugged?" Leita's brows flew up. "Laudanum—that's a sleeping potion, isn't it? Something they give to teething babies."

"Yes, but you were given much, much more than that. Enough to render you unconscious."

Leita's thoughts darted wildly back to that night and the next morning. "How do you know this?"

"The doctor assured us that was what had happened."

"But how, how did it happen? Did other people get sick?"

Armand shook his head. "No, it was intended solely for you. And there was a reason."

"But why? If this really happened, why? Why would anyone want to drug me and make me sick?" She was utterly bewildered.

Armand hesitated. Here was the crux of the matter. Perhaps it would be better to be startlingly direct. To state it barely.

"The reason was lust. The object was to render you unconscious so that this lust could be satisfied. And it was."

"What are you saying?" She had a sudden, sick feeling in the pit of her stomach.

"You became ill while dancing. Sir Charles saw you

311

leave the floor and a little later went in search of you. You had been taken to a room off the side gallery. You had been rendered unconscious and were violated while you were unconscious." He enunciated these words clearly, all the while watching her face.

This must be a dream—some kind of nightmare! It was so absurd, hearing Armand's measured, gentlemanly tones describing something so ridiculous.

"I have never heard anything so ridiculous!" It wasn't real—it couldn't be.

"Ridiculous? In a way, yes. But horrifying. You see, Sir Charles entered the room where you lay, just as your attacker finished the act. Only minutes too late to prevent it."

"You are saying that someone violated me while I was asleep. In fact, put me to sleep for that purpose? Oh, this is too bizarre!" Leita's mind was still incapable of embracing this as fact.

"Exactly. And he escaped," Armand said flatly.

Leita said nothing, made no response. It was like some gruesome fairy tale that had nothing to do with her. She was mildly surprised that Armand seemed to believe it.

He read her thoughts. "He was still masked and in costume. In short, he was unidentifiable, and he fled from the room by another door when Sir Charles entered from the gallery. He was wearing a Pirandel costume—of which there were many—and his identity was and is unknown."

Leita sat up straighter. Armand was right. There had been many Pirandel costumes—it was a favorite role for masked balls. Even Jack Hidel had been wearing one. Mary Jo had commented on his lack of originality.

"But if I don't remember it, and this, whoever he was, ran away, why are you so certain it happened at all?"

"Because of your position when Sir Charles entered the room, and the action of the man." I am going to have to be specific with her, or she will not believe it. "Your dress was so arranged, or disarranged, as to facilitate his actions. You had plainly been assaulted. And he—here I must be even more indelicate—he was fastening up his trousers when Sir Charles surprised him."

Leita's nose wrinkled in disgust.

"It was undoubtedly someone who is mad. It was the act of a madman."

"If this really happened, why did no one tell me?" Leita asked, still unable to take it seriously.

"In the beginning, it was thought that you would be better off not knowing. You hadn't been injured. Doctor Veaubain made certain of that. It was decided that since it could only distress you, and the culprit was unknown, it would be better that you weren't told, since you remembered nothing of it. But now it is necessary that you know."

Leita's expression of perplexity didn't alter but she made no response.

Armand drew another deep breath. "You see, my dear girl, that heinous act has resulted in your being with child."

He waited for this to sink in.

She blinked and seemed relatively unmoved. It was obvious that his words made no sense to her. He deliberated a moment, then pulled the bell rope to summon a servant. Leita hadn't uttered a word.

The servant entered almost immediately and left after Armand requested coffee.

He walked back to the bedside then and looked down at her. "My godmother has been beside herself with worry. I may say, I think she would approve my telling you, that the tisanes you have been dosed with were given with the hope of effecting an end to your condition. But I understand they have been of no avail."

Leita frowned again. Questions, questions about her last flow. And those endless cups of hot, herb tea. She hadn't minded them, had taken them for the natural solicitude of a kindly woman. Could this possibly be true? She pressed her hands to her breasts. They had been tender and swollen for some weeks now. She had taken it to be the result of the disruption of her flow, had expected it any day but had not been concerned. The flow had come twice in the interval since Breve held her in his arms. Her eyes misted. If this hideous joke were really true, why couldn't it have been his? But it can't be!

"I was unaware of this until yesterday, though I had been growing more concerned with your health. I knew it wasn't natural for you to faint so unexpectedly—so frequently. Yesterday, after it happened again my godmother was so distraught and I so concerned that she finally confided in me. Even the doctor had hoped that your injury might result in ending your pregnancy. But it did not."

Armand sat down suddenly on the bed and took her hands in his. "I lay awake the whole night thinking of your plight. My first thought when the situation was brought home to me was that you needed a man's protection. What could be more obvious than the solution I immediately thought of? You cannot—you must not—bear this child while you are still unwed."

Armand was so vehement that Leita closed her eyes for a second, as if to evade the force of his speech.

"This is actually true?" she whispered. "You say that I am going to have a child, as the result of a rape?"

"That is the case," Armand said heavily.

"Oh, dear God!" Dismay flooded her. What was she

to do? She didn't even know who the father was! And what would she tell her own father? He would be wild with—with what? Not anger at her, certainly. But he would blame himself for having allowed her to come. An illegitimate child, in that town! It would be an object of gossip, of scorn, this unreal baby that she would bear. She recoiled in horror at the image of herself, unwieldy and pregnant, being whispered about, being ostracized. Her whole life, and the life of an innocent baby, blighted because of some madman.

The maid entered her sitting room with the tray and Armand got up quickly, took the tray from her and returned to the boudoir.

"Yes, I would like some coffee." She took the cup from Armand and sipped at the frothy sweetness. "I have been ill in the mornings," she said suddenly. "The hot chocolate makes me ill. Was that because of—"

Armand nodded. "Undoubtedly."

She emptied half the cup before she spoke again. "And that is why you asked me to marry you."

He smiled gently. "Partly. I am not being totally unselfish, you understand. My life is empty. If you become my wife my solitude will be relieved, my sadness diminished. I will welcome the child. And I have great affection for you, Leita. Otherwise it would not have occurred to me. I want you to understand that. For my part, I would not be entering a loveless union. I didn't ask for your hand out of charity, my dear girl. It would give meaning to my life." He was choosing his words carefully, watchfully. She was subdued, even calm. He had expected an outburst of despairing tears, but her pale face was quiet.

"Does Lady Hidel know—know what you have asked me?"

"Yes. My godmother is one of the kindest women alive. She has been crucifying herself over this."

Leita closed her eyes and sighed heavily. "I need to think, Armand. I need time to think about this. You understand that, don't you?"

He rose. "Of course I do. I never thought that you would be able to make up your mind right away. I will leave you now, if you like, and whatever you do, you must remember that I am and will remain your devoted friend."

Leita gazed at him solemnly. "There is something splendid about you, Armand. I don't think I have ever admired anyone so much in my life."

He took her hand in his and brushed it with his lips, then left.

Leita got up late that evening and shakily walked the floor, finally stationing herself in the window where she looked up at the flowering stars in the dark night sky. She felt no hunger, hardly any thirst, she felt only numbness as she faced the import of the tale Armand had told her.

It was one o'clock in the morning when the ache in her chest spread and her shoulders shook as the sobs she had suppressed rose, almost choking her. She clung to the curtain, bowed in a defeat and a heartbreak so agonizing that she felt her body must break in two. She wept, wept as if she would never stop, could never stop. The bitter, salty tears flowed down her cheeks and she clasped her arms across her breast, bending until she knelt on the floor by the open window. The cool night air bathed her trembling body, chilling her till she finally crept to the bed where she lay sobbing into the pillows. Occasionally through the rest of the night she would fall asleep, exhausted, but there was no surcease from her memories of Breve. In these dreams he always looked at her with tenderness, his voice true and clear in her sleep. His tall figure astride his horse, his smile

316

warm on her as they galloped side by side down tree-lined roads, as they waltzed, his arm firmly around her and laughter dancing in his dark eyes.

The sky was pink when she stood by the window, her face tearstained and pale, her eyelids so swollen it was difficult for her to see. It was by the first, soft light of dawn that she came to her decision.

Chapter 20

"SHE IS NOT EVEN CATHOLIC. IN MY ANXIETY I OVER-looked that. It is going to take some string-pulling, Armand." Lady Hidel was bustling around her morning room, her face alight with excitement.

"And that is precisely what I am on my way to do—some very selective string-pulling." Armand straightened his cravat and gave a cursory sweep of his hand to his fine, blond hair. He felt pleased, rejuvenated even, and there was a lightness to his step that had been missing for a long time when he took himself out the door.

Mary Jo was standing with her mouth open, quite literally gasping with astonishment, watching Leita as she dipped a brioche in her coffee and leisurely ate it.

"You aren't! You can't! You're just saying this to tease me and get me all riled up."

"Now when did I ever do that?" Leita smiled and wiped her mouth with the napkin. Chilled cloths had reduced the swelling of her eyelids until it was only barely noticeable and she presented a picture of relaxed assurance as she sat up in bed, concentrating on the breakfast before her. Now that her decision was made, her predicament comprehended and faced, she felt strangely peaceful. She hadn't eaten for some thirty-six hours and she was relishing the hot, buttery brioche. She missed the breakfasts of home, when, after her early morning ride she was accustomed to filling her plate with a succulent slice of ham and an egg or two, along with the hot biscuits and preserves.

"It is to be sometime this evening, that is, if Armand is able to arrange everything by that time. And I am truly happy about it. Now don't make such a face. You are fond of Armand, I know you are."

"Of course I'm fond of him. He's so near perfect I don't know how anyone could help but be fond of him. But I haven't seen even one little tiny sign to say that you are in love with him!"

Mary Jo stepped closer to the bed. She had recovered sufficiently to feel hunger, and now she broke off a piece of brioche and popped it into her mouth. "Giselle brought an extra cup. I'll pour you some coffee," Leita said, and proceeded to do so. Mary Jo was looking at her piercingly.

"Look at your eyes—all swollen up like a poisoned pup! You've cried half the night. It was the news about Breve eloping that made you do this!" Mary Jo dropped down onto the bed. "Leita honey, you just can't! You can't just up and marry someone you don't love—even that sweet wonderful man, because of Breve. When I came back in the room that day and you were gone, I said to myself she's gone upstairs to cry her eyes out, and I decided I'd better leave you alone for a while. When I found out later that you had fainted and hit your head I was just positive it was the shock of what that ninny said about Breve. Now it's one thing to

320

get your heart broken, but it's another thing entirely to throw away the rest of your life just because the man you love took it into his head to go off with somebody else!"

Leita had dropped her eyes at the beginning of Mary Jo's outburst and then, unable to bear any more, she threw back the covers and snatched at her robe. Putting it on she took her hairbrush and began brushing her hair with great energy. Please don't let me cry, please don't let me cry, she prayed silently. Mary Jo was so much a part of her life, her presence so tied in with those long, golden days when they rode beside the wagons on the way north. She went on brushing her hair. What can I say to her? She knows, she has always known that I love Breve, love him desperately! But I can't bear to talk about it now—to talk about his being married to someone else.

Mary Jo's torrent of words continued and she stood beside Leita, her eyes flashing with feeling.

"Oh, stop, Jo! Please stop! I just can't bear to be nagged and bullied on top of everything else that's happened!"

"You poor darling!" Mary Jo was instantly contrite and threw her arms around Leita. This was Leita's undoing. Her thin hold on composure was broken and she dissolved in tears, weeping into Mary Jo's scented curls.

"There, there now. You just go ahead and beller." Mary Jo patted Leita's heaving shoulders. Her face was contorted with sorrow and her eyes perplexed. She was obviously searching for something—anything to say that would relieve Leita's tortured feelings.

"I'll tell you this," Mary Jo burst out with indignation as Leita sobbed bitterly, "when I get my hands on him he'll be sorry that he ever did such a fool thing—he'll just be sorry."

Leita began hiccuping and the hiccups gradually mixed with laughter. The absurdity of it! The picture of Breve cowering before an angry Mary Jo, being castigated because he had been so unwise as to marry someone other than Leita was so ridiculous that her tears were stanched and she drew back.

"Well, that's some better," Mary Jo said emphatically, and going to the china basin, wrung out a cloth in cool water and began to bathe her friend's face.

"I'm goin' to tell you something I've never talked about before. It may help some." She looked at Leita speculatively. "If anything can."

"When I was fifteen I fell in love—just head over heels in love. He was the best-lookin' man I ever did see, and he was the sweetest talkin' man that ever walked the face of the earth. He was twenty-four, he said." She took up the cup of coffee that Leita had poured for her and sipped it. "He sweet-talked me into runnin' off with him. We were goin' to be married. He was new in Greensboro. Said he was rich. His folks were supposed to be back in New York and we were goin' to get married on the way there. Well, come to find out he was already married. He was the father of a baby, too. He was countin' on my daddy to pay him money—a lot of money—to go away and leave me alone." She sat down heavily on the small slipper chair, the cup cradled in her hands, and there was a bleakness in her blue eyes as she continued. "My daddy paid him all right, and it was a real-for-sure scandal around those parts. I think that was one reason Daddy was so all-fired set on movin' north. Nobody worth anything would have asked to marry me around Greensboro, not after that. Well, you might think that I would have been mad, bitter-mad, at bein' so fooled." Her voice dropped and she was silent for what seemed to Leita a very long moment. Then she raised her face and looked squarely at Leita who stood still holding the hairbrush. "I wasn't. I was just heartbroken. And I stayed in love with that man for the longest time. I couldn't forget him—I thought no one else would ever do for me. So I've got some idea of what you're goin' through, Leita." There was a little catch in her voice that brought Leita to her side. She knelt on the floor beside her with her arm across her friend's knees.

"I do love you, Jo. I'll never have another friend in my life like you."

Mary Jo's eyes were bright with a film of years. "Then you better listen to me, because there's more. About three months after that happened, one of the boys I'd always known came courting me. It didn't take him long to ask Daddy for my hand. When Daddy told me I said yes—right away. He was surprised, but Mama came up to my room that night. She was real worried. You see, she knew something of how I had felt about Tom, and she knew I was still pining for him. She had a long talk with me—and I changed my mind about tearin' right off to the church to marry John. She said, you see, that she knew my heart was just broken over what had happened, but trying to pretend I loved someone else and trying to forget Tom by getting right busy being married to a man I didn't love would do nothing but bring me real unhappiness in the long run. She said that no matter how hard it was to believe, someday I wouldn't love Tom anymore—I would always remember him but I wouldn't be in love with him—it wouldn't hurt anymore. Now you know how calm and sweet Mama is; not a thing like me. She liked John and he had always been stuck on me. Anybody else might have jumped at the chance to marry me off, all things considered. But she was thinking of my happiness and I knew it, so I listened." She gazed steadily at Leita. "And she was right. I wouldn't have him now if he was the President."

Leita laid the hairbrush down carefully and remained silent. I cannot imagine not loving Breve, she thought.

"And I'm everlastingly glad that I didn't marry John," Mary Jo added meaningfully.

When Leita spoke it was with finality. "I'm going to marry Armand, Jo. It's settled, and someday I'll tell you the whole story."

"What more could there be?" Mary Jo asked.

"There is a very important 'more.' It has to be, Jo, and believe me, I'm not going into it lightly. I'm not marrying Armand out of spite, or because of my broken heart, and I'm going to be as good a wife to him as it's in me to be. You'll understand some day. I just can't talk about it now."

Mary Jo tapped her lower lip with her fingertip. "All right. I'll not harangue you anymore, honey. But I'll tell you something else. I, for one, don't happen to swallow that story whole—about Breve, I mean. I've got a deep-down feeling that he didn't run off and get married at all. One reason is that I think for sure that he is in love with you—and don't forget, I know him!"

"Mary Jo," Leita's voice was earnest, "if we had never made that trip to Chicago I might agree with you. But I know, know for dead certain now, that he doesn't love me. No man would act the way he did if he loved a woman."

"What way?" Mary Jo asked sharply.

"I can't ever tell you that. But I know," Leita answered, almost in a whisper.

Leita lay down after Mary Jo left. She felt the fatigue that comes with vanquished hope, with great disappointment, and she lay quietly, staring at the bed hangings. Her thoughts moved in random directions as

324

she wondered what it was going to be like—this life that was offered her, as the Comtesse du Favre. She chuckled once as she thought of Mrs. Ridenour, their housekeeper at home. She could see her, heavy, freckle-spangled arms akimbo, eyebrows raised in mock dismay. "So it's a countess you are, is it? And I suppose you'll be lordin' it over a castle now? One of them Frenchies picked you off, just like I told your pa would happen." No, no castle, Mrs. Ridenour, a chateau in a green valley where I will have to learn how to be happy again. She wondered about the chateau. Armand spoke of it with such proprietary love, describing the clear blue waters of the river below the summit on which it rested and the fields of staked grape vines and the wheat, and the horses. It will be nice to ride again, my own horse, every day. But for how long? When would she have to retire from society, as was customary when one reached a very obvious state of pregnancy. And what of this baby? Her hand stroked her abdomen hesitantly. How difficult to believe, that a child was growing inside her. She examined her feelings carefully. I don't feel bitter toward it, she concluded with relief. It couldn't help it. But who—who in God's name could have drugged her and caused this? She had wrung her memories of that night dry; it was no use. She could remember nothing after dancing with Jack Hidel, when she had been so hot and thirsty and dizzy from the champagne. She thought of the courtiers, the effete aristocrats who flirted with her, every other partner she had had all evening, and she grimaced. So many of them could be imagined capable of such a thing. The open dalliances she had observed at the balls and public gardens and receptions had shocked her deeply in the beginning. She had talked about it with Lady Hidel, who had told her, in her sprightly, good-natured way, that marriage for the most part was a question of finances and solidifying important family connections. One couldn't be blamed if, subjected to a loveless marriage, one took one's pleasure where it could be taken. Most men kept mistresses, their wives took lovers. It was all to be expected. One had to be very careful that one's children were born on the right side of the blanket, to borrow a peasant expression, since heredity and the progression of titles was of extreme importance. But then again, one could never be certain. She herself had been fortunate; she had married for love and the love had flourished, therefore she had led a far less complicated life than her friends and acquaintances. Leita pondered the dissolute ways of so many of the men in the circle she had entered and decided that what she viewed as horrible would probably be considered a diverting prank by many of them. And one quickly forgotten, she thought bitterly. But not by me. She forsook this train of thought and speculated on her responsibilities as Armand's wife. Probably a score of servants, at least, she thought with alarm. And the townhouse, which he is scarcely ever in, that will be a responsibility, too. Good, she thought decisively—it will be good for me. I will have so much to learn, so many things to do that I won't be able to think about anything else. Not if I'm careful. And Armand had promised her this morning that they would journey to America regularly. She would not be separated from her family for years on end. The planting and the harvest were great occupations with him, and the pressing of the grapes and the supervision of the wine-making. Armand was not a disinterested landowner. Everything that happened on his estate was directed by him, but there would be free periods when his presence wasn't required and they could spend them in Indiana with her father and mother and brothers. Daddy will like him, she thought, and that is like balm to my heart. He must never know what happened here—it must always be kept from him. There was a knock at the door and Armand entered, his eyes bright and his glossy brown cravat slightly askew.

"My dear, are you feeling better now?"

Leita forced a smile. "I am feeling much better. And what are all those papers?"

Armand waved a thick sheaf of papers at her. "The result of great and untiring activity. The Abbé Longquist will be here at eight o'clock to read the service. This arrangement was made after no little pressure was applied to the good Abbot by the Bishop, who fortunately was a close friend of my father's and was delighted to help me expedite my marriage. In fact, he plans to attend. Godmother and Miss Tillett are qualified as witnesses, and now all that is required is your signature on only a hundred or so of these documents."

He is happy, Leita thought. I have never seen him so animated. He is actually happy at the prospect of marrying a girl he is not in love with and becoming a father to her child—a child whose paternity is unknown. She felt a rush of warmth for him. I knew he was sad, but I never realized the depth of his loneliness until now. She went to him and put both her hands in his.

"I want you to know how deeply grateful I am to you, Armand."

He blushed and looked like an awkward boy for a moment. She raised on tiptoe and kissed him.

That's good, Lady Hidel thought, as she swept into the room. The Lord moves in wondrous ways—this union may be blessed already. "You two are dallying!" she cried. "And so much to do." She indicated the mass of white satin hanging from her arm. "I've been to see Felix and he sends his most fervent congratulations.

327

Also, this dress was taken in to your measurements exactly, and I think it will be beautiful, particularly in candlelight."

And the day sped on.

At eight o'clock that August evening the candles were lit in the main drawing room and the Abbé Longquist performed an abridged ceremony, joining in marriage Armand Francois Auguste de la Penseans, the Comte du Favre, and Leita Caroline Johnston in holy matrimony. The ivory-tinged white satin shimmered in the light as Leita knelt. The film of tears in her violet eyes were thought no more than to be expected under the circumstances. Armand stood erect, his mind wandering occasionally to another ceremony when he had been younger and convinced that life held everything for him and the girl beside him. The two little sons of the Duc de Maine had been brought to hold the traditional yoke of white satin above the couple and their eyes danced with excitement as they played their part. Mary Jo stood resolute and solemn beside Leita. In her mind's eye she was seeing a girl in a frothy pink dress laughing up at Breve Pinchon who looked down at her, oblivious to everyone around him. Mary Jo sniffed. Lady Hidel thought she was moved by the moment, but she was wrong. Mary Jo was thinking of how Leita and Breve looked that first night in Greensboro, when their love had just begun.

Chapter 21

COLD WINDS GUSTED ACROSS THE ATLANTIC AND THE night was dark and cloud-soaked, but the main saloon of the French liner was bright with gaslight. The red velvet curtains were closed against the blackness of the night outside and soft, blue cigar smoke swirled in hazy ellipses around the heads of the men seated at the baize-covered tables.

Breve Pinchon picked up his glass of lightly watered bourbon and bid a goodnight to the other men at the table. "You have enough of my money for this evening," he grinned. Amiable hoots of derision met this remark.

"If I play with you every night of this voyage I'll be pauperized before we reach Le Havre," one man with a cadaverous face laughed.

When Breve sauntered off he was joined by a tall, slender man with slick dark hair and a skin so white that any woman on board would have envied it.

"If you're going to take a turn around the deck I'll join you, if you don't mind."

"Come along," Breve smiled.

"I'm getting off at Southampton. Where are you headed for?" the man asked.

"Ultimately Geneva. I have some business there. But I'm going to stop off in Paris and take a look at it first. Are you hungry? I intend to try to scare up something to eat before I turn in."

"I can always eat," the other man said amiably. "But aren't we too late?"

"Not if we handle it right," Breve chuckled.

The major domo was overseeing the laying of the tables for early breakfast in the morning when Breve approached him. The elderly man shook his head sorrowfully, then accepted what Breve pressed into his hand and Breve returned to his acquaintance. "Sit down. We've been promised some cold turkey sandwiches and a bottle of claret."

Breve looked at the man with curiosity. He was tall and well-favored. Has a rakish gleam to his eye, Breve thought. He extended his hand. "If we've met I don't recall your name. I'm Breve Pinchon."

The other thrust his hand forward and grasped Breve's in a strong, dry grip. "Daniel O'Connell. I'm traveling to Cairo, posted there at the consulate, but I'm stopping off in England first. I have a few more days of leave and I intend to use them."

"With the Consulate in Cairo? Well, you don't have dull work," Breve reflected. The claret was uncorked and the sleepy-eyed waiter poured an inch or two in Breve's glass. He tasted it and signified his approval.

"It isn't dull now. It's a fascinating place, if you can stand the heat and the flies. Jam-packed with adventurers from almost every country in the world. Small chance they stand against the populace, though."

330

Daniel O'Connell tasted the claret and lifted the top of his sandwich and pelted it with salt.

"I wasn't there before the canal was begun, of course, but they tell me it wasn't the same."

"What an undertaking," Breve remarked. "If De Lesseps hadn't had the tenacity of a bulldog it could never have been done."

"True, true," Daniel agreed. "England didn't just throw stones in his path, they rolled boulders into it. If Napoleon hadn't bailed them out, that ditch would be filling up with sand right now."

"It was over fifty million francs, wasn't it?" Breve asked.

"Over eighty million! But he had to do it. The Bourse would have collapsed if he hadn't. Two hundred and some thousand shares of the company were taken up in France. When England worked on the Sultan and got him to pull all the Egyptian labor off the canal back in 1863, the whole project would have folded if Napoleon hadn't stepped in. Victoria's government has greased every palm in the Orient to keep that canal from opening, but they're going to have to eat crow now," Daniel remarked with satisfaction.

"Irish, aren't you?" Breve grinned.

"To the core," Daniel smiled.

"Strange place for an Irishman, Cairo," Breve remarked.

"It was a plum. A few more years, if I behave well and stay out of brawls, I can look forward to being posted in Paris. There is a lot to be said for that, as compared to Boston." Daniel laughed.

"What sent you into the diplomatic service?" Breve inquired. The young man beside him was so vigorous and imbued with such unmistakable intelligence that Breve was puzzled at the choice of a career which left him so little leeway for his own initiative.

331

"My father sent me into the diplomatic service, simple as that. He makes soap—O'Connell's peerless soap, maybe you've heard of it?"

"Lord yes—that must be a thriving concern. Chicago is plastered with posters advertising it."

"Thriving it is. He's richer than Croesus," Daniel stated affably. "But Boston is Boston. If you're Irish you had *better* be rich—then they don't spit on you quite as freely. He decided early in my life that he didn't want his shining heir to be buried in the soap works—I was to get out in the world and take advantage of being a rich man. He made such a healthy contribution to the Republican party that they could refuse him nothing—ergo, I'm a vice-consul. I could have had London, but my spirit recoiled at that. I prefer to learn the ropes in a post where I'm not under such close and critical observation. So I chose Cairo to make my gaffes, and I haven't been sorry. It's a fascinating place—exotic, colorful, and slightly dangerous. You can buy anything in Cairo, and sell anything. There isn't a vice in the world, nor a piece of thievery that doesn't thrive there. You ought to come down there when you finish up in Geneva, see the canal. It's a wonder. Port Said is growing—rising up like a Phoenix from marshes and flats where Lake Menzala lay before. The whole enterprise is so damned impressive. Did you know there was a canal there over two thousand years ago?"

Breve lifted his brows.

"There was," O'Connell asserted. "There was a channel from the Nile to the bitter lakes and from there a channel to the Red Sea. When old Darius conquered Egypt he enlarged it. The Persians were enterprising and the Ptolemies kept it open after that until the Cape route to India took the trade that way. And now it will cement France as a power. That canal is one hundred miles long and every ship that passes through its locks will pay a toll. Imagine controlling the waterway for shipping from the East to every European port."

"Not to mention the advantage to France in any future war. They will control Mediterranean traffic, won't they?"

"You bet your boots they will!" Daniel chuckled, and then changed course abruptly. "Are you married?"

Breve swallowed the mouthful of sandwich before he answered. "No, I'm single."

"What do you do?"

"I sell stocks, bonds, railroad shares, mining shares."

"A bandit without a gun." O'Connell laughed.

Breve chuckled. "I'm above reproach; no reason to be otherwise. You can make money easily if you use your head, not to mention a little imagination."

Daniel O'Connell put his head to one side and ran the napkin over his broad mouth. "You're a southerner, aren't you?"

"Born and bred in Charleston—Chicago's my home now, though."

"You carried a gun, didn't you?" Daniel had looked him over appraisingly before this question.

"Yes I did, carried it on a horse," Breve assented. "Tenth cavalry."

"I was a Lieutenant, and I survived too," Daniel said, with a faroff look in his blue eyes. "Do you run into any enmity now that you're up North?"

"Not a bit. I think it's the South that cherishes its hate—with reason. Being conquered is a very bitter pill. Then too, northerners are a more practical bunch by far. We southerners are romantics." Breve made a small grimace.

"You must come to Cairo. I personally will show you the time of your life. Since you are single I have another inducement. Egyptian females are definitely off-limits—they're muffled up to their ears in veils and only the almehs live free lives."

"Almehs?"

"Prostitutes. Cairo is alive with them. There are some really beautiful ones, but I have no truck with them. Disease, man. They're riddled with it. I leave that to the others, but there are the Europeans. Numerous unattached ladies, sightseeing. Eager for a view of the pyramids and adventure in the Orient. Lovely ones too. Something about being that far away from home in such an exotic place brings out the wanton in the most protected and refined. You've got to come. We'll turn the town upside down."

Breve laughed. He liked this fellow, liked his enthusiasm and the ready twinkle in his eye. He considered the invitation for a moment or two and then drained his glass. "This trip of mine is full of imponderables. I can't say how long my business will take me—probably not long in Geneva; that part is open and shut." He refilled Daniel's glass and then his own before he continued. "But if I have time left, I'll take you up on your invitation."

Daniel's response was hearty and sincere. "Good! You won't regret it. My duties aren't so demanding that I can't come and go as I please, so I will be free to take you around. The Khedive is building a new opera house for the canal opening. We can even get a river boat and go up the Nile a ways, you can see how the Egyptians live outside the city. You will sail to Alexandria and there's a train down to Cairo. It isn't too bad either. Just let me know when you will arrive and I can arrange my schedule accordingly."

When they parted, they arranged to meet the next day. Daniel went to his stateroom, but Breve decided to take a turn around the deck. He was restless, though it was late and he had slept little the night before. He stood at the rail and listened to the slap of the waves against the hull. He walked on, intending to head for his bed, then stopped again and lit a cigar. The sigh that escaped him was tremulous. What would she say when she saw him? It won't be easy, not after what happened, he thought. She may well refuse to see me at all. I will just have to persevere. We will need to be alone, uninterrupted for long enough to tell her the whole story at my own pace. He drew on the cigar, lost in memories, memories of Leita cantering along the road ahead of the wagons, her straw hat tied with emerald-green ribbon, that shining mane of hair bouncing on her shoulders. She had loved that life, up at dawn, greedy for breakfast, then starting off with the early morning birdsong a melodious clamor from the trees. By noon her cheeks would be flushed from the sun. He bit his lip at the memory of that night beside the river when he had first felt the softness of her body against him. He had taken her in his arms without forethought, driven by a love for her that surmounted his knowledge, certain then, that he could never have her. The softness of her mouth under his, and the second kiss, when her lips had parted and his rushing passion had forced his tongue between them and her shuddering intake of breath. He had been lost, the scent of her skin and the fullness of her breasts straining against him till he had forced his hand down her nightdress to grasp and caress her stiffened, projecting nipples. The supple heat of her body against him in the cool night, his delight in her sweetness, her fiery candor, her sharp intelligence, all the qualities that had given birth to his love for her swept over him that night when he bore her to the ground, laying her gently in the bed of soft leaves. He had forgotten everything as his hand swept under her gown and he ran his fingers over the pounding pulse in her groin, caressing the soft dampness between her thighs. Her legs had felt like satin against his hips and he had felt the beat of her heart in his mouth when he seized her nipple in his lips. She had gasped, then pressed his head closer to her throbbing breast and his mouth had grown fiercer, more tenderly devouring until he thrust into the enveloping heat between her thighs and knew nothing but the surging fire in his own loins as his hands gripped the sweet fullness of her hips under the sheer gown and she rose to meet his thrusts with little moans of ecstasy, her tongue darting over his lips, her arms locked around his back. He remembered one moment when he had looked down into her face, transfigured with the love they were consummating there in the darkness of the trees, her hair spread out on fallen leaves. . . . Breve sighed and tossed his cigar far out onto a cresting wave. He had known passion, known desire, many times. That he was hotblooded he had acknowledged to himself long ago, but never had he known the searing tenderness, the glory of possession, the fullness of heart that he had known when Leita lay breathless in his arms. Love and lust are so far apart, he thought. Sated lust is like sated hunger: you satisfy it and it's over—but love, love is so powerful that you stay drowned in it. One small body, one ringing laugh, one shining presence becomes life's necessity. And what if she recoils from what I have to tell her, must tell her? What then? His step was purposeful as he walked toward the stateroom. If she does recoil, then I will have to wait until I fall in love again. I won't spend my life yearning for one female, he thought, as his key turned into the lock.

Stephen de Jean stood looking down at the roiling waters of the Ruhr. He was on his way to Essen. He had journeyed first to Ems, where General von Roon's

336

reception of the Frenchman had been marked with stolid dignity, and had ended with a chuckle.

"I can do nothing for you. I would advise you to see Alfred. He holds the funds you have come to redeem. The greatest foundry in the world, but Alfred is always short of kronen." The General had chuckled tolerantly, seemingly unaware of Stephen's tension.

"You will enjoy the trip. Our waters are beautiful, particularly now at this time of year. We are famous for our forests, as you know. You will be impressed. Ah, I envy you wealthy Americans; time to travel, time to enjoy."

Stephen had itched to grasp the rolls of fat around his throat. Unctuous and patronizing, General von Roon had exuded cordiality, and Stephen had shaken his sweat-dampened hand, afterward scrubbing his own hand vigorously with his fine cambric handkerchief.

Now the waters of the Ruhr, which had been blue and crystal-clear for miles, began to roil and darken. The sludge from the sprawling, gray, fire-brightened Krupp steel works began to change the river even at this point. A dull, far-off thumping reverberated in the air—the sound of the steam hammer pistons. The thick, deep forests absorbed the light from the sky and beyond them its blue was browned by the sulphurous fumes.

Later that morning Stephen alighted from the carriage and viewed the spectacle before him with a kind of dismay. Boiling smoke filled the air, swirling over one gray building after another and Stephen stared round him at the sprawling iron and steel works where cannon was turned out and sold indiscriminately to Russia, France, any country that required armaments and could pay. He had come to see Alfred Krupp,

337

overlord and erratic guiding hand of the largest arma-
ment manufacturing business in the world where rolling
mills boomed and scorching fires raged. And where a
crazy man is seated at the helm, Stephen thought
bitterly, a man who thinks of nothing but iron and steel
and amassing funds wherever he can to fire his mania.
Stephen shook his head wearily. He was tired, furiously
angry, and full of foreboding at the coming interview.
He had wired ahead; Krupp knew he was coming, and
from now on he must be artful and watchful and
persuasive. He drew himself erect, chin thrust forward,
and strode up to the guard, swinging his walking stick
as he did so.

One hour later Stephen sat in an anteroom, still
waiting. The plush of the two ancient chairs which
graced the otherwise bare room were darkened to the
color of dried blood by an overlay of grime.

He rose when the man entered the room, a man with
his head set squarely on his shoulders, seemingly
without benefit of a neck, and a soot-studded white
shirt collar pressing his jowls upward.

"Yes, Mr. Reischoff. I trust you have word for me. I
have been waiting for one hour now." Stephen's voice
was cold, his glance haughty. He was aware that Ernest
Reischoff was a brother-in-law of Alfred Krupp but he
was damned if he would curry favor with him. If he was
to gain his end, his dignity would have to be asserted.

"I am so sorry, so very sorry, Herr de Jean." Ernest
Reischoff spread wide palms apart. "He is frantically
busy just now—he sends his deepest apologies to
you—it cannot be helped. A forge is not functioning,
you understand."

"He troubles himself with forges?" Stephen inquired
coolly.

"He troubles himself with everything—everything!"
Ernest wiped a sweating brow. "But Herr de Jean,

wait!" Stephen had turned on his heel, preparing to leave for the moment, so angry was he.

"Herr Krupp has asked me to beg of you your company at dinner tonight—at the Gartenhaus. Then he will be able to talk and to enjoy your company. He is most desirous of this, Herr de Jean."

Stephen deliberated. This was a happy chance. Dinner was a much more propitious environment for explaining his mission than a hasty conversation in the midst of this goddamned noise and dirt. A few bottles of wine, conversation, a little judicious flattery if the occasion seemed to warrant it. He bowed. "I will be happy to accept Herr Krupp's kind invitation. And the hour?"

"Eight o'clock. And a happy farewell to you, Herr de Jean." Reischoff beamed and Stephen bestowed a restrained smile on him before bowing his way out.

At five minutes till eight that evening Stephen had found his way to the front step of the Gartenhaus. The man is demented, he thought, not just demented, stark, raving mad. Krupp's home was situated in the middle of his works, within the sprawling mass of buildings and annexes and the sound of the hammers still rang in the evening air. The house rose heavenward, a pile of gray stone that looked as if it might have been tossed there by drunken giants. It was an orgy of towers and turrets and mullioned windows and carved fretwork. Its periphery was marked by hothouses, hothouses containing God-knows-what, Stephen thought. Their panes of glass were so darkened by soot and smoke that nothing could be seen of their interior. Perhaps baby cannon, Stephen conjectured and smiled, the first time that day.

Stephen handed his silk hat and cane to the stark-featured butler and looked around in the gloom. The interior was even worse. He followed the man into a drawing room where the furniture was covered with dingy antimacassars. Heavy velvet drapes shut out the sight of the smoke and Stephen was joined by a man who looked to be at least seventy. Alfred Krupp extended a scrawny hand, a hand whose tendons were prominent and whose fingers were curled. His face was long, gray and pinched, his eyes a piercing gray with pink-tinged whites. His hair, what there was of it, was iron-gray and straggled in wisps down to his collar, hanging over his corded and somehow pitiful looking neck. He looked at Stephen quickly and furtively and shook hands with haste, as if he were going to hurry from the room.

"Such a pleasure you could dine with me. I am alone. My wife is gone—to the waters. She is not well—her health is delicate." The speech was delivered haltingly, in a dry staccato, and Stephen assured him that he was delighted to receive the invitation. Alfred Krupp's eyes darted again and again to Stephen's face and he turned and led the way through the open doors into a dining room that was at least the length of a ballroom. The vast expanse of the mahogany table was graced at one end with a silver candelabra and two places were laid with gold-rimmed china. The plates and goblets were shivering and the dishes on the sideboard trembled. The house, so solidly and massively built, reverberated rhythmically to the thudding steam hammers. The man is a millionaire, Stephen marveled, and he lives here in the middle of this dirt and hellish noise. It has to be by choice. Stephen had expected to be offered a glass or two before dinner, while he made his host's acquaintance, but such was not the case. Alfred meandered his bent body to the table where the butler stood waiting and beckoned Stephen abruptly to the chair on his right. Stephen seated himself and his host's harsh voice went rushing on.

"My son, you know, it's a trial, my son's absence.

Friedrich is a blooming boy—growing fast into manhood. Good health!—he has good health! That is what matters."

Stephen agreed, thinking privately that it was well that the boy was absent. These surroundings surely were not conducive to anyone's health.

He watched as the butler poured pale yellow liquid into the goblet before him and when he put it to his lips it was with a little trepidation. But it was a good wine, thankfully, nut-rich and dry. None was poured for Herr Krupp. He sipped from a glass of water. Stephen fortified himself with the wine and decided to wait until the main course before broaching his subject—but he would wait no longer than that!

The soup plate set in front of him was thick with floury noodles, and glistening pools of chicken fat formed on its surface. Herr Krupp was served with a bowl of hot milk and his crabbed fingers jerked and pulled at the bread which he dropped into it, piece by piece.

"Eat—eat!" he commanded almost jovially. Stephen had been watching him tear at the bread with some fascination. "My cook likes company—not like some cooks. You are fortunate, young man, to have good digestion—good health. Myself now, my days are spent fighting the malfunctions of my body." He inserted a spoonful of milk-soaked bread into his sunken mouth and Stephen nodded genially. I don't believe he's over fifty-five, he thought, with no little wonder, yet he looks as if he is at death's door.

The entree was rabbit, fried, spiced, and flanked by a mound of boiled potatoes and carrots. Stephen tasted it gingerly. Not too bad, he thought with relief. His host set himself the task of a meager pile of steaming potatoes and they ate in silence for a few minutes. Then Stephen told the tale of his errand.

"I am sorry for your partner's death. Very sorry." Alfred Krupp's dry voice choked out the words. "I understand you to say that you wish to recall the investment—the monies that Mr. Wenzler has invested here in my little business." He spooned up a piece of boiled potato and eyed it suspiciously. "When is the note due?" The question shot out sharply.

"A year from now. But you understand that Mr. Wenzler's death has made it necessary to consolidate his estate; that is the only reason I seek to withdraw the investment," Stephen said, thinking privately that this was a very sharp old bird.

"I wish that I could comply with your request. But it is impossible."

"Surely not," Stephen protested with a smile.

"Oh, but it is, Herr de Jean. So many thousands of kronen! I am in the position of a poor man, poor in gold. Always it takes so many kronen for machinery, for all the expensive things to keep my small business afloat. That is why I so welcomed your partner's investment. Gold is a problem—a great problem."

Stephen sighed. The poorer they talk the richer they are! He was aware that Alfred Krupp's steelworks was always scratching for money because the man's enthusiasms for new tools, new machinery, was indiscriminate. But he intended to get that money and he decided to set about it with no more preliminaries.

"I am empowered with several orders for you, large orders for railroad wheels. I collected them before I left and they will be placed with you on the condition that Mr. Wenzler's investment is liquidated and paid to me before I leave Essen."

The old man's eyes darted sharply to Stephen's face and then circled the room and came to rest on the candelabra before him.

"What do you call a large order, Herr de Jean?"

"One thousand. The total runs to five thousand—five thousand wheels, to be paid for on delivery. On the one hand you have a profit, a very healthy profit, I might add. On the other hand you have nothing to gain, only interest to pay." The hook is set, Stephen thought. The old man's cupidity was aroused. Stephen had taken care to arm himself with this incentive before he left Chicago. It hadn't been difficult, with his contacts, and he knew that Alfred Krupp's avarice for business was exceeded by no man's. Accordingly he changed the subject suddenly, asking Herr Krupp about his trip to London. The remainder of the dinner, including an excellent cherry tart, was taken up with Krupp's recital of the virtues of the English and his own accomplishments in the realm of iron and steel.

When Stephen took his leave his host said, almost as an afterthought, that if he would come to the ironworks tomorrow morning they could talk about business. Stephen made his way back to his hotel and stretched out on the cool, clean sheets with a glass of champagne, more relaxed than he had been in weeks. The greedy old devil won't let those orders get away from him! He'll pay up. Stephen, he told himself, it's a rare day when you can be bested.

The next day at noon found him at the Bank of Essen with a draft for four-hundred-twenty-thousand kronen which he presented and when it was honored he requested that the funds be telegraphed to his offices in Chicago. He boarded ship for Dusseldorf, relieved as well as satisfied. He had no way of knowing when Prussia planned to either attack France or incite them to attack, but he knew well that once war was declared he would never have been able to liquidate the investment. He chose a table on the promenade deck and ordered a stein of beer from a waiter whose ginger-colored beard reminded him of the dead Hugo.

343

The warm summer sun beat down on the raised parasols and music from an accordion rose on the air as the ship followed its course to Dusseldorf. Now for some pleasure, Stephen thought, and blew the foam from the beer.

The restaurant in Dusseldorf was a lighthearted place. An orchestra played its strains into the evening air and Stephen poured the pale, golden Leibfraumilch into his companion's wine glass. The roast pork steamed on his plate and for once he felt hungry. The night promised well, he thought, letting his glance fall on the lush contours of the girl's bosom. Blonde and apple-cheeked with a ravishing swing to her rounded hips, Anna whatever-her-name-was ate daintily but heartily of the pork and dumpling.

She is quite a dumpling herself, Stephen thought with amusement. He had spotted her sauntering by the entrance to his hotel and had plucked a handkerchief from his pocket and presented her with it. When she accepted it, lending herself with a smile to the masquerade that she had dropped it, he congratulated himself on his perception. It was a point of pride with him, that he could spot a prostitute immediately, no matter how ladylike her demeanor or how sedate the dress. Pretty she was, though a trifle plump for his taste, but his spirits were too high to be dampened by such a petty fault. She ate and drank dreamily, quite as pleased as he. The old brewer who kept her in lavish comfort was ill and this would be a pleasant vacation from his boarlike gruntings. This man was quite handsome and obviously rich. He would pay well and the necklace of opals and pearls that she had been coveting would be hers after all. If Ludwig weren't subject to these bouts of penury she would have had it long before this. She thought with languid satisfaction of how it would look, the pale greenish stones and the rosy pearls on her pink and white skin.

When the cab delivered them at the door of the imposing brick house which Ludwig had purchased for her she led Stephen into the hall and up the stairway, dismissing her maid with a cheery nod. Entering her bedroom she began matter-of-factly to undress and Stephen watched in high amusement. She does very well, he thought, glancing around at the silk-covered walls and the heavy, gleaming furniture. The headboard of the bed was decorated with raised figures of cavorting cherubs amid mother-of-pearl patterns. Very well indeed, he thought, pulling off his boots. He folded his trousers neatly across the back of a glaringly pink divan and turned.

"My God, you are like a Rubens!" he exclaimed, a smile of pleasure curving his mouth.

"And what is a Rubens?" his paramour asked pleasantly.

She stood before her dressing table, taking the combs from her blonde curls. Her hips curved fulsomely, marked by two deep dimples at the base of her spine. Her legs were plump and rounded like the arms that were reaching up to her hair. Her breasts gleamed like whipped cream with large, pale-pink nipples jutting out. Her waist, though not small, was gracefully curved and her throat was a soft ivory column. Stephen felt a surge of lust, felt it with satisfaction since this was the first time in quite a while that he had felt any desire to bed a woman. I've been through a quiet, little hell, he thought, and I am very ready for you, young woman.

"A Rubens is a painting," he replied in his serviceable but limited German.

"As long as it is pretty." She smiled archly, and tossed the last gold comb onto the table-top.

She padded on bare feet to the bed where she lay down rather stolidly, waiting for him.

Not a very fiery creature, he thought, as he walked toward her. Well, we will have to see. He bent over the expanse of soft, white flesh and ran his hands slowly down the sides of her body, pressing her hips, her thighs, and running down to her gracefully small ankles. The flesh gave beneath his hands and a scent rose from her that seemed to be a combination of apple blossoms and musk. Stephen felt desire building in him as he stroked the line of golden down that ran from her navel to the mass of golden hair between her thighs. She sighed then, voluptuously, and reaching up, drew his face down to hers and caught his mouth with her lips. They parted slowly, very slowly; their texture was soft and full. Finally, he shivered as her tongue flicked gently into his mouth, stroking his own tongue ever so lightly. He thrust his own tongue over her lips and then into her mouth, at the same time sliding his arms under her waist. He worked his hands down to cradle the soft flesh of her buttocks and she drew him down against her, at the same time moving her hips voluptuously against his clutching hands. She freed her mouth and ran her lips over his neck, caressing his skin with her tongue. He trembled, shivers of desire ran through his body like electric currents as her mouth moved down over his chest. She slid her hand down his abdomen and stroked his hard, throbbing organ. She gave a small giggle of pleasure as she took it into her hand and raised her mouth to his again. This time she pulled at his lips, almost gnawing at them, at the same time darting her tongue in and out of his mouth as she ran her fingers delicately over his swollen member. He was groaning when she parted her legs and then raised up, both arms around him, turning to lie on top of him.

"Oh, this is good," she breathed huskily in German
346

and raised up on her elbows. She brushed her breasts across his chest, rubbing the nipples over it. He grasped one heavy breast in his hand, kneading it in a transport of pleasure. It was creamy white and the nipple spread over it as soft as satin. He raised his head and she bent forward. His tongue darted out to run over the nipple. She sighed heavily and moved her breast over his lips as he clasped her thighs. The huge nipple was puckered and red now and he took it in his mouth, biting gently. She gave a little whimper as he closed his lips over it, pulling it hard into his mouth. His desire had mounted to a frenzy and he pulled her legs apart and she raised her hips, fondling and caressing him before guiding him into the moist recess between her thighs. His hips rose as he plunged into her and she thrust her own rhythmically, meeting his frantic probing while his mouth left one breast and began to devour the other. Her creamy, billowing flesh enveloped him and she breathed heavily, panting and gasping as he forced her buttocks down in a convulsive rhythm. Her mouth was hot and wet when it covered his and his body arced in a final thrust. Anna fell onto him, limp and perspiring at the same moment.

"My God," he breathed. "I needed that." She smiled happily. He was going to get more. She wanted this man well-satisfied when she told him how much she needed for the necklace.

Stephen had always found that bouts of carnality were an ideal antidote in times of stress, and his pent-up nervous energy was expended frenetically that night. Anna's body alone was an aphrodisiac and her seemingly spontaneous skills incited him afresh through the night. Wholeheartedly erotic, she knelt before him, her long blonde hair trailing on the pillows, her body aquiver with excitation while he gripped her abundant hips and pounded his loins against their soft flesh.

When he thought he was spent, he napped, to be awakened by her wet mouth. He looked down where she crouched over his hips, her curls brushing his legs while her tongue moved artfully, rousing him to a hard, hot lust, so intense that it seemed fresh. He waited, writhing, prolonging it, watching her lips and fingers on his engorged manhood, and then flung her over and impaled her fiercely, his body charged and violent as he plunged into her again and again.

Afterward he slept, his head pillowed on her melon-like breasts. He awoke at mid-morning refreshed and calm. He had his gold, the murder of Hugo seemed far in the past, and his face was as smooth and unlined as a man of twenty. When he asked her what she would like as a gift to remember him by, her response was demure. She told him of the necklace and he smiled, his smile tightening a little when she hesitantly named the price. Then he smiled fully, aware of his loose, relaxed, sense of well-being.

"You are well worth it, my dear," he said as he laid the bills on her dressing table, and she kissed his cheek chastely, then did a little impromptu dance to celebrate her windfall.

Noon found him at the train station, waiting peacefully for the train that would carry him to Paris.

Chapter 22

THE CITY OF TOURS LAY ON THE HORIZON, AND LEITA looked up at the spire of the cathedral soaring above the curling, early-morning mist off the river. They had come down by train and the carriage that met them at the station went rolling off down a dirt road. Far ahead a pile of gray loomed on a promontory and when the carriage turned off to career down a poplar-lined avenue Armand squeezed her hand. She knew that her reaction to his estate meant a great deal to him and she summoned a resolve to like it no matter what. The carriage had wound around, climbing higher until they came out suddenly and ahead of her was an expanse of green lawn, dotted with beds of brilliant flowers and shaded by trees. The chateau itself spread gracefully over its site with two L-shaped wings enclosing the semicircle of turf where the gravel drive drew up in front of the steps. Urns filled with flowers lined the edge of the terrace.

Leita sighed. "I think it's the loveliest place I have

ever seen," she breathed, relieved that her admiration was genuine. She turned her eyes full upon him as he sat beside her. His fine, blond hair brushed the collar of his frockcoat and the smooth planes of his face were glowing with the pleasure of being home. A fountain stood on the oval in front of the terrace and the full-limbed figure of a woman held a cornucopia out of which streamed water to play over the marble porpoises around her feet.

"That is Demeter, the earth goddess," Armand said, gesturing toward the white marble figure whose feet were greened with lichen. "And she needs to be cleaned," he chuckled.

Leita adjusted her wide-brimmed straw hat and tossed the streamers back over her shoulder before the coachman handed her down. She took a deep breath and held her shoulders back. The massive front doors had opened and a stream of servants were marching onto the terrace. The woman who led the procession was dressed in black silk, tucked, high-necked and severe, despite the balmy heat. Her skin was sallow and pale above the black, and her cheekbones were flat, giving her an almost Oriental countenance. She turned her head sharply and the line of servants evened up almost immediately. What a harridan! Leita thought.

"What is her name?" she whispered to Armand as they ascended the steps of the perron.

"Madame Dechinard."

They curtsied, bowed, threw her piercing glances or shy ones. Wind rustled in the trees. It had come up quickly and when they reached the end of the line Armand opened the door with a sweeping gesture.

"Before the tour we will lunch," he said, and Madame Dechinard disappeared down the hall. The floor was set in black and white tiles, the table in the center, and the side chairs set against the walls gleamed from hours of hand rubbing. Armand took Leita's arm and guided her to the right-hand side of the horseshoe staircase. An immense circular window of stained glass shot sparks of colored light over the first floor landing and when he opened the door, their sitting room was almost as bright. The walls were covered with lemon-yellow silk, and the Louis XV furniture with its gilded wood and lavish tapestry made the room both graceful and restful. Leita untied the ribbons of her hat and flung it on a chair.

"This is a perfectly lovely, perfectly beautiful place, and I can hardly wait to see the rest of it."

"I am gratified." Armand smiled broadly. "And I can hardly wait to show you the rest."

She changed her dress, first washing the dust of the road from her face and hands, presented herself to him, and they made their way downstairs.

A small table was set on another terrace, one that looked out over the winding ribbon of the river below the promontory. They lunched on a cheese tart, carrots newly pulled from the ground and a soft, white wine. Leita had learned a few things about her husband in the days intervening since their marriage. Though they had slept apart these past nights in his house in Paris, she had heard him in the night and twice gotten up to find him; once, pacing in the hall and another time reading in the library at three o'clock in the morning. He was an insomniac, he explained a little sheepishly, had been for some time. He joined her in her boudoir for breakfast and she had found he was inclined to be waspish on arising. As the day progressed his good nature took charge but woe be to the maid who happened to let a drop or two of his morning chocolate slosh into his saucer. Leita had no doubt this was due to his lack of sleep and suspected that the insomnia had dated from the death of his wife and child. He treated her with warmth and affection, yet gave no sign at all that he desired more in their relationship. She supposed that this was due to her recent injury and possibly her pregnancy—or perhaps simply the fact that he wasn't in love with her. She was still fatigued and bemused over the circumstances she found herself in and the present state of affairs didn't disturb her. They had been friends since her arrival in Paris; she was at ease with him and surprised to find herself so content. What would come would come.

"Do you feel well enough to ride?" Armand asked, plucking a ripe red cherry from the bowl in the center of the table.

"Yes. I feel very well, you know," she replied, and pushed her chair back.

Horses were brought round and she felt full of anticipation as they cantered off to the outbuildings. They stopped when they reached them and Armand presented a swarthy, barrel-chested man named M. Barthez. He was in charge of the vines and therefore held a position of prime importance. Leita listened to their lively conversation and when they rode off again it was to cover the perimeters of fields where the silver-gray undersides of grape leaves glimmered mutely in the hot afternoon sun. The stakes, yellow because of new wood, rose like a forest in what looked to be miles of vines. Armand dismounted to show her the new vines and their ancient boles, looking over each one as if it were a child. Grapes hung heavy and pale pink was beginning to cloud their cool greenness.

"Six more weeks and they will be rich purple and sweet as honey," Armand announced, testing the weight of a cluster. "And then the pressing! It is an exciting time, the harvest, but we need rain now." His hazel eyes swept the sky but it was bright blue and cloudless. "It will come," he said, "hot sun and cool rain make wine the gods would treasure."

They rode on and surveyed golden fields where wheat swayed. They rode slowly past orchards with apricots and peaches ripening on squat trees and taller trees where women in white headdresses, their skirts pulled up and fastened to their belt, stood on ladders to pluck the bright-red, slightly sour cherries. Their wooden clogs were ranged on the ground under the trees. Armand spoke to them and introduced her. They smiled and giggled and descended from their perches to curtsey and nudge one another, their red-cheeked peasant faces alive with curiosity and good will.

"And now into the village to see how things are going, not to mention a glass of wine," Armand announced. His own cheeks were flushed with pleasure and his hazel eyes bright.

Well-being and relief were coursing through Leita, as they cantered down the road past the fields gold with wheat and green spears of corn. No wonder he loved it here. The chateau was not dark and gloomy, as she had feared, but a beautiful place, full of light and richly and comfortably furnished. The grounds were breathtakingly lovely, with fountains splashing and groups of trees, each with its bench as a resting place. And the countryside, all this reminded her somewhat of the home she had left in South Carolina, the vast expanse of fields, the busy, peaceful activity. Her heartbreak would heal here; life would turn with the seasons, each with its own excitement and sense of plenty. For the first time since the news of Breve's marriage she felt the pull of life and a surge of hope.

They came into the village and hats were doffed as the few who were not at work somewhere greeted them. The inn was small and they dismounted and took

chairs at a table outside, where they were soon surrounded by the inhabitants, old men, children, a
younger man or two who were waiting for the employment of the harvest. She was surprised that Armand
knew each one by name and after the presentations
were made, quite as naturally as if they had been
strolling along the Boulevards Italiennes in Paris, the
conversation became animated. Leita sipped lemonade
and ate carissons, candy-coated almonds, and tried to
keep pace with the flurry of news and heated discussion
of crops, the birth of baby pigs and the winter market
for dried fruit. In the chatter of voices Armand leaned
forward, his elbows resting on his knees and one hand
fondling the arm of a rather grimy child who sheltered
by his side while staring at Leita with a concentration
that was flattering for its simplicity. Leita was enjoying
this, wondering at it. She had never seen Armand so
full of interest, so voluble. So this is his milieu, she
thought. A polished, elegant aristocrat, tactful, an
attentive listener, held in regard by all, but here, in this
small French village on his own land he came alive,
interested and concerned by every birth and death, the
drying of apricots, the bushel yield of the cherry trees,
the weather, and above all, the grape harvest.

That night when they sat at dinner eating fish which
had been caught that afternoon she looked at him, her
eyes twinkling.

"Now what is amusing you?" he asked.

"I have married a farmer!" and she burst out
laughing.

He laughed too, but looked a touch disconcerted at
the same time.

"But you don't understand. I love it, I feel at home in
it. Don't you realize I am a farmer's daughter?" She
could hardly speak for laughing. "The people in Fort
Wayne will know that I am married to a French Count

and will imagine all kinds of pretentious nonsense. They will never believe it when I tell them my husband is a farmer."

Armand stared at her for a second and then broke into laughter too.

"I grew up with talk of the fields, the crops, the harvest. Weather was the most important thing in the world for most of the months of the year. My great treat was to be allowed to disturb the hens by looking for eggs. And now I will lead the same kind of life again."

Armand raised his glass to her. "All of which means that I married well," he pronounced, and they both fell to laughing.

Stephen's steps rang out on the marble floor and his walking stick tapped along. He felt no need to restrain his exuberance as he looked around. The Grand Hotel of Paris, facing onto the Boulevard des Capucines, was the height of luxury for Parisian visitors. Eight hundred rooms, richly furnished, a plethora of servants to attend to your every wish, and outside the boulevards of the City of Lights. Now this is more like it, Stephen thought, as he signed his name to the register with a euphoric flourish.

He followed the bellboy and surveyed his suite with satisfaction; striding through the open French doors out onto the balcony, he leaned on the balustrade and looked off in the distance to the spire of Notre Dame. The boulevard below was athrong with carriages and strolling pedestrians and he sighted four open-air cafes from his vantage point. He rang then and ordered a bottle of champagne and caviar "with much lemon." Then he threw off his jacket and seated himself at the escritoire where he proceeded to dash off two notes, one to Leita, the other to Lord and Lady Hidel. A reply was delivered as he lay in the steaming water of a bath, a glass of champagne in one hand and a cracker spread with caviar in the other. He dried his hands and opened the envelope. Annette Hidel's handwriting sped over the heavy notepaper—"So delighted! Come for dinner, we are at home tonight. Also there is some news that will surprise you."

Stephen pursed his lips. Only Lady Hidel had replied. Perhaps Leita had been out when her note was delivered. He finished the bottle and scraped the last black pearls of caviar onto a cracker and savored them together. It was seven o'clock now—he would dress. This proved to be fraught with decisions. He discarded two frock coats and settled on a burgundy velour trimmed with gold stitching which made a rich contrast with the yellow drainpipe trousers. He chose a burgundy cravat and swore when the nick on his jaw commenced again to bleed.

"My God, I am excited," he muttered as he applied a plaster to the small wound for a minute or two. Small wonder, I've dealt with the damndest set of circumstances these last weeks, and dealt well, he complimented himself complacently. But now only one thing remains to come to fruition. He paused while he waited for the plaster to staunch the drops of blood and thought of Leita. That mane of red-gold hair and the deep velvet of her violet eyes, her proud independence and her unsettling candor, and the lushness of her body. What a prospect, he breathed, to awaken that body, to summon up that passion she carries deep within her. Rome, that is where I will take her to honeymoon, orange-scented Rome and down to the Mediterranean. For as long as she likes, and then— what a prize she will be on my arm when I return to Chicago! He remembered with satisfaction the flurry of admiration she had aroused during her visit and preened himself in anticipation of his return with her as Mrs. Stephen de Jean.

There were several guests in the drawing room of the Hotel Bouvait when Stephen entered. Lady Hidel emitted a little trill of pleasure and kissed him warmly. Sir Charles greeted him with a little less warmth, but his usual benignity, and Stephen looked around the room. Where was she? After being presented to the guests he asked Lady Hidel in an aside if Miss Johnston wasn't going to join them.

"That is the news I mentioned," she smiled gaily. "Your friend is in the country." Darcy was watching Stephen, a look of serene composure on her face while she waited for Lady Hidel to break the news. She had never relayed to her hostess the extent of Stephen's interest in Leita and now she was glad she hadn't. She knew that Lady Hidel regarded him as just another suitor.

"In the country?" Stephen repeated.

"Yes, Stephen. Your beautiful little friend has married, and married none other than Armand. You remember him of course. Leita is now the Comtesse du Favre."

Stephen's face blanched and his pupils turned to pinpoints. "Leita married? Surely you are joking."

Annette Hidel was slightly taken aback by the intensity of his question. "Yes, Stephen. It was very sudden, but they make such a charming couple. It will be a very good thing for Armand. You remember his tragedy and we are all so happy that now he is not alone," she chattered on. Mon dieu, she thought, he is very distressed by this news. He must have been in love with her, though it is rather hard to credit. Stephen is so cool, so self-involved, I never thought of him in connection with a grand passion.

"She mentioned him in her letters, but only in

passing, I thought. I had no idea they were so seriously involved." Stephen's voice had risen and was almost shrill.

Lady Hidel shrugged. "Neither did anyone else. But there you are. One never knows about affairs of the heart. Here they both were, under our very eyes and no one thought of it until they announced they were going to be married. It was a quiet ceremony. Leita's parents were informed right away, but then I suppose you were en route and that is why you didn't hear."

Stephen subsided and shot a dark glance toward Darcy. "Well, I must offer my congratulations. I hope they will be very happy. I gather you are quite pleased about it." Bitterness laced his voice and Lady Hidel touched his arm soothingly.

"I am simply delighted. You know how close Armand is to me, and while your friend was here I learned to love her too. She is an extraordinary young girl. And now you must have an aperitif," and she beckoned to a footman.

Stephen was seated beside Darcy at table and picked at his squab with a remorseless fork.

"Why wasn't I informed of this?" he whispered.

Darcy shivered a little at the vicious current in that whisper. "Simply because I knew nothing of it till the wedding was announced. And that was the morning of the same day. I sent word immediately—I left the house on foot solely to wire you the news."

Stephen was not mollified. "You must have seen it coming—right under your nose—" then broke off as his partner turned to him with a burbling question about America.

Darcy sighed with relief at the interruption. Mary Jo had been watching this exchange from her place further on up the table and she sighed too. I feel much better that Leita has married Armand than I would if Stephen

358

had caught her on the rebound; perhaps things have worked out for the best, she thought, sadly.

Stephen left early, pleading fatigue from his journey, but inquired if Darcy wouldn't care to take a drive with him the next afternoon. She granted his request graciously but looked forward to it with something less than pleasure as she undressed that night.

The day was cloudy, almost gloomy, and the air was humid on the Champs Eliseés. On the table before them the sorbets were awash, melting at their own pace while Stephen pelted Darcy with questions.

"I have told you, Stephen. She saw a great deal of him but never at any time did I detect an atmosphere of courtship. He might have been one of her brothers. And you are acquainted with Armand, I know. He is a gentle man, dreamy even, and certainly in the throes of melancholy."

"Not now he isn't," Stephen snapped.

"I suppose not. However, they took up residence in his house here in Paris and left for the country shortly after that so I have no way of knowing how his new situation has affected him." Darcy was keeping a good deal to herself. She had overheard Giselle, Lady Hidel's maid, discussing Leita's pregnancy with her husband, who was one of the footmen at the Hotel Bourait. Giselle had been in Lady Hidel's service for too many years to count and in one way or another was privy to everything that happened in the house. Trustworthy and loyal, she did not regard a discussion of the affairs of the house with her husband as indiscreet and Darcy had been making her way to the kitchen one night when she was unable to sleep because of a headache. Deeming it too late to call a servant, she was going to heat some milk which she did frequently in the wee hours since Jack Hidel's departure. She had paused in the butler's pantry at the sound of voices and overheard the conversation between Giselle and Louis. It was the second night after the marriage and Darcy had stood stock still, frozen in dismay as Giselle repeated the circumstances of Leita's conception, which she herself had overheard the very night Leita was brought home unconscious from the ball. She and her husband were rehashing these events, speculating again as to the identity of Leita's attacker. They were up at this late hour for the same reason as Darcy; Giselle had been unable to sleep and Louis had accompanied her to the kitchen and was enjoying a brandy while Giselle drank chamomile tea. Darcy had glided softly back to her suite and spent several hours wide awake, staring at her bed curtains as she pondered this. The precipitous wedding ceremony was explained now. Undoubtedly it had been someone drunk, insanely intoxicated, at that ball, and she had known nothing of it. She hadn't even attended because she had been feeling unwell that evening. She felt sympathy for Leita, but a touch of envy too. How like that girl to fall right into the arms of a handsome count, pregnant by another man, but still wrapped in fortune's arms. She had deliberated during dinner as to the wisdom of repeating this to Stephen as a means of avoiding his ire, but decided against it. The secrecy surrounding the situation had not been breached and she would not be the first one to pass on the tale. There would be little point, after all; Leita was married now and quite out of Stephen's reach. Whether he knew the truth or not was of no consequence.

"I read your letter aloud and your arrow hit its mark, Stephen. The poor girl fainted dead away and struck her head on the hearth. A doctor was called and she was put to bed with a slight concussion."

Stephen grimaced. "Terrible! I had no thought of any such misfortune as that."

Darcy gazed at him levelly. "She was obviously very much in love with the man."

"Not irrevocably. Witness her immediate marriage."

"A broken heart and wounded pride had unforeseen results there. It was an outcome that never occurred to me," Darcy said, and drew her sorbet toward her. At least he seemed to be less angry. He won't mourn long, Darcy thought wryly—not Stephen.

"Cupid's arrow flew too fast and hit the wrong mark." Stephen's mouth was twisted with disdain. "I would never have considered the Comte du Favre as a likely rival though. He always struck me as a colorless character, not given to whirlwind courtships by any means."

Darcy shrugged. "One never knows."

Stephen straightened in his chair. "And now I have some news for you, unpleasant news, I'm afraid. Hugo Wenzler is dead."

Darcy's spoon clattered on the marble top of the table and she turned wide dark eyes on Stephen. "What are you talking about?"

Stephen felt a tiny flutter of satisfaction. It was a pleasure to see her taken aback too.

"Died at the hand of thieves, Darcy. He was robbed and murdered in his office on a Sunday afternoon. That is the reason for my delay in arriving. There was a great deal to do and I had to appear at the inquest, of course."

Darcy took out a handkerchief and dabbed at her forehead. He had told her so coolly. The man had been associated with Hugo for years, as friend and partner, and he announced his death with a detachment that shook her almost as much as the tragedy. She pressed the handkerchief against her upper lip for a moment and breathed deeply. How right she had been to be wary of him. His coldness was beyond belief.

"Did they find the thieves?" she brought herself to ask, finally.

Stephen shook his head in negation. "Afraid not. They have no idea who they were. His safe, his private safe was cleaned out and he was stabbed and left on the floor. Nothing was known of it till the next day when the clerk found him."

Darcy felt a wave of nausea at the thought of Hugo's fleshy body lying bloodsoaked and alone through the night. "Oh, my God, how dreadful!"

"Yes, very." Stephen said quietly.

They parted finally and when Stephen called at the Hotel Bourait the next day Darcy was as composed in manner as always. He even looked closely to see if her eyelids were swollen with weeping; they were not. Stephen was puzzled. I thought she was rather fond of the big bear, he mused. Well, she will have to look further afield now, and he mentally cast up a list of middle-aged widowers who might make a husband for Darcy. After all, he was under some obligation to her. She had played her part.

Chapter 23

"TEN O'CLOCK IN THE MORNING, AND THE GODDAMNED fog hasn't lifted yet!" Jack Hidel walked along Fleet Street, cursing as other pedestrians jostled him. The stairway he ascended was steep, and as he opened the door marked Mr. Hovington-Smythe, Esq., Solicitor, he entered a muggy, airless room and brushed the droplets of moisture from his jacket. The clerk who looked up at him had black hair brushed damply over his skull and his skin was a livid white.

"Might you be Mr. Jack Hidel?" the clerk inquired.

"Yes, I am," Jack answered shortly.

"Mr. Hovington-Smythe and Lord Hidel are await-ing you, Sir. I will just take you in." The clerk led the way down a carpeted hall. His fleshy derriere in the striped pants bobbled officiously and he opened the door with the air of an undertaker seating a member of the immediate family.

The man at the wide mahogany desk in the window embrasure rose and extended his hand. Jack took it languidly. "Good morning, Mr. Hidel. Rather dim out there in the streets, isn't it?" Mr. Hovington-Smythe wore a black cutaway over his gaunt, long-limbed frame and his face was marked by weak blue eyes that seemed to roll around behind the slits that enclosed them. His hair was gray and fell in kinky waves over very large ears with only the pendulous lobes visible beneath.

"Yes, very dim." Jack answered diffidently and nodded to his uncle who had maintained his sitting position through these amenities. Sir Charles nodded curtly back at him.

"This won't take long," he said quietly.

The clerk entered with a tea service on a tole tray. Jack took his cup and sipped, grateful for something to do. The office was somber. The trio of windows gave onto a view of swirling gray fog. Gaslights burned in sconces, adding their flares to the yellow light of the lamp.

"Sir Charles spoke accurately, I believe. I have here the documents which are to be signed by you. If you care to look them over."

Hovington-Smythe handed Jack a sheaf of papers, after untying the red tape that bound them. Jack took them and read them swiftly. Two red spots burned on his flat cheekbones before he finished reading. His breath was coming fast and when he spoke he began with a slight stutter.

"And if I don't choose to sign these? What about that? Because I do *not* choose to sign them!" The hand that held the papers was shaking.

Sir Charles sighed heavily and set his cup carefully down in the saucer. Hovington-Smythe rose from behind the desk and turned a circumspect back to his client, looking out the window at the veils of fog with quiet concentration.

"Jack, the choice is yours. But I urge you most fervently to consider the consequences. If you do not sign these documents, you will be arrested and gaoled. The circumstances of your conception, which automatically disinherit you, will become a matter of public record. The shameful facts of your private life will be on every tongue."

"I could have simply left the country, you know. I didn't have to subject myself to this degrading—this humiliating—" Jack's chin was trembling and he sought vainly for words.

"If you had done that, Jack, firstly I would have set the law on you. You might or might not have evaded them; that point is moot. But at the same time, your true origins would have been exposed. Of course, I would have had no other choice." Sir Charles spoke crisply.

"You would have done that to my mother?" Jack's voice rose to a shriek. "You would have disgraced my mother with your disgusting tale?"

"Your mother knows the truth better than anyone. The disgrace she laid at her own door. And I have no children; I am quite prepared to make my home on the continent permanently, that is if this skeleton in my closet must be brought out to clatter its bones on the London streets. Quite prepared," Sir Charles finished calmly.

Jack seized the pen on the solicitor's desk and Mr. Hovington-Smythe turned.

"If you will but wait one moment, Sir. A witness will be necessary."

He stepped to the door and called hoarsely and the plump little clerk bustled in almost immediately.

The clerk stood by, his plump white hands folded over his waistcoat, while Jack scrawled off a signature, six signatures, with his whole arm trembling and the spots of color on his face looking as if they would take fire. He flung the pen at the desk and it rolled, then fell to the floor. The clerk bent over and retrieved it, then affixed his name to the first document.

Jack turned on his heel and threw the door open. Then he turned and inhaled deeply as he braced his shoulders. "I will return to Paris—my mother stays there until September. I wish to stay with her until then. When she leaves for England I will leave for Italy, ostensibly on holiday. I want her to know nothing of this—nothing." His eyes were suddenly beseeching and Sir Charles felt a tremor of compassion.

"I think that arrangement will be satisfactory. Your departure will attract less attention that way and I assure you, I have no intention of divulging any of my knowledge to your mother."

Sir Charles stressed the last phrase and Jack swallowed once, then lurched through the doorway and down the hall. Out in the fog he turned one way and another, then bolted across the street while a coachman grabbed at the reins of his four-in-hand in a face-reddening effort to prevent the lead pair from trampling Jack. The coachman's oaths followed Jack into the warmth and light of the pub.

He drank two whiskey and sodas, then bethought himself that the place would be frequented by solicitors and their clerks, some of whom might know the reason for his presence here this morning. He looked furtively around, imagining he was being stared at, then left quickly. He had intended to return directly to Paris after meeting with his uncle and his solicitor, but he had underestimated the humiliation attendant on the ordeal. He was sick with it now, and impotent rage made the whiskey roll in his gut. He stood at the curbside, being splashed with mud flying from the wheels of the passing carriage, insensible to it, lost in vacillation.

366

Finally, his jaw set, he hailed a cab, had it wait while he collected his things from the inn, and then to Victoria Station. He was en route to the small manor house in Berkshire where his mother had retired when he was twelve. He spent the next two weeks there, alone with only the housekeeper and butler, lying drunk in his chambers through the night and the better part of the morning when he rose to pace broodingly about the grounds. Many of his waking hours were spent in devising tantalizing and air-tight schemes for murdering his uncle, entering the solicitor's offices by stealth and destroying the incriminating papers, then returning to Paris. But they had to be discarded in his sober moments. The solicitor knew his history and he was positive that Annette knew, and his life was ruined, totally ruined.

Not until two days before he left did his face soften into a cunning smile. He drank two glasses of bicarbonate and had a tea tray before him laid with hot scones which up until a moment ago had turned his stomach. Now he leaned back in his chair and pulled the lapels of his robe together. Staring at the ceiling he tapped his fingers on the arm of the chair. No fugitive nonentity he, the last laugh would be his! It would be easy; he was sure it would be easy. He poured a cup brimming with strong tea and milk, then sat on the arm of the chair and wolfed the hot scones, speckling his unshaven chin with crumbs and dollops of butter.

He rang for the tray to be cleared and ordered a bath, then bounded up the stairs. He inspected himself closely in the standing mirror. His long flat cheeks were sunken and covered with a ginger-colored stubble mixed with gray. His fleshy eyelids were swollen and hung over the vein-marked whites of his eyes. He had lost weight and the robe hung on his frame like a scarecrow's costume. He squinted at his reflection and then struck his fist decisively against the highboy, making the brass handles rattle. He scrubbed himself long and luxuriantly in the hot water of his bath, then rang for the butler, requesting that he shave him. This done he dressed and spent the rest of the day on a horse, riding through the lanes and downs, coatless in the warm summer air. He returned and ate a hearty dinner, soaked in another hot bath and went to bed immediately where he slept till the morning sun was high.

The housekeeper remarked to her husband that she was glad that particular siege seemed to be over while she prepared the brimming breakfast tray that Jack had ordered. He devoured ham, eggs, hot scones and a bowl of Scotch oatmeal before taking to his horse again. The next two days were spent in this regimen and the morning of the third day found him peering into his mirror with a satisfied smile. The eyes were no longer bloodshot, his cheeks, though still thin, were not gray and sunken but shone tinged pink with sunburn. He rang for the butler and sent him into the village with a message to be telegraphed. His wardrobe was brushed and aired, and he departed the next morning by an early train.

Midday found him at lunch on the channel steamer. He sighed luxuriantly as the waiter removed the remains and lit his cigar, then he leaned back, stretching his legs full in front of him and savored the coffee, while he sent rings of blue smoke into the air. A secret marriage could be effected quite easily. They could leave, be in Florence within two days, and be married there. Then sail from Italy for the United States. He would be ensconced as the husband of an heiress, shielded by the width of the ocean from any reprisals his uncle might care to take. And what could he do? Nothing. There would be no point in airing the whole shabby business; he was certain Sir Charles didn't want his name dragged through the mud. As for being disinherited, that was simple enough. He had already told Darcy that his uncle had never liked him, had always been prejudiced against him. She had enough money for both of them—he would be well set up, inured forever against the threats Sir Charles made. And in a short time he would send for his mother, poor little thing. She would live with them in Chicago. Simple, simple and beautiful; why hadn't he thought of it earlier? He could face everyone now without a tremor. He knew what they didn't, he would emerge the victor.

That evening on the Rue de Monceau when Darcy entered in answer to his note he embraced her tenderly, then apologized for taking the liberty with an almost abject description of how sorely he had missed her.

They dined at the Maison d'Or in a private room, but it wasn't till during their drive that Jack came to the nub of his mission. His voice was shy and diffident as he spoke, and the words came haltingly.

"I've never done this before and I am sure I shall do it poorly. You must excuse my awkwardness, I have never been glib and now least of all." Jack was surprised to find that he really was feeling timorous. Darcy was a touch intimidating—not a new emotion for him; he had always found composed, self-assured women intimidating. He was only at ease with those who were fulsomely flirtatious, and best of all, far from ladies.

Darcy's ivory skin glowed with a faint flush and her oval eyes shone dark and lustrous in the night. She wore a gown of Sebastapol blue, inky blue in the folds and an ivory egret plume pierced her curls which were dressed high off the nape of her neck. She clasped her gloved hands tightly in her lap. It was coming, finally.

She had been slightly disturbed at Jack's explanation of their meeting at his house instead of calling for her at the Hidels', but if he and Sir Charles were suffering a temporary coolness in their relationship, that was no concern of hers. It had happened before, Jack had said indifferently, and would undoubtedly happen again, but at present he didn't wish to encounter him. It was simply another instance of his uncle's dislike for him coming to the surface again, and would pass in time. The quarrel had been of no moment—simple irritation. So much for that, and Darcy had dismissed it. Now she gazed steadily ahead as the horse clip-clopped down the street. He was going to propose and he was suffocating with embarrassment, but she couldn't help him. Or could she? She unclasped her hands and placed her right one over his and felt a sighing tremor run through him.

"I want you to be my wife, Darcy. I am deeply devoted to you and I believe we could be happy together." He blurted the words out, relieved by the pressure of her hand on his.

She turned her liquid gaze on him. "Oh, Jack," she whispered. "I am so very glad you asked me. All my plans to leave for Florence were saddened by my reluctance to part from you."

I knew it, he thought triumphantly, and lifted his eyes from his knees. He leaned forward then and kissed her cheek. Darcy grimaced inwardly. How can he be so tepid? she thought with irritation. She responded by pressing her lips to his cheek and he placed his arm around her shoulders then and drew her to him.

"I don't know how to say this—perhaps you will be disappointed. But I can't help it. You know how shy I am." Darcy stiffened slightly. What in the world was he talking about? He felt the rigidity in her shoulders and hastened on. This part of it was vital; it was vital that she should concur in his feelings, cooperate in his plans. "To go through the ritual of a public wedding would be sheer torture for me; to be stared at and congratulated and have all those people descend on one. To me marriage is a very private thing and I do so hope you will agree with me." She turned her face and placed her cheek against his. He is only concerned about the ceremony, she thought with a thudding sense of relief. "In short, I want us to elope," he continued almost in a whisper. "We can elope to Florence; it is a beautiful city and their marriage laws, for Protestants at any rate, are much more lenient than those of France. We will send word back as soon as we are man and wife. But I do so want it to be our own ceremony, only you and I, without all the silly clamor and fuss of a lot of people we aren't at all interested in."

Darcy nodded her head. She would have agreed to being married on an ice floe if he had insisted; as long as they were married it was irrelevant where and how. She did experience a pang of regret; she had looked forward to a grand ceremony in Chicago, not least of all for the sake of rubbing a few noses in her triumph, but that could be forsworn.

Jack kissed her cheek again. "I am so glad—so very glad you don't mind too much. It will be beautiful, I promise you. And after that we can go to the United States, directly from Italy. I am most anxious to meet your father, and I will need to make amends to him for stealing his beautiful daughter."

Darcy smiled with satisfaction as much as excitement. Their return would be a tour de force. But when? Before she could ask, Jack continued, on the crest of the wave now.

"Could you possibly be ready by the weekend? I am most anxious. I have waited so long for such happiness. I know you will have your wardrobe to see to and I don't want to rush you, but it will be so gay, so wonderful, when we step aboard the train and are gone—just you and I."

Darcy's heart quickened. It would be exciting. Of course she could be ready and said as much. Before they parted he kissed her full on the mouth, after having been assured that their secret would be shared by no one, and she felt the rather dry pressure of his closed lips as he sealed their bargain. She lay awake that night, tossing with anticipation and victory. It wasn't till they met again the next afternoon for a drive in the Bois that she remembered to tell him of Leita's marriage.

He was her confidante, her husband-to-be, and she told him of the evening wedding, a surprise to everyone. His pale blue eyes were opaque and his face almost expressionless as he reflected on this news.

"Very odd, wouldn't you say? I never noticed anything brewing between those two. Very sudden and very odd." His fingers were twitching with their habitual unrest and Darcy, having spoken to no one of the conversation she overheard, now proceeded to tell her fiancé, in strictest confidence.

Jack listened, his face a mask, while she told him of the speculation between Giselle and her husband as to who the father of Leita's child might be—the attempts to abort her, and the final gallant decision of the Comte du Favre. Jack rubbed his index finger over the bridge of his nose. "She is definitely going to have a child, from what happened that night?"

"Most definitely. I gather that Lady Hidel has been in a terrible flurry about it, but now their problem is solved. Armand will claim the child, and Leita will be saved from disgrace." Jack continued rubbing the bridge of his nose and Darcy felt a trifle perplexed. Jack's habitual Jeremiads about Leita's brazen behavior, her freedom with suitors, her scandalously loose demeanor, would seem to have been verified by this happening. In fact, she had almost not confided the secret to him, anticipating that he would maintain that Leita herself probably incited her attacker with her loose ways. But no such denunciation was forthcoming. He seemed lost in thought.

Back in Paris they sat at a cafe and instead of his customary lemonade Jack ordered a brandy and soda. Up until now he had seemed almost gay, relishing their romantic conspiracy. He explained his preoccupation by saying he had suddenly been afflicted with a headache. During a silence he suddenly remarked, "What a bloody mess!" Darcy blinked at the energy of his statement and he explained by saying that Armand took a great deal on himself by taking charge of another man's unborn child. Darcy replied emphatically that she thought it was admirable on Armand's part and she felt vastly relieved that the whole sordid mess was resolved, and resolved so well. After all, Leita had been her responsibility, and although she couldn't have prevented what happened, still, she hadn't been there that night and that could have been construed as negligence on her part.

Jack agreed with her hastily, saying he had meant no criticism, had only been appalled at the situation, including its outcome. Mollified, Darcy brought up the ball to be held at the Marquise de Sivry's that evening and they agreed to meet there, with Darcy remarking that it was really delicious that no one there would suspect that he and she were to be married in less than a week. Jack agreed, with a rather distracted smile, and they parted on the best of terms.

Stephen descended the broad carpeted stairway of the Grand Hotel, stopped at the foot and gave a luxurious pat to his gleaming white dress shirt. He had been enjoying himself thoroughly. Well acquainted in Paris, he was always welcomed with glad cries. Handsome, rich, and of good French family, he was never at a loss for invitations and this visit particularly he regarded the round of festivities as his just due. He had no guilt about the murder of his partner; he regarded his action as both necessary and justified. The man had proved to be, however unexpectedly, a traitorous embezzler and merited his execution, for such he regarded it. His strivings in the matter of recovering his funds had exercised him and he felt that he had surmounted a series of obstacles and now was most deserving of reward in the form of rest and entertainment. He had begun a most promising flirtation with the eldest daughter of a court chamberlain and he looked forward with pleasure to seeing Louise Violaine tonight. Witty, very pretty, and certainly a maidenly innocent, he could smell a satisfactorily sensuous liaison in the offing. He had penned a note of fulsome good wishes to Leita and experienced a pang or two of regret as he thought of his dampened hopes. She had been a marvelous girl and he had been monstrously unlucky. But fate had called the tune and he hardly filled the role of a heartbroken and inconsolable lover. Tonight promised to be splendid. The Marquise de Sivry was giving a ball to celebrate her return from the country and all of Paris that hadn't fled to provincial estates for the summer would be there. Stephen decided to have a brandy before he got a cab and deflected his steps to the right, then he stopped dead. By God, it was him!

Breve Pinchon's wide shoulders were conspicuous in the sedate lobby as his surefooted, confident stride carried him through the door. Stephen pursed his lips and made a little sucking noise, then smiled softly. He met Breve midway, slapped his shoulder and at the same time extended his hand. Breve cast a surprised look down at him. He was a good three inches taller, a fact that always irritated Stephen.

"Now this is a surprise. When did you get to Paris?" Stephen asked, his face wreathed in a welcoming smile.

"About fifteen minutes ago." Breve grinned. He was in good spirits. He was here now and the die was cast. He looked around the ornate lobby with an appreciative eye. "Are you staying here?"

Stephen nodded. "I always stay here. You'll get no better service in town. You've made a wise choice."

"I'll trust your judgment," Breve remarked.

"And now, come and have a drink with me to celebrate your arrival. Is this your first time in Paris?"

"A drink would be welcome. And yes, this is my first time in Paris." Breve accepted his invitation, wondering why the spurt of bonhomie on Stephen's part.

It occurred to him that Stephen had no idea of his love for Leita. Why should he? He was of course glad to see a familiar face, as most people are when they encounter an acquaintance far from home.

They sat sociably over their wine, Stephen giving Breve a running commentary on what he shouldn't miss in Paris. They spent several minutes discussing business with the single-minded attention of men whose lives revolved around investments.

"You have just arrived and therefore you must be baptized in Paris society, Breve," Stephen stated at one point. Breve's dark brows lifted momentarily. "I'm serious. I was on my way to a very festive party which the Marquise de Sivry is giving. It promises to be splendid and you can meet all the haut monde. Now you must come along with me—or did you have other plans for the evening? If you did, cancel them."

"My plans for the evening were a hot bath and a soft mattress," Breve smiled. He was turning the invitation

375

over in his mind. It was too late to do more than write a note to Leita, telling her he was here and asking to see her. That thought gave rise to another question. If Stephen was inviting him so freely, why wasn't he with Leita? He hadn't mentioned that he was calling for her. Breve felt suddenly lighthearted; Stephen wouldn't be seeking his company, he was sure, if he were escorting Leita tonight. Things might not be going so well for his dapper acquaintance where Leita was concerned.

"I'll take you up on it, but I'll have to get presentable first."

"Excellent! I can promise you a marvelous time. I'll wait here for you."

The Marquise de Sivry held out a long, thin hand for Stephen to kiss, meanwhile sweeping her eyes over Breve. Tiens! she thought, what an intoxicatingly handsome man! What is he? Italian—Greek? No, he is far too tall for either. Breve's tailcoat of finest black wool woven with silk heightened the sparkling white, lace-trimmed shirt. His thick hair gleamed like the wing of a blackbird and ended in long sideburns against the bronzed skin of his face where his white teeth shone in a polite smile.

"I have taken the liberty of bringing a friend, newly arrived from America. May I present Colonel Breve Pinchon," Stephen said.

"Aah, an American! Of course, I should have known. M'sieur, you are a handsome giant!" the Marquise smiled, and allowed herself a small tremor as Breve's lips brushed her hand. "I am delighted that you brought your friend, Stephen, and what part of that vast and mysterious country are you from, Colonel Pinchon?"

"From Chicago, which explains my acquaintance with Mr. de Jean," Breve smiled.

"How exciting, and now you must allow me to conduct you around the room. You must be introduced to at least a few of my guests. They will be charmed."

The Marquise was a sprightly little woman, indeterminately thirty and dressed in scarlet and white voile. Breve had a certain amount of French at his command and was able to acquit himself creditably in conversation, to the Marquise's delight. His dark eyes roved over the guests as he made his way through the throng with his hostess's hand tucked in his arm. Once he drew in his breath at the sight of a pile of red-gold curls and then exhaled in disappointment when the lady turned. It was on the tip of his tongue several times to ask his hostess if she had made the acquaintance of a Miss Leita Johnston but he restrained himself. His nerves were keyed to a high pitch and he accepted a glass of champagne with relieved readiness. He savored the cool, slightly tart liquid and then emptied another glass. It took three more glasses before he began to feel a tingling sense of relaxation flow through the tight muscles of his neck and shoulders. Breve, you're like a lovesick boy, he chided himself. I would rather see her for the first time alone, but it has been so long. He had dreamed of their meeting in so many variations, and now it will probably be different than any of my imaginings, he thought. He drank more champagne to quell the trepidation and excitement that flowed through him, all the while he carried on one conversation after another, answering questions about Chicago, explaining that one rarely saw a savage Indian, let alone having anything to fear from them in that booming metropolis.

His mind darted back to the indulgence he had permitted himself before leaving, back to the red-brick neo-Grecian house on Rush Avenue that he had seen and bought quickly, in a flush of optimism. There was a lily pond at the end of a path leading from the rear terrace, a lily pond graced with a marble statue of a girl whose hair was tied behind and flowed over her shoulder in the way Leita's did when she intended to spend the day on her horse. The house was for Leita; it was Southern in style, with tall white columns rising up three stories high and a long front veranda that overlooked an expanse of lawn so green it looked as if it had been sprinkled with dew-dampened emeralds. But the lily pond, gracefully oval and lined with teal-blue tiles, had been the crowning touch. He remembered her saying how dearly she loved the lilies. She had spent many hours beside the pond that lay in the ellipse of manicured grass at Wisteria Hall. This was where he would bring her—they would finally be together— together for the rest of their lives.

He realized suddenly that a question had been addressed to him and turned quickly to the woman beside him.

"I have interrupted your reverie! I am so sorry. It must have been a lovely one; you were smiling while your eyes were so far away."

"Please allow me to apologize. It was rude of me, but I have had a great deal on my mind lately," Breve said graciously. What in hell is her name? he wondered. We were introduced, but I have forgotten it completely.

The lady laughing up at him had dark hair swept back into a chignon which was pierced by a tiny, gold dagger. Very striking, he thought, looking at her dark eyes and milk-white skin. Her dress was of soft, gold tissue trimmed with massive scallops of lace where it was molded only partway over her breasts.

"And you have forgotten my name," she laughed. "I can tell by the wild look in your eye. I should torment you by not telling you, but I can't be so cruel. I am the Baroness Hequet, but you may call me Simonne if you

378

promise not to forget it again. The Baron is in Florence, attending to some tedious government matter and I have come alone, which is why the Marquise made us known to one another so swiftly. But there, I shan't attempt to monopolize you. I have the feeling it would be impossible, at any rate."

"I could only consider it the highest of compliments," Breve rejoined. Very charming, and very seductive, he thought. Has made it plain immediately that her husband is out of the picture for this evening, at any rate, and I would be most welcome in her bed. It's remarkable, he thought, how stale and ordinary these liaisons are when you are in love with another woman. This creature is beautiful, and probably interesting, and yet I couldn't be more indifferent; even primed with champagne I'm indifferent, he chuckled to himself. He realized he was very near to being drunk, not disgracefully drunk, but happily, freely intoxicated.

He asked her to waltz, which she did beautifully, light as a bird in his arms. They strolled out onto the grounds afterward to the huge, purple tent where a buffet was being served by two chefs. Breve realized that he hadn't eaten at all since noon; no wonder he was lightheaded. Dancers filled the terrace and the strains of a Metas waltz filled the soft night air. Breve saw that the Baroness had a plate piled high with delicacies and had just filled his own when he looked up at the open French doors at one end of the terrace to see Leita emerging on the arm of a slenderly built man with pale blond hair and an evening coat covered with decorations. His heart leaped into his throat and pounded there. He set his plate down quickly; his hands were trembling. My God, she looked lovely! Pale blue gauze sprinkled with silver moons swayed luminously around her and a handful of white gardenias were pinned at her breast. Her hair flamed in the light of the torches set around the terrace and cascaded in curls down her back and over one shoulder. Her face was slightly fuller than he remembered, her cheeks flushed and her eyes dark and purple under those thick lashes. She was surrounded in that instant by a laughing group. I wonder who in the devil that fellow is, Breve thought. At any rate, it looks as if de Jean hasn't made the running and that's all to the good. He swallowed in an effort to still the throbbing in his ears. What I want to do is march over there and plow through that crowd and just pick her up in my arms and carry her out of here. Who the hell is that man with her? Breve hadn't noticed Stephen de Jean sidling along toward him.

"Of course I will go over and extend my felicitations," the Baroness was saying between mouthfuls, "but I have no intention of doing it until that crush dissolves. I thought they were staying at Tours anyway," she said rather petulantly.

"The crush is understandable. This is the first time they have appeared in society since that deliciously secret wedding. What a thunderclap!" The speaker was a small man devouring scoops of melon as fast as he spooned it up. He dabbed now at his shirtfront where a drop of juice had splattered. "Astonishing really. One of the oldest families in the nobility, the de la Penseans, and the one remaining branch allies itself with an untitled American from some incredibly wild frontier. Armand's grandfather is no doubt spinning in his grave," the little man chuckled maliciously.

Breve felt a tightness between his eyes, a sudden tightness that threatened to explode. "Who are they talking about?" he said to the Baroness, unmindful of the harshness in his tone.

She looked at him, surprised at the abruptness of his question. "They're talking of the Comte du Favre. We just saw him come out on the terrace with his new bride."

"Someone said he married an American," Breve pursued.

"Yes, Colonel, he did, and in secret, only a fortnight ago. The charming little thing came to Paris as a guest of Lord and Lady Hidel and absolutely swept Armand off his feet. There has been a great to-do about it." She dabbed at her mouth and scanned Breve's face with a puzzled look. Dear me, the man is quite pale, she thought.

"It was such a surprise, you know. The Comte was widowed, rendered widowed and childless by a most tragic accident not two years ago and he has been quite inconsolable since."

"Never came out, avoided people like the plague," the small man injected. "Would never have married a commoner if he hadn't been in that state of mind. Most felicitous really, her presence. Lady Hidel is his godmother and he was an absolute fixture there. The only place one saw him really, until he began squiring his godmother's delectable young guest."

"You are being dreadful," a vivacious blonde spoke up. "Everyone thought that Miss Johnston was absolutely charming. I think it was very fortunate that she came on the scene when she did. You all know there was a time when we feared for Armand's reason—his grief was so intense."

"Commoner or not, she is absolutely beautiful. I think he did well," a portly older man wearing the red ribbon of the Legion of Honour said decisively.

"Pish and tush," the small man disposed of his melon rind and made a face. "France is full of beautiful women and the name of de la Penseans is not one to be bestowed so lightly. If you ask my opinion he should

381

have made her his mistress until he recovered his senses. What would happen to France if we went about marrying unknown little creatures from the wilds of the provinces? One knows how eagerly they pursue titles."

There was mingled agreement and vehement protest at this last pronouncement and Breve sat down, heavily. His fingers curled numbly around the stem of his glass and he poured it full from the bottle on the table at his side. His eyes never left the terrace, but he listened to every word of the clamorous conversation around him. He sat there, drinking steadily, his food untouched for the next twenty minutes. Torches illuminated the terrace and he watched Leita as she danced, smiling up at her partners, radiant and graceful. Then he stood up.

"Baroness, I recall your saying you intended to extend your felicitations to the newlyweds. I will be glad to accompany you. I am acquainted with the bride."

The Baroness took his arm and strolled off with him. His pallor was gone and now his face was covered with a dull flush and his eyes glowed like black coals.

"You are certain you care for nothing to eat?" Armand asked solicitously.

"Positive. Truth to tell I'm a trifle nauseous. I know it is because of all those cherries I ate this afternoon. I was positively gluttonous, but I had such a craving for them I couldn't stop," Leita replied with a shamefaced smile. She looked over the dancers and was glad they had come. She had been a trifle anxious as she anticipated her reception tonight. She knew full well that Armand's title dictated his choice of a wife and though she had been graciously received as a visitor to the country she feared that their reaction might be different now. But it hadn't been the case. She had been embraced and welcomed quite as freely as if she had been one of the nobility herself. Mary Jo and Etienne should arrive at any moment now and she wondered if Stephen would appear. She had been surprised to get his note and was looking forward to seeing him. She felt certain his life wouldn't be blighted by her precipitous marriage to someone else—not Stephen. But oh, she would be glad to see Mary Jo; she had missed her.

Then her heart stopped beating for a second. The glare of the torchlights had fallen on a man who looked so much like Breve that it might have been him. Now he passed the point where the glare distorted his features and she gasped. It couldn't be! He was only a few steps away, his eyes so dark on her they seemed to be boring through her. She was with him—that nameless woman he had fallen in love with, leaning on his arm and smiling. Leita rose, her arms tingling and trembling and her legs weak; she felt as if she really must fall. Armand gave her a bemused look.

She stood speechless and numb as Breve bent over her hand. The woman was speaking, was saying something to her, but the throbbing in her ears blotted it out. Now thankfully she was speaking to Armand. Breve's voice came through, his tone sharp and clipped as he uttered polite phrases and the next moment she felt herself being moved onto the terrace. The music was playing and Breve swept his arm around her and took her limp hand in his. They swept off in a waltz and she spoke the only words she could think of.

"Your wife is beautiful, Breve."

"My wife?" His mouth curled sardonically and one dark brow lifted. "You must think marriage is a contagious disease. You are the only bride here, Leita. And such a beautiful one." His tone was hard and mocking. The words she had spoken to him that night on the deck of the boat, when she had said, "I will go anywhere with you, Breve, anywhere!" were ringing in his ears.

The nausea rose up in Leita's throat with a vengeance. No wife? It hadn't been true? He was whirling her, his grip on her waist hard; she felt dizzy and little beads of perspiration sprung out on her upper lip.

"How well I remember your saying you were going to see the world and marry whom you chose, and when you fell in love you would know right away. You're quite a little prophetess. It all came true, didn't it—but you had to come to Paris to fall in love."

"Breve!" She almost whimpered. She was feeling so wretched. If he would only stop, if she could only talk to him in some peaceful, quiet place. Not here, in this whirling mass of near strangers.

"Breve, you don't understand. I didn't fall in love with Armand," she whispered weakly.

He looked down at her face. "What did you say?" he asked sharply.

She swallowed. "I didn't fall in love with Armand—I didn't marry him because I was in love with him."

"Well, you always were one for the truth, my dear. And now you admit it without a blush. So you fell in love with being a Countess? Very understandable. All young girls would like to grow up to be a Countess. Most of them aren't as pretty as you, however, and can't effect it so easily. How you have changed! The forthright, headstrong, girl-child I knew has grown up into a conniving little wench!" His eyes were like black diamonds as they swept over her scornfully. His hold on her waist tightened and he looked over her head. She turned her face away and he didn't see the tears wet her cheeks. They had reached the edge of the terrace and he released her suddenly and strode off, striding through the dancers as if they were so many inanimate objects to be swept aside. Leita closed her eyes, overcome with despair, then felt an arm around her shoulders.

"Who was that drunken lout?" Armand inquired angrily.

"He was just someone from home that I used to know," Leita answered finally, trying to catch her breath and at the same time swallow the sob that would betray her emotions to her husband.

"What did he say to you? What did he do to upset you like this?" Armand's tone had grown angrier as he surveyed her flushed and tear-stained face.

Leita sighed. "He thinks I am a conniving little wench who came over here title-hunting. That is the long and the short of it. Pay no attention, Armand. He had been drinking and he was never known for his gentle ways."

Armand led her to a chair, seated her, and then whispered in her ear, "I will return in a few moments. Can I bring you anything, my dear?"

Leita nodded. "I would very much like a glass of lemonade."

He patted her shoulder. As he walked through the open doorway a small muscle in his jaw could be seen to be jumping. He was fiercely angry. He searched the room with his eyes, having seen Breve go into the house from the terrace. But he was nowhere in sight. Then he walked into the hall. Breve stood with one hand on the doorknob and a footman stood behind him glowering; the man had evidently been rebuffed. Mary Jo Tillett stood in front of Breve, her hands raised in a gesture of supplication. Breve made some statement in reply, opened the door and disappeared into the night. Mary Jo turned and the look on her face was one of such dejection that Armand was spurred to her side.

"I was coming after him, but the devil has gotten away! What has he been up to you with you? He danced with Leita and left her in tears."

Mary Jo avoided Armand's eyes. She had never seen this mild man so agitated, but she was at a loss for an explanation suitable for his ears. She had just finished pleading with Breve to remain a few minutes longer so that she could talk to him. He had refused, not just refused, but coldly and angrily dismissed her.

"Whatever you find so necessary to tell me can be told in a letter. I will be at the Hotel Nestor in Geneva. And I wish you good night."

She knew full well why he had been so angry, but her frustration was intense. If he had let her she would have explained to him about the letter Darcy had received telling of his marriage. Then at least he would have understood part of it. God knows what he had said to Leita.

"Why is this boor such a mystery?" Armand inquired. "He comes in here, leaves my wife in tears, treats you with the utmost rudeness—I could see that. And yet I am not to be told who he is."

Mary Jo stopped suddenly. "Armand, that is the man who was in love with Leita. And he evidently didn't know she had married. I would guess he came to Paris unheralded to surprise her and he is in a rage now."

Armand faced her. "But she told me there was no one. I inquired when we were discussing marriage."

Mary Jo sighed deeply. "It is a long story, Armand. I'm sure Leita felt she was telling you the truth. Since the day they met it had been—well—complicated, to put it mildly. A tale of misunderstandings and cross purposes."

"And what is to be done now?" Armand spoke after a long moment of silence.

Mary Jo shrugged. "There is nothing to be done. He has gone charging off like a mad bull and for that matter, I don't know what his intentions were when he arrived here tonight. They have known one another over a year now and nothing ever went right between them. Don't worry about it."

Armand was subdued and walked slowly down the length of the hall with her. Mary Jo looked at his face, then put her hands on his shoulders.

"Armand, I was watching Leita tonight. I came in before Breve confronted her and I know she is happy. Leita isn't good at feigning happiness, and I know her too well to be deceived. What you have given her means more than even you could know. And Leita would never deceive you, it isn't her way. If she repented of her bargain she would tell you. Otherwise my advice is to leave well enough alone. And let sleeping dogs lie, too," she concluded with a laugh.

"Hardly a sleeping dog." Armand smiled. "More like a thunderstorm."

"One that has passed over." Mary Jo nodded prophetically.

On the terrace Leita awaited Armand's return, unaware that she was being watched. Jack Hidel stood further on in a group of guests, his eyes on her so intently that he scarcely blinked. He had seen Breve approach her, watched her on the dance floor with him, then seen them part, but their meeting held no interest for him. He was unaware that anything of importance had happened to her—his eyes and his thoughts were riveted on her person. This pink-cheeked creature held his child in her body. And she was laughing, oblivious of him. Another man stayed at her side, intending to receive the fruit of his own loins as if it belonged to him. The hours between parting with Darcy and arriving here had been spent in a white heat of thought, and now Jack was smoldering in the grip of obsession. Never, never through all the years of his life had Jack received his just due. This conviction was the lodestone of his personality. The withdrawn, diffident man who at the best received only tolerance from those around him was a walking inferno of resentment and suspicion, a slave to towering jealousies. His mind churned now over his past; he had been disdained by his mother, her favors reserved for his uncle and his sister. His gorge was high as he recalled how she had pandered to Uncle Hugh's every whim, and he had many of them, the uncle who was always visiting, generally unwell, his tastes at table dictating their menus, his headaches requiring that Jack step quietly, and his tempers that reduced Dora to pitiful tears. Jack must always be careful not to upset Uncle Hugh; if he did his mother would suffer. Jack Hidel's face was hard and tight, remembering how he had been discriminated against, ignored, disliked in school and cast into the background at home where his sister had basked in the limelight. Betty had been a bossy, mean girl, well aware of her favored position. He had hated her, and now he understood the tacit assumption he had himself absorbed, that he was somehow not quite right, that he was lacking. Of course it was taken for granted by his mother and his uncle that he was short a few pence, the common term for deficiency. He had rejoiced when word came of his uncle's death, then fell into a maudlin guilt for his joy over the removal of one of his rivals. He had never really wanted to marry, had been tongue-tied in the company of girls, only at ease if they were married. Then he enjoyed ingratiating himself with them, to the discredit of their husbands, with his quiet, understanding ways. His teeming feelings of rivalry were gratified by this exercise, but otherwise he had never thought of himself as the head of a family. Now, that was changed. He had been humiliated, degraded, told that he was an imbecile—an idiot, a fate he couldn't escape due to his conception. But this glowing girl was going to have his baby, and it would be perfect, absolutely perfect! The baby belonged to him! She belonged to him!

Chapter 24

JACK HIDEL SCREWED THE STOPPER INTO THE SILVER FLASK and asked yet again: "Are you certain it won't hurt the child she carries?"

Madame Charbonnel smiled tolerantly, but a sigh of exasperation escaped her. "It will not hurt her or the baby, I assure you, M'sieur Hidel. And now we must set about transforming you."

Jack nodded and removed his shirt. The story he had told to Madame Charbonnel had had a thread of truth running through it. A young paramour of his, a housemaid, was going to have his baby. She refused to leave her husband, a lout who beat her regularly. In truth, Jack assured Madame Charbonnel, she was afraid to leave him. She was temperamental to the extreme, and would no doubt put up a fight if Jack attempted to abscond with her. But she was a good girl, really, and she was going to have his baby. He intended to marry her, after procuring a divorce for her, which

391

terrified her in the extreme. She was convinced her husband would kill her—would find her wherever she went. Jack had hit upon the idea of sedating her, in order to get her out of the country. Then he would set about the divorce and marry the girl. But, it was essential that no one should recognize him when he went for her. Hence, the need for a disguise. Madame Charbonnel was charmed by the romance of all this. In addition, she was more than a little delighted at the prospect of getting this client at a far remove from her establishment. Since the night when Sir Charles had called for him, with blood in his eye, she had determined that he must be discouraged. She had no intention of jeopardizing her hard-won business by stepping on the toes of a man who had the Emperor's ear, as Sir Charles did. Altogether she had fallen in with his scheme with a certain amount of enthusiasm.

She had procured and filled two flasks with a solution of poppy juice and sugar water, had sent a maid out to rouse a chemist and now she took up a comb and began to apply the solution to Jack's pale brown locks. He sat quietly, rather like a small boy, while she did this, darting his eyes again and again to the mirror on the wall. When she finished his hair shone black as tar in the light from the chandelier.

"It suits you, my dear. Suits you very well," she smiled, making a valiant attempt not to laugh. He looked like a different man—rather like a racetrack tout or a prosperous pimp, she thought privately.

Now she busied herself applying spirit glue to two limp pieces of hair backed by a light canvas. When she completed this she turned with one of the pieces held between her fingertips.

"Now you must hold very still," she cautioned him, and pressed the backing and tapped it with her fingers till she met the end of his chin. It was an Imperial, a well cut one, in the popular spade shape and she was wholeheartedly pleased with the result.

She descended on him with the mustache before she would allow him to turn his head, affixed the hairy fragment and stood back.

"Now you may look. And I swear to this, your own mother wouldn't know you."

Jack's china-blue eyes lit up at the sight of his reflection. Madame Charbonnel was right. No one would recognize him now. He had started to rise when Madame Charbonnel waved her hands.

"No, no! There is one more touch." She took a small bottle that held a dark brown liquid, dampened a piece of cotton with it and began to stroke his face. His fair skin, highly tinged with ruddiness, disappeared under her application and became swarthy. She continued down his neck with the cotton and then applied the mixture to the back of his hands and his wrists, halfway up to his elbow.

"There now. You have the complexion of a sun-burned Italian. If that girl's husband should see you now he would never know you. You are incognito, my friend."

Jack viewed his reflection with satisfaction. Dark skin, dark hair, mustache and beard had transformed him into another person entirely.

"I quite like it, you know," he said shyly. And Madame Charbonnel shook her head. The man was half-mad, she was certain of that. The look in his eyes when he came in her house that night had frightened her. He was obsessed. And here he was admiring himself like a girl. But what of it? She would be rid of him for a good long while at least and for a goodly sum too. She glanced at the pile of gold louis on the table. He paid well, one could say that for him.

Jack took his leave, carrying a long, rectangular box,

and went back to the apartment where his mother lay sleeping. He opened the drawer of his desk and took out a sheaf of notes and began to study them. Then he took pen in hand and began to write, looking intently every moment or two at the notes in front of him. He discarded one page after another, crumpling them impatiently into the willow basket beside the desk, and continued writing.

Leita wakened the next morning to sun streaming in the windows. She blinked her eyes and stretched, then flinched. She felt groggy and her head pained her. Then she remembered. She had drunk several glasses of champagne last night in a fruitless quest for relief from her feelings. She felt nauseous now and rang for the maid who brought her a basin. After she had thrown up she felt weak, but somewhat better.

"No coffee this morning, Marie. Some tea, with lemon." Marie hastened out and Leita reflected tiredly how easy it had all been. The servants had welcomed her, they did their utmost to serve her and so far there hadn't even been any quarreling among them. The housekeeper at the chateau had unbent finally, after Leita realized the extreme possessiveness she felt toward her master. The housekeeper had been certain that a marriage that had taken place so quickly must come to some bad end, and the fact that Leita was a foreigner had cemented her fears. But even she was amicable now. No one despised her or looked on her as a fortune hunter, no one but the man she had fallen in love with over a year ago. She writhed inwardly as she recalled the expression on his face. A conniving little wench, he had called her. How dare he? Brutish, as ever, refusing to listen to her, scorning her so furiously that her eyes had stung with tears, though she had clenched her teeth to stop them. And he hadn't married after all. It had been as Mary Jo suspected—a rumor. She had realized later that the woman with him was one she had been introduced to in Paris. A Baroness something or other. But she had been so shaken at the sight of Breve, tall and dynamic, walking toward her, that she had barely glanced at the lady on his arm. Now she trembled at the memory, trembled as she thought of his closeness to her, his face tanned and handsome, his white teeth flashing and his eyes so dark and piercing that everything within her had melted in an anguish of love for him. Would it never end?—that wild beating of her heart, the need she had felt for so long, just to be near him, near the vigorous strength of that hard, muscular body, his quick, deep laughter and the mellow sound of his voice when he spoke to her, even carelessly.

Well it had ended—it ended last night when he walked away from her after insulting her so deeply she knew she would never, could never forgive him. Her marriage hadn't ended it, this still unbelievable pregnancy hadn't ended it, but his treatment of her last night, the harsh cruelty of it, had killed her love for him.

She drank her tea and bathed, her eyes alight with anger and her heart hardened with fury. Then, when she began to dress she began to cry. She wept with a mounting pain. She would never see him again, never see that resolute stride of his bring him to her, never feel the soft tenderness of his lips. Her tears brought no relief; it seemed that her heart must burst with the pain it contained. She sat down and attempted to write a letter to Jerome Knox, partly because Jerome had been close to Breve. The tears dropped on it and she surrendered to them yet again. She washed her face and walked out onto her balcony. Paris stretched away in the distance, soft blue and mauve under a cloudy, overcast sky. Carriages rolled along the boulevards, their occupants laughing, flirting. She leaned on the iron railing, drinking it all in. This was to be her home from now on till the end of her days, here and the chateau near Tours. Stephen de Jean had extended her his good wishes last night, remarking that she did credit to her station. He had looked very well, complacently handsome as always. She shuddered to think she had ever even considered marriage to him. Armand was so different. His grace and kindness were bred in his bones. There at least she was fortunate. Without Armand's protection she would be in a dire strait indeed. What if she hadn't married Armand? What if Annette had been forced to inform her of what had happened to her and there had been no Armand to rescue her? She would have told Breve. She knew that with certainty. And then what? She thought of that night in Chicago, when he had as much as told her that she was only a temporary pleasure. He had never asked her to marry him—in fact had always ended by rejecting her, forcefully too, and repudiating his love for her. No, her dilemma would never have been solved by Breve. A sword of sunlight pierced the low clouds and struck the tower of Notre Dame over on the Isle de la Cité. Somewhere in that mass of gray buildings, Breve was walking, sauntering down a boulevard or sitting at a table. It was inhuman, it was cruel, that he was out there, so near to her but so oblivious, occupying himself happily without her, without even thinking of her. She felt a wild urge to go look for him, to find him and make him hear her out. She would do it. She would hire a cab; Armand had taken the carriage to the Bourse earlier that morning and probably wouldn't return till late afternoon. She sped into her boudoir and unbuttoned her morning dress, looking about wildly for something to put on. She answered the knock at the door distractedly and Marie handed her a note in a pale mauve envelope. Oh my God, perhaps it was from him!

She tore it open but it was only Darcy's handwriting that filled the page. She read it quickly, then stopped and read it again carefully.

Dear Leita,

Something very important has happened. I need you to come to meet me at the Gare de Lyon. I will be waiting in Car 4, the third compartment, of the train to Marseilles. Please do not fail me, and please, please, keep this in utmost confidence.

Yours in need,
Darcy Rankin

What on earth could have happened to Darcy that she would need me? And at the train station? Cool, competent Darcy. Somehow she couldn't imagine Darcy really needing anyone. She had said "the utmost confidence." Darcy with a secret she could imagine; it seemed in character somehow, but if Darcy was imploring her, she had better go, and make haste about it too. It was well after one o'clock now and it would take some little time to cover the distance between here and the station. She dressed quickly, her fingers flying over the buttons of a pink and white striped cotton dress. She grabbed a hat, threw it back and grabbed another, one whose streamers matched the pink in her dress. Running out of the room she met Marie in the hallway.

"If the Comte should return early you may tell him I have gone out for a drive, but I intend to be back before he arrives anyway."

"But Madame, the carriage is not here," Marie protested.

"That doesn't matter," Leita called back over her

shoulder. "I will get a cab. I simply must have some fresh air." And she ran down the stairway and out into the street where she hailed a cab and directed the coachman to take her to the Gare de Lyon.

The note from Darcy had fallen to the bottom of the armoire when Leita plunged her hand in in search of a dress. It lay there still.

In the Gare de Lyon Breve purchased his ticket for Geneva and hoped devoutly that no one else would share his compartment. His head pounded from the quantities of brandy he had drunk the night before, his eyes felt inflamed and scratchy from lack of sleep and he was in a black mood. The train was to be late and that didn't improve his disposition. He decided to take his malaise to the bar in the station and accordingly made his way through the bustle and ordered a glass of brandy, on the theory that more of the same couldn't make him feel any worse. He sipped it gloomily; the cafe was crowded and he left the bar to sprawl in one of the chairs outside the door, taking advantage of a table just vacated. The scowl on his face discouraged a hesitant pair from seating themselves and he sat back and surveyed the crowd.

I can't get out of here soon enough, he thought, and I'll never come back. I'll never see her again and that will help, after a while. What in hell is that fellow doing—and where have I seen him before? The man in the uniform of the Imperial Guards had been pacing up and down and consulted a pocket watch anxiously twice in the short space of time since he caught Breve's eye. It's his walk, Breve decided; I've seen someone that moved like that—recently, too. The man walked with one shoulder higher than the other, his neck drawn back into his chest and his head jutting out. Like a camel with a hump, Breve chuckled. He beckoned to a waiter and ordered another brandy. He intended to

398

sleep for the length of the journey, regardless of who invaded his compartment. The Baroness Hequet was to join him in Geneva the next day. It seemed her husband's stay in Florence was to be an extended one and she liked Geneva. Breve had put the stamp of approval on her plan, more out of fatigue than anything else, but now he decided that it would probably be a very good thing. She was beautiful, passionate, and would certainly help to take his mind off what had brought him here in the first place. And it wouldn't last long; she would have to return to Paris and he would be free to do as he chose. That fellow was certainly worried. He watched the officer in the Guards' uniform peer down through the throng of travelers. Whoever he is waiting for is late and he is on the verge of a nervous fit. The soldier suddenly darted between a mother and two children and apprehended a waiter, asking for a whiskey and soda, and directing the waiter to be quick about it. Breve frowned. He had heard the voice too. Rather high and thin, and a very marked English accent to his French. Must have been someone at the party last night. He searched his mind; it was annoying to him that he should be so familiar and the memory still elude him.

The officer gulped the whiskey and soda so quickly that he came near to choking and darted back to the spot he had been pacing. Breve emptied his glass and rose from the uncomfortable little iron chair. About time to saunter over to his own platform. He strolled along, looking at the crowd to pass the time when at the far edge of the travelers he saw Leita. She was hurrying, almost running, holding a wide-brimmed straw hat in one hand. Her curls bounced on her shoulders and it was obvious she had a destination. Her eyes looked straight ahead purposefully. Now where was she going in such a hurry? Breve's heart leaped into his throat at the sight of her and he turned, unwilling to lose sight of her so quickly. His footsteps took him along in the same direction she pursued. How pale she looked! She looked as if she might be ill. And he had been close enough to see her eyelids were puffy and swollen. Regret stormed through him. He had been vicious to her; he had hurt her. There was no excuse for the way he had spoken to her, the way he had left her on the terrace. He had behaved as if she had been promised to him and had willfully deceived him. His temper again, his bitter disappointment, above all his love for her. She looked so small and vulnerable as he watched her back while she shouldered her way through the crowd—so vulnerable and so young. He was gaining on her—he should reach her, tell her he was sorry, perhaps even tell her why. Then his brows drew together in perplexity. The Guards' officer had materialized suddenly and now he spoke quickly to the hurrying girl. She looked up at him, puzzled. He spoke again. Breve heard his words. "Miss Rankin asked me to meet you and assist you to her. Come, we must hurry." Leita nodded in a bewildered kind of way and the pair of them sped on, the officer's hand at Leita's arm.

Breve stopped dead. Too late now. So it was Leita that queer fellow had been waiting for. And Darcy Rankin was somewhere around here. Breve drew on then but when he saw Leita climbing the steps into the train with the officer close on her heels he stopped, sighed, and then shrugged. He walked dispiritedly to the platform where the Geneva train sat waiting, found his compartment and put both feet up on the seat. He stared bleakly out the window when the train finally commenced to roll. Something was gnawing at his mind, something wrong. It would have to be, he

400

thought grimly. There is certainly nothing right. Then it hit him. That officer, his English accent! What was an Englishman doing in the elite Imperial Guard, Napoleon's own company? Breve sat up, frowning. No Englishman would be allowed to serve in that. Englishman? He slapped his knee. That was the fellow—the fellow he had seen Darcy with last night. He had been introduced and he remembered that thin, rather high voice. And that walk. He had observed him with some interest because it was obvious that Darcy attached considerable importance to him and he had been reminded of Hugo Wenzler and the fact that she had been almost constantly in his company. He had assessed her new escort with a little curiosity because of that. He recalled now—the blue eyes and that lop-shouldered walk. But that fellow had been smooth-chinned; no beard or mustache, and his hair had been a brownish, gingery color. Breve rubbed his jaw thoughtfully. Something was very strange here. He would take an oath that the two men were one and the same. And Leita hadn't seemed to recognize him—she had obviously been puzzled—quite as if he were a perfect stranger. And this man was the nephew of the people she had been staying with. Darcy had informed him of that. Well, they did look very different. The dark hair and the beard changed him, but he wasn't, he couldn't be completely disguised unless he changed his posture and his walk, and his voice. No, Breve thought, that was Hidel, and now why in hell was he gotten up like that, and why did he want to deceive Leita? He felt sleepy no longer and made his way to the dining car where he ordered and consumed a heavy luncheon. Finally he dismissed his questions with a grimace. It doesn't matter anyway—and then again I may have been imagining things. I had better get my mind on business and away from mysteries that I'm fabricating myself. And he returned to his compartment. Gnawing over who is meeting her at a train station is no way to forget her, you idiot. And I have just seen her for the last time. He settled himself to sleep, but it was a long time coming.

Chapter 25

THE TRAIN FOR MARSEILLES GAVE A JOLT AS LEITA SPED
down the narrow corridor outside the compartments.
Then it began to move. She turned wildly to the strange
man behind her.

"But the train is leaving!"

"Never mind," he spoke soothingly but hastily. "She
is in the next compartment. It will only take a moment."

She felt his hand on her back as she opened the door
and the next moment she was catapulted into the empty
compartment. She fell forward onto one of the seats
and the officer turned her over quickly. She opened her
mouth to scream and kicked wildly but a handkerchief
soaked with some overpowering scent was thrust
against her mouth and nose. She strangled, choking
and trying to cough and breathe at the same time. Her
fingernails clawed down the face of the man whose arm
held her pinned to the seat. She gasped, the stench of
the handkerchief was overpowering and her eyes stared

up into the man's face. Dear God! She knew him. It was Jack Hidel—those eyes—it could be no one else. It was her last thought before she lost consciousness. Jack pressed the ether-soaked cloth harder against her face even though her thrashing had subsided. When he was absolutely certain she was unconscious he straightened and expelled a long breath, then sprawled his long frame onto the seat opposite. He rested for a moment, still breathing heavily, then got up quickly and arranged her body to look as if she were only sleeping. Little drops of perspiration marked his forehead, tokens of his fear. Now, with Leita unconscious and the blinds to the compartment pulled, he allowed himself to relax. He even allowed himself a smile. It hadn't been at all difficult—went off perfectly, he congratulated himself. The conductor's knock brought him to his feet just as the door opened. He placed a warning finger to his lips as he rummaged in his breast pocket.

"My wife is not well," he whispered, offering the tickets to be punched.

The conductor cast a disinterested look in the direction of the sleeping young woman, touched his hat brim and closed the door.

Jack Hidel spent the next few minutes in divesting himself of the uniform and dressing in his customary garb. He was just beginning to feel hungry when Leita's eyelashes fluttered. Her first sensation was nausea, a gripping, roiling nausea and she groaned, turning her head from side to side. Jack leaped up and bent over her.

"You are to make no sound—no sound, do you hear me?" His voice, though he whispered, had risen high with his anxiety.

"Oh, I am so sick," Leita moaned, then tried to raise up. He put his arms under her shoulders and helped her to rise. She looked blankly into his face. Her own was pale and distorted.

"You must listen to me. I am going to take you to a lovely place, a place where you can have our baby. But you must not try to get away from me. You have to understand that you are with me and you are going to stay with me until our child is born. If you attempt to escape me, if you attempt to raise an alarm, I will exact a reprisal."

Leita frowned. His face was wavering in front of her and she began to retch. Oh God, she was so sick. What was this lunatic talking about? That she must not get away from him? She could hardly move! She fell back down on the seat and her head lolled over. She began to throw up. It was completely involuntary and her retching continued as she turned her head and threw up onto the floor beside the seat. The strange man rose quickly and rummaged around on the opposite seat, then held a hat under her mouth. A hat of all things! This must be some terrible nightmare. Finally her retching subsided and the sour smell of vomit permeated the air in the compartment. She sighed. She felt better now but her head continued to spin.

Jack took the Guards' jacket and began wiping at the pool of vomit on the floor. He gagged once. He had certainly never done this sort of thing before. Madame Charbonnel had said nothing about the ether making Leita ill. The train clattered on and Jack swiped ineffectually at the mess, then covered it with the jacket. Leita lay back now with her eyes closed and her hands folded on her bosom.

"Are you all right?" he whispered.

"Of course I'm not all right!" she snapped. She was beginning to regain a little energy. "I am dizzy and I am ill, and who in the world are you?" She had forgotten her recognition of him, and he had changed out of the uniform.

Jack drew his breath in, his keg-like rib cage expanding. "I am the father of your child." It was a whisper, but emitted with a certain demented pride.

Leita's eyes flew open and she looked him full in the face. Now she remembered. She looked in those eyes, alight with an expression she couldn't understand, but one that frightened her nevertheless. The skin was dark, the beard and mustache were unfamiliar, but the lines of his face again revealed his identity to her.

"Where is Darcy?" she asked.

"Darcy is in Paris," Jack replied cryptically.

"You are Jack Hidel! Why are you wearing that ridiculous beard? It was you who pressed that cloth over my face and held me down! Have you gone mad?" Leita started to raise up, then fell back onto the seat. Her head spun and the nausea had begun to rise again when she moved. Now she became aware of the speed of the train clattering along on its way to Marseilles. What could be happening? She had hurried so to find Darcy, wondering what sort of trouble she could be in to have sent such a frantic note, and now here she lay on a speeding train, sick and in the company of this strange man who had surely—yes, he had shoved her ahead of him into the compartment and she had fallen. Now she remembered it quite clearly. He had lunged at her, choking her with that stinking rag!

"You had better tell me very quickly why Darcy isn't here, as she said she would be, and give me an explanation of your actions. If there is a sane one!" She was getting very angry, in spite of feeling so weak.

Jack swallowed once and commenced. "It was I who sent the note to you. Darcy is in Paris and knows nothing of what we are going to do."

"What we are going to do!" Leita repeated in a voice that rose to a shriek.

"You must be quiet. I tell you, you must not cause a disturbance!" Jack said darkly. She felt a little shudder run through her as she looked into his contorted face. His eyes were gleaming, pale, blue and intense with something that looked very like madness.

"I told you before, if you attempt to escape from me I will exact a reprisal. I have a man watching Armand. He will trail the Comte du Favre's footsteps. If you elude me, if you try to get away, I will send a wire, and the Comte du Favre will be killed. My man will not hesitate. He has killed before, and it will be nothing to him to carry out my orders!"

Leita raised up on her elbows. He was mad—his mind had snapped, she thought. She felt terror now. No one knew where she had come; and what did he intend to do to her?

He read the fright in her eyes and felt relief. Now he had some power over her. The tale of the waiting man had been a fabrication, but she had no way of knowing this. He took heart and continued.

"You are going to have a baby—the baby is mine."

"Yours? What in God's name are you talking about? And how did you know I am pregnant?"

"I fathered that child, and that child is mine!" He spit the words out viciously.

She cast about in her mind for some means of getting away from this madman. She must humor him. He would have to sleep eventually, and then she would get to someone—the conductor. She must agree with him, listen to him, and wait to get help. Her head was clearing now and she raised up to a sitting position.

"How did you know of my pregnancy?" she repeated, watching him carefully.

"Darcy told me. Otherwise I might not have known until it was too late. They would have deprived me of my child—they schemed and plotted to take my son away from me!"

"Who schemed and plotted? Who are you talking about, Jack?" she asked softly, trying to still her trembling. He seemed to be on the verge of a fit. And how did Darcy know? She had never told her and she was certain Annette hadn't confided in her. "And what did Darcy tell you?" she asked, still softly, controlling the tremor in her voice.

"Darcy told me enough," he said darkly. "They have always plotted against me—always! They never liked me, not from the time I was a child! But they will have to change when I bring them my son. I will have my rightful place back then!"

"And why do you think you have a son?" Leita asked. She was totally bewildered by his ravings but decided to draw him out, get him to talk.

"Because I do!" he shouted then. "And he will be perfect! And my uncle will have to take back his lies then!"

She said nothing, fearing to incite him further. He was drawing deep breaths and staring wildly at her. She felt a lurch of nausea and closed her eyes, fearful that she would have to throw up again.

"You seduced me, you know," he said suddenly and almost primly.

She looked at him in astonishment, then broke into laughter. Of all the ridiculous statements! This silly man, with his silly false beard. He had always irritated her, bored her to yawns, and now he sat there saying that she had seduced him. Her laughter rose higher, a relief from her feelings of terror.

"Oh, you can well laugh," he said petulantly. "I've watched you—all of your little tricks. You are a heartless, scheming little flirt. Carrying on with every man you see."

She choked on her laughter and he glared at her. "I know what you are. No one knows better than I! But the fact remains that the child is mine! No matter how it came about, I will have my son! If you hadn't been so drunk you would remember!" He turned his head aside sulkily and stared out the window. His cheeks were flushed even through the stain Madame Charbonnel had applied.

Leita looked at his stony profile with distaste. "I do not get drunk, Mr. Hidel."

"Oh, but you did get drunk. You knew what you were doing. You knew quite well! I was only being helpful because you said you were ill, but you seduced me as soon as we got in that room!"

Leita's brows began to draw together and her heart thudded in her breast. Her hands began to shake and she clasped them tightly in her lap.

"What are you talking about?" she asked, her tone even.

"It wasn't my fault. It was all your actions. But I am going to shoulder my responsibility now. So the Hidels married you off to her godson, simply to avoid embarrassment. No thought of me! No thought of my rights! I wasn't to be told. Only disinherited— deprived of my name even. That's what he attempted to do to me! Well, their shady tricks won't work for them anymore. It doesn't matter what kind of ceremony they had performed. I will have it annulled! They were going to give my child to another man! The highhandedness of it! Typical. Typical," he smoldered and turned his face again to the window.

Leita's mind was flying. Annette had said that Sir Charles saw her attacker, but did not recognize him. It wasn't possible that she had lied. Jack had been in costume that night, but Sir Charles would have known him. There would have been no question. It couldn't be. The man was raving, talking about something else.

"And why would they want to give your child to another man?" She decided to draw him out further, anything to keep him talking. Somehow she would get to the bottom of this—learn what his hallucinations were, what he was raving about.

Jack was silent then. Leita opened her lips to repeat her question, then decided against it. He spoke finally. "Because they are liars, and because they have always despised me, me and my mother. They despise my mother because she was the daughter of a draper. Not one of them! Not an aristocrat! They have always scorned her."

"But she married your father. I always thought they were very friendly to your mother, Jack," she said.

"Snobbery! Snobbery! They always made it plain what they thought of us," he fumed.

Leita fell silent. Then she framed another question. She thought it unwise but she had to know what he had been alluding to. "You said something about 'that room.' What room were you speaking of, Jack?"

"Why the room at St. Cloud, of course," he said, as if marveling at her stupidity. "I only took you there because you said you were ill. I thought you should lie down," he said with a sanctimonious air.

Leita felt a wave of dizziness overcome her again and she leaned her head against the back of the seat. She had been dancing with Jack, she remembered. In fact, that was the last thing she remembered, telling him she was ill and dizzy. Now he was talking about taking her to a room; he said she had seduced him.

"What happened in the room?" she finally asked. Her lips felt parched and dry and the words came out a little thickly.

"You know what happened. Or you would know if

you hadn't been so drunk. Of course, I had been drinking too."

"You said something about my seducing you," she probed further. The nausea was growing stronger now.

"That's what it amounted to. But of course it was nothing new to you. I discovered that," Jack said righteously.

Annette had told her that she had been drugged, drugged with laudanum. She remembered nothing. Was it possible that the man who drugged her, who attacked her, was this peculiar creature sitting across from her? She closed her eyes. He had pushed her into this compartment. He had gotten her onto the train by trickery. He had overpowered her with an ether-soaked rag, and furthermore he had told her that he had a man waiting in readiness to murder her husband. Was it so impossible to believe after all that had happened in the last hour that he was also the man who had drugged her with laudanum and raped her while she was unconscious?

Sir Charles had made a trip to England shortly after that night and she remembered now Darcy saying that Jack had gone off to England to take care of his affairs. They had known! Sir Charles and Annette had known and kept it secret. But why? Because he was a member of their family? No, that didn't seem possible, somehow. They would have been all the more anxious to make amends for what had happened. It would have been much simpler to have arranged a marriage when it was certain that Leita was pregnant, a marriage in name only. But they hadn't, and furthermore they hadn't wanted anyone to know that the attacker had been Sir Charles's nephew. There was only one explanation for that. They hadn't wanted him connected with her in any way, would have done anything to avoid giving him any right over the future of her child. Because of his character? That certainly seemed reasonable enough. Witness his actions today. The man wasn't just unstable, he was mad, truly insane. They had wanted to keep him out of it at any cost.

"You said you were disinherited?" she questioned gently.

His features froze. "Of no importance. That will all be taken care of." He lapsed into silence.

She watched him narrowly. If this horrible thing were really true, how did Darcy come to know of it—and to discuss it with him? Anger flared through her. Darcy was supposed to have been her chaperone, to have her, Leita's, interests at heart, and she had been talking of such a terribly private matter to this idiot? She felt her cheeks grow hot with fury.

"And what did Darcy tell you?" she said icily.

"What did she think of the part you claim to have played in my misfortune?"

He remained silent.

"What did she think of her fine friend who put laudanum into my drink—drugged me and then attacked me? What did she think of you then—you unspeakable beast?"

Jack started. He hadn't realized that Leita knew of the laudanum. His uncle hadn't mentioned it and he had somehow assumed that they hadn't known of it. His glance shot around to her eyes, dark with hatred.

"I didn't drug you. That is a fairy tale. You were drunk," he said viciously. Jack's talents as a liar had been refined long ago. Furthermore, he had so gone over the tale of her having seduced him that he half-believed it himself. Leita's beauty, her indifference to him, and the numerous others that paid her court had enraged him. This had been his customary reaction to very pretty girls since he approached manhood; he hated them for ignoring him.

"You drugged me! You drugged me and raped me!

412

You are so foul—!" Leita burst out, her rage and disgust exploding.

"Be quiet—be quiet or I will make you quiet!" he hissed, with a frightened look at the closed door of their compartment.

"You didn't tell me—you didn't say what Darcy thinks of her fine friend now!" Leita taunted him. She was frightened, but her anger overcame her fright.

"Darcy knows nothing—nothing about us!" he shouted.

"You said, you said that Darcy told you. Now you are lying again!" she shot back at him.

"Darcy told me only what she overheard—that you were pregnant from the night of the ball at St. Cloud. She overheard Lady Hidel's maid talking about it with her husband. I do not lie—I never lie!" He was shouting now, and the perspiration had sprung out on his brow again.

"And you didn't tell her? You really didn't tell her that you were the one who raped me? How modest you are! Not every man could drug a girl into unconsciousness and then rape her! It was quite a feat on your part, wasn't it?" Leita shouted.

"Stop it! Stop it!" He lunged forward and pressed his hand over her mouth. She opened her lips and bit as hard as she could and when he jerked away there was blood running down his palm onto his wrist.

"Enough! Enough of this!" he said in a hoarse whisper. I am going to put you to sleep again and you are to stop this hysterical behavior. Remember what I said would happen if you raised a disturbance. Do you want the Comte to die because of you?"

The salty taste of his perspiration was in her mouth and she spit on the floor. "That is what I think of you," she said. "A creature who would stoop to what you have done would think nothing of murder."

"I do what must be done," he shouted.

"And where are you taking me?" she cried.

"Far away, far, far away," he said. "And now you must eat something. You are not to go without food."

"I will not eat," she snapped.

"We will wait then," he said complacently, and sat back and commenced staring out the window again.

She maintained her silence and the train hurtled on. By the time night had fallen she was well over her illness from the ether and her healthy body demanded food. She had not eaten since the evening before and the nausea she felt now came from hunger.

She walked to the dining car with Jack behind her. They ate without speaking and walked back to the compartment. She was convinced that he held Armand's life in his hands and resisted the temptation to run from him. They took their places again without exchanging a word and the evening wore on.

Jack yawned once, then again. Then he went rummaging in the portmanteau that he had put in the compartment before he took up his post to wait for Leita. He rang for a porter and requested two glasses of lemonade. When they were brought he unscrewed the cap of a flat silver flask and poured a few drops of milky liquid into one of the glasses.

"This will help you to sleep," he said, offering it to Leita.

She shook her head firmly. "I don't need anything to make me sleep," she said coldly.

"But you do. I am going to sleep and I need to know that you won't be so foolish as to run out of here and tell the conductor some wild tale. Now drink it." He spoke harshly at the last and she drew her head back.

"You have drugged it. I won't drink it."

"But you will. It is only a drop or two of laudanum. You will sleep soundly, and you will drink it." His eyes had taken on that mad glint again and he pressed the glass in her hand. She was truly frightened. He had prepared for this, had contrived the whole scheme to lure her out of her house and onto a train where she would be at his mercy. There was nothing else to do; she was afraid of him. She drank it and some minutes later began to feel drowsiness steal over her. It was almost peaceful—a relief, she thought, and pillowed her cheek in her hands as she slid down in the seat. She slept deeply, and he sat up, wide awake, staring at her.

Jack stirred and stretched his arms. The window emitted a cold gray light. It was the first hour of dawn and the train was slowing as it came into Marseilles. He closed the portmanteau and smoothed his hair with his palms. Leita slept on and he gave a silent thanks to Madame Charbonnel. When the train ground to a halt Leita wakened and sat up. Where in the world was she? She looked through sleep-dimmed eyes at the man opposite her. Then it all came back and she closed her eyes again and sighed deeply.

"We will be getting off now. I want you to take my arm and go with me quietly. I know you will, since you realize the consequences." He spoke as if he were commenting on the weather and Leita looked out the window at the almost deserted platforms in the station. Now was her chance. She could break away from him and get word back to Paris. First the police—they would send a telegram to Armand to warn him. She began to feel hope as she smoothed her hair and straightened her dress.

The conductor assisted her down the steps of the platform and Jack smiled at her, his stiff, humorless smile. "We are going to have some breakfast."

"That will be nice," she replied coolly. She had seen a gendarme at the entrance of the station. He stood there, looking over the crowd. She would make a run for it and plead for protection. Thank God this nightmare would soon be over.

"But first I must send a wire," Jack remarked. His eyes had followed her gaze to the waiting gendarme.

"A wire?" Who in the world would he telegraph from here?

"Yes, to my assistant who is watching over Armand. If he does not hear from me, then he knows that something is amiss and he will carry out his task. That is our arrangement. I wire him at the times we agreed upon, in the code we agreed upon. I leave nothing to chance, you see." Jack congratulated himself on his inventiveness as Leita's face fell. Oh, dear God, she thought. I can't take the chance, I simply can't. I will have to go along with him now. At least until I can think of something—some other way.

Outside the station he hailed a carriage and asked the driver to take them to a restaurant. Leita asked for tea and sipped it. Finally she said that she must have a bathroom and Jack spoke to the waiter who escorted her. When she returned she ate a croissant, finished her tea, and then said, angrily, "Now what are you going to do? Haven't you come to your senses yet? Don't you realize that the police will be looking for me now and that you will be caught, and very shortly too?"

Jack emptied his cup and rose. "No, my dear. Where we are going the police will never dream of seeking. Come along."

She rose wearily. Her dress was mussed, she hadn't washed, and she felt a wave of despair. Up till now it had seemed like a nightmare. This man could not possibly kidnap her and elude the search that would be made. She had to remember that.

He hailed another cab and when it stopped she saw that they were at the harbor. Jack walked along purposefully but she was feeling very strange. Her eyes felt cloudy and she felt as if she might fall. He gripped her arm and guided her as she walked waveringly beside him. She felt so sleepy and the walkway seemed to be moving and trembling under her feet. She stumbled and clung to his arm. What could be the matter?

"Here we are." Jack stopped in front of a storefront and propelled her in. She sank into the chair he pulled out for her and closed her eyes. She didn't even trouble to listen to what he was saying to the man behind the counter.

When he came back to her he had to lift her up out of the chair. She made an attempt to walk energetically. "I think I am ill again," she whispered.

"Never mind. We are almost there," he replied and she tripped. She had tripped on the edge of a gangplank. The side of a ship was facing her and he was half-carrying her up the gangplank!

"Wait! Stop! Where is this you are taking me?" She leaned against him weakly, but her voice had carried. The man at the top of the gangplank looked curiously at the strange pair who had halted at the foot.

Jack whispered in her ear. "You are to be very quiet now. You are attracting attention. You are to come with me and not say one more word!" She recoiled at the viciousness in his voice but then was forced to support herself again by clinging to him. She moved with dragging footsteps beside him and heard him tell someone that his wife was very ill and could they please be shown straightaway to their cabin.

"You drugged me again, didn't you?" she gasped as she reached for the post by a bunk bed.

"Just a drop or two. Nothing that will hurt you. It is necessary to insure that you behave properly." He was very relieved. The strength of her protest when she saw the ship had surprised him. It was most fortunate that he had dropped the laudanum in her tea at the restaurant. She was a strong girl and even though he had her thoroughly frightened, she still was quite capable of doing something foolish. I will have to keep her in here for the length of the journey, he decided. That rebellious nature of hers could well overcome her good sense, even though I have convinced her that Armand's life will be in danger if she bolts.

It was almost noon before the ship heaved anchor and made its way out into the blue waters of the Mediterranean. The steamer carried only a few passengers in addition to its cargo and since the staff was not overburdened, Jack had no difficulty in seeing that all their meals were brought to them. At first Leita refused to eat or drink, fearing that everything she touched would be drugged.

"It will make it easier for you. You are distressed, overwrought. It is a very mild sleeping potion and you should not object to it." Jack strove to convince her. Then she became ill from the motion of the boat and this served to incapacitate her so that she was truly incapable of leaving the cabin to enlist the aid of anyone she might convince of her tale. He went to some pains to leave the impression with the other passengers that his wife was afflicted with a case of nerves and he was taking her to sunnier climes in the hope of restoring her to full health. He used the laudanum judiciously, since she was forced to drink something now and again, being depleted by her retching.

They had been at sea for six days when Jack brought a bottle of dark liquid from the depths of his portmanteau and told Leita to remove her dress. She had been feeling better for the last few hours, had at last been able to eat something, and now he must take advantage of this to complete his preparations.

418

"I am most certainly not going to remove my dress," she snapped.

"If you don't it will be stained by this dye. I suggest that you do, since that is the only gown you have." He spoke dryly and busied himself with rinsing out the bowl which had recently contained soup and emptying some of the liquid into it.

"And what do you propose to do with dye?"

"I am going to dye your hair, Leita. I had intended to do this on the train to Marseilles, but you were far too rebellious, and then far too sleepy. You are going to have black tresses. Just a little further precaution, you understand."

She objected strenuously, but finally acceded to his demands. There was really nothing else she could do. He would simply drug her and do it while she was unconscious. She wrapped herself in a sheet from the bunk and sat sullenly on a low chair while Jack combed the evil-smelling stuff through her shining hair. She had not bathed for three days and had no change of clothing and she felt completely and utterly wretched as she sat there, with the ship rolling and the dye making dark, cold little drips on her white shoulders.

She hadn't wept, not once. She would never let this beast see her weeping and defeated. He would be caught—wherever they were going someone would find her—the police would be looking for her everywhere, she knew. Oh God, let someone find her soon! She felt as if she could not bear much more of this.

Her hair was lank and wet when he opened another bottle and began to stroke her cheek with a pad of cotton.

"It is only a little stain to darken your complexion. More in keeping with your new coiffure," he smiled. He was actually enjoying this—this defacement.

When she finally rose to look into the tiny mirror on

the wall she drew in her breath sharply with dismay. Her skin was swarthy and her hair lay in limp, damp strands, chilling her where it touched her shoulders. Her eyes blazed out from the pale brown skin, their deep violet color darkened by the contrast with her skin.

"I look hideous!" she cried.

"No, not hideous. But you would not be recognized easily. And that is the whole point. Not that anyone would know you where we are going," Jack added smugly, and began to clear up the things he had used to effect the metamorphosis.

"And where are we going?" she demanded, tears starting into her eyes despite anything she could do.

"You will see," he murmured enigmatically. "Now, I think it is time for a nice cup of tea. We will be docking late this afternoon."

Chapter 26

THE STEAMER HAD BEEN DOCKED FOR A LITTLE TIME BEFORE Jack opened the door of their cabin and guided Leita onto the deck. He carried the portmanteau in one hand and kept a firm grip on her arm with the other. At the top of the gangplank she stopped and drew a breath of astonishment. The docks were alive with bony, dark-skinned men, their loins wrapped in dirty white rags as they scurried about at their task of loading bales of copra and cotton. The sun beat down heavily on the scene below her and a din of dissonant music from drums and flutes added to the shouts and curses that filled the air. A camel plodded awkwardly along with a man on its back and another man raised a cudgel and brought it down with a thwack onto the back of one of the workmen standing beside a tall jug.

Speechless, Leita allowed herself to be guided down the gangplank and halfway into the milling throng before she turned. "Where in the name of God have you brought me?"

Jack's smile betrayed excitement as well as satisfaction. "We are in Egypt, Leita. This is Alexandria and we are going to Cairo."

Leita nearly fainted. Egypt! She would never be found! This maniac could keep her prisoner here forever and no one would ever know where she was! Fright made her legs weak and desolation brought tears to her eyes. The harsh syllables of a totally strange language flowed around her as she stumbled along blindly beside him. She wouldn't be able to make herself understood to anyone! She was lost, totally and completely in his power!

The train station was an open-air platform, packed with men in robes, men in white loincloths, their heads bound in yards of white cotton and many with short black hats that reminded Leita of flowerpots. Women draped in black, their faces covered and only their eyes and a scrap of brow exposed, stood silent and solemn, many of them holding children by the hand. Babies were slung from their shoulders, their dusky little cheeks pressed against the folds of black cloth. Flies were thick, lay on the children's cheeks, their eyelids, and buzzed in black throngs around the few who were eating a yellow-fleshed melon, tossing the rinds down onto the dry dirt where they immediately turned black with the ravenous flies. The babbling, strange tongue sounded in Leita's ears as she looked around wildly, shrinking from the press of those unwashed bodies.

The train was not much better. Open at the sides, the narrow seats made of woven reeds, and the aisles jammed full. A live chicken hung by a string from the arm of a woman standing in the aisle next to Leita's seat and the beating wings flapped at her arm. She moved to sit next to the open side and the train began to pull out.

Leita felt sure she was going to be sick. The sun beat down and clouds of dust spun up and into the cars as the train moved slowly out of the town. It gathered speed finally and swayed so precipitously that she was sure it was going to derail. The horde clinging to the sides tightened their grip and swung in rhythm with the swaying cars.

Jack followed her eyes. "What you see is the annual flooding of the Nile. It is high in August and covers the land for miles on either side of the river. It is receding now and next month they will begin to plant."

Leita kept her eyes fixed on the distant coolness, hoping to distract herself from the nausea boiling up in her throat.

"And when we reach Cairo? What do you plan to do then?" she asked listlessly.

"Then you will see the place where you will stay until the child is born. I am assured that it is most pleasant and luxurious," he answered stiffly.

"How could there be a place for me in Cairo? You have never been here before. You know nothing of it," she objected.

"I have a friend. A good friend. She has an acquaintance living in Cairo. He is a man of wealth and maintains a large household. You will be very comfortable." Jack only hoped that the name on the slip of paper in his breast pocket would prove to be cooperative. Madame Charbonnel had simply said that where gold is concerned, Muhad Bey was amenable to any arrangement. He dealt in slaves and was wealthy, but had never slaked his thirst for money, she had said. He would see to Jack's requirements, she had assured him. And Jack was well provided with gold; he had cleaned out his accounts before leaving England.

Leita wiped her perspiring face. Somehow, some way, she would escape from him. She must wait and think. Then something occurred to her. Cairo—and the Suez Canal being built just a few short miles away! The place was overrun with Europeans. She had heard

423

conversation about it by the hour in France. De Lesseps was a cousin of the Empress Eugenie; and his company, composed of Frenchmen, and others who had bought stock, was centered in Alexandria. But Cairo, she had heard, was far larger than Alexandria. Foreign though it was, and how terribly foreign, Leita thought as she stared around at the occupants of the train, Cairo swarmed with Frenchmen. The trap isn't as tight as he thinks, Leita decided with a tight, little smile. I will find someone to help me; he can't watch me every minute of the day and night. All I need is pen and paper and someone to carry a message! And we will be going to a hotel in Cairo. Surely someone there will help me!

The train finally reached the center of Cairo and Leita got down stiffly. Two narrow spires pierced the air where she looked off above the crowd, and a massive blue dome glittered in the sunlight. It was her first sight of a mosque, and that the grandest one in Cairo. The air was clear, except for the dust being raised by the donkeys that trotted along, carrying their passengers willy-nilly, while the people scattered out of their way. The noise was intense; flutes and drums played their own strange melodies and the cries of the water vendors, the fruit sellers and the keening pleas of the beggars made a roaring clamor in her ears.

Jack's hold on her arm had loosened and she looked around, searching for a light-skinned face in the crowd, someone in European dress. But she was surrounded by Egyptians, Greeks, and Armenians and while she scanned their faces Jack began a conversation in French, mixed with sign language, with a wiry, grizzled old man who sat in the coachman's seat of a dilapidated carriage. Jack showed the man a slip of paper and they bent their heads over the writing. Aid was summoned in the form of a younger man who wore a dirty, gray robe instead of the loincloth. Laboriously he went over each letter of whatever was written on the paper while Leita continued to search the teeming mass of people for a friendly face. The younger man uttered a cry of recognition finally and spoke in quick, sharp syllabled words to the old cab driver, who grinned as he finally understood. He signified by many nods of his head that he would carry the man to the place marked on the paper. Jack gave a coin to the younger man and told Leita they were to go in this carriage. She climbed up with no reluctance. They were going to a hotel, she knew, and there surely would be Europeans staying there. And, oh heavenly thought, there would be a bath! She could sink down into warm water—she would soak for an hour at least. Then, when she was fresh, she would find a way to get someone—anyone—to send a telegram for her. It shouldn't be so very difficult. She would take some of Jack's money. He had to sleep sometime and she would only pretend to drink whatever he gave her. She wouldn't sleep now, not until she was able to steal some of his money, and bribe someone to send a telegram to Armand. Then she could relax, confident that Armand would be safe and she would be set free.

But now the carriage entered a narrow street and the walls of the mud-daubed buildings pressed in on either side. Leita looked behind her at the broad avenue they had left, and wondered what kind of place lay ahead of them. Jack knew nothing of Cairo. It was possible he had the address of some dingy hole. Well, no matter, they would turn around and return. She knew that he was fastidious and would never put them up in the kind of filth that surrounded them now. The scent of rotting fruit was incongruously mixed with the scent of jasmine and the carriage tilted precariously around one corner after another, turning and entering streets so narrow that they were nothing more than lanes. She felt so tired she thought she would faint from the heat! What a terrible climate! And what a terrible place, she thought, trying not to see the scrawny limbs and open sores that afflicted so many of those clustered against the buildings. But now the street they turned into opened out and whitewashed walls ran along it with the waving fronds of palm trees towering up from behind the walls. The grizzled little driver ceased lashing his horse and the carriage came to a sudden stop. The driver jumped down and made excited gestures in the direction of the gated wall. Jack nodded, helped Leita down and by sign language signaled to the driver to wait.

He walked to the gate and rapped briskly on it with the head of his walking stick. There was no answer and he rapped again, banging at the gate energetically. When it opened a crack he searched in his breast pocket and extracted an envelope and placed it in a brown hand that emerged. Leita watched this wonderingly. This was not a hotel, she was certain. The street here was comparatively quiet and deserted. Now the gate opened wide and a brown man with an enormous belly stepped out and bowing low, swept his hand in the direction of the interior. His head was wrapped in a turban, but it was sparkling white. Jack paid the driver and took Leita's arm and they walked through the open gate.

She looked around, astonished once more. A pool of water lay at her right, rimmed with blue tiles and a fountain cascading into the center. Tubs of flowers in bloom and green shrubs were set at intervals in this wide courtyard and a pillared walkway lay ahead of her, its cool shade enhanced by the green and white tiles that floored it. She walked along as if in a dream, following the wobbling hips of the man who led them.

426

They passed through an arched gateway after a wrought iron gate was opened by a thin man in a loincloth and found themselves in a second courtyard, this one laid with blue and gold tiles and graced with another fountain. It was surrounded on four sides by pillared and arched walkways and shadowy arches were cut into the cool white walls. Leita sagged with relief. Her face was smudged with dusty grime. The purplish blue of her eyes looked out of place in that brown face. Her hair, still stiff with the dye since there had been no opportunity to wash it, was pulled back into a chignon and wisps of it came straggling down over her neck. The pink and white dress was spotted with vomit, and streaked with dust. Her palms felt sticky and gritty as she smoothed at her wrinkled skirt. She wouldn't tell them—wouldn't try to get anyone to help her, until she had bathed and was presentable, she decided miserably. They followed the portly man into a semicircle of yellow and white tiles and there he bowed low, his forehead almost scraping the tiles. Leita peered into the gloom ahead of her. The scent of coffee rose in the air and she almost fainted with pleasure. Then Jack's hand pulled her forward up two steps.

"Curtsey!" he whispered.

Obediently she dropped a curtsey, hoping she could rise without tottering; she felt so shaky and fatigued. Then her eyes became accustomed to the deep shadow and she saw before her a brown face with glinting black eyes. The man's head was covered with a white cloth, banded round with a scarlet cord and a small black mustache prickled out over his narrow upper lip. His chin was pointed and a diamond shaped black beard projected out from it. He was sitting on a cushion, and other cushions of wildly clashing colors were scattered around beside him. Two very plump brown hands lay in his lap. Their fingers, shiny with grease, were crowded with rings glittering with precious stones. He coughed, placing one bejeweled hand on his belly as he did so, then, coughing again, he beckoned with the other hand in a signal for them to be seated.

Leita sank down onto a cushion. If she hadn't she would have fallen down, so dismayed and heartsick was she. She had thought this was a European household. It had never occurred to her that they were entering the house of a native. Why they had come here she couldn't imagine. What a time to pay a visit! Hot and dirty and just off that dreadful train. She reflected again that it was impossible to anticipate the workings of Jack Hidel's mind. He was demented, beyond all doubt.

"I received the wire from Madame Charbonnel, telling me of your mission and your need. You have arrived in good time."

Leita's head snapped up. The man was speaking in English, slowly, but a clipped, surprisingly precise English. She felt a flare of hope. At least she would be able to make herself understood. And who was Madame Charbonnel? Now she saw that the figure beside the larger man, the figure that sat so quietly, picking at his teeth with a sliver of ivory, was a younger man. He was dressed in an identical fashion but his face was leaner and he wore no beard, simply a small black mustache. He was watching her, his eyes black and velvety in the shadows.

Jack began to speak but the older man waved one plump hand in dismissal of his words. "We will have to speak of money—of gold, and of time," he said clearly. Then he clapped his hands and when the servant's head materialized he gestured toward Jack and Leita. The servant set two cups in front of them and picked up a bronze bowl, shielding his hands with a cloth. He removed the cover from the bowl and a rich scent rose up in the air. Leita was hungry, fiercely hungry. The

428

older man waved his hand at her, obviously signifying that she should eat. She looked around in front of her for utensils and a plate and then looked up quickly at the sound of a chuckle, a definite chuckle, coming from the younger man. A word or two and a small bowl was set before her with a pearl-handled spoon. She spooned out some of the mixture—it appeared to be rice mixed with a meat of some kind and vegetables. She took a bite of the steaming food and then choked, her eyes watering. It was hot, hot with pepper and the meat was mutton, strong and rank. Her face went pale from her effort to quell her nausea. The sound of a clicking tongue came from the younger man and he whispered something to the man beside him. Jack was watching her disapprovingly while he spooned food from the bowl in front of him. In a few moments the servant materialized again and set a silver plate in front of her. On it was a cold breast of some kind of fowl. Then he put a small brass pot down beside her plate and an empty cup beside it. She looked up gratefully at the older man.

"Thank you very much. I am afraid I am not accustomed to hot food," she said.

"And you are with child," the man nodded, his small mouth curving in a smile.

She started. How in the world did he know that? She looked at Jack who looked straight ahead.

"And now as to the time. When will the baby be born?" The man was speaking to Jack, she realized. What in the world was happening here? But she was terribly thirsty and there was a tantalizing fragrance coming from the little brass pot. She lifted it and poured. It was a clear, golden liquid and she sipped at it tentatively. It was mint tea—how heavenly, and sweetened with honey. She drank it greedily, feeling it revive her, then decided that no matter what was happening

429

she would eat. She would need her strength for whatever efforts lay ahead of her and she cut into the fowl. It was delicious, flavored with rosemary and lemon, and she ate quickly.

"It will be born in March of next year," Jack was saying. "Her health is rather delicate and she will need the best of care. She is accustomed to ease of living and Madame Charbonnel told me, accurately, I can see, that your home was luxurious."

"She will be well taken care of. Nothing in the way of comfort is lacking here, Mr. Hidel."

"I will remain here in Cairo, of course. I will visit her regularly."

"My home is your home, Mr. Hidel." The man inclined his head slightly with the stately phrase and his eyes ran over Leita. Her bewilderment was apparent. It sounded as if they were talking about her—about her staying here!

"Your wife seems surprised, Mr. Hidel," the dark-skinned man said thoughtfully. "Surely she was aware that—" his words trailed off while he watched Leita struggle to her feet.

"I'm not his wife!"

Jack had unfolded his long legs and scrambled into an upright position. He put an arm around her shoulders and said sternly, "Be quiet now and sit down."

"I will not sit down, and I will certainly not allow anyone to think I am your wife. I would die of shame if I were." She spit the words out and turned to the Egyptian.

"I don't know who you are, sir, but I am the Comtesse du Favre, wife of Armand Francois, the Comte du Favre of France. I am an American and before my recent marriage I was Miss Leita Johnston of Fort Wayne, Indiana."

The Egyptian spoke quietly. "I am delighted to make your acquaintance, Countess. And now, if I may introduce myself, I am Muhad Bey, and this unworthy is my son, Fadim, my eldest." He indicated the younger man beside him. "Perhaps at this point it would be interesting to hear your explanation, Mr. Hidel." The man spoke smoothly but his eyes were intent.

Leita interrupted without hesitation. "I was kidnapped by him, tricked into boarding a train in Paris by a forged note from a dear friend of mine. He strangled me with ether and kept me drugged till we—"

Jack broke in feverishly, his hand covering Leita's mouth. "She is raving. She has not been well since her pregnancy commenced. Pay no heed to her. She is out of her head now." Leita bit down hard and Jack jerked his hand away quickly. The son's hand crept over his mouth to hide the smile that broke out and Muhad Bey, alert and interested, motioned to Leita to continue, which was unnecessary. She had every intention of being heard out.

"He kept me drugged with laudanum and forced me to board a steamer which brought us to Alexandria. He forced me to do this by threatening me with the murder of my husband if I did not accede to his wishes." Her voice rose in a combination of horror and indignation.

"But where *is* your husband, Madame?" Muhad Bey asked.

"He is in Paris, but this craven coward has a man following him who will murder him if I escape. He is insane—completely mad!" Oh, what a wonderful relief it was to tell someone—to ask for help, to reveal finally what was happening to her.

Muhad Bey pursed his small mouth and sucked on his teeth for a second or two. "But you are with child, are you not? And by this man?" He inclined his head in Jack's direction.

431

"I am with child as the result of a criminal act by this man." She decided that the whole truth should come out now, at last. "He drugged me with laudanum and while I was unconscious he raped me, then fled. That is the reason for my pregnancy, and that is why he has kidnapped me."

There, that should be reason enough for them to summon the police immediately.

She continued. "My husband, the Comte, undoubtedly has every police prefect in France alerted and looking for me. This man must be brought to justice and I must be returned to my husband."

"This has the ring of truth, Mr. Hidel," the Egyptian remarked blandly. Fadim was watching the Englishman intently.

"She is carrying my child. It is I who have the right to it. After the child is born I have no more concern with her, but until then she is my property," Jack stated hotly.

Leita stood triumphantly scornful. She had told her story. Now he would rot in some prison and at last she would be free. Oh, how glad she would be to see Armand and Mary Jo again! She raised her head proudly.

Muhad Bey deliberated for what seemed an unnecessarily long time to Leita. He took a sip from the tiny cup before him and when he spoke it was Jack he addressed.

"And how much are you prepared to pay, Mr. Hidel?"

Jack expelled a long breath. "I will pay whatever is fair, Muhad Bey."

Muhad Bey laughed. "Ah, the English! Always what is fair—what is proper."

Leita stood paralyzed for a moment. Now she burst out. "What are you saying? Why don't you summon the

432

police now? I have told you the truth. I was kidnapped by this man and you talk to him of money?"

"But what is of more importance than gold, Countess?" Muhad Bey murmured, indifferent to her indignation.

"I am a French subject! You are cooperating with a criminal in the kidnapping of a French subject! I am also a citizen of the United States. You must call the authorities at once!" she cried.

"Quiet yourself, Madame. It is true, you are a French subject. But this is Egypt, Madame." He spoke quietly, almost languidly. "I am ruled by the viceroy and by Mohammed. The Khedive Ismail Pasha may dictate to me; Louis Napoleon may not. Now I beg you to subside." He turned to Jack again.

"I will require eight hundred piastres each month in payment for sheltering the Countess. I will require it in one payment, now, or tomorrow if you so wish."

Jack blanched. It was a monstrous sum.

Leita stared unbelievingly at both of them, then picked up her skirts and ran. Fleetfooted she made her way through the courtyard, turned and ran down the pillared walkway. Coming out into the first courtyard she ran to the gate. The man squatting on his heels beside it looked up at her, puzzled, as she pulled at the iron handle, pounding with her fist at the thick wood of the gate. The handle would not turn. It was locked from the inside. The servant had a key on a thong around his neck, a huge iron key. She beckoned to him, signaling frantically that he should unlock the gate. He shook his head emphatically and the next moment a hand dropped onto her shoulder. She turned and struck at the heavy jowls of the portly man who had escorted them and he stepped back and then caught both her arms in a pair of surprisingly strong hands. She saw that she was defeated. The man said nothing and she bowed

433

her head, her shoulders shaking with the sobs she had contained until now. She wept bitterly, despairingly.

The guard of the gate resumed his squatting position and watched her, his eyes fathomless. Finally the strong hands released their hold on her arms and the man swept one hand up to her face. In it was a soft, perfumed cloth and she took it and wiped her cheeks and eyes. She drew a deep, shuddering breath and then threw her shoulders back. Her eyes were bleak with despair, but she would not let them see her bent with weeping. She would still find a way to escape, later, when she was stronger.

At the moment when she fled, Jack had started after her but Muhad Bey had stopped him quickly. "There is no need," he remarked phlegmatically. "She cannot leave us." Fadim had risen, however, and stood now as Leita re-entered the courtyard, her head held high.

"Since I am imprisoned here, I would like to bathe now," she announced coolly.

The young Fadim eyed her admiringly and Muhad Bey spoke.

"Hussein will take you to the seraglio, Madame Countess. I have every expectation that you will be comfortable there."

Leita turned to follow the portly man and Jack called out to her.

"I will come and visit you."

She wheeled and spoke deliberately, her eyes as cold as a stormy sea. "I will never see you—never. Armand will kill you, you know. You have signed your death warrant." Then she walked away.

Jack felt a shiver run down his spine, and he blinked his hooded eyes. Nonsense. He tried to dismiss the sudden fear he felt.

"Do you prefer to pay now or tomorrow?" Muhad Bey asked apathetically.

Jack pondered this. "I will pay the eight hundred piastres, but I will pay them every month. I will call each month to assure myself that she is in good health. I will need to have my money exchanged and I will return tomorrow with the amount for the first month."

"Allah go with you," Muhad Bey replied. It was a dismissal, Jack realized, and he was escorted to the gate.

They were following the line of the outside wall, Leita realized, as she walked along the cool tiles. Pools of lily pads floating on the cool blue water were laid in a line ahead of her and the fountains tinkled. Entering the shade of a long room she glanced indifferently around her. The walls were snowy white, open archways let in whatever breezes stirred and the floors were tiled with elaborate designs. A fountain played in the center of the room and on a low, ebony table a board lay. It was evidently used in playing some game or other; it was marked in colored squares and there were colored discs scattered over the table top. They walked through another arched doorway and the servant stopped. This room was smaller, less of a gallery, and there were scarlet and blue cushions scattered on the blue tiles. A table stood in the center; on it was a bowl piled high with pale green grapes and ripe peaches. A round bronze tub was being filled with water by a very fat, dark woman with splayed, brown feet and a feathery black mustache on her upper lip.

The man bowed. "Your bath is being prepared. My name is Hussein, and I am in charge here. I will make every attempt to acquire anything you request." He bowed again, his fleshy jowls wobbling, and left her alone with the woman filling the tub. Leita made no reply to him. His fluent English had rendered her wordless.

435

She looked at the woman who was emptying pitchers of water into the bronze tub. "My name is Leita. What is yours?" The woman looked at her and broke out in a smile. Leita flinched. The woman's teeth were black with the exception of one gold one. The smile, though, was definitely friendly.

"Do you speak English?" Leita asked hopefully. No reply, just a broader smile. Leita resorted to French, her only other language. No response to that either. She sighed and began to unbutton the front of her dress. The woman spoke then, but in Arabic, set down the pitcher and planted herself solidly in front of Leita and began to struggle with the buttons. Leita realized, watching the fat fingers fumbling, despite the concentration, that she was unfamiliar with buttons and she smiled, for the first time in days, it seemed to her, and patted the well-meaning hands. Then her own fingers flew down the dress front and she stepped out of it. The woman's brown eyes looked wonderingly at her ribbon-trimmed corset cover and the petticoats that brushed the floor. Leita untied the petticoat strings and the ribbons to the corset cover and stood naked except for the corset which pushed her breasts up and was laced tightly around her small waist. The woman's eyes opened in surprise at this device and she ran her plump fingers over the whalebone. She touched the lacings and looked questioningly at Leita. Leita nodded and the woman pulled at the string, then unlaced the corset and Leita flung it to one side in a gesture of joyous relief. The woman's tongue had commenced a concerned clacking and she ran her hands over the red welts on Leita's skin, welts made by the whalebone stays biting into her flesh. She began to massage them vigorously and Leita motioned to the bath, walked over and stepped in. Clouds of jasmine scent rose from the warm water and Leita felt she would perish with pleasure as it laved her body. She removed the pins from her hair and sank into the bath. The woman handed her a square of clear, pale green soap. It was strong with jasmine scent and Leita used it lavishly, soaping her hair and her body twice over. She was lying still in the water when another woman entered with a bucket, and returned with several more. The heavy-set woman motioned to Leita and lifted her by the arm pits, indicating that she should step from the tub. Then with a heave of her mighty arms she tipped the bronze tub and sent the water cascading over the floor. Leita watched this in surprise, then saw that the tiles were sloped to a drain in the corner. The tub emptied, the woman proceeded energetically to fill it again and then poured the contents of a bottle of alabaster ointment into the warm water. The scent of jasmine was heavy in the room by now and Leita lay in the perfumed water, luxuriating in the scented heat. A cage with a brilliantly colored bird hung from the ceiling and Leita watched it sleepily. Finally the woman who she supposed was to be her servant stood beside the tub with an immense towel stretched out and Leita stepped up and allowed herself to be enfolded in its softness. Her hair was toweled dry and when she felt it, it was soft again. She was led to a pallet on the floor covered with a finely woven, silky linen and she lay down, sinking into its softness. Then the servant's hand slathered oil onto her back and buttocks and began to massage her. The plump hands were strong and skillful, kneading and pressing away the tightness, the fatigue that had held her in a vise. She closed her eyes, for just a moment she told herself, then she must think, think of a means of escape. During that one minute she fell soundly asleep, her cheek pillowed on her crossed arms, the hands kneading her heat-pinkened flesh and massaging the tired muscles. When the woman ceased her massage she took a silken sheet and spread it over the girl. Then she stood up and looked at her, a perplexed expression in her dark brown eyes. She had never seen flesh white and pink like this before, never. Yet her face was dark. She must be ill, very ill, this strange, tired girl. She went about putting the room in order, then left, carrying the damp towels. Before she went through the archway she turned and looked at the girl's sleeping figure again, then her tongue clucked, expressing her wordless concern, and she left her alone.

Leita slept on through the stillness of the afternoon. A lacy, carved fretwork covered a section of the wall nearest the pallet, dividing it from a sheltered walkway. Late in the afternoon a white-robed figure glided along the walkway and stopped. Two black eyes peered through an opening in the carving, and rested on Leita's body. She had turned on her side and the sheet, worked downward by her turning, left her pink-tipped breasts exposed. She breathed gently, her heavy breasts rising and falling. The dark eyes scanned her body intently for some minutes. Then the figure glided noiselessly on. Fadim was very curious about this young woman, very curious.

Chapter 27

M. Pietri had been the prefect of the Paris police
for more years than he cared to count. He had had few
days that could be spoken of as trouble-free, yet the
difficulty he faced now was almost without precedent.
He looked nervously around, adjusted a chair, held a
wine glass to the light and assured himself that it was
sparkling clean, then started as the door burst open and
the Comte du Favre, his face pale and his brown eyes
burning, entered.

M. Pietri bowed. "We are honored, M'sieur le
Comte."

"That you are honored matters not at all to me. It
has been five days, five days during which any horror
could have happened, and you still have not located
Madame la Comtesse. What are you doing man? What
are you about? Do you have every man employed in
the search?" Armand struck the tip of his walking stick
on the floor.

M. Pietri had met the Comte du Favre many times before this past week. He himself was an habitué of court society, and he had known Armand as a gentle-mannered, young man, a young man of piercing intelligence, mind you, but benignly gracious. The fastidiously polite Comte du Favre had metamorphosed into a veritable beast from Hades during these last few days.

"I am delighted to tell you that we have at last located a cab driver who says he carried Madame la Comtesse to the Gare de Lyon on the afternoon of Friday last. The man has been abed with grippe and only just yesterday returned to his cab. That explains why we have not, up till now, that is, been able to find anyone who remembers picking her up."

"The Gare de Lyon?" Armand's brows had drawn even closer together. "What in the name of God would have been her reason for going there?"

"That is the mystery, M'sieur. So far we have grilled everyone who was in the Bois that afternoon, assuming, from what she said to your servant, that she would have gone there for the fresh air she mentioned. But to no avail. No one recalls seeing her there. No hansom driver took her there. The Gare de Lyon was her destination, it seems."

"But are you certain he knows who he is speaking of? Do you believe him?"

"I believe his memory is accurate, sir. He was hailed by the Comtesse shortly after one o'clock in the afternoon, directly in front of your residence. He describes Madame as wearing a dress with a pink and white stripe and a large, white collar. He also recalled that she carried a hat, a large hat he said, with pink ribbons hanging from it. He was struck by her appearance, if I may say so, M'sieur."

440

"That is exactly what she was wearing according to Jeanine, and that particular dress and hat are missing to be sure. But there, her description was published in at least three newspapers, and several times. He could have gotten it from that and be leading us astray."

"That is possible, of course, but in my judgment the man is speaking truth. He is quite concerned. Says he cannot imagine what could have happened to her there in broad daylight. As he tells it, he remained with his cab in front of the station for some time before he got another fare. He did not see her come out and he was watching, simply because he was watching for another customer."

"So, it must be true. I agree with you. But—did he take her anywhere before dropping her at the Gare de Lyon?"

"He says not. He remarked at her anxiety about getting there. She directed him to hurry, to drive very fast, and, in fact, paid him extra for getting there with dispatch."

"Mon Dieu!" Armand dropped into a chair. "What earthly reason could she have had? I am confounded, utterly confounded! Wait, we must find all the trains that leave from there during the early hours of the afternoon."

"I have here a list of trains that left between one-thirty and three o'clock of Friday last." He handed Armand a closely-written sheet of paper.

Armand perused it once and then groaned. "Seven—seven trains. All to different destinations. And we haven't a hint of a reason for her going there in the first place."

"Only that it must have had something to do with a train, one that was arriving or departing," M. Claude Pietri remarked a little dryly. "However, we do know that a note was delivered to her shortly before she left the house that afternoon."

"But not a glimmer of its contents. Not a glimmer," Armand said despondently.

"It hasn't been found?"

"No, oh no. She evidently took it with her. Not unusual at all for her to thrust a note into her reticule."

"We must consider it the key, but we are without a key at present."

"There is only one thing to do. Each of those seven trains must be combed. Everyone who worked on them must be asked to identify her. If she even boarded one of them, it is possible that she can be identified. You have the miniature I gave you?" Armand asked.

"Even now my men are interrogating everyone who worked on the trains in question. The conductors particularly. If she was one of them we shall soon know."

"I daresay you are doing all that can be done." Armand sighed. "I waited two days before notifying her family in the United States. I couldn't believe that she was truly missing. I have received a wire from them. Her elder brother Eugene has already taken ship and should arrive by the end of next week. I cannot bear the thought that she will not be found before then. She must be! I imagine her lying ill somewhere, ill and helpless. If she had been kidnapped I would have heard. Some demand would have been made. If only someone would notify me that they have her, that all they want is money."

"That would surely simplify matters. But if that were the case you would have had some message before now. Abductors do not care to be burdened with their prisoners for long. They usually make an immediate demand," M. Pietri observed.

"An impenetrable mystery," Armand lamented

darkly. "However, I will leave you to set about it. You will notify me at once, of course, if any—"

"Be assured," Mr. Pietri replied and accompanied him to the entrance of the Surete. He realized that he had forgotten to offer his caller the wine he had ordered so carefully. Most disconcerting case I have ever had, he thought grimly, as he returned to his office. Just as the Comte had said, an impenetrable mystery.

Darcy Rankin viewed Leita's disappearance as a mystery too, but with one possible answer. Even perhaps an obvious one. She had been intrigued by Breve's appearance at Madame de Sivry's, unexpected, and certainly a shattering surprise to Leita. She had watched them carefully as they danced, observed the tumultuous emotion in both their faces, and had seen them part, abruptly, part with Breve obviously quite angry and Leita's eyes filled with tears. They had quarreled, and surely neither of them would have allowed that state of affairs to remain the same. An apology must have been forthcoming some time the next day, in all probability tendered by Pinchon. She assumed that Breve was in love with Leita, partly because she couldn't imagine that any man could be the object of Leita's love without returning it in full measure. The girl was enchanting and any other possibility seemed very farfetched to Darcy. It seemed obvious that Breve had come to Paris expressly to see Leita and had been catapulted into a jealous rage when he found that she had just married someone else. No doubt with Stephen maneuvering Breve into the position of being taken completely off balance by the news. She had watched Stephen too, that night, and his malicious pleasure had not gone unnoticed by her, at least. No, Breve would have gotten in touch with Leita, she was certain. The mysterious note delivered to her was undoubtedly from him. That would explain why she hadn't left it lying somewhere in her room, but had taken it with her. She herself had ascertained that Breve Pinchon had left his hotel the same day that Leita disappeared. She wondered a little that this had gone unremarked; at least Mary Jo should have noticed the coincidence. She had wondered at first if Mary Jo had not been privy to Leita's intentions, but dismissed it. Mary Jo was so sincerely distraught that she couldn't possibly know her friend's whereabouts. But far be it from her to introduce the possibility that Leita had simply gone off with Breve Pinchon, although it seemed the only reasonable answer to her disappearance. Eventually they would be heard from.

Her mind had been traveling along these paths while she sat with Mary Jo and Etienne in an outdoor cafe in the Bois de Boulogne. Mary Jo was speaking with enthusiasm of Eugene Johnston's coming arrival. She seemed to feel that once Eugene was in Paris, all would right itself and he would find Leita at once. Darcy had a more urgent preoccupation. She was at a loss as to the reason for Jack Hidel's sudden and unexplained departure. He had left a note for his mother, saying that he had decided to jaunt off to Italy for a while, on the spur of the moment. Dora Hidel seemed quite undisturbed by this but Darcy was disquieted and angry. Why hadn't he left a note for her? Why hadn't he mentioned his plans the evening before? She assumed, in groping for reasons, that he had gone to make arrangements for their marriage, possibly to rent a pension for them. But he should have told her. It was terribly inconsiderate of him. Of course, he would write to her from Italy and there hadn't been time for her to receive a letter yet. But still. Her anger rose again. She would let him know in no uncertain terms that she had no intention of being treated in this summary manner. He could be very peculiar at times, she reflected.

Mary Jo too was waiting. The night after Leita's disappearance she had written to the hotel in Geneva where Breve had said he would be staying, had written the full particulars of Leita's disappearance, and the full particulars of the letter to Darcy by which Leita had learned that Breve had finally married, then the sudden surprise of Leita's marriage just forty-eight hours later to the Comte du Favre. Mary Jo knew nothing of Leita's pregnancy and ascribed her sudden marriage solely to a fit of heartbreak over Breve. Now she waited. She was confident that when Breve learned that Leita had possibly been kidnapped, and why she had married Armand, he would come racing back to Paris and tear it apart to find the girl he loved.

So they sat, each one with her own thoughts, while Armand learned belatedly that Leita had journeyed in haste to the Gare de Lyon, only to vanish into thin air.

Chapter 28

LEITA WAKENED AND SAT UP QUICKLY. WHAT IN THE world was that strange sound? A soft cotton robe had been laid across the end of her pallet and she pulled it on over her head. Seeing a sash she belted it round her waist and then her eyes lit on a pair of slippers, embroidered in gold and stitched with beads. How pretty! She slipped into them. They were a trifle large for her, but stayed on. Meanwhile the eerie sound went on and she went through an archway and out into a courtyard.

She crossed the courtyard and pattered down a walkway, then stopped in amazement. The adjacent courtyard was filled with bodies, women obviously, since dark hair fell over their shoulders. But their faces were pressed to the tiles and their arms stretched out before them. Now they rose and fell back on their knees, their mouths forming the words of a call that sounded oddly like the strange man's keening. She could distinguish the word "Allah." Then they fell forward again, stretched supine. There must be a dozen women here, Leita thought; their robes were all the colors of the rainbow. She stood entranced. She knew now what they were doing. She had read of it. This was their morning devotional. These people were Mohammedans. Then she decided that it was probably rude of her to stand and stare while they were performing a religious rite and she betook herself back.

She wandered back to the room in which she had awakened and spied the dish of fruit on the table. As there were no chairs she seated herself on a cushion with the bowl in her lap and began eating a peach. It was delicious, and she felt almost happy. She had slept for hours, peacefully and dream-free. She was clean and fragrant, her robe was clean, and best of all, that dreadful sheepface was no longer opposite her every time she raised her eyes. She grimaced and drew her brows together. Having him constantly beside her, loathing him! Apart from his villainy and his madness, he was the most tiresome and tedious person she had ever met. Now at last she was free of him. She could think now. And she thought of Muhad Bey. There was certainly no hope there. He was another villain, definite and unredeemable. His son? He had not uttered a word during the whole interview but she had felt his eyes on her. It was likely that since the father was so fluent in English the son would be too. But would she ever see him? She must, must at least find out if he were a possible ally. She had little hope of the women she had just seen. She was informed enough to know that they were probably the wives of Muhad Bey, and in all probability illiterate. She knew that she must be in a harem or seraglio and she suddenly realized that Hussein, the man who had escorted her to this room, the very fat man, was probably an eunuch. She had read that only eunuchs were allowed in harems, and he had said he was in charge here. What an exotic place she found herself in! She would observe everything carefully so that she could tell Armand in every detail. And Mary Jo—she would be entranced. Leita thought of the wall surrounding the courtyards and buildings. It must be over six feet high. But, it might be possible to get over it, if she had something high to stand on. She looked around the room. No chairs, not one, and the table was low. She finished the peach and began plucking at the pale green grapes. She was thoughtful, casting over the possibilities for something high enough to get her comfortably over that wall and away. She supposed that actually few people would want to escape from here. Not his wives, in all probability. Nor his children; he probably had at least a score. And the servants would be slaves and marked as such. It was quite likely that no one before had really bent all their efforts toward escaping from here, but she most certainly would. And she would succeed, too! She was thinking how lovely it would be if someone would walk in with a soft-boiled egg and some biscuits when she heard a rustling noise. She looked behind her in the direction of the sound and her eyes widened in fright. The fretwork was filled with black, staring eyes. Then she laughed aloud. The brightly colored robes were visible too. They were staring at her, staring as if she were a strange animal in a zoo. When she laughed the rustling increased and she got up and ran out into the walkway. Still laughing, she made gestures of welcome, which evidently sufficed, because they gathered round her then, pushing back the sleeves of her robe and remarking to each other about the color of her skin. They were friendly, at least, Leita thought. Taking her arms they walked into the long room and pulled cushions around, seating themselves crosslegged on them and murmuring and laughing to each other. Leita herself sat down then and the woman beside her rattled off a few words in Arabic. Leita shrugged helplessly, then said good morning in French. To her pleasant surprise the woman replied in the same tongue. She was actually a girl, Leita observed. Young, with a merry little face and dancing black eyes which were outlined darkly with a powdery blackish substance. The girl asked her name in somewhat halting French, offering the information that she was called Yaquim. The heavy-set serving woman entered then, followed by another. They carried massive metal trays with pots of coffee and small cups without handles.

"Where did you learn to speak French?" Leita inquired. This cheerful, smiling girl would hopefully become her accomplice, she thought.

"I had a teacher. My father employed her. I can read also," the girl stated with no little pride.

"Are most Egyptian girls taught to read?" Leita asked.

Yaquim shook her head decisively. "No, no. But my father was educated in France and he believed that I should know these things. However, they made me very unsuitable to be a wife, you understand. It was also his feeling that I should choose my own husband. My mother was very angry about these things. But of course she could not prevail against him. Then they died of the cholera. They both died, one week apart." Her merry little black eyes grew sad at this memory and Leita laid her hand on the girl's hand. Yaquim looked at her affectionately and squeezed Leita's hand. "You are nice lady. I am very happy that you are new wife of Muhad Bey. We will have many friendship together."

Leita's eyes widened and then she laughed. "We

certainly will have many friendships together, but I am not a wife to Muhad Bey."

"Then you have not been in ceremony yet. So the reason why he not with you on your pallet last night," Yaquim said.

"I am not here to become the wife of Muhad Bey," Leita explained. Oh dear, how to relate her mixed-up tale to this girl? "I am here because a man brought me here, all the way from France. He stole me from my husband and kept me prisoner, then brought me here and he is paying Muhad Bey eight hundred piastres every month to keep me here—to keep me from going back to my husband."

Yaquim's perplexity was evident. "You have husband? And another man stole you? Far away this happened?"

"Yes," Leita answered simply.

"But if he steal you, then why keep you here, and not with him?"

"Because he knows I might escape from him."

Yaquim fell silent and sipped her coffee. Leita continued, now that she had the girl's attention. "My husband doesn't know where I am—where the man took me. He probably has no idea that I am not in France and I know he has the police searching for me."

Yaquim looked her in the eyes. "You have much trouble then."

Leita sighed. "I certainly do have much trouble. I have to find some way to let my husband know where I am. Then he would come with many policemen and get me."

"Much trouble. Many difficulty," Yaquim sighed. "But Muhad Bey—does he know of your trouble?"

"I told him. He knows," Leita said angrily. "He only cares about the eight hundred piastres he is being paid."

451

Yaquim nodded. This evidently didn't surprise her in the least. "He buy many slaves. Muhad Bey very rich man. He loves gold."

"And you are one of his wives?" Leita asked.

"Yes. When my mother and father die no one want me for wife. A girl who can read and write make bad wife they all say. But Muhad Bey bought me anyway," she ended philosophically.

"He bought you?" Leita repeated.

"Yes, he gave much gold to my uncle for me. He is proud to have a wife who can read."

The serving woman set a tray in front of them. On it were flat pieces of something that looked like a kind of bread. Then she set down a bowl of dates. Leita nibbled on a piece of the bread. It was actually very good. She felt she had given the girl enough to think about for the present. Later, when she knew her better, she would ask for her help.

The group had begun to disband and Yaquim sucked on her fingers. She had eaten several of the sticky dates with great relish. "Now you must dress. You come with us," she smiled. And Leita followed the chattering women across the courtyard and into another pavilion.

An hour later Leita had been massaged with oil and now she stood before a mirror examining her new raiment. She wore a pair of ballooning trousers. They were made of silk and striped in yellow and white. The band around her hips was set with sparkling yellow stones. A long-sleeved blouse of a very sheer material was tucked into the low-cut pantaloons and over this she wore a vest of yellow silk, richly embroidered in scarlet and blue. She looked at the palms of her hands with distaste. Yaquim had massaged them with her fingertips coated with a reddish substance which she said was henna and they looked as if Leita had been

452

carrying bricks. Yaquim had been vastly pleased with the result, deeming her very beautiful now. Leita's hair, black and long, hung down over her shoulders and the darkened skin of her face was decorated with black kohl circles rubbed around her eyes. She shook her head despairingly. The others had twittered around her, exclaiming, and Yaquim had told her they thought her very lovely, except that she was far too thin. Leita laughed at this. The group had all performed their toilette together and each of them was roundly plump, with two or three of them frankly fat in Leita's estimation.

Now several of them had fallen to playing at the board decorated with squares and Leita decided to take a walk in search of something that would aid her in her planned escape. She strolled through two courtyards and two other pavilions. Servants were at work sponging the tiled floors. Nothing was to be seen that might help her in her plan of getting over the wall. Cushions lay about, tasseled and embroidered. Low tables were set here and there. Apart from that there wasn't a single item of furniture. She walked beneath the wall, judging it to be over six feet in height. Then her eyes lit on a tall jar. There were many of them set along the wall. Painted in brilliant colors they obviously served only as decoration. She looked around and after making certain that she was not observed, she attempted to move one. She was unable to budge it, not even a quarter of an inch. It was quite tall enough to raise her to her goal, if it were overturned. She dusted her hands together and sighed. She was disappointed, but not discouraged. She would think of something.

At least, she thought, strolling back to the pavilion, it is a lovely place to be imprisoned. Colonnaded, shaded, set with brightly colored flowers and graced with lily ponds and beautiful tiles, the house and grounds of Muhad Bey were truly a beautiful oasis.

Back in the pavilion where Muhad Bey's wives and concubines were gathered Leita was being introduced to the game that several were playing with the small, colored discs when suddenly the women scattered like leaves before a November wind.

Leita looked up to see Hussein entering the room and behind him was—yes, it was the son of Muhad Bey. Every wife had disappeared and Leita sat alone on her cushion. Fadim faced her.

"Are you quite comfortable here?" He spoke in English and Leita felt a surge of joy.

"I am comfortable, of course, as comfortable as one could be in my circumstances," she replied.

"I have brought you something." He extended his hand and in it was a book.

Leita accepted it and looked at the cover. She suppressed a smile. It was a copy of "Robinson Crusoe." She had read it when she was a child. "Thank you. It was very thoughtful of you," she said graciously.

"It is a nothing. I only thought that perhaps time might hang heavily for you here. Do you speak any Arabic?"

"None at all. In fact, I never heard the language before."

"It is as I thought."

"And how is it that you speak English?"

"School, when I was a young boy. I was sent to school in England for several years. A very strange country. So wet. You have been there?"

"No, I am afraid not. We sailed directly to France. I had planned to go to England this fall." Her eyes fell on Hussein who stood immobile behind his master's son. His expression was one of definite disapproval. He doesn't like it that Fadim wished to visit me, she thought. Well, I intend to be very courteous to him. I need every friend I can find, she thought.

He talked on, telling her about the little village in England where his school had been situated. And all the while Hussein stood, unblinking, looking off into the distance.

Leita listened attentively, questioning him now and again when he paused. If I was ever charming let me be so now, she thought. I didn't expect to see him again, and from the way the women scattered it is obvious this visit is an unprecedented one. I must make a friend of him. Somehow, some way, he might be of help to me.

His face was a little feral, but not unpleasant. His chin was long and pointed like his father's and his liquid brown eyes held warm lights. When he rose to leave Leita rose too and offered her hand. "Will you come back to see me?" she asked.

"I will be most delighted."

"I am glad. I will be lonely here," she replied with honesty. He left with Hussein following at his ponderous gait. Fadim was quite pleased with his conduct, pleased with his conversational expertise. At least she does not despise me as she does that Englishman, he thought. I will not marry her, of course, she is a Christian—but I will have her for my household. I must wait though—wait before speaking to my father. There is the problem of the child she carries.

Leita felt encouraged and when food was brought she ate heartily of the smoked fish and hot rice mixed with vegetables. She was surprised to find that the rice in her bowl had not been seasoned with the burning peppers. She could see bits of them in the other bowls. She was touched for a moment at this evidence of consideration, but hardened her feelings very quickly. After all, she thought, he is being paid well to keep me, and I must be fed with something I can eat.

455

After the food had been removed the other women lounged around, quite obviously intending to nap. Leita went to her own pallet which had been rolled up and set against the wall. She unrolled it and lay down. Nothing very dreadful has happened so far, and I have made some progress. Two who speak a language I can understand, and at least one of them is my friend. She pillowed her cheek on her palm and fell asleep while the hot sun beat down on dusty, teeming streets of Cairo.

Fadim visited the pavilion every day after that. Usually he came in late morning, before the food was brought for the noon meal. Then he came in the evening, right after the muzzein's call to devotions had ended. Leita entertained him with stories of her own country in which he evinced a deep interest. He wasn't at all difficult to talk with, quick-witted and gracious. She found that she enjoyed his visits, looked forward to them even. As for placing her trust in him, she thought not. Not yet at least. She felt that there was more beneath his manner than he revealed and so far she was reluctant to enlist his help.

Yaquim was another matter. Warmhearted, full of merriment, she was embarassingly explicit about sexual matters and made a habit of recounting the details of the nights that she was honored with the attentions of the husband she shared with the others. When Leita remarked on her frankness, she said cheerfully that everyone talked about it. It seemed that the other wives shared the details of their cohabitation with lustful merriment and Leita was amused.

"Where do you go when you go out?" Leita asked one day.

"Out?" Yaquim said, in a puzzled tone.

"Yes, don't you go out for drives or to visit your friends?"

Yaquim laughed. "My friends are here. Only men go to other places to visit friends—to cafes and houses."

"Do you mean to say you never leave here?" Leita asked in dismay.

"No. It is not the custom. The women of the fellahin go into the streets. They go to buy the things that are needed for their household. But we do not go out—it is not necessary. Everything is brought to you when you are the wife of a wealthy man."

"Are you telling me that you expect to spend the rest of your life within these walls—a prisoner?" Leita's astonishment was so apparent that Yaquim laughed her rich little laugh.

"Where would we go? A woman cannot worship in the mosque. If I desire new clothing, the merchant comes with the fabric and Hussein brings it to me. What would we do if we went out in the streets?"

"Well, for one thing, it would be nice to take a drive in a carriage, to see other faces and other surroundings." Leita was determined that once outside these walls she could enlist help, and if she could persuade Yaquim to accompany her, perhaps she could pass through the gate.

"Why see other places? They are all the same, except for the streets of the poor, and one would not go among them."

"Well I for one want to go out. I am not accustomed to being forever within the same four walls. Wouldn't you like to dine in a restaurant? If we went together we could do that."

Yaquim looked puzzled. "You wish to do this thing very much?"

"I certainly do," Leita declared. "You don't know how much I wish to do this thing, she thought with desperation.

Yaquim shrugged. "I will ask Hussein, though it will

457

be thought very strange." She disappeared for a while and came back with a look of chagrin on her round little face.

"Hussein tells me not to be so foolish. He also tells me not to speak so much with the French lady. He was angry."

Leita's heart sank. Yaquim had seemed to her to occupy a place of some importance among Muhad Bey's wives and she had hoped that perhaps a dispensation would be allowed in her case. But no. She was appalled at the mindless passivity with which these women accepted their lot in life. Bedecked with gold ornaments, their dusky skins oiled to a glowing softness, they spent their waking hours in a kind of languor, broken only by the excitement of their gambling and the passion with which they devoured food. Dates, all kinds of sweetmeats, bowls of rice and roast fowl and the eternal mutton, were consumed in vast amounts. They played with their children, who ran in and out of the pavilions, watched over and disciplined by servants. But they were hardly occupied with their motherhood. They are in a prison as much as I, Leita thought despairingly, and they neither know nor expect anything else.

She had asked Fadim if she might have some paper and he had brought her a tablet of drawing paper and some watercolors. The small paintings she executed were the object of delighted interest there but her attempts to encourage the others to try their hand at it were met with embarrassed giggles. She was definitely a foreigner and was expected to do such strange things. Actually, she had requested the paper with a different end in mind. If she were to be allowed outside the walls with Yaquim she would have a message ready, hidden in the folds of her robe. It would be comparatively simple, she thought, to slip the message into the pocket or hand of any European she might see. She dreamed of this, spent long hours planning the transmission of the note. But it all depended on getting outside these walls and so far that had proved impossible. She was well-fed, rested, and her every need was met quickly. But her early enthusiasm had died and now she became morose and despairing. Fadim would not help her; if there was one thing she had learned about him it was that he held his father in great fear. As the eldest son he occupied a position of great importance, one which he had no intention of jeopardizing. The eunuch Hussein treated her with a cold watchful eye, and he was the only other person in the woman's pavilion who had access to the outside. Leita knew he went outside the walls. Yaquim had mentioned it. What was she to do?

Fadim was pacing the tiles around a lily pond, and retracing his steps. Hours of thinking had brought him to one conclusion. His father would never give the European woman to him as long as he was being paid so richly for her. He could wait, of course, wait until the child was born. The Englishman had said very distinctly that she would be of no importance to him after that. But that would not be for a very long time, and he was impatient. He would not, could not wait that long to have her. He had seen her white flesh, seen her abundant breasts and the curve of her graceful hip. He wanted her for his pallet and he wanted her now. Two weeks had passed and he hadn't found a solution. No, that was not true, there was a solution, but it was a dangerous one. Highly dangerous if his father found out. But why should he learn of it? He could effect it with no one knowing, if he were very careful.

He betook himself through the gates with a decisive stride and walked along the streets into the poor section. There he visited a little old man in a hole-in-the-wall shop and came away after the space of an hour with a small pottery jug hidden in his sleeve. Ten whole piastres had been put into his hand and a dire threat whispered into his ear before Fadim left his dark little quarters and hurried back to the walled house of his father.

Fadim knew that Leita enjoyed the hot rice mixed with vegetables. He entered the pavilion the next day later than usual, just at the time the servant was carrying the food in. He relieved her of the bowl he knew was Leita's since there were no peppers visible in it and carried it into the pavilion, but not before he had shaken his sleeve over it. The tiny cloud of white powder fell into the rice and disappeared between the hot grains.

The other wives scattered when he entered and seated himself on a cushion across from Leita. "I will take food with you if you don't mind."

Leita looked around at the backs of the fleeing women. "I don't mind at all, but they won't like doing without their meal," she smiled.

He shrugged. "They will be served in another room." He requested the servant to bring him something and she set two bowls carefully before him. She was obviously horrified and not a little frightened by this departure from protocol, Leita thought.

They talked while they ate. She asked him questions about the progress of the canal and he answered with interest.

"I would dearly love to see it," she said wistfully. "I asked Yaquim if she could get permission to go out for a drive but Hussein refused it, summarily."

Fadim looked at her in surprise. "Moslem women do not go out onto the streets of the city."

"But Fadim, I saw women in the streets of Cairo."

"The women of fellahin. The poorest of the poor. No Moslem wife would wish to mingle on the outside." He was evidently still astonished that this request had been made.

"I saw women on donkeys, richly dressed women, not in the black robes of the poor. They had rings on and silken robes," Leita protested.

He shrugged. "There are some perhaps. An occasional few. But it is against the law of Allah."

Leita's temper escaped the leash she had kept it on till now. "That is unthinkable! That a woman should spend her life as a prisoner behind stone walls. In America we visit our friends, we go to the theater, we dine in restaurants . . ."

Fadim eyed her calmly. "But you are a foreigner. Here in Egypt a man's wife remains in his house." He was totally unfazed by her indignation, as well as by her comparisons. "A good Mohammedan does not allow other men to look on his wife. In Cairo there are many Greeks, many Turks and Armenians. They are not all of the same customs. Their wives occasionally go into the street—to a bazaar perhaps. But their purchases are made for them by servants. They do not speak with strangers, ever."

"I think it is appalling. It is no different than being in jail. In my country one must commit a crime to be treated so," she declared.

"Perhaps their crime is being born a woman," Fadim answered, laughing at his own witticism.

"Well, then, I am not a Mohammedan. There is no reason for me not to go out. Would you take me for a drive, to see the canal perhaps?" She had intended to make this request sweetly and subtly, but the words were out, borne of desperation.

"Oh, but that could not be done. It would be against my father's wishes," he replied imperturbably.

Leita sank into a despairing silence.

When he left her he looked a little uncomfortable.

461

He knew how angry she was and sought for some means of placating her.

"Tomorrow I will bring you another book. It is a very thick one which I have obtained at much difficulty. It is a book of plays."

She sighed and her thank you was grudging and a little sullen. There was nothing to be gained from this man but books it seemed.

Chapter 29

THE HEAT IN THE PAVILION THAT AFTERNOON WAS SULTRY and for the first time felt overpowering. No breeze seemed to stir as she tossed and turned on her pallet. Anger, disappointment—and fear that she would not be able to escape this prison—took possession of her. Finally she fell into a fitful sleep but awakened after only a few minutes. A rolling, painful nausea had awakened her and she folded her arms over her stomach. This wasn't like the sickness she had felt in the mornings; this was strong and wouldn't stop. The others lay flung out on cushions, sleeping soundly while they were fanned by servants. Leita sat up. Her forehead was dripping with a cold perspiration and she got to her feet with difficulty. A servant materialized at her side. The woman wore an expression of concern as Leita hugged herself tighter and shook her head from side to side, moaning. What could be the matter? It was dreadful! Then the retching began. The servant trotted away and returned as quickly with a pottery bowl. Taking Leita's arm the woman led her back to her pallet and squatted on her haunches before her, holding the bowl quietly while she made soothing, cooing noises. Leita retched for a short time and then lay back exhausted. She thought of the illnesses, the diseases, that were endemic in this country. Diseases which she as a foreigner would be subject to more readily. Good God, I could die here! Desperation seized her. No one would know! She would simply die and that monster would return to France as if nothing had happened. She retched again, her whole body trembling in panic. She must do something—get a message out of here some way! She lay back again and her thoughts darted feverishly. I will ask Yaquim. I must! I will ask her if she knows of any way to get a message out of these walls. She is not stupid, and if she is too afraid to help me I will promise to get her out too, to take her to France with me and take care of her. I must prevail upon her somehow! There is no one else. She lay ill for the rest of the afternoon. She had expected to feel better after all the retching she had done but instead she felt weak and helpless, still nauseated, and her head spun every time she attempted to rise.

It was thus that Fadim found her. He came earlier than usual and knelt beside her pallet.

"I am told that you are ill. I am very sorry. Perhaps the food didn't agree with you." His voice was soft and soothing and Leita turned her head tiredly toward him.

"You must help me, Fadim."

"That is what I came to do," he answered solemnly.

"No, I mean you must help me get a message to my husband. I could die here and no one would know. You must help me get a message to the French consul."

Fadim clucked his tongue. "You are most certainly

464

not going to die, my lady. Do not worry yourself with such dire predictions."

"Fadim, you must—you must take a message for me."

His dark eyes filmed over then. He did not enjoy being put in such a position. To aid her, to do as she asked, would be to place himself in unthinkable jeopardy. No one betrayed Muhad Bey with impunity. To admit this to this beautiful girl was extremely distasteful to him. He would have preferred to do something heroic in her eyes. His pride was immense—how could he tell her that he could not do as she asked without revealing that he was afraid to? Furthermore, he had no intention of having this prize plucked from him. His infatuation was as immense as his pride and they both equaled his fear.

"It cannot be done. I regret it deeply. I have the highest of feeling for you, but it would be to dishonor my father." That was partly true, at any rate, he thought.

"Dishonor!" Leita echoed. "You speak of dishonoring a man who is taking gold to keep a kidnapped woman prisoner!" Leita's eyes blazed and she pushed herself up.

Fadim dropped his eyes. "It is that our customs are different," he said lamely.

"'Customs' to aid and abet a criminal—a madman?" Leita grew paler with the force of her emotion and suddenly the room spun and she fell back on the pallet.

He grimaced in concern. "At least you looked a touch ashamed of it," she whispered weakly. He looked away, avoiding her eyes.

"You must not exert yourself further. You are with child and you are ill. Try not to think of such disturbing things," he implored her. Then his hand crept into his sleeve and brought out the little pottery jar. "I have brought some medicine for you. It is very sweet and will not taste too bad. It should be of help to you."

"What a strange man you are," she said weakly. She watched indifferently as he poured the greenish-brown liquid into a small cup, careful to let the last drop fall from the pottery jar before setting it aside. He put one arm under her shoulders to raise her so that she could drink. This surprised her. He had never before touched her. She sipped it tentatively. Under the heavy sweetness it was sour and brackish, but there was so little of it that she managed to drain the cup and then asked for some water. The water was cool and flavored with orange blossoms.

"I think I can sleep now," she said wearily. "And thank you, thank you for the medicine at least." She gave him a quavering little smile. These people were so strange, she thought, with their multiple wives and their multiple devotions—five times a day they knelt and faced the east at the call of the muzzeins—they shunned alcohol—and they made slaves of captured prisoners without a qualm. Their lives moved in an ellipse that didn't touch the boundaries of what she knew as civilization. To speak of morality to them was as hopeless as beseeching a cat to act on principle. This young man was obviously infatuated with her—his dark eyes burned on her with an intensity that wasn't open to any other interpretation, yet he would not lift a hand to help her. His grasping, slave trader father was his unquestioned ruler, and Fadim would someday rule his own household with the same whip-hand of absolute power. It was a nightmare that she lived in—a nightmare that wouldn't end until this accursed child was born. And then what? Could Jack Hidel allow her to go free after that, to accuse him of kidnapping her and paying for her imprisonment? Mad he certainly was, but he knew that his position would be a very dangerous one if she were free, even months from now. A chill ran through her—a chill of fear as she wondered what steps he would take to be assured that his crime would never be found out. It would be so easy for her to die here; he could say that she had died in childbirth and no one could prove otherwise—not from this sanctuary of wickedness. Definitely—he wouldn't let her escape to accuse him! Dear God, she must get out of here! She realized for the first time that it wasn't a question of imprisonment only—it was her life that hung in the balance. A chilling fear gripped her and her legs quivered. She huddled her body into a little ball on the pallet.

Fadim was darkly thoughtful as he walked back through the courtyards. A breeze had come up and the stiff palm fronds crackled and rustled overhead. He was searching for Hussein and found him reclining on some cushions by the pool that lay outside his own quarters. It was still the hour for the afternoon rest and Hussein lay sprawled with a bowl of fruit at his side, his mountainous belly falling in folds over the belt of his brightly colored trousers. The eunuch sprang up when Fadim approached and bowed, touching his forehead with three fingers.

"Be at rest, Hussein," Fadim said distractedly. "I have just come from the seraglio and I thought it wise to speak to you of the condition of the French lady."

Hussein stood silent but his brows quivered and rose slightly at this. Fadim's visits to the seraglio were a little disconcerting at best. He was well aware that his master's son lusted for this strange white woman and he foresaw complications that could rest heavily on his own shoulders. A Christian woman, and a prisoner at that; there was no wisdom in such a choice. Hussein wasn't convinced of the wisdom of keeping her at all. He moved freely outside the walls and was well aware that a French Countess was a person of no little importance in the world. Whatever power her husband commanded, and he knew it was a good deal, would fall in unwelcome blows on the heads of all who were involved in keeping her prisoner. Cairo was full of influential Europeans and he wondered what would happen if, somehow, one would get wind of the fact that a titled European lady was being kept prisoner in the house of his master. And she herself was of a disconcertingly rebellious nature, intelligent, and quite capable of plotting some kind of contact. Though how he couldn't imagine. He had gone over every possibility, but still felt uneasy. He knew that the Khedive was sensitive to the demands of the French, particularly now that the opening of the canal was planned for the following fall. He had no desire to see his master divested of his property, which would be the inevitable result of his being apprehended for the role he played in the Countess's forced exile. He, Hussein, had lived here for a good many years and he looked forward to a comfortable old age as the trusted servant of this wealthy man. He had piled up gold for himself, true, but not enough to ensure a life of such luxury as he was accustomed to. A eunuch who had lost his master was not in an enviable position—and he had no intention of seeing his master's household jeopardized by an unpredictable white woman.

"She is quite ill, Hussein, and I think a servant knowledgeable in such matters should be in attendance on her. My father would not like it if her illness became serious. Is there someone who can wait upon her who is skilled?"

Hussein nodded, his eyes hooded. "I will see to it now. There is such a servant, a woman who has a touch with sickness. You may be easy in your mind, Sire."

Fadim nodded as Hussein made another low bow.

He walked back to his own quarters, still uneasy. The old man had warned him of the dangers of the potion he had sold him. Death was a possibility, he said, but if she were healthy she would be safe, and no longer with child. Fadim couldn't dismiss his foreboding—and he began pacing again, back and forth beside the lily pond with its tinkling fountain. It had been necessary to drop the powder in her rice to make her ill, so that his ministering the potion would follow in a logical sequence. The stuff was too foul to have been offered as anything but medicine. Now he wasn't so certain he had been wise—and he continued pacing, head down, staring with unseeing eyes at the delicate gold tracing on the blue tiles.

Leita had fallen into a light sleep and then awakened. A dark-skinned woman sat beside her pallet, legs crossed and hands folded. She offered her a cup and raised her head gently. It was sweet and cool, tasting of peach nectar and honey. Leita drank gratefully—her lips felt dry and scaly. Then the pain struck, a pain that seemed to rip her body in two. She screamed and tensed, bending over nearly double on her pallet. It was a moment that seemed like an hour and the sweat started out on her forehead and upper lip as she gripped her knees. Then, just as suddenly, it stopped. The woman beside her looked at her with a questioning alarm and Yaquim materialized at her side. "What, oh what, is making you hurt?" Yaquim's face was sober with concern and Leita shook her head, gasping.

"It was such a pain—a terrible cramp," she whispered, almost fearing to breathe.

Yaquim turned and said a few words to the servant who nodded.

"You did not tell me, but it is gossip among the women that you are going to have a baby," Yaquim said.

"How did they know?" Leita replied, more to herself than to Yaquim.

"So it is true. It must be very early then, you are so slender."

"Yes, it is early—not three months yet," Leita said bitterly. Then she arched her back suddenly, as the pain gripped her again; griping, cramping, it seemed to tear through her vitals like a knife. The servant's strong arms went round her shoulders and she squatted behind her, rocking back and forth. Leita bowed her head on her knees, pressing her cheek against the soft silk of her trousers. When it faded, Yaquim took a soft cloth and wiped Leita's face. The sweat poured between her breasts, yet her skin felt chill to the touch. Her eyes were dark and wide now and her skin under the stain was pale, blanched of all color. Yaquim said a few words to the servant who had risen and was scurrying out of the room. She returned in a few moments with a cup full of some milky liquid and held it to Leita's lips.

"She says it will help the pain," Yaquim whispered tensely.

Leita forced it down—vaguely sweetish, it stuck in her throat and she swallowed convulsively. The servant pressed a cupful of honeyed water to her mouth and that helped the thicker liquid go down. Yaquim and the servant were conversing—Yaquim with ill-disguised alarm and the servant responding in quiet monosyllables. And then—Oh God! Leita curled up into a ball, paralyzed by a girdle of fire and iron that tightened around her abdomen and pressed against her spine with hot claws. She shrieked and rocked back and forth, clutching her drawn-up knees in a spasm of agony. She was dying—she was surely dying. She felt a gush of hot stickiness then and the pain faded as quickly as it had commenced. The hot stickiness ran down between her legs and she uncurled slowly, afraid to move lest that

470

terrible searing pain grip her again. Yaquim drew in her breath as she looked down. The silk trousers that covered Leita's legs were scarlet with blood! The servant drew in her breath and her brown hands flew to the fastening of Leita's belt, uncoupled it and tossed it to one side. Then she pulled gently, pulling the wet silk off Leita. She called out something and placed her palm against the small of Leita's back, rubbing firmly.

Leita looked down in amazement. Her inner thighs were covered with bright red, sticky blood and she could feel it oozing out of her body. She was dying—she had known she would. She was bleeding to death in this terrible place and no one that she loved would be beside her or ever know what had happened to her!

She looked up into Yaquim's face and saw tears streaking down her brown cheeks.

"Oh my friend—my dear friend. I am so sorry," the girl said in a hushed voice.

Leita closed her eyes, then caught her breath. It felt as if she were being pierced with a red-hot poker and she flailed into an arc of pain, her nails piercing the skin of her ankles as she gripped them, bending double, trying to escape the searing, cramping torture.

When she lay back finally, too weak to move, the servant bathed her legs with warm water and laid a soft, silken sheet over her lower body. She was surrounded by concerned faces, dark eyes resting on her with sorrow. The wives had gathered round and stood with their hands clasped, their braceleted arms quivering with tension.

At least someone cares—a little, Leita thought wildly, before the pain seared through her again.

It went on and on. She remembered Yaquim's soft voice at one interval, telling her she wasn't going to die. She must have been screaming that she didn't want to die here and Yaquim had whispered that she wouldn't,

471

she was losing her baby and she was so terribly, terribly sorry. Leita's glazed eyes fell on the tall figure of the eunuch time and again as she rolled on the pallet with soft hands stroking her and the strong arms of the servant holding her. She was in a fog—the milky liquid had been laced with opium. Time and again she was sponged clean of the hot blood that poured out between her legs and then she was lifted and carried to a clean pallet. Finally the cramps lightened and the time between them drew out. She had refused more of the milky liquid; she could not have swallowed it and was afraid she would choke. Now she lay limp with a burning ache in her lower abdomen. She could not raise her head and was too weak to speak.

Hussein stood beside a pillar—looking at her with his hooded eyes. He had hoped for a while that she would die. It seemed impossible that she should live—the amount of blood that spurted out of that small body had convinced him that she would die on that pallet, and he would be rid of his fears. He could dispose of her corpse easily enough and no one would need to know—no one outside these walls. Whatever inquiry was raised would not touch them here—no one would have seen or heard of her. But no—she lay, pale as death but still alive. He sighed and reached for a peach. He had given serious thought to poisoning her—so fearful was he of the consequences of her presence here—but he well knew that he would come under his master's suspicion and that would be as good as sudden death. And now her pregnancy was ended. Of that he was certain. Malech—he shrugged. Now it was to be seen if she would live through the rest of the night. With luck she would die. He went to tell Fadim.

The servant stayed beside her through the night. When she wakened, which was often at first, Yaquim's small plump figure was always sitting next to her pallet. Finally she slept, soundly and for hours. The dawn call of the muzzeins went unheard by her and it was with a special thankfulness that Yaquim prostrated herself this morning. She thanked Allah for the life of her friend and then scurried back to her side and placed a small, brown hand on Leita's forehead. The servant had said the thing to be watchful of was fever—if it came Leita would die. Her forehead was still cool and Yaquim sighed.

They watched beside her for two days, feeding her the cool, green grapes and tiny pieces of melon. There was no more retching and Leita began to regain strength. It was only then that the servant brought a tiny bowl of hot rice mixed with chicken. She had been allowed no hot food until the danger of fever was past—nor could she have swallowed any. Now she ate the rice greedily and drank deeply of the honeyed orange water. A burning ache still lay at the pit of her abdomen and her legs were weak, but her head spun no longer and the nausea was gone—finally. She had not seen the times that Fadim appeared noiselessly beside her pallet, his brow creased with anxiety. He never lingered for more than a few moments but he went without sleep until the danger of the fever had passed.

Now Leita looked around the pavilion, at the brightly colored cushions and the cluster of wives, their plump bodies bent over the gaming boards or reclining while they chewed the sticky dates and gossiped. They had one and all stroked her forehead and held her hands and keened over her and she had been touched by their warmth. To a woman they had regretted that she had lost her baby. Aside from their duties of the pallet, the bearing of children was their sole reason for existence and to lose a baby was a tragedy unparalleled to them. She thought of this now and she sat up weakly. The servant quickly piled cushions behind her to support her back. She looked around for Yaquim who came pattering over when she beckoned.

"Will you tell her I would like to swim in the pool?" Leita asked.

Yaquim's velvety dark eyes widened. "But you are not strong enough," she protested.

"Oh, yes, I am. And it would be so refreshing. Please!" Leita beseeched her.

Yaquim pondered a moment then spoke a few words to the servant who made a gesture of denial. Yaquim spoke more and then the servant rose grudgingly and supported Leita with one arm about her waist as they walked out into the courtyard. Yaquim was removing her bright yellow pantaloons and pulling off her vest and she stepped into the pool, her plump little brown body aglow with the oil that was rubbed into her skin daily. The servant helped Leita to undress and Leita stepped into the cool water. The hot sun beat down onto the pool and the water lapped deliciously around her thighs. She had done this daily before her illness and loved the cool, bright depths of the pool. The other wives never failed to gather round when she swam. They tittered and giggled at the sight of her white body and golden pubic hair. Leita had realized that they weren't making fun of her, they were simply amazed at such colors on a woman's body. Also, their own pubic area was kept cleanly shaven. Now she stroked her abdomen. She had noticed an increase in the size of her waist and a slight fleshy fullness before, now her abdomen was smooth and taut, her waist tiny again. A glow of happiness surged through her. She was not carrying the fruit of that night when Jack Hidel had attacked her; she was no longer pregnant with his child.

She had been delivered. Oh glorious day! She was herself again! Muhad Bey would release her—there was no longer any reason for her to be imprisoned here! She laughed aloud and skimmed into the water, turning and rolling like a happy child. Her nightmare was over!

Fadim had not come; she had not seen him since the night the pain had struck her down. He waited until she was past the danger of the deadly fever that often set in after miscarriage; then he went to his father.

Muhad Bey listened imperturbably to his son's request. He had been informed earlier of the nature of Leita's illness by Hussein and had been displeased. He had not only questioned Hussein closely but had called on other servants in the seraglio, had learned what Leita ate and drank, what her activity had been, and finally satisfied himself that the incident had not been caused by carelessness on the part of any of the servants as to Leita's well-being, nor had she had any opportunity to effect the abortion herself. He well knew that there were certain potions which could be used for such a purpose, that almehs availed themselves of these methods due to their profession, but it was unthinkable for any other woman to do such a thing, and he saw no way that Leita might have procured any potion which would have rid her of the child. It was an act of Allah—but one which irritated him immensely. He had named the sum of eight hundred piastres—an outrageous amount of gold—in expectation of a bargaining session. Instead the mad Englishman had agreed to pay. Such a sum was unheard of; it was the profit that could be expected on the sale of at least three firm-bodied young girls. He reminded Fadim of this impatiently. He had decided to simply say nothing, the girl would remain in the seraglio as if nothing had happened. The Englishman had called, but she had refused to see him. For that matter, if she changed her mind there would still be no way she could see the Englishman to tell him that she was no longer pregnant. Not unless Muhad Bey himself commanded it. She would be kept in the seraglio. There were six more months to be paid, a sum of forty-eight hundred piastres, which he had no intention of allowing to slip through his fingers. If, at the end of that time, Fadim still persisted in his wish for this scrawny, white-skinned creature, then so be it. In the meantime, of course, he was free to do whatever he chose, now that she was no longer with child. She was only a woman, and unworthy of such a long discussion if it were not for the gold involved. He had spoken. And he turned his back sullenly and dipped his fingers into the hot mutton, sucking on them loudly as he licked the hot fat from them.

Fadim continued his own meal in silence. What he had been granted was as much as he could ask, and he dared not bring up the subject again. He hadn't thought of the possibility that Muhad Bey would simply keep the girl as before without informing the Englishman that his hopes for a son were blighted. But he should have seen the logic of it—forty-eight hundred piastres! He had been too anxious, too single-minded in his desire and his impatience. But there, he was free to do whatever he chose, that is when she had recovered, of course. Fadim's only association with women had been with almehs—Mohammedan girls were closely guarded before marriage as well as after. But he knew that he was attractive to women—the almehs often quarreled over whom he was to choose and not just for his gold either. He would have Leita, and on his own terms, before his father made him a formal gift of her. He smiled contentedly as he chewed his mutton. He would not wait six more months before availing himself of that

476

rose-pink skin and those sumptuous breasts. He had acted with decision and the prize would be his. The novelty alone of embracing those white buttocks entranced him.

"But you will take me to him. I must see him, and you know it full well!" Leita cried, stamping her foot in the little gold slipper.

"Muhad Bey does not hold audiences for women." Hussein spoke the word "women" almost as if it were an obscenity. "He is well aware of the fact that you are no longer carrying a child. Your home is to be here, here in the seraglio, and I have no more to say."

"You are a fool!"

Hussein flinched at this and his eyes darkened ominously. "The only reason for my being held prisoner here is because that lunatic wanted me to bear his child. Apart from that I am no good to him—for anything! Now I no longer carry his child so I must go free! Don't you comprehend this?" Leita was in a frustrated rage. Her request for an audience with Muhad Bey had been made with perfect confidence. She was well now and expected to leave that very day, or the next morning at least. Now this fool was balking her—talking nonsense—totally without logic. She wondered if he really understood everything she said.

Hussein drew himself up, his broad belly made his robe jut out and his splayed brown feet were planted wide apart.

"It is you who are the fool, madame," he enunciated bitingly. "You are good for one thing—your presence here calls down a shower of gold piastres. That and that alone is the reason you will remain quietly in the seraglio." He turned and his buttocks wobbled under the white cotton as he walked away.

477

"But he won't pay now—the Englishman will not pay now that I no longer carry his child!" Leita shrieked after him and then ran and pulled at his sleeve.

He shook her off as if he were shaking off an insect. He stared at her mordantly. "And how is he to know this, pray tell?" He smiled then, an icy smile that struck horror into Leita's heart.

He walked out of the pavilion, hurrying a little to get away from the scene of such uproar. He didn't really dislike this strange girl. But she was a great bother, a not inconsiderable source of worry to him, and he of all people would have rejoiced if she had been pushed out the gates. Her independent airs, her obviously strong character gave him a feeling that the reins of control were shaky in his hands. But, at bottom, he had no ill will toward her. But she could—and of this he had no doubt—she could bring this household tumbling about their heads. He reached his quarters and picked up a dish of sweetmeats. He selected one and chewed fretfully. Perhaps he could help her to leave. If she escaped, that is if she promised him she would bring no accusations against this house, perhaps that would solve the matter. For her part she would be only too glad simply to be set free. She would find the French consulate, he would direct her to it, they would reach her husband the Count, and she would be free to take up her old life. He had the feeling that if she promised not to implicate him and this household, that she would keep her word. He chose another sweetmeat carefully. It would be so simple. To awaken her in the night, to unlock the gate and see her through it. He could attend her perhaps through the dangerous streets—or enlist the aid of his brother. Him he could trust implicitly. He chewed, barely tasting the sweetness of the honey and crisp sesame seeds. Then he spat suddenly. If she

478

escaped the blame would be laid at his door. He was in charge here, the undisputed master of the seraglio. He was held responsible for everything that happened in these pavilions. If the women quarreled he was expected to bring peace—if they desired something he was expected to see that their wishes were fulfilled. If the American woman was to escape, no matter what his protestations might be, he would be held responsible. Muhad Bey did not take gold lightly—it was food and drink to him. The loss of eight hundred piastres every month would throw him into a towering, hot rage, and he, Hussein, might very well find himself with his tongue cut out at the roots. His master would not hesitate at such a punishment, not for negligence that resulted in so much loss of gold. He would be relegated to emptying slop bowls, would feed off the scraps left in the bronze dishes. No! And he spat again, the honey sour in his mouth; he would not feel the cut of the knife again. He had lost his manhood years ago, not against his will but in exchange for food and shelter. The act of a desperate young man had turned him into a capon. But he was neither starving nor begging now. And he wasn't selling his body in the baths to every lecherous pederast that could pay a few gold coins as his brother did. Though Allah knew that his brother didn't have to commit sodomy to live. The boy was as greedy for gold as Muhad Bey; though Hussein kept him supplied with enough to live decently and well, he continued to ply his trade in the baths despite this. Greed! Hussein thought with despair. Some day the boy would find himself beaten up and stabbed, lying in some alley in the poor quarter. That was the frequent fate of the prostitutes who plied their own trade and refused to share their earnings with the men who ran the houses where pederasts gathered and paid well for beautiful boys. But there—he, Hussein, was not going to have his tongue cut out for allowing the American woman to leave. No, he would have to bend every effort to see that she didn't conceive and accomplish some such plan herself. He would put nothing past her—she was disturbingly intelligent.

Chapter 30

Darcy was worried, very worried, and worse, she was forced to conceal it. Every other day she called on Dora Hidel, receiving a cup of milky tea and enduring her recital of morbid gossip, in expectation of receiving a letter from Jack. There had been no word, not a scrap of paper, and though Mrs. Hidel assured her that she herself had not received a letter from him, Darcy was not certain she believed this. She had begun to suspect that Dora Hidel's saccharine ways concealed a nature that was quite the opposite.

Dora assured her blandly that Jack often took himself off for a few days or a few weeks without corresponding—then returned to continue his routine as usual. Darcy was very careful to conceal her desperation from this woman. She had become fairly certain that any female that threatened to come between Jack and his mother would feel the iron hand of her power. She was in her boudoir now. Expecting Jack's return every day she decided to occupy herself with sorting her wardrobe—to prepare her trousseau for a hasty departure in case he should arrive with plans for their wedding laid. Too, it gave her something to do. Piles of lacy lingerie lay on the bed and she was examining a corset cover when Mary Jo entered.

"I am so utterly, dreadfully depressed," Mary Jo sighed and flung herself down onto the satin-covered chaise in a sea of crinolines and petticoats.

What do you have to be so depressed about, was Darcy's irritable thought. But she suppressed it. "Isn't Etienne coming for you?" she asked.

"Oh, yes, he'll be here at four o'clock. Where could she be, Darcy? What on earth could have happened to her in a train station?" Mary Jo spent most of her days fretting in this way. She had had no word from Breve and waited with diminishing hope to hear from him. There had been time, since she posted her letter, time for him to have received it and return to Paris. But no word!

"If she were found—if only she were found. We could get on the first boat—the very first—and go back home!" Mary Jo cried. "But I won't leave—not till she is here. Though I want to."

"And what about Etienne?" Darcy asked mildly.

"Oh, fiddle! That sounds unkind, I suppose. I do like Etienne, but I want to go home." Mary Jo rose and pattered around, making a distracted little tour of the boudoir. She picked up a chemise, fingered it idly and put it down.

"Are you sorting your things out? I should do that I suppose. I have bought so many gowns here. More than I will have room for in my trunk. And the hats! They take up so much space."

"Yes. I decided it was high time I got my belongings in order. We have been so busy this summer, running here and there, that I have simply let them pile up. The maids are going to have a field day with my castoffs. And the hats—I cannot resist them either, the Paris milliners are so imaginative."

Mary Jo stood in front of the open armoire. It was bulging with gowns, bright silks and airy voiles. "I will help you," she announced with decision. "It will give me something to do."

"Anything to keep from fretting," Darcy replied philosophically.

Mary Jo drew out a gown of ruby-colored silk and held it up in front of her, turning this way and that before the tall standing mirror. "You mustn't discard this one. That color is heavenly on you. You look like a Borgia princess in this."

Darcy eyed it speculatively. "I think you're right—about keeping it, that is—not about the Borgia princess." She smiled. Mary Jo was always diverting.

Mary Jo was pirouetting now with an emerald green voile trimmed in embroidered white daisies. "Not my color at all. I look sallow," and she laid it on the bed before drawing out another—this time a pale yellow voile caught up with yellow silk tulips around the bodice.

"Now this one is delectable," she exclaimed. "If you give this to the maids I shall be heartsick."

"Take it—I've worn it three times and I'm bored with it. But will you have room for it?"

"Wonderful. I'll make room for it." Mary Jo eyed her reflection; set off by the clear yellow, her dark curls glowed and her white skin took on pinker tones. Matthew will like this, she thought with pleasure. He always remarks when I wear yellow. Oh, to see him again—and soon! What a glorious return it will be! She was so sick of Paris now, sick of lying awake and wondering where Leita could be, frightened for her, terrified each morning for fear news would have come in the night that her body had been found in some Paris alley. She longed to hear her laugh, to see her running up the steps, her bright mane of hair bouncing on her shoulders.

She sighed and surveyed the double row of hatboxes on the shelf of the armoire. "You have even more hats than I do."

"It's a vice with me, I'm afraid," Darcy replied.

Mary Jo pulled a stool over, stood on it and brought down a hatbox. Opening it, she withdrew a wide-brimmed leghorn, trimmed with yellow silk tulips around the crown. She popped it onto her dark curls and peered into the mirror.

"That goes with the yellow dress. You must take it, too," Darcy laughed. "You look delicious in it."

"Merci, madame." Mary Jo laughed and made a curtsey. She began pulling down the hatboxes, opening them and trying on bonnets and sun hats and elaborately trimmed leghorns.

She's like a little girl sometimes, Darcy thought, glancing at her now and then as she tied ribbons under her chin and adjusted the brims, pirouetting in front of the mirror.

"Now this one is beautiful!" Mary Jo exclaimed as she opened another of the hatboxes. It was a wide-brimmed lacy straw, trimmed with scarlet silk strawberries, brilliant against the white crown. The brim was so wide that it caught on the tissue paper lining the box and drew it down. Darcy was examining the ribbon on a chemise, absorbed in deciding whether or not it should be replaced, when Mary Jo pulled the letter out from between the tissue paper and the side of the box. Mary Jo read the address on the letter automatically and then stopped. It was addressed to Miss Leita Johnston. She turned it over. The return address was Breve Pinchon, Esquire, Chicago. Suddenly Mary Jo's smile faded and she glanced at Darcy who was straightening a pile of lingerie, smoothing the lace carefully. Mary Jo had a queer, prickling sensation in her throat. She deliberated for one second only, then thrust the letter down into her bosom quickly. Her mind was racing. Why would a letter directed to Leita be hidden, unopened, in Darcy's room? Furthermore, the letter was from Breve. The only one, to Mary Jo's certain knowledge, that Leita had received—but she hadn't, she hadn't known of it! Something was very much amiss here. She was alarmed to find that her hands were trembling and she managed to dissemble her agitation, pulling down a few more boxes and then replacing them before she excused herself to dress for the drive with Etienne. Darcy went on about her task, distracted by her unease about Jack Hidel, sorting and discarding one item after another in an effort to occupy her mind and ease her distress.

In her own boudoir, Mary Jo turned the letter over and over in her fingers. Should she open it? She was most certainly dying to. And Darcy—why had she done this—this underhanded thing? What possible reason could she have had for stealing Leita's mail and then hiding it? Eugene was expected momentarily. She would wait until he came and show him the letter. He would know what to do.

When Mary Jo arrived back at the Hidels' after the drive with Etienne, there was a note from the Comte du Favre. Eugene Johnston had arrived and would they please come for dinner to discuss what steps could be taken now. Thank heaven, Mary Jo thought, and stuffed the letter into her reticule.

Eugene looked dreadful, Mary Jo thought. His dark eyes were ringed with smudges and his cheeks were gaunt.

"You look as if you haven't eaten or slept, Eugene,"

she said sorrowfully as she kissed his cheek and relaxed in the curve of his arm.

"Damned little, if you'll excuse me," Eugene answered. "But I feel better now that I'm here on the spot. Can you imagine how helpless I felt, all those miles away? Now that I'm here we'll get things moving," he said grimly.

The dinner seemed endless. She was glad to see that Eugene ate heartily and relished the wine. Armand looked almost as bad, his fair skin paler than ever and his own eyes sunk in hollows. Mary Jo waited impatiently. Darcy was here and she couldn't present what she had found in her presence. Thankfully they didn't linger over dessert and she trailed along with Darcy and Lady Hidel to a small drawing room to wait while the men enjoyed their cigars and port. She managed to excuse herself in very little time and skimmed along the passage back to the dining room. She opened the wide double doors and entered, to the combined surprise of the gentlemen seated at the table, their heads ringed in clouds of blue smoke.

"You will have to excuse me for barging in like this, but there is something I must show you in private." She spoke quickly and pulled the cords of her reticule open. She extracted the letter and handed it to Eugene who turned it over in his hand reading both sides, and then looked up at her questioningly. Armand had risen and pulled out a chair for her and she sat down heavily in the silence.

"I found it only this afternoon," she began.

"But it hasn't been opened, and the postmark is certainly not recent," Eugene broke in.

"That's just it," Mary Jo cried. "She never got it. It was hidden, hidden in one of Darcy Rankin's hatboxes in her room. I came on it this afternoon and pushed it down the front of my dress. I don't know what it means. I can't imagine why Darcy took it and then hid it, but that's the case. I thought you should know that something very strange is afoot here."

The men looked at each other. "And who is this letter from?" It was Armand who spoke first.

Eugene pursed his lips for a moment, waiting for Mary Jo to answer. Then took the bit in his teeth. "It is from an old friend of ours, a Mr. Breve Pinchon. He accompanied us on the trip north."

"But why in the world?" Armand stopped. "Breve Pinchon? Wasn't that the name of that boorish drunk who reduced Leita to tears at Madame de Sivry's party? He upset her terribly, I recall. Could he be involved in her disappearance?"

Eugene looked startled. "Breve is here? Here in Paris?"

"He was," Mary Jo replied. "But he left the next day for Geneva. As a matter of fact, I have written to him, telling him of Leita's disappearance, but I have had no answer. At least none that I have seen," she concluded. The thought had just crossed her mind that perhaps Breve had written, and it had been intercepted as this letter had.

Eugene tapped the letter on the cloth. "No, I don't think that Breve could be involved in her disappearance. He's an honorable man. An unpredictable one, but honorable."

"I found him most objectionable." Armand spoke decisively.

Eugene smiled thinly. "I don't doubt that Leita was upset at seeing him. They quarreled, roundly and frequently." He chose his words carefully here. "They were, in point of truth, quite attached to one another I believe."

Armand's pale brows lifted. "You mean there had been a romance between them."

487

Eugene sighed. "A very stormy one. But yes, there was. Though, for reasons I cannot reveal, there was no possibility of their marrying."

Armand fell into a thoughtful silence at this and Sir Charles spoke for the first time. "We are sitting here with only conjecture at our service. We must leave no stone unturned and though this letter was dispatched and concealed long before Leita's disappearance we will have to ascertain if it is in any way connected with it. To do that we will need to speak to Miss Rankin."

"Immediately," Eugene said firmly, and ground out his cigar.

Lady Hidel's face wreathed itself in one of her sparkling smiles as the group entered the drawing room. "Well, gentlemen, you join us sooner than we expected."

Sir Charles seated himself on the divan beside his wife and took her hand in his. Eugene remained standing, the letter hanging from one hand as he spoke.

"Miss Rankin, there is one thought uppermost in all our minds, and that is the fate of my sister. I have just been informed that this letter, addressed to Leita, was found in your room. To be exact, it was hidden in your room. I speak bluntly, but you will excuse me, I know. I must ask you the reason for this—" He held the letter up and Darcy's pale skin turned a deathly white.

"Where did you get that?" Then she turned to Mary Jo, as she realized belatedly the outcome of Mary Jo's helpful rummaging. Good lord, what now? What could she say? Her nerves were raw enough, and to be confronted with this! She was aware that everyone was looking at her.

"I never saw it before. Never. I have no idea how it got in my room. What are you accusing me of?" Her countenance was marked now by two bright red spots high on her cheekbones.

488

Eugene looked at her quietly. *She is lying—lying in her teeth. What kind of plot was afoot here?*

"No one accuses you of anything. My sister has disappeared, under suspicious and threatening circumstances. Anything connected with her is of extreme importance, particularly something so mysterious as a letter to her that was intercepted and hidden. I am sure you must have an explanation, Miss Rankin."

Armand had remained silent but now his voice lashed out at the silent, quivering woman. "My wife has disappeared, she is undoubtedly in the hands of some criminal element, her life in danger. There is no time for lying, for subterfuge. We must bend every effort to find her and if you know anything of her whereabouts, if you are party to any kind of secret knowledge you must tell us immediately!" His harsh words cut the air like a knife.

"I have no secret knowledge. How can you all be so stupid? She has probably run away with that Colonel Pinchon. She is mad about him. They are probably hidden in some hotel somewhere while you are browbeating me. You are so stupid, and so blind." Darcy's rage was surfacing now, all the tension she had been enduring for these past weeks tore through her like a spring uncoiling. "Leita, Leita, I am so sick of hearing about Leita. I am frantic with worry over my fiancé. He has not been heard from for three weeks. I am certain now that something has befallen him. No one is searching for Jack—no one cares about him—but I know something dreadful must have happened to him. I haven't heard a word—"

"Jack—Jack, your fiancé?" Sir Charles' voice broke through her words. "Yes, my fiancé—and your nephew! No one expresses a word of concern about him, and I am frantic." Darcy's quivering hand drew a lace handkerchief from her bosom and she dabbed at her perspiring brow. There, it was out, and just as well. They had better start concerning themselves with Jack's disappearance too.

Sir Charles' face had turned an ashen color and Lady Hidel looked up at him in bewilderment.

"Do I understand you to say that you are engaged to marry Jack Hidel?" Sir Charles said unbelievingly.

"Yes, we are affianced. And he has disappeared! His mother thinks he is in Italy. He left a note to that effect just three weeks ago, but I am convinced something has happened to him. She says she has received no letter from him and I certainly have not." She looked Sir Charles full in the face.

"We were to be married in Florence—secretly, because he is so shy. You would all have known afterward. We were going to return to America after our marriage, and now—and now." She broke down into tears.

Armand and Eugene exchanged glances and Mary Jo never took her eyes off Darcy. She was certainly a deep one—never a word, but she had accomplished her intent.

"Marry? Do you mean that cur asked you to marry him? And you accepted?" Sir Charles shouted, maddened and confounded by the turn this interrogation had taken.

"He is not a cur!" Darcy shouted back through a storm of tears. "You are contemptuous of him, all of you, just because he is shy and soft-spoken and—he knows you despise him."

"How long since he left?" Sir Charles asked quietly and coldly, a strangely intense expression in his eyes.

"Just three weeks ago. The day after Madame de Sivry's party, in fact. He was to call that afternoon and he didn't. I haven't received one word," Darcy sobbed.

Sir Charles met his wife's eyes. The same thought

was born in both their minds. Sir Charles put his head in his hands and then raised his eyes to Eugene and Armand who stood speechless with astonishment at this outpouring.

"I have concealed too much for too long, with the best of intentions, but that is what the road to hell is paved with, I daresay." Sir Charles spoke so softly it was almost a whisper. He took Annette's hand. "I am about to wash some dirty linen, my dear. You agree that I should, do you not?" Annette Hidel nodded wordlessly, her own face pale now.

"I have reason to fear that Jack Hidel is at the root of Leita's disappearance. I was aware that he wasn't around, of course, but Dora said he had jaunted off to Italy, and that was where I intended he should go. The further off the better. But now I must tell you my story, and it is a most unpleasant tale to unfold."

Darcy was blowing her nose into her handkerchief as Sir Charles poured a glass of absinthe from the decanter on a side table, handed it to Eugene, and proceeded to fill two more. "Jack Hidel is not really my nephew. Not in the bloodline you understand." He paused and grimaced. "He is the son of Dora and her brother, a brother who died in an asylum, raving mad." Mary Jo looked at him with wide blue eyes and Darcy froze in her chair. He continued. "I have kept careful watch over him. Under the circumstances, of course, it was most important that he not marry, that he never beget children, and fortunately, he was so tied to his mother's apron strings that he never has, until now." The room was hushed as he spoke and the hush was unbroken as the meaning of his last words impinged on each one listening.

"I have disinherited him, and he has signed legal documents forfeiting his right to use the name of Hidel. This came about because—because." How to tell this?

491

He fell silent for a moment and his wife rose and touched his shoulder comfortingly.

"Leita was attacked," Lady Hidel spoke up. "Attacked and raped while she was under the influence of a drug. It happened the night of the ball at St. Cloud." Darcy was relatively unperturbed by this news, and wondered what it had to do with the subject at hand but Mary Jo and Eugene were galvanized. "What did you say?" Mary Jo cried.

"It is true," Lady Hidel nodded. "Her attacker was Jack Hidel, my husband's erstwhile nephew, whom he had lavished such care on. Sir Charles went to look for her and surprised him after—just after, the act had been consummated. Leita was still unconscious, of course, and Jack fled. Our one thought was her well-being and we took her back to the house before my husband went in pursuit of his nephew."

Armand was thunderstruck. "But I thought Sir Charles didn't recognize the man!" he cried.

"I couldn't tell you, Armand. I simply couldn't reveal this secret that Sir Charles had kept. He was in England if you remember, and didn't return till after your wedding. Then we discussed whether or not you should be told—whether Leita should be told—and it tortured us both. Do you understand, my dear? Do you understand why I alone couldn't tell you?" Annette's eyes were filled with tears now and Armand went quickly to her side.

"Of course. Or at any rate I am making the attempt," he said, laying an arm about her shoulders.

"I don't believe it." Darcy's sibilant whisper filled the room as if she had shouted.

"I don't blame you," Sir Charles said brusquely. "A nice fellow you gave your hand to."

"What is this?" Eugene's voice rose. "Am I to

understand that my sister was raped and nothing was done about—the man is running free?"

"I must admit to that, Mr. Johnston. And it is my doing. If I had turned him over to the police it is quite possible, I shudder to say it, that we would not be gathered here tonight. But I didn't out of the pride in my family name, out of distaste for having the facts in every journal in Paris and every muckraking newspaper in London."

Eugene's eyes were blazing and Sir Charles refilled his own glass with absinthe and offered the decanter to Eugene. He refused it with a curt gesture.

"I searched him out that night, Mr. Johnston. I gave him an ultimatum. He was to go to England and sign papers forfeiting his right to the title and his right to use the name of Hidel. Then he was to take himself to Italy and remain there, never to leave—never to return to England or France again. He is an abject coward, in addition to being a depraved and licentious man. I left him groveling on the grass of the Bois, facing the consequences of his actions. . . ."

Darcy was huddled in her chair, her hands to her face. Mary Jo was riven to her seat, paralyzed with astonishment and horror at the story that was being revealed.

"And now comes the difficulty—or the worst difficulty up until now. Despite my wife's care, which was born of our concern and great affection for your sister, in addition to our sense of terrible responsibility for the fate which had befallen her—we discovered that Leita was going to have a child. She had been under the doctor's care from the night of the tragedy, of course."

"Jesus Christ!" Eugene's head had jerked up.

Armand looked at him and nodded. "Annette told me of her plight. Leita knew nothing of it. I felt that someone must protect her from the calumny she would suffer. I told her the truth, and I proposed that we marry. It was her decision. We were married the next evening."

Eugene got up and reached for the decanter. "You are saying that not only is my sister missing—disappeared without a trace—but she was pregnant by this madman?" He was trembling with anger and Armand answered him evenly.

"That is the substance of it. She was well, you understand, but a little over two months pregnant."

Mary Jo felt as if she herself would faint. Leita *pregnant?* And she *knew* it? And that was why she had married Armand so quickly? She thought of Breve's face, dark with smoldering anger that night. Oh, if only she had known! She could have told him then. Perhaps he would have taken Leita away and all this would never have happened. She clenched her hands in her lap but kept silent, her mind racing. She must reach him, somehow he must learn of this!

"I have told you all this because it seems to me to be far too much of a coincidence, that Jack Hidel has disappeared too and even more important, that he left on the same day that Leita was taken captive by someone! He did not know that she was going to have a child, of course, but he was obviously besotted with her in his perverse way. I speculate that he took her, that he made off with her on some pretext; she would never have gone with him willingly, of course, so we must assume that he used force."

Darcy had walked to the side table and was pouring a glass brimful of the powerful absinthe. She sipped the liqueur and turned toward the group, her face swollen with crying.

"He knew she was going to have a child," she said dully.

Lady Hidel turned. "What did you say, Darcy?"

"Jack Hidel knew that Leita was going to have a child. I told him," she repeated and swallowed down half of the absinthe.

Sir Charles stood stock still and Eugene's eyes narrowed as he stared at the dark-haired disheveled woman.

"How did you know of it?" Lady Hidel cried.

"I overheard Giselle talking to her husband about it, one night when I couldn't sleep. And I told Jack." Her speech was devoid of feeling, and her face bleak and ashen in the candlelight.

Sir Charles looked at Annette. "There you are. That is settled, then. Now we know why she disappeared, and who lured her away. His hold on sanity must be very thin. I am sure that the news that he was to become a father was enough to tip him over the brink into some wild scheme."

"We know damned little," Eugene exploded, setting his glass down with a crash. "We know that she is in the hands of a lunatic, but we don't know where she is."

Armand rang for a servant. He was pensive now. When the footman appeared he whispered a few words to him, received a negative reply, and then made a request. The footman disappeared. The group in the drawing room sat still, in a torpid kind of misery. Sir Charles was lost in thought. Eugene was pacing, his jaw clenching and unclenching. Darcy was staring with blank eyes at a portrait above the mantel and Mary Jo was plucking at a rose on her skirt, wondering impatiently when Breve would reply to her. Perhaps he had already returned to America. The letter he had written to Leita lay unopened on a small table, forgotten in the aftermath.

The doors opened then and the footman re-entered, followed by a small figure wrapped in a robe.

"Ah, Marie, I am sorry to have had you awakened. I know it is late." Armand rose and went toward the girl. "But I wanted to ask you something, something that couldn't wait. I want you to think very carefully now. Did a gentleman named Jack Hidel ever call here on your mistress?"

"Jack Hidel?" Marie repeated the name, then shook her head. "No, M'sieur, I do not remember such a name."

"He was tall, Marie. An Englishman. His hair was brown, a gingery color, I believe." Armand glanced at Sir Charles. "And he had blue eyes, pale blue eyes. He was a touch timid. Now, does that description help you?"

Marie shrugged. "No, M'sieur, I have never seen such a gentleman call here. I am sorry."

Armand frowned. "That is all right. Go along back to your bed now."

The girl pulled her robe around her and went to the door. Then she turned. "M'sieur, if you will pardon me, but you asked me to search for a note in Madame's chambers, you remember?"

Armand stopped. "Yes. But you found none."

"No, M'sieur, there was nothing that you thought important. But I found a note this afternoon, while I was seeing to Madame's gowns. It was at the bottom of the armoire, crumpled up. It is probably of no importance, and you were out till late. I had no opportunity to tell you earlier." She smiled hesitantly, her piquant little face creased with sleep.

"Well, get it, Marie! Hurry now. Everything about Madame is of importance, you understand."

"Certainly, M'sieur." She scampered out the doorway.

The girl returned and tendered him the piece of mauve paper, which she had gone to great pains to

496

smooth out. He read it, frowning, glanced again at the date, and handed it to Sir Charles.

"What now, Miss Rankin? You are a very strange woman," Sir Charles remarked acidly as he handed the note to Darcy.

Darcy read through it once. Then wiped her eyes with her handkerchief and handed it back to Sir Charles. "I didn't write that. It is signed with my name, but I haven't the faintest idea what it is about."

"Is this your handwriting?" he asked, knowing full well that it was. Armand stood by him, looking with expressionless eyes at Darcy.

"It looks like my handwriting. But I didn't write it. Here, give it to me." Darcy took it and examined it closely. "This is an imitation of my handwriting. Someone has gone to some pains with this."

"Well what does it say, Charles?" Annette burst out, exasperated.

Sir Charles read the note requesting Leita to come to the train station, to the train to Marseilles.

"So that was what sent Leita rushing off to the Gare de Lyon. She was on her way to aid a friend, a friend who had asked her to keep her request in confidence." Armand glanced at Darcy. "You were a party to this, Miss Rankin. Now you are going to tell us the rest."

"I was not a party to anything, Comte du Favre," Darcy answered, quietly and totally without umbrage. "Someone has imitated my handwriting, imitated it very well, that is all."

Sir Charles' eyes narrowed with sudden thought. "Was Jack Hidel familiar with your handwriting?" he inquired.

"Of course he was," Darcy answered tiredly. "I wrote to him while he was in England, attending to some business he said, and I occasionally wrote him a note here in Paris."

"He kept them then. He kept them and used them to forge that note to Leita. A note he knew she would respond to." Mary Jo burst out with this.

Eugene smiled for the first time since he had entered the drawing room. "Very astute of you, Mary Jo. That is in all probability what happened."

"The man should be guillotined," Armand said sharply.

"I agree with you," Eugene replied.

"Now her trip to the Gare de Lyon is explained, and we know her destination there. It is possible he kept her on the train to Marseilles," Sir Charles offered.

"Possible and very probable," Armand replied. He had taken paper and quill pen from the small secretary against the wall and had seated himself. "I will pen a note to M. Pietri and send my man with it. We will follow shortly after. I think only one train need concern us now—the train to Marseilles. He is, I know, exploring that avenue, but now we can be fairly certain that is where she was taken.

The group finally disbanded, the ladies to ride home in the carriage alone, leaving the gentlemen to go on to M. Pietri's.

Darcy lay awake all night and then watched the sun come up over the mist-shrouded skyline of Paris. She had no future—not here, not anywhere, she thought dispiritedly. She, with all her cleverness, had been taken for a fool, and how successfully!

Chapter 31

Breve Pinchon opened his eyes slowly, carefully. The morning sun was glaring through the sheer white curtains, but thankfully they were floating in a strong breeze. The room opened onto a balcony facing the east and though this made for coolness during the afternoon, the morning sun hadn't failed to awaken him early these past mornings. And this is the last morning, he thought, yawning expansively, the last morning in Italy. His outstretched arm touched the raised shoulder of the woman lying next to him. Not that it hasn't been fairly pleasant, he mused. Simonne made an entertaining traveling companion; well-traveled herself, she had guided him through the streets and museums of Florence and Rome, enjoying his interest and enthusiasm. Just what I needed, he mused on, a long, entertaining holiday with a compliant and passionate companion. The Baroness Hequet had felt no need to hasten back to Paris. She assured him that her husband's enforced absence from his mistress would propel him directly into her arms when he returned from Florence, and he was quite tolerant about his wife's pursuits, as long as they were not vulgarly conspicuous, which of course she was not capable of being. Breve had shrugged his shoulders. It was up to her; if the Baron didn't require her presence and she preferred to accompany him as he wandered down through Italy, then he certainly wasn't going to object. But today she would entrain back to Paris and he, he would be at the docks at four o'clock to board a ship that would glide out into the blue waters of the Mediterranean. He was going to Africa, and a thread of excitement ran through him at the thought. Ten years ago his future had been clear cut; he would join his father's cotton brokerage business, take his place in Charleston society, marry some coy South Carolina belle, of good family, of course, and never stir from lush, flower-bedecked, graciously rigid Charleston. And here I am, working in a raw city that is growing rich so fast that it astonishes itself, with clients scattered through Europe—and now I am off to Africa, to view a canal that will change the shape of commerce for years to come, and about to say goodbye to the Baroness who has been sharing my bed. He smiled; wandering must be in the blood. He got up quietly and walked to the open French doors. The sea was visible from here, choked with the high-masted ships that lay in the harbor. He pulled the curtain aside and breathed deeply of the salty, already warm air, his strong, bare chest expanding.

A quiet knock sounded at the door and he wrapped his tall body in a robe and answered it quickly, taking the proffered tray and returning to the bedside. He poured the rich coffee out and Simonne wakened to the fragrance. She ran slender fingers through the mass of dark hair that fell to her shoulders and reached out for the cup. He pushed away the memory that crossed his mind, the memory of Leita sitting up in the early morning beside the dead embers of a campfire, running her fingers through her tangled, red-gold hair, and smiling sleepily as she took the granite mug of coffee from his hand. He sighed and drank deeply of the hot, creamy coffee. It will take time, more time than I've given it. Someday I will have forgotten, but not now, not yet.

Simonne was nibbling at a piece of thick-crusted Italian bread. "Sometimes you are so very pensive," she remarked with a smile and brushed a crumb off the sheet. "Everyone has a heartbreak in their past, you know. The art of life is in the forgetting." She reached across and ran a cool fingertip over his brow.

"I am more than content, my dear," he grinned, and stretched his long, smoothly muscled legs out on the bed, holding his cup carefully.

She drained her cup and set it aside, then slid her hand into the opening of his robe and stroked his chest, plucking gently at the thickly curling black hair. He caressed her arm absently at first, then tightened his fingers as her hand stroked gently down to his flanks, brushing his groin lightly as they passed down over his thighs. He turned toward her and pulled the sheet down as he covered her mouth with his, working his lips gently and teasingly over hers, forcing her mouth open and then darting his tongue between her lips. Her hand had found his swelling manhood when another knock sounded at the door. "Damn," he breathed and she jumped up and covered herself in a long silk robe. Two porters entered, carrying an oval-shaped tub filled with water.

"It is my fault. I ordered my bath early, remember, because we were leaving," she laughed.

The porters, who understood no English, gazed at

her admiringly as she handed them a few coins. With a knowing glance in Breve's direction, they bowed out of the room.

Her robe dropped to the floor and she stepped into the tub, gliding down into the warm water. The dark, brownish-red of her nipples shimmered as she soaped her breasts and her creamy-white shoulders. Breve lay on the bed, watching her and when she rose from the tub, her body glistening wet and lit by the warm sun he went to her and wrapped the towel around her. She stepped closer to him and tilted her head up, offering her mouth, and his hands cupped her rounded buttocks, pressing her tightly against him, while he caught her parted lips and devoured them. She slipped her hands under his robe and ran them down over his flanks pressing his heavy thighs tightly against her soft, damp flesh. A sigh drifted through her parted lips as she felt the throbbing of his manhood against her loins and she ground her hips against him, darting her warm little tongue in and out of his mouth. He tore the towel open and threw it aside, then gathered her naked body in his arm, crushing her moist warm breasts against him while his hands caressed her hips and buttocks. She went limp in his arms and he carried her down to the thick rug beside the tub, running his mouth over her body, nibbling at the white skin. He rubbed his cheeks over her white, blue-veined breasts and slid his sun-browned hand between her legs, caressing her fiercely. She arched her back and gave a little cry of desire and he bent his head over her breasts and seized one taut nipple between his teeth, nibbling it and circling his tongue over it before he drew it into his mouth. Her legs were parted now and she was gasping; her hand found the throbbing redness of his member and she grasped it, pulling roughly with her fingers. Breve moaned, took her other breast in his mouth, pulling on the nipple so fiercely that she gave a little cry. He raised his head and looked down into her flushed face, then knelt over her while she wrapped her long white legs around him and guided him into her, arcing against him with a ferocious passion, rocking her hips to meet his. They were locked together, gasping in the rhythm of desire. She pulled his head down and crushed his lips against hers, thrusting her tongue deeply and quickly into his mouth. Her legs gripped him tighter as her hips moved in a convulsive abandon, matching his deep thrusts. When she cried out and her tense body grew limp, he smiled and thrust more deeply into her until he finally fell spent and gasping over her.

"You know well how to say goodbye, mon cheri." She smiled wickedly against his cheek.

He laughed uproariously. "Simonne, you are a marvelous woman."

"I know," she laughed. "It was a delightful chance that threw us together, was it not?"

Breve nodded. "A very delightful chance, my dear." He got up and stepped into the by-now tepid bathwater.

"It has been charming and you will miss me, of course," she said philosophically, scrubbing his back with the sponge, "but a man like you will never be lonely, not for a lover."

It was later, when they were in the carriage on the way to the train station that she said something in a surprisingly serious vein. She had turned to him and lifted the rosy veil that covered her hat. Her dark eyes were intent looking into his. "Someday, mon cheri, I have no doubt of it, you will gain what you came here for."

Breve's brows lifted. "And what do you mean by that?" He was genuinely puzzled. She smiled enigmatically.

"A quarrel can be more revealing than a kiss. That, and a man who makes love with only half of him." The enigmatic smile flashed again and she dropped her veil. Breve made no reply. The carriage had stopped outside the station and he helped her down and saw her off, then ate a hearty meal of pasta and wine before getting his bags and heading for the wharf.

He did not linger in Alexandria but took the first train to Cairo. Daniel O'Connell was expecting him.

The domes of the over three hundred mosques in Cairo glittered in the intense rays of the sun, gold and blue shimmered over the city and Breve breathed deeply of the scent of jasmine and melon and hot spices. Breve strolled, the smaller passers-by instinctively making way for his tall, richly dressed figure. As he walked he dropped coins into the bowls of the mutilated beggars and soon carried a tail of urchins who clamored at his heels until he stopped and bought them all a cup of the sweetish-warm orange drink sold by a vendor. The streets lay in a haze of golden dust, roiled up by the camels, the countless little donkeys and hundreds of splayed brown feet. Drums beat and tambourines tinkled, mingling with the cries of the hawkers.

He was deep within the city now and on the fringe of a crowd. Curious, he pushed his way through and found himself at the edge of a great square. Men walked back and forth, their galabiahs swirling over the polished stones. There were women lined up in rows; black women from Nubia with heavy gold circlets drawing their ear lobes down. Their skins were oiled and gleamed blue-black and they were nude except for the necklaces that a few wore and the gold circlets around their upper arms. Girls, lighter in color, their hair smeared with yellow clay and their hands brick-red with henna dye, stood erect, staring over the heads of the men who slapped at their flanks and tweaked their conical, dark-pointed breasts. This was Cairo's open-air slave market, packed with traders and the representatives of wealthy men, where girls were bought and sold as if they were bundles of twigs for a kitchen fire.

Muhad Bey sat on a pile of cushions, the stem of a jewel-encrusted pipe in his mouth. His eyes were slitted in concentration as they rested on each oiled body, sweeping from head to toe and assessing the probable worth of each slave. To his left there were about a dozen young females, chattering to each other, their long fingers traveling idly over their bodies, fingering their bracelets and their necklaces that dangled down to their navels. This was Muhad Bey's stock-in-trade for the day and he received the offers he was given with an enigmatic bow of his head, the clerk standing beside him inscribing each price that was settled on in a wide book. Gold clinked into the bronze bowl beside him and he puffed on his pipe, satisfied with the day's proceedings so far. When Breve passed him, Muhad Bey's dark velvety eyes flicked over him with a moment's curiosity. The man was too tall to be a Frenchman, he thought idly, then his attention went to the emissary of a wealthy Cairo house who was presenting an offer for two of the girls.

Breve noticed the heavy-set Egyptian only in passing as he made his way through the rows of gleaming, dark bodies. He had heard that the Viceroy himself granted contracts to these traders, authorizing them to capture and sell whom they would from the villages that lay along the reaches of the upper Nile. And a roaring business they do, too, he thought, taking in the crowds of men in their gleaming white robes and their plump, beringed hands.

He left the square finally and found the verandah of a hotel where a fountain played and waiters scurried with trays so heavily laden it looked as if their thin limbs would collapse under the strain of carrying them. He ordered a bottle of wine and found to his surprise that it was very good, and then threw himself on the mercy of the waiter when it came to choosing his food. When it arrived he ate heartily.

A man seated himself at a table on the far side of the sunny terrace and something about his gait impinged on Breve's sleepy awareness. He sipped his brandy and then glanced over at the stranger who was perusing a European newspaper. He was dressed in gray, gray frock coat and trousers and a darker gray cravat decorated his white shirt front. He wore a black imperial, the tiny, spade-like beard looking a touch ridiculous on the tip of his long chin; the thin black mustache inadequate over the narrow line of his almost lipless mouth. The cup of thick Turkish coffee sat cooling in front of Breve while he searched his mind. Then he shrugged and emptied it at one gulp. He disposed of the rest of his brandy in the same manner and paid his bill. While he was counting out the unfamiliar coins the stranger rose, folded the paper under his arm and walked down the steps of the terrace into the street. Breve saw him out of the corner of his eye and snapped his fingers in sudden recognition. That walk, with one shoulder higher than the other, and the turkey-like projection of his neck! That was the fellow who had met Leita at the train station in Paris! The one with the strange English accent overlaying his fluent French. But he had been in a Guards' uniform then—now he was in civilian dress. Odd, that was damned odd when you came to think of it! How could you account for an Englishman in the French Imperial Guards turning up in Cairo?

Breve walked down the street and stood looking after Jack Hidel's receding figure. Finally he turned and walked in the other direction. He dismissed the puzzle after a while, caught up with interest in his surroundings. He decided to tour the bazaars. He had better turn up with an interesting package for Mae Schneider when he got back to Chicago and he would take care of it now, while he was looking over this strange, exotic city.

He sauntered through the street of the ivory workers, watched the nimble brown fingers carving the pieces of tusk into unbelievably delicate traceries and he stopped and bought a fan whose ivory spokes were carved into lilies. That will do very well, he thought, and with this necessary task off his mind he turned into the next street, intending to explore it and then find the hotel where his trunks had been delivered. It proved to be the street of the gold workers and he soon became enraptured with the ornate work that was displayed, necklaces, collars, bracelets, all gleaming softly against the hanging black silk and the countless men bent over their work, their tools laid beside them on strips of cloth.

He was looking at a wide gold collar, made of gold chains so tiny they looked as if they could be drawn through the eye of a needle. It was decorated with pieces of turquoise and, he thought, the most beautiful piece of gold work he had ever seen. The slender man standing in the wide arched doorway beckoned to him to enter and Breve deliberated, then shook his head. He took a step and bumped into a man standing by the tier of stone steps. The man stepped back quickly and the slender man in the doorway barked some ill-natured words at him. "It's all right," Breve said in French, hoping the man understood him. The slave who stepped aside had dark brows, one of which was slashed with a wide scar and a dark purplish spot decorated one cheek. The spot was slightly concave and Breve had noticed them before on other men. The man's nose swept into a curve that almost touched his upper lip and he bowed low, backing away quickly, and took up the bridle of a donkey. The bridle was hung with gold medallions and the little saddle was made of emerald green velvet richly worked with gold. Breve nodded in answer to the bow and took another step before stopping again.

This must be the finest shop in the bazaar, Breve thought, and glanced up into the opening where the man who was evidently the owner was displaying a necklace to an Egyptian woman. The sun was lower in the west now and its rays illuminated the cool darkness of the interior. The woman wore a pale yellow robe and the veil that covered her face below the eyes was of sheer yellow silk. She was gazing apathetically at the necklace and Breve narrowed his eyes against the sunlight. Her eyes—the eyes outlined in black kohl—were a dark violet color. My God—she had eyes exactly like Leita. The strangeness of those velvety, purplish blue pupils against the dark skin struck him. She seemed totally indifferent to the splendors of the necklace that the man was holding.

Another man stood beside her, a plump Egyptian whose broad belly thrust his white robe out. He was looking questioningly into her face and she met his eyes and shook her head. The movement made the sweep of yellow that covered her head fall back slightly, exposing the black hair that swept over her temples and circled her forehead. Breve sighed and remained watching her while the shopkeeper drew another necklace from behind him. The sunlight struck her face full, outlining familiar cheekbones and the curve of a small mouth which remained unsmiling. A slight smile moved over Breve's own lips. The girl's face and eyes were a duplicate of Leita's. What mixture of blood had resulted in those violet eyes, that straight little nose? He stared for a moment, then sighed and moved on. He felt in need of company—a little gaiety to take his mind off—off what? Off the girl I have to forget, he thought viciously. He would find the American Embassy and see Daniel. Right now, he wouldn't wait till evening.

In the goldsmith's shop Leita stood quietly while the bearded goldsmith drew out one example of his art after another and held it caressingly, proudly, for her inspection. A thin little smile marked her face when she told Hussein to thank him, to say that his work was beautiful, but she was really not interested in having anything today.

Hussein felt a frustration that mounted into anger. A man long experienced with women, it had never crossed his mind that she would refuse—refuse a gift from the finest goldsmith in Cairo. He, Hussein, was going to pay for it. He had to do something—anything to raise her spirits. And when he thought of this it had seemed to be the most effective means of pleasing her. The situation was becoming serious. Since the day she had pleaded to be released on the grounds that she no longer carried the child of the Englishman, not a bite of food had passed her lips. She had refused even coffee, contenting herself with sips of orange water. She refused implacably to eat and already she was quite weak; she had fainted twice according to her woman servant. He had not yet informed Muhad Bey of this development, having finally hit upon the idea of taking her out, thereby granting at least one of her wishes, and making her a gift of jewelry. He had been well satisfied with this inspiration, thinking she would be cheered and diverted. Any one of the other wives would have been deliriously happy to be standing here with the contents of the goldsmith's shop at their disposal. But no—she refused, and not sacrificially either—she simply was indifferent.

He tossed the goldsmith a coin and preceded Leita

down the steps. The slave assisted her up onto the donkey's back and drew up the second donkey who took Hussein's weight dolefully and began to trudge through the dust. Hussein, instead of riding behind Leita, rode abreast of her. He was taking no chances of her catching someone's eye, perhaps tugging at a sleeve. He was well aware that her desire to leave the confines of the seraglio was based on the chance of approaching another European and he rode close beside her, never relaxing his watch. He would have to think of something else—but what? The girl was in a weakened condition already from the strains of the miscarriage, and painfully thin to begin with. Muhad Bey would simply tell him he must force her to eat—the responsibility would be his. He brushed the flies away from his jowly cheek with an impatient hand. All very well for him—but what is there to do? She is determined, and I am certain of this—Muhad Bey has never made the acquaintance of a woman whose determination matches this one.

Leita adjusted her body to the rise and fall of the little donkey's back. She felt faintly dizzy, as she did now most of the time. They would have to do something soon. She would be no good to them if she became ill—really ill. Muhad Bey's eight hundred piastres wouldn't be forthcoming if she continued this fast. And it wasn't difficult now; the very thought of food made her ill.

Daniel O'Connell came loping out into the marble-paved hall of the American Embassy and shook Breve's hand with enthusiasm.

"By God, old fellow, you got here! Can't tell you how pleased I am. Do you have a hotel yet?"

Breve grinned with pleasure at his vigorous, cheerful, newly-made friend. Daniel was tall and broad chested with straight black hair and a small, neatly trimmed black beard. The pink and white of his Irish complexion was tinted darkly by the Egyptian sun and clear, cornflower blue eyes peered out from under heavy black brows. He had a strong grip and only relinquished Breve's hand after drawing him into his office, a rather imposing one, too, Breve thought, looking up at the fiercely glaring American eagle on the wall over the desk.

"And now for a drink," Daniel said expansively. He poured bourbon into a glass, siphoned soda over it and dropped in an ice cube. "Compliments of the house, Breve. And here is a toast to a pleasant and informative visit. When did you get in?"

When Breve replied that he had been in Cairo a scant three hours Daniel laughed.

"Well, you haven't had time yet for the heat to destroy you. Actually I just came back in from the siesta. From one o'clock to five everything closes down here, as far as Europeans are concerned anyway, and most of the Egyptians for that matter. The bazaar stays open but the trade is minimal."

"I know. I walked through there."

"Well, you will see more than that. Now, there's no point in our sitting here when we can be out and around. Drink up, man, and we'll be off."

Breve grinned and downed the rest of his drink. They were in the hall when Daniel struck his forehead.

"I forgot. You have quite a pile of mail waiting for you. I've kept it in my office." He dashed back in and returned to hand Breve a leather pouch.

They went to the Hotel du Nil with Daniel leading the way. He inspected the room that had been allotted to Breve and approved it while Breve stripped his shirt off and splashed himself with cool water and then shaved before they set out.

511

"Don't you want to look at your mail?" Daniel inquired.

Breve shook his head. "It's only business. It can wait." He hadn't opened the pouch.

"Well, I didn't exactly steam anything open, old man, but several of your missives were penned in a very feminine hand, and there is quite a bit of recent mail from Paris. I'll be glad to wait and stare at the ceiling while you take a glance at it. Better still, I'll pour us both a drink."

Breve hesitated. The feminine hand could be explained as Mae Schneider, but the mail from Paris? Quite a bit of it? He may as well look and at least see who it was from. Could Leita have written to him?

"All right, but make mine light. We have a long night ahead of us and I want to be able to see what I'm looking at," he laughed, and untied the pouch.

Several thick envelopes from his office in Chicago, and sure enough, three letters from Mae Schneider. He was going to have to do something about breaking that off when he returned. He had entered into the liaison more from a gentlemanly inability to refuse her than for any other reason. Well, he would simply tell her straight out. He had no desire to add any more horns to Schneider's already decorated brow. Ah, but Mary Jo Tillett, now that was a different matter. He remembered with a sharp sting of contrition how harshly he had put her off, refusing to listen to her. He would read her letter and write to her immediately. But there were two—he opened them both and chose the one with the earliest date. Daniel handed him a tall, cool drink and gave him a friendly smile, then walked out onto the balcony where he stood sipping his own. He's a considerate fellow too, Breve thought. I'm glad I came. Then he began to read the flowing, hasty handwriting. The story of Leita's sudden marriage to a man she had only been friendly with unfolded in short, sharp sentences. Breve's brow drew together sharply at the recounting of the news of his marriage and the effect on Leita. Her marriage had taken place only forty-eight hours later.

He finished the letter and threw his head back against the chair and a long sigh escaped him. Who in hell was the fool who had written that rumor, and all the way to France? A rumor that had changed two lives, changed them irrevocably. His face was dark with anger and he rose and paced the room twice, then struck his fist against the wall. What could be done? Nothing could be done! It was that simple—or was it? So that was what she had meant when she said she was not in love? And he had torn her to pieces with his scorn when she had been trying to tell him. Jesus Christ! Daniel looked in at the sound of Breve's fist hitting the wall and decided to maintain his exile on the balcony. He wished he hadn't urged his friend on to whatever bad news had been contained in the pouch.

Breve picked up Mary Jo's second letter, already opened, and scanned it, then with brows raised over eyes still bloodshot with anger he read it again. Disbelief fought with alarm and he rummaged through the pile of envelopes. There—the crest of the Comte du Favre! He slit it open and read it carefully, read again the story of the confrontation with Darcy Rankin and the subsequent truth about Jack Hidel and, unbelievably, Leita's pregnancy following his attack on her at St. Cloud. Breve threw the letter down as if it had been a live, quivering snake. God above, the man he saw meeting her was a near-lunatic! And she had gotten onto a train with him, obviously not recognizing him in his disguise! And he had stood there and watched it! That had been the very day she had disappeared, because of a note in a forged hand! He seized the

513

decanter of liquor and poured a glass half full before he siphoned the soda water into it. But at least they knew something. Marseilles had been scoured. Every hansom driver questioned, every dockmaster and the passenger lists checked. They had found the hansom driver who had taken a young woman matching Leita's description to the wharf. She had been accompanied by a man whom Breve knew to be Jack Hidel, since he had seen him in his false imperial and mustache. There had been some confusion about his identity in Paris, but the Comte du Favre was of the opinion that it was Hidel, despite the disparity in description. Damn well it was him, Breve thought, and I know where he is now. He is right here in Cairo. The ship captain remembered Leita as a very ill young woman. "Could barely walk," was his report, and Breve's jaw clenched. What in God's name had he done to her? What had he done with her now, here in this stinking, teeming city—a sick and pregnant girl in heat that robbed even healthy Europeans of their vitality.

He called Daniel in from the balcony. "I'm afraid our evening's outing is off, Dan. There is someone I've got to find here in Cairo and it can't wait."

"Someone you've got to find? Tonight? Where is he?"

"That's just it. I don't know. I saw him today, as a matter of fact. That's why I know he's here. Otherwise I would be off to Alexandria because that was their destination." Breve's eyes were diamond hard and far away.

"He's no friend, believe me. And he doesn't know me. Or at any rate he probably wouldn't remember me. That much will be in my favor at least."

"You're rambling. The heat and lack of food has gotten to you," Daniel said cheerfully. "Come along, and we'll take care of at least one thing. You have to eat, you know. In this climate food every few hours is a real necessity."

In the hotel dining room which was vast and half-empty at this early hour, the overhead fans whirred like giant locusts and the white cloths and sparkling glass-ware denoted a careful hand somewhere.

"You'll find some of the best food in Cairo in the hotels run by the French. They bought two in order to accommodate their own tastes and they're usually overrun with customers."

Delicate little crab claws were set before them with a red, spicy sauce and Daniel dug in. Breve considered for a few moments. He had no appetite, none at all. The waiter brought the wine, turning the label for inspection and Breve nodded without looking. When his glass was filled he took a sip and dismissed the waiter.

"Something has really set you back on your heels," Daniel observed, gnawing on a piece of the flat Egyptian bread.

"Yes, and I'm going to tell you what it is. If you can stand a long story, that is. Furthermore, I'm going to need your help."

Shortly after Breve began his recital Daniel set down his fork and listened raptly. His crab legs went untasted and the wine reached room temperature as Breve continued on, not leaving out a detail, from the reason for his trip to Paris to the story that Sir Charles Hidel had revealed.

"My God man? This loony has actually kidnapped this girl—and she is going to have a baby?" Daniel was wide-eyed, his brows almost touching his forelock.

"Exactly, Dan. And I've got to find her," Breve stated unequivocally and finally took a deep swallow of the pale wine.

"But all you know is that he got her onto a steamer

headed for Alexandria. There are thousands of Europeans in Alexandria. That is the main center for the canal affairs."

Brève held up his hand. "I didn't finish. I saw him this morning, Dan. Quite by accident. It was around midday really and I had stopped to eat on the terrace of the Luxor Hotel. He wasn't wearing the Guards' uniform. He was done out in gray and I didn't recognize him at first. There was just something vaguely familiar about him—you know the feeling."

Dan nodded.

"It was when he got up and walked away that it came to me. It was the very same man, I'm dead sure of that. So I know he is in Cairo now. I intend to spend this evening in finding them. He must have her locked in a hotel room somewhere."

Dan pursed his lips thoughtfully. "There are only four other hotels in Cairo where a European would put up. The rest of them I would dismiss—no European would tolerate the conditions. It won't take long to cover the four. We'll go to it, just as soon as we've eaten. I really think you ought to eat a little. This has been what you might call upsetting and you had better keep yourself in tiptop shape."

Breve ate indifferently of the fish, which tasted rather like mud, he thought, and hastily gulped down half a slice of roast lamb and a bowl of rice. When he stood up, Daniel rose just as quickly.

At the reception desk Breve was relieved to hear that Daniel's Arabic was surprisingly fluent. He wrote down the name of the man they were seeking and displayed his credentials as the Vice-Consul which served to put the desk man on his mettle. The guest book was presented to them and they pored over its pages. The clerk had already told Daniel that he could recall no

516

one with such a name as having been registered there but they checked back over the thickly-written pages just in case. Then, at Breve's behest, Daniel described Jack Hidel. The desk clerk watched and listened; Daniel employed gestures too, but the clerk finished by a negative movement of his sleek, dark head. He was most sorry, but no; he knew of no such man.

The two men left the hotel and strode out into the dusty street. The sky was a fiery pink and the heat was at its most intense. Breve loosened his cravat as they hastened on to the first hotel on Daniel's list.

At the end of an hour they were no further ahead. Daniel's throat was dry from his graphic descriptions of the man they sought, to no avail. There was no one by the name of Hidel registered in any of the four hotels, and no one answering that description. At the last hotel the desk clerk had been cooperative, but ignorant.

"He says he knows nothing of the man. Besides, he is only here for this evening, replacing his cousin who is sick," Daniel told Breve.

"Ask him if someone will be here tomorrow that might know." Breve said impatiently.

Daniel repeated the question in Arabic, received an affirmative answer and they left, after sprinkling a few piastres in the clerk's palm to insure that he spoke to no one of their quest. Breve insisted on this. He was not going to have Hidel forwarned. The chance of his taking Leita away quickly made Breve's blood freeze in his veins. Hidel was in Cairo now, and he mustn't be alarmed into dashing off to another spot in this teeming, God-forsaken country.

Daniel spoke earnestly over the bottle of chilled wine he had procured in a street cafe. "We have to consider that the fellow isn't using his real name. He was divested of it back in England, if I have the story right."

517

Breve nodded, his eyebrows furled in concentration. "I have to face the possibility that he isn't in a hotel where we could easily find him. He may very well have taken a house of some kind where he can keep Leita locked up more easily than in a hotel."

"Damn and blast! I hadn't thought of that!" Daniel struck his fist on the table.

"That's probably why we've run up against a stone wall," Breve said angrily. "He could hire someone to watch over her while he goes strolling around Cairo."

"You can hire someone to do almost anything here," Daniel assented gloomily. "What you describe could be managed, with enough gold, that is."

"Oh, he's well supplied there. The Count's letter said that his uncle had ascertained that Hidel emptied his bank accounts in England, and the one he kept in France. They were sizable, too. It seems the fellow has always been a tightwad and just sat on his money." Breve's tone was morose. "He came prepared, the devil did. But he hasn't got long now. I'll hunt him down—and he'll know what fear is when I find him."

Daniel glanced quickly at his friend's face. Breve's eyes were dark with fury and the muscles in his jaw were jumping as if they had a life of their own.

"And what are you going to do when you find her? What about the two of you, I mean? Things are very tangled up, aren't they?" Dan inquired with a worried frown.

Breve's face hardened. "She'll have to be returned to her husband. She's a married woman." He drank down the rest of his wine and refilled both their glasses.

"What if she doesn't want to go back to him, now that you're here?" Dan asked gently.

"Her husband and her brother are on their way to Alexandria right now," Breve said shortly.

Daniel drew in his breath and then shook his head. "I see," he said and took a thoughtful sip of his wine.

"I have an ace in the hole, you know," Breve remarked. "Even if Hidel has taken a house somewhere in this labyrinth of a city, I know he goes out. I saw him today, remember. And I'll find him. There are only so many places a European in Cairo would frequent, right?"

Daniel concurred. "A few restaurants, some cafes, the better hotels, and of course, the bazaars. Can't think of any others."

Breve pondered this and Daniel watched him with curiosity. He sensed the latent strength of the fury Breve contained and Daniel hoped that someone else was around when Breve found this Hidel. He's quite likely to kill him on the spot, Daniel thought, and that could be messy—that could cause some trouble for this forceful man.

Breve stroked the stem of his glass. "Do you have any friends here, Dan, anyone we could bring in on this?"

"You mean watchers, someone else to spot him?"

"That's right. We have quite a bit of territory to cover. A couple of others, here and there at the hotels and cafes—it would help."

Daniel spoke without hesitation. "It will be done. I'll charge off now and round up a couple of good fellows I know." Daniel rose and Breve stretched out his hand.

"I can't thank you enough, Dan."

Daniel O'Connell smiled a wide, Irish smile. "Don't mention it. And don't tear yourself up any more than you have to. This fellow Hidel is a dead duck."

Breve laughed. "Maybe you'd better give me the names of a few places to drop in now—places that might attract that murderous idiot."

Daniel obliged and agreed to meet Breve in two hours at a cafe that was frequented by both Egyptians and Europeans, then left on his quest.

Breve went off on foot. He visited one cafe after another, finding a seat in the dusky, smoky interiors, peering through the lamplit gloom at tables occupied by a mixture of Frenchmen, English, Greeks, Armenians and a heavy scattering of Germans. He made the acquaintance of quite a few of these and managed to inquire after other Englishmen in the city—saying that he was looking for a cousin named Prewitt who might be traveling with a friend whose name he couldn't remember, but could describe. The description had elicited no information so far, but Breve didn't despair. His jaw was set; sooner or later he would come on his trail. But all the while something was troubling him—some memory was eluding him, and he knew it was important.

In the cafe where he had arranged to meet Daniel he sat at a table in a corner, watching two male dancers. Daniel had said that the place was noted for an accomplished and popular dancer named Abydos. The music was loud and shrill as the muscular Egyptian moved his body sinuously on the dance floor. Tambourines and drums and two high-pitched flutes accompanied his gyrations and the crowd was stamping and calling out as a clatter of piastres hit the floor now and again. Daniel's tall frame hunkered through the low doorway and he joined Breve.

"The fellow is a bardash, you know. Richer than Croesus by now. He's one of the most popular in the city," Daniel observed.

"What is a bardash?" Breve inquired.

"A male prostitute." Daniel laughed. "I told you that anything can be bought here, remember? But Abydos is getting a little long in the tooth, now. It's the younger ones who are the most sought after. The other fellow that just got up to dance with him—he's on his way up in the world."

Breve watched the younger man's slender frame, oscillating, thrusting his hips forward, while the little gold cymbals on his fingers clanged together. "Christ almighty! What's next?" Breve breathed.

"Exactly. But the Arabs are pretty strong on that kind of thing. There is a time in a Moslem's life when he is supposed to do without women, and they think this makes a nice change. The bardashes do a roaring business in the baths."

"The baths?"

"That's right. You haven't seen them yet. Big, cavernous places with huge pools of heated water. Everyone goes to them. Water is quite a valuable commodity in Egypt, as you can imagine, and the public baths serve a real purpose. You can have a nice, warm loll in the water for a moderate sum, and a massage and a rubdown, and they also get anything else they might care to pay for from the bathboys. Seriously, they're very sociable places. Men meet there every day or so, precisely as they would in a club back home. They're patronized by the Europeans, too."

Breve looked at him.

"Of course—I hadn't thought of that. We'll have to keep a watch on the baths, definitely. Johnny Devlin is going to cover the restaurants and Mike Laren will see to the cafes, with my help, of course."

"And I'll cover the baths and spot-check the other places," Breve said, and sat back to watch the spectators, his eye on the entrance. Something still nagged at the periphery of his mind, some small detail that he felt was important, but couldn't put his finger on. He let his mind wander now as he looked around, hoping it would come to him.

521

It was odd, this city; he had eaten in a hotel dining room, drunk in an outdoor cafe and visited several others—and had seen only men. No rustle of skirts, no brilliantly colored gowns, no white shoulders and shining curls. There had been female dancers in several of the cafes, but their dark skin and balloon-like trousers were so exotically foreign that they seemed unfeminine. The audiences, the people frequenting the streets at night, were all men. He had seen a few women that afternoon, most of them draped in the black of the poor, their faces obscured by the yashmak, or veil. Leita would certainly be conspicuous in Cairo. There were a few European women, Daniel had said, but so far Breve had seen none and he could imagine Leita on the terrace of one of the hotels, her red-gold hair shining in that brilliant sun. The girl he had seen in the bazaar, with her big, violet eyes in that dark little face—if her skin had been lighter, say, and her hair a different color, she would have been Leita's twin. He recalled the planes of that face, thrown into stark relief by the bright sun, the dark hair swept back from her forehead. Then his whole body grew still.

He drew in his breath and sat with his eyes closed for a moment, a long moment, as he held the vision in his mind. Then his fist struck the table, knocking over Daniel's glass as well as his own and tipping the oil-filled lamp onto its side.

Daniel grabbed at the lamp and set it upright, then jumped and began mopping at the front of his trousers. Breve brushed at his own clothing where the sour wine had scattered over it.

"Did you decide to set the place on fire?" Daniel asked, only half-joking.

Breve clasped his friend's shoulder. "I just remembered something, Dan! Something that has been nagging at me for hours now. Something that I saw without noticing, if you know what I mean."

"Well, out with it." Daniel grinned and beckoned to the turbaned waiter for more wine.

"I saw her, Dan! I hadn't been in Cairo two hours when I saw her. I saw Leita!"

"You saw her, and you forgot it?" Daniel was wonderfully puzzled.

Breve told him about the dark-skinned woman in the goldsmith's shop—the woman who looked so much like Leita.

Daniel relaxed. "There's a lot of mixed blood here Breve, from centuries of intermarrying. Egyptian women usually have black eyes, but there is an occasional exception. You just happened to see one."

"That's what I thought, too. Until just a minute ago." Breve's chuckle was so lighthearted that Daniel felt a pang of anxiety for the disappointment he knew Breve was headed for. "I told you earlier that something had been nagging at me, something I couldn't remember. Well, I decided a minute ago to quit trying to remember and just let my mind wander where it would—and then it happened. I was thinking about that woman standing there in the bright sunlight. She moved her head and the headcovering slipped back a little. Her hair was coal-black, a dull, dead black."

"And you said Leita was blonde," Daniel protested.

"But, that's what I saw, without it registering till now. Her hair was black, yes—but it was gold at the roots!"

Daniel blinked and stared at Breve.

"Don't you see? Her hair had been dyed! The sun illuminated her face sharply, and her hairline. That hair was a bright gold at the roots—a good half-inch of bright gold!"

Breve rose. "Come on, let's go out and get some fresh air."

Daniel followed him through the low arch of the doorway and into the cool, night air. The moon hadn't risen yet and the night was dark, but stars were brilliant in the indigo sky overhead.

"For Christ's sake, Dan! She had hair the color of Leita's! And no one has hair that color and light brown skin. It was Leita. He disguised her the same way he disguised himself—hair dye and stain on the skin. Now do you see what I'm talking about?"

"It's the damnedest thing I ever heard of. Egyptian women don't dye their hair," Daniel said wonderingly. "You say she was dressed in yellow?"

."Yes, a yellow, silky stuff."

"The clothing of a wealthy woman. Are you actually saying that you believe this fellow has gotten her up to look like an Egyptian woman?"

"What better way of hiding her?" Breve said.

"None, when it comes right down to it," Daniel assented. "But, was he with her?"

"No." Breve reflected for a moment, remembering vividly the scene he had walked away from just hours ago. "There was a big man beside her. Not too tall, you understand, but fat, and dressed in a white robe with a striped one over it. Had a belly like a barrel."

"Sounds like a eunuch."

Breve looked at him quizzically.

"They work in the seraglios—the harems. The Moslems trust them with their women, of course, because their 'boules d'amour' were cut off when they were young. They can be pretty tough, though. They're crafty fellows."

"That would be logical—to hire a eunich to guard her. A man strong enough to see that she couldn't get away, but she couldn't influence him either. My God, it was her, Dan! And I looked at her and just walked away!"

"You didn't even know then that she had been kidnapped," Daniel offered.

"No—but I should have known something, from the way I felt when I saw her. This probably means that he took a house and is keeping her in it, with the fat fellow as a guard."

"Sounds like it. Which makes our task a little more difficult. Do you remember the shop? Could you find it again?"

"I'll find it like a shot. In fact, that's where we're going now," Breve said determinedly.

"It will be closed, man, closed up tight with bars too, most likely, considering what they sell in there."

"I'll get him up," Breve said brusquely. Daniel shrugged. "Wait—that might not be a good idea. It would make my search pretty conspicuous. I'll wait till morning before I buttonhole that old fellow."

"That's a better idea," Daniel said, with relief. "Don't go tearing down the bazaar your first night here. You could use some sleep, too, I expect. And I'm ready to drop right here in the gutter."

"All right. Till morning then," Breve agreed.

Breve stood on the balcony outside his hotel room. The sky was a nappe of blue velvet with brilliant white stars cut out of it. The shadows of the buildings were marked with orange lights here and there. Cairo stretched out before him with the Nile a shimmering gray silk ribbon running beside it. And somewhere, somewhere in those shadows Leita lay. He saw her in his mind's eye as he had seen her many times, her cheek on the palm of one hand, her lashes still on her cheek. Somewhere, but where? He came near to dressing again and going out into the streets to search for her. It was maddening—that she should be so near and yet hidden from him.

"Wherever you are, I'll find you!" His hands clenched the still-warm railing of the balcony as he spoke his vow aloud.

Chapter 32

THE NEXT MORNING HE BREAKFASTED QUICKLY AND headed for the bazaar. The shop was open, but just barely. A spindly-legged boy was plying a rush broom tiredly over the steps. Breve entered the still-cool darkness and looked around. The smell of coffee was heavy in the air and the old gentleman with the white beard sat cross-legged on a beautiful carpet, sipping at a tiny cup of coffee. He pressed his chin against his chest as he inclined his head in Breve's direction and waved his bony hand toward the counter, mumbling something in Arabic. Breve decided to exercise diplomacy and spent some time looking at the pieces of jewelry. A slurping sound came from behind him and he turned to see the old man dipping his fingers into a bowl of something that looked like hot gruel, sucking it off his fingers with grunts of pleasure and dipping them again. Breve smiled at the sight.

"What are you eating?" he asked companionably, but with little hope of an intelligible answer.

The old man held the bowl out to Breve and made dipping motions with his fingers. "Pulse," he said. "You are welcome to share it with me."

"You speak French!" Breve was as relieved as he was astonished.

The old man's mouth opened in a toothless cavern. "Many French in Cairo." He smiled, and motioned again with his fingers. Breve decided that it would be impolite to decline the invitation and scooped up some of the hot gruel. He tasted it and grinned. It was good, a little like cornmeal mush with scraps of meat mixed in. He thanked the old man and wiped his fingers on his handkerchief, then he pointed to a gold chain. Tiny crowns were set along it and each crown was centered with a blue sapphire.

"How much?"

The old man pursed his lips and wiped at his beard as he rose. "One thousand piastres. It is very beautiful piece of work. The stones are without flaw."

He drew the necklace out after unlocking the case, and held it up. The sapphires glinted in the gray light and the gold was mellow, so finely worked that the chain folded softly in the old man's hands.

"I will give you six-hundred piastres," Breve offered.

The old man groaned. Sorrow contorted his features. "Nine hundred piastres, because you are a gentleman. Then I am robbing myself," he lamented.

Breve appeared to consider this, while the old man eyed him appraisingly. Breve's handmade boots shone and the cream-colored trousers that covered his long legs were sharply creased and of a finely woven light wool. His frock coat was a chocolate brown and beautifully cut, his linen shone and the cravat he wore was pinned with an opal stickpin. The old man noted the firm line of his jaw and decided to hold the line at eight hundred piastres. This man would pay that much, he was certain. He was not a haggler, and was obviously very rich.

"I will pay seven hundred and fifty piastres, and consider it well done." Breve smiled, aware that the old man was enjoying this.

The old man appeared to be close to tears. "My bowl would be empty if I took such prices! I will let you steal it—steal it, I tell you, M'sieur, for eight-hundred and fifty piastres!"

Breve reached into his pocket and the old man sighed. He should have held the line at nine hundred piastres. Ah well, it was still two hundred and fifty more than an Egyptian would have paid—and a Greek would have held him up even more. He took the money with pleasure and wrapped the necklace in a piece of blue silk and tied it with a blue velvet cord.

Breve put it in the breast pocket of his jacket. When his eyes had alighted on the blue sapphires he could see them adorning Leita's throat as surely as if she had been standing there. It was a good luck charm for now. He had purchased it knowing he would fasten it around her throat with his own hands. The morning was beginning well.

"I think you can help me with something else," Breve said.

The old man scurried back to the counter in anticipation of another sale, but Breve shook his head when he held up a bracelet for his approval.

"No, not that. Yesterday, when I passed your shop you were showing a necklace—that one," he pointed to a heavy pendant, "to a lady." The old man looked at him, his rheumy eyes blinking.

"The lady wore a yellow robe," Breve described, "and she had dark blue eyes—almost purple."

The old man's own eyes hooded over then, like those of a reptile.

"There was a man with her, a man with a large stomach." Breve made a gesture, a rounded sweep of his hands covering an imaginary paunch and the old man's mouth wrinkled slightly at the corners.

"She spoke French," Breve continued, determined not to leave out a detail that might jog the old man's memory. "I would like to know who she was—and who the man with her was."

The old Egyptian sucked on his lips. In the name of Allah, this big fellow was mad! To be inquiring for a woman who caught his eye just as if he had any hope of meeting her. He would not last long in Cairo if he continued at this rate. A Moslem's woman was sacrosanct. Even Europeans knew that—or should! But still, these foreigners were incomprehensible.

He shook his head, his brownish pate catching the light from the first rays of the sun entering the shop. He would not pretend total ignorance, of course, or the fellow would know he was lying. A Moslem woman who spoke French would surely be remembered.

"I do not know. They bought nothing," he shrugged. "I never saw them before," he concluded dispiritedly.

"You never saw them before? Not even the fat man?" Breve was hugely disappointed. Daniel had said that the eunuchs were well known in the bazaars. They were great jewelry buyers themselves, and being in charge of the women, they were courted by the shopkeepers.

"He was a eunuch, I think," Breve added hopefully.

"Yes." The old man's eyes twinkled. "But I do not know him. There are many such in Cairo, many. I am very sorry, M'sieur. I wish that I could help you further."

He bowed low, then swept his hand toward the

coffee sitting on the tiny burner. "Will you take coffee with me?"

Breve shook his head and declined politely. As he made his way down the narrow street the old man hobbled to the top of the steps and looked after him. A man on his way to folly, the old man thought, watching Breve's broad back as he shouldered his way through the pedestrians. His eye is caught by a woman of Muhad Bey's household, and he is mad enough to be searching for her. He reflected for a moment on the advisability of telling Hussein this choice morsel. He would, the next time he saw the eunuch. His shoulders shook with silent laughter.

That night Breve's head ached violently and his eyes burned from the dust and the searing sun. He had looked at a thousand faces, every hotel, every restaurant, every cafe that would come within the periphery of a European's patronage had been visited by him. Now he sat with Daniel, comparing notes over tall glasses of soda laced with lime juice and arak, the colorless Arab liqueur.

"He said he didn't know, but I'm positive he did. There was a flicker in the old man's eyes, by God," Breve swore.

"These natives won't tell you anything. I know that from experience. Europeans mean one thing to them—money. Aside from that they consider us animals, and incomprehensible ones at that. We're not in their club. The cultures are so far apart I wonder that we mix with them as well as we do. Centuries of invaders have flowed over them like water over stones. The old man would keep what he knows to himself, unless another Moslem was interested."

Daniel went on to report that there were a good many Europeans wearing the black imperial beard and mustache, but none had proven to be English. All Frenchmen—and furthermore none knew of the Englishman that was described to them.

"Well, we can make the rounds of the cafes before we eat. Then we'll eat in a hotel—better chance of spotting him," Breve concluded, unfazed by the day's lack of success.

They went from one cafe to another, then to the Hotel Cheops, where a quick survey of the crowded dining room proved a disappointment. They continued their search in the gathering coolness of the night and ended up at Breve's hotel at two A.M. They took a nightcap in the almost deserted bar and Breve bid his friend goodnight and went to his suite. The air was scented and cool as he leaned over the balcony again.

His body felt as tense as a spring; he was poised to act, yet powerless. Sleep was far away, he knew, and he went back down to the lobby, now dimly lit by the hanging bronze lamps. Cream-colored moths fluttered and thudded against the lamps in a suicidal frenzy. The clerk sat on a stool, his dark head resting on the desk, the papers beside his cheek trembling to the rhythm of his sleeping breath.

The air outside was cool, almost chilly, and Breve picked his way through the curled up bodies of the homeless. They slept where they could, pressed against the sides of buildings where the sunbaked clay held the heat of midday and warmed their backs. The scabby, thin limbs of the street-sleepers anguished him and he took to the middle of the street to avoid seeing them. The poor were like grains of sand here, he thought, with no future but the overpowering necessity of gathering enough scraps of food to keep alive till they were rescued by death—after which they believed they would live at ease. Perhaps that's hope enough, Breve thought dispiritedly.

The magnitude of the need defied any efforts to alleviate it; the coins dropped into the bowls held in bony hands helped for the moment only. Slavery was better, he thought. At least a man looked out for his property, kept it fed and reasonably clean.

He walked swiftly, still tense, walked till he had cut through the eastern part of the city and stood at the edge of the Nile. The water was as dark as charcoal in the night, lapping softly at the banks as it flowed past the hulls of the fellucas, the triangular-sailed ships that plied its waters. Lanterns bobbed at the prows, casting a soft light on the brightly painted hulls. Cairo was asleep; the palm fronds rustled in the breeze and the moon shone down brightly, picking the tops of the waves with an iridescent light.

The languid, monotonous murmur of the water soothed the knife-edge of his tension. He yawned, relishing the quiet after the ceaseless pandemonium of the daytime. He finally turned away from the river, reluctant to leave its phantasmic peace, and traced the dark streets back to his hotel. He sat on the edge of the bed to pull off his boots and sank back onto the pillows to think for a moment. When the muzzeins wailed at the hour before dawn he wakened; pulled the quilt up over his chest and slept again.

It was eight o'clock and the sun was beating down relentlessly when he opened his eyes. He got up and shaved, wielding the long, straight-edged razor quickly over his tanned cheeks. He shrugged into a shirt of soft lawn, picked out a jacket and then discarded it. He would go coatless and etiquette be damned.

He decided on the Hotel Luxor for breakfast. It was situated across the street from another large hotel patronized by Europeans and was a good vantage point, since he could see whoever entered or left if he sat on the terrace. He had just taken the first sip of coffee when Jack Hidel came swinging jauntily up the steps, a newspaper under his arm. Breve stopped, the cup midway to his lips, and his eyes raked over Hidel's figure as he took a seat not three tables away.

Garbed in gray again, the imperial still affixed to his chin, Jack opened his paper. Breve picked up his cup and carried it to a table at the far edge of the terrace, behind two other occupied tables. He kept a carefully concealed watch as Jack sipped coffee, cleaned a plate of its contents, and packed a pipe full of tobacco. Breve's fresh, flaky croissant went untouched.

When Hidel finally rose Breve waited a minute or two before following him. There was a good chance that Hidel would recognize him from their meeting at the Marquise de Sivry's, more so here where a European was fairly conspicuous. Jack walked swiftly, the paper still under his arm and his neck jutting forward. He skipped across the thoroughfare between two donkeys and an oncoming camel and Breve followed well behind. When he entered a stone building graced with a ceramic dome Breve's steps quickened. Hidel was going into the baths—it should be easy from now on!

The Egyptian at the counter took Breve's coins impassively and waved him on in through the wide archway. His steps resounded in the cavernous building. Before him was a spectacle, the spectacle of a high-domed ceiling where light came streaking down, reminding him of the shafts of sunlight that pierce clouds after a rain. The walls were set in brilliantly colored tiles, scarlet, turquoise, peacock blue, veined with gold; they gleamed in the faint half-light. Huge, rectangular pools, lined with the same tiles, were spaced across the floor. Steam rose from the water and the air was heavy and humid. Men lay about in the pools and lounged at the sides. Young, swarthy Egyptians walked along between the pools and squatted on their haunches, gabbling to one another.

Breve went to one of the cubicles and shucked his clothing off. When he emerged he was accosted by a young man, who spoke to him in Arabic. Breve gestured his incomprehension and essayed a sentence in French, which was understood. The young man instructed him that the first pool was cool water, the other three warmer in ascending degrees. It was customary to enter the coolest pool first. Breve decided quickly that it would be best if he and Hidel were not in the same pool, regardless of how vast they were, and, explaining that he liked warmer water he lowered himself into the second pool and lay submerged up to his neck.

And just in time, too. Hidel appeared; the skin of his body was white, an almost livid white in contrast to the stain on his neck and face. Barefooted, he walked gingerly, clutching the towel wrapped around his loins. He lowered himself into the water of the first pool hesitantly. The young man who had followed him retained his towel, squatting beside the pool while Jack laved himself with the water.

Breve's body was rigid. He was exercising all his self-control to keep from lunging at Hidel. It was essential that he be able to follow him undetected and no matter how he longed to jerk him upright and pound him into senselessness he would have to restrain his desires in order to find Leita.

Breve hoisted himself out of the last pool finally. He had been watching and saw that the other bathers went through a further archway after leaving the last pool. He walked leisurely along and the young man who attended him motioned to the open door of a small room with a high table. Breve stretched out on the table and when the young man attending him closed the door he signified that he wished it to remain open. The young man's eyebrows lifted slightly, then he set the door ajar and proceeded to smooth oil over Breve's back. Breve saw Hidel pass his doorway, then heard the door of the room next to him close.

The hands of Breve's attendant were strong and adept, gathering the hard flesh over Breve's muscles and pulling and smoothing it.

"You are not very relax, M'sieur. Muscles very tight," he observed in his heavily accented, almost unintelligible French.

Breve gave a snort of laughter. He was certainly not "very relax." That bastard lay in the room next to him and he wouldn't be "relax" until he could feel his fist strike hard into his flesh.

The massage continued. Breve could hear conversation and muffled laughter from the next room and when the attendant finally asked if that were sufficient Breve said yes, but that he would like to lie there and doze a while longer. He would pay him when he dressed. The attendant nodded, left, and returned with Breve's clothing. Breve pulled several coins out of his pocket then and there, paid the attendant and lay back down on the table. He had heard no click of the door to the next room and he intended to stay there until Jack came out. He wasn't going to lose him now. Breve lay quietly, his jaw clenched, resting his chin on his arms. The time passed slowly.

That's a hell of a long massage, he thought, feeling a second of alarm as it occurred to him that Hidel might have left the room so quietly that his ears had missed it. There was a certain amount of noise in this section. The conversations echoed off the tiles and Breve got down and pressed his ear to the partition. It was quiet—not even the sound of hands slapping flesh! Then he heard a moan. The partition was made of woven reeds and Breve quietly spread the reeds apart, making a tiny aperture.

Jack Hidel sat upright on the table, the boy attending him was bent over, his head almost pressed into Hidel's lap. Breve frowned, puzzled for a moment, then enlightenment swept over his face.

The boy, who was sixteen or so, had one hand cupped around Hidel's engorged member as his mouth moved up and down in a sliding motion. The faint moan came again and Breve turned away and began to dress. The moaning came through the partition, a trifle louder now, and finished with a gasp. Breve jerked his boots on and waited till he could hear conversation from the next room. He listened to the clink of coins and tapped his fingers impatiently on the table top. At the sound of the door opening he waited, then walked out and followed Jack onto the street.

Staying carefully behind, he followed Hidel along the main thoroughfare and then he turned off into a narrower street. Jack went into a hotel, one which Daniel had dismissed as not patronized by Europeans. It was a large, Moorish structure of clay bricks and looked rather sumptuous. Hidel walked purposefully through the lobby where a few robed Egyptians were seated, puffing at their chibouks, the black, wooden pipes which they carried with them. Jack went up the stairway at the end of the lobby and Breve turned and approached the swarthy old man at the desk. He was sipping a cup of coffee and lifted grizzled eyebrows at Breve.

"You want bed and room?" he inquired hoarsely. Breve saw that his neck was swollen; the front of it was a huge mound of flesh spilling out over his collarbone. The man has a thyroid disease of some kind, Breve thought, looking at the bulging, yellowed whites of his old eyes.

"No, I don't want a room, but I do want some information, and I will pay for it handsomely." Breve reached into his pocket and pulled out a handful of piastres. He counted out twenty and saw by the expression of astonishment and avarice on the old man's face that it would be enough.

"An Englishman just walked through this lobby. He wears a little black beard and mustache—dressed in gray. I want to know if he is staying here and, if so, what name he is using." Breve's expression was bland as he held out the coins. The old man reached out a brown-spotted hand but Breve drew back.

"My answer first," he said, just as blandly.

The old man drew a sheet of paper toward him and with trembling fingers inscribed something on it. Breve looked down and read the writing. Jack Byron, it said. Jesus Christ—he's aping Lord Byron! Breve thought, almost laughing aloud.

"How long has he been here?" he asked.

The man held up one hand and extended two fingers of the other; he closed and opened them three times.

"Three weeks, about?"

"Yes, just about," the old man repeated, carefully.

Breve dropped the coins into the dry palm. In an instant the clawlike hand disappeared into the folds of the robe. Breve pulled out ten more piastres.

"I will pay you this—ten piastres more. That is for your silence. It is important that Mr. Byron does not know that anyone has been asking about him, do you understand?"

The old man's head nodded energetically. Then he

spat onto the floor. "I not speak to the English," he said with contempt.

"Now, and this is most important. Is a lady staying with him?" Breve asked, his whole body still as he waited for the answer.

"A lady? Woman?"

Breve nodded.

A cackle burst out and the old man covered his mouth with three fingers. "English have no lady. Never see lady with him. Boys!" He made a graphically obscene gesture and Breve smiled wryly.

He left, after cautioning the man again regarding his silence. He hurried down the street, ran up the steps into the bath house, doled out a coin to the attendant and walked into the pool chamber. He looked carefully at the attendants hunkering beside the pools, then started off after one he saw just coming through the archway from the massage rooms.

"I beg your pardon, but you speak English, I think?" The question was a statement and the boy turned. He had a long, oval face with wide, dark brown eyes and a nose that curved downward. His shoulders and arms were those of a boy, still undeveloped but wiry and muscular.

"Yes, sir. I am called Tahir. You like another massage? I saw you here before."

Breve shook his head. "I need your help. And I will pay you well for it. How much do you earn here? How much money?"

Tahir eyed Breve silently. "About fifteen piastres every week." He spoke softly, looking round as he did so. There was no need for any of the others to be aware of what he garnered here. It was a large amount. He was sought after and was prone to preen himself on his popularity, but he had no intention of drawing down

539

any more jealousy from the others. They were quite capable of conspiring together and attacking him, injuring him enough to make him unable to work.

Breve considered. "I want to employ you—pay you, you understand—to follow a man. From morning through the night I want to know every place he goes, everyone he sees."

Tahir shrugged. "What will you pay?"

"I will pay you every day, when you report to me, fifteen piastres. As much as you make here in a week."

The brown eyes lit up with cupidity, then dulled. "You are lying," Tahir said flatly.

"I am not lying. This is very important work and well worth fifteen piastres every day."

"Come." Tahir led him out a side door which opened into a miniature garden. Geranium bloomed there and a jasmine bush scented the air.

"Who is this man you want me to follow?"

"The man you attended almost an hour ago. The Englishman with the black beard and mustache."

Tahir's face crinkled into laughter. "Mr. Beeron? You wish me to follow him? That is all?"

"That is almost all. You must be very careful, very sly, so that he doesn't suspect. And now, listen carefully."

Tahir craned his neck forward.

"Mr. Byron knows the whereabouts of an American lady—a lady called Leita. She wears the dress of an Egyptian woman now, but she is American. He has her hidden somewhere in Cairo. He will lead you to her, I know that. When you find where she is hidden, you are to tell me immediately—you understand?"

Tahir nodded.

"When you find her, and when I have gotten her from the hiding place, I will pay you one thousand gold piastres."

Tahir sat down suddenly on the stone bench. "You are truly lying now!"

"I am not in the habit of lying," Breve said harshly.

"You pay one thousand gold piastres to find this American woman?"

"Most definitely. Yes!" And I would pay much more than that, Breve thought, watching the boy carefully. Tahir's eyes were veiled now and he appeared to be lost in thought.

"How long are you being in Cairo?" he asked finally.

"Until the lady is found. And that had better be soon," Breve replied.

"I will go now," Tahir said, and started up.

"I am at the Hotel du Nil. My name is Breve Pinchon and my room number is 108. You will report to me there each evening at sundown, but you are to follow Byron at night, too, until he finally goes to bed—and be there early in the morning."

"Yes, yes," the boy said impatiently. "I go now. He always returns to the Hotel Mamun after the bath. I go now."

"Make sure you're careful," Breve said to him finally when they reached the street.

"Tahir slyer than many jackals!" the boy crowed and started off, his long legs forking through the crowd.

Breve hurried off to the American Consulate and collared Daniel, taking him to a cafe where they ordered a vast meal. Breve poured the wine, a smile creasing his face into more jovial lines than Daniel had seen since they sailed together.

"All right, out with it! You look like a tomcat that's been into a bowl of cream. Something has happened, hasn't it?"

Breve sipped the wine and sat back. "Wait till you hear, Danny boy. Success has crowned this morning!"

"You found him?"

"Did I! And in the flesh, very much in the flesh."
Breve's spirits were high and he stretched his arms out,
his teeth flashing in a smile.

"I had barely gotten a taste of my morning coffee—I
was on the terrace of the Hotel Luxor, and he walked
right up."

"Did he recognize you?"

"God no! He didn't even notice me. I moved off and
waited while he ate and then I followed him. He went
straight to the baths."

"He must not go every day. Paul was there yesterday, half the day. He says he's wrinkled as a prune."

"Evidently not. Might be a little rich for his blood,
every day—with what he does there," Breve said
meaningfully. "He's got a young fellow named Tahir
who gives him a massage and goes on to more personal
things."

Daniel's brows rose. "Has truck with the bardashes,
does he? Quite a fellow, our kidnapper!"

"When I think of that vermin with his hands on
Leita! I could tear his neck right off his shoulders!
Christ, what a pleasure it will be—when I'm free to get
my hands on him." Breve's face was dark with anger.

"It sounds as if it won't be long." Daniel smiled.
"Did you find out where he is staying?"

"The Hotel Mamun. Off on a little side street. Big,
imposing place, though."

Daniel scowled. "I ignored that one. It's clean
enough, luxurious even by Oriental standards, but I
never heard of a European staying there. Thought they
didn't cater to them—just rich, traveling Greeks and
Armenians."

"Well, he has been there for over three weeks. Calls
himself Jack Byron. There's a flight of fancy for you! I
talked to the old fellow at the desk, crossed his palm

542

with plenty of gold and I think he'll stay quiet. Hidel has never had a lady there, though."

Daniel frowned.

"That means one thing," Breve continued. "He has her hidden somewhere here in Cairo, in all probability with that fat eunuch watching over her. I went back to the baths and found Hidel's paramour and hired him."

"You hired him! To do what?"

"Hired him to follow Hidel. The boy knew where he was staying, and he's going to dog his footsteps and report on everything he does. He'll see me every night at sundown and report. He knows what he's looking for, too. I've promised him one thousand piastres when I have Leita back."

"One thousand piastres! Do you realize how much that is to an Egyptian?"

"I've got a faint idea. Young Tahir took off like his shirttail was on fire. I expect great things from that boy." Breve drained his wine and forked into the smoked fish.

"Breve, these catamites can't be trusted any further than a eunuch, unless you own them, of course, and then they steal you blind!" Daniel protested.

Breve gestured with his fork, emphasizing his words. "Ah, but don't forget—he doesn't get the money until I have Leita. And as for his daily wage, I will pay him every evening, but not for long. He knows I mean business."

Daniel rubbed his chin. "It's an unusual device, a bold scheme, actually. Those bardashes are cunning—have to be, they live by their wits."

"All we need do now is wait. And by the way, ask your friends to dine with us tonight, as my guests. I have to say it again, Dan, you'll never know how I appreciate all you've done."

543

Daniel grinned and finally began on his fish. "I never judged that things would be quiet around you—and how right I was."

Tahir was cooling his heels and eating a sticky, sweet sherbet, his third, while he waited for Jack to appear. He sat on a wall across the street from the Hotel Mamun. His mind was darting in and out of the shoals of his knowledge of the foolish Mr. Beeron, as he called him. He was also calculating how long he would be able to draw out this employment of his. At fifteen piastres a day it was well worth a little thought. But then, the final prize of one thousand piastres made the other seem insignificant. Should he or shouldn't he warn Hussein? Sooner or later, and probably sooner, he would have to lead the tall American to the house of his brother's master. Would Hussein take steps to foil the American's aim? If he told Hussein all of it he would definitely want half the money for himself. Would he cooperate in allowing the girl to be abducted by the American? He knew that Hussein was not happy about her presence. He had spoken of it sulkily when they met last week. Hussein should be joyous at the prospect of being rid of her. But there again, he would be afraid that the blame would fall on him if she were to escape, and Muhad Bey's wrath was no small thing. Hussein had even mentioned having the Englishman done away with, which would have been simple enough to accomplish. A few piastres would see that he was garroted in some alley. Then the monthly sum of money wouldn't have been forthcoming and Muhad Bey would not care what happened to the American lady.

In the name of Allah, he had almost forgotten! Hussein had said that the eldest son was lusting after the girl like a street dog after a bitch in heat. That made

544

things more complicated, much more complicated. Perhaps it would be best not to tell Hussein at all. Never mind, he would think it over carefully. There was time, plenty of time.

Tahir ducked down behind the wall as Jack descended the steps of the hotel. Then he padded off on his slippered feet, eeling his way through the crowd, still licking happily at his sherbet. Allah had smiled on him. Nothing to do but follow this son of a dog and eat sherbet!

That evening Tahir reported to Breve. Mr. Beeron had engaged in the most innocuous pursuits. There was no sign of an American lady. He would run back now to pursue him through the evening. He received his fifteen piastres impassively with orders to search Mr. Pinchon out at once if he came upon the American lady. He took his leave with much bowing and forehead touching and loped down the street, back to his quarry. Tahir had rather large, white teeth and they gleamed in his brown face as he ran along, listening to the chink of his piastres. Sixteen, almost seventeen, he was between a man and a boy, in many ways still boy, except for his cunning, which had been sharpened to a knife edge on the whetstone of circumstance.

The next day Daniel and Breve set out on horseback to view the Suez Canal. A horde of workmen and a waterway wide enough to accommodate ocean-going vessels lay before their eyes.

Another year at the most and the canal would be completed. The Empress Eugenie was to sail to Egypt to officiate at the opening ceremonies and a huge, ornate opera house was being built on the edge of Cairo. Tannhauser had been commissioned to compose an opera to inaugurate the opening. Egypt was prosperous and the European investors were full of optimism.

They rode hard back to Cairo to be in time for Tahir's appearance at Breve's hotel. Breve left Daniel, having arranged to meet him later for dinner and walked quickly from the train station in the direction of the Hotel du Nil. When he passed the side street that led to the Hotel Mamun Breve hesitated a moment, then turned and walked down the narrow street. He had ample time to reach his hotel before Tahir and curiosity drove him to the spot where he had last seen Hidel.

Breve was on the wrong side of the street and cut across through the crush of donkeys and camels. He was walking behind one little beast when his eyes lit on the saddle. It was a brilliant emerald green, ornamented with gold thread. A camel driver shouted an Arabic obscenity at him and he made a dash for the curb, narrowly escaping the sharp hooves of the camel. Then he stood and searched out the donkey again. The man holding its bridle—a purplish spot shone dark on his cheek! Daniel had said they were plague spots, a third of the people in Cairo had them—souvenirs of survival of a dreaded disease. Not a distinguishing mark, certainly. The man made a half-turn then, pulling on the donkey's bridle as he led it around a cart. There it was—the brow with the wide, livid scar cut through it! That was the fellow he had bumped into outside the goldsmith's shop! Breve tensed and his eyes narrowed, never leaving the donkey as he strolled leisurely through the crowd. The scent of pulse, the hot gruel that was the common food of so many, steamed in the air and the slave—he surely was a slave, plodded forward on slippered feet.

He may not have been awaiting Leita that day, but I'm not leaving that to chance, Breve thought. Where he goes, I go. Then Breve stopped and backed up against the warm brick of a shop building. The slave had stopped outside the Hotel Mamun—directly in front! He drew the donkey close to the curb and stood there, immobile as a statue. Breve waited, scarcely moving. The donkey was not for hire, he knew. The little beasts that were rented as taxis were not done up so handsomely as this one. It was young and well-fed, its sides sleek and its little hooves painted black. The gold on its bridle denoted it as the possession of a family of wealth.

Breve's eyes never left the slave, who watched the passers-by with the air of one who was detached from this fetid, milling mass of humanity. His galabiah was clean, he was lean but not emaciated, and he was obviously prepared to wait. Five minutes passed, then another five. Then Jack Hidel appeared in the shadow of the arched entrance and descended the steps. The slave stepped aside, not hastily but with a minimum of courtesy and Jack mounted the little donkey.

Breve expelled a long breath. This was the connection! The plague-marked slave *had* been awaiting Leita that day, and now Jack Hidel was on his way to her. Chance and tenacity, plus his usual good fortune, had led him to this spot at the right time.

It was chance that led me to Egypt, Breve thought as he beckoned to a donkey driver, or maybe it was fate. He mounted the little donkey and signified that he simply wanted to ride. He had decided on the spur of the moment that he would be more conspicuous on foot.

The buildings blotted out all but a few rays of the setting sun as Breve followed Jack's mount into ever narrower streets. The dusk was short here; no long twilight, just a brilliant scarlet sunset and then night. All to my advantage, Breve thought.

He kept well behind Hidel and the slave who loped alongside the donkey with the green saddle. The streets were no more than narrow lanes now. Breve kept a careful watch at each turning since Hidel was far enough ahead to be lost easily in the maze of intersections that sprang up every so often. Breve patted one trouser pocket lightly. The small derringer that he carried was effective only at short range, but its finely rifled barrel was trustworthy at six feet or so. He regretted that he hadn't worn his coat. His revolver fit well in the specially padded breast pocket of all of his coats. He shrugged. The derringer would be enough, if it came to that.

Dark had fallen inexorably in the fifteen or so minutes since Hidel stepped out of his hotel. Breve deliberated, then jumped down from the donkey and pressed several coins into its owner's grimy hand. He could travel as fast as the donkey trotted and his movements could be more flexible now.

He loped along in the shadows of the buildings, picking his way through families seated cross-legged around their braziers, enjoying the first cooling breezes of evening while their supper cooked. The narrow lane led into a wide thoroughfare and Breve strode along easily on this less congested pathway. Then he drew up sharply and stepped into a doorway. Hidel's donkey had stopped.

Across the way was a long white wall, covered with vines. The slave's galabiah was a faintly luminous white in the shadowy night when suddenly there was a flare of light. A gate opened and a blazing torch illuminated Hidel slipping down from the donkey's back. The slave followed him through the gate and then slowly, the gates shut behind them, blotting out the light.

Breve stood in the darkness. So this was it. Leita must be behind those walls. His tall, muscular body was tensed and his heart thudded, the blood pounding in his ears. He jumped and struck out when something pulled at his sleeve. Then he looked disbelievingly at Tahir who had materialized at his side out of nowhere.

Tahir's whisper cut through the night. "I followed you, M'sieur. When you were not at your hotel I went back to the Hotel Mamun. I have a friend there, who told me that Mr. Beeron went off on a mount attended by a slave. I followed, and saw you. I have something to tell you, M'sieur."

"Well, what is it?" Breve muttered. This fellow was a slick one, all right. It hadn't occurred to him to look behind him.

"The lady you search for is in this house. It is the house of the slave-trader, Muhad Bey."

"How do you know this?"

"Because my brother serves Muhad Bey. He is no longer a man—he is a eunuch and in charge of Muhad Bey's gynacaeum."

"What is a gynacaeum?" Breve whispered impatiently.

"The harem, M'sieur—Muhad Bey's wives and concubines. My brother Hussein told me this afternoon of the American lady." Tahir had decided that this lie was as good as another. While following Breve he had realized that he could retain his knowledge of Leita's captivity no longer. It was obvious that Breve would pursue Hidel all the way to the house of Muhad Bey and Tahir would lose the fortune he had been promised if Pinchon learned of Leita's imprisonment on his own. The news must come from him and quickly.

Breve bit his lip. The wall was a full six feet high. And what would he do when he was over it? He would stand out like a sore thumb.

"Tell me, where is the lady? Where is the harem inside those walls?"

Tahir frowned. "It is at the far end, the last pavilion

to the south. I have been inside a time or two, but not in the gynacaeum. It is certain death to go there."

"If I am caught, you mean," Breve said wryly. "Now listen, I want you to run fast and get me a robe like yours. It must be broad across the shoulders and I don't care how you get it. Just run like hell back here." Breve sprinkled coins into Tahir's palm.

Tahir disappeared into the night. As he ran his mind raced. The crazy American was going to try to get into Muhad Bey's house now, dressed as an Egyptian! Why else would he want the robe? He would be caught—his throat slit without ceremony, and Tahir's one thousand piastres would be only a dream. He must do something!

Chapter 33

LEITA WAS BEING DRESSED, AND LISTENING TO THE outcry Yaquim was making. Yaquim's voice rose in shrieks, the Arabic syllables following one another like waves in a brook. She was having a tantrum, screaming that she was ill—that she had been poisoned! Dear little Yaquim! She had promised Leita that she would find out when the Englishman was to call and somehow insure that Leita could get out of the seraglio and into the other part of the house to see him, even if it meant drugging Hussein. Yaquim's velvety eyes had flashed with indignation. Seeing Leita so ill had roused her spirit and she felt that though a life of impoundment in a harem was in the natural scheme of things for her, for Leita to be held prisoner with no kin or countryman to aid her when she lay near death was an injustice not to be borne. Leita was a foreigner, far away from her own land, and as such to be pitied, particularly since she would undoubtedly fall seriously ill again if her dangerous, self-imposed fast continued.

551

That morning Yaquim had learned through a servant that the Englishman was to dine with Muhad Bey that evening. Up till now Jack had only seen Leita through the tracery of a latticed partition. She had refused to see him prior to her miscarriage but he had called frequently to assure himself that she was being well-cared for. But now, when everything depended on getting to him, she was to be kept away!

The pitch of Yaquim's shrieks was rising. Her ruse would be effective, she had assured Leita. Rivalry among the wives was a common thread of discord in any seraglio. It was not unusual for one or all of them to drug the drink of a favorite when they knew that their lord and master was to pay a nocturnal visit. The favorite, drugged, could not be awakened, and this induced irritation and displeasure in the husband. The ways of a seraglio were contorted and kept in an uproar by such intrigues. A servant could be bribed to bring in a tiny vial of opium. Yaquim was definitely the favorite of Muhad Bey and the likely focus of such a scheme. Now she ranted and screamed. Hussein was attempting to mollify her and the other wives stood around sullenly, angry at the accusations pouring from the girl. In a minute or two she would offer the cup of apricot nectar to Hussein, insisting that he drink it if he were so certain it was harmless.

Leita sat down heavily. She was weak, so very weak. Yaquim had drawn her a little plan of the pavilions, pointing out the courtyard where Muhad Bey entertained visitors. It was the same one where Leita and Hidel had met with him on that fateful first day which seemed so long ago now. Leita wondered if she would be able to walk that far without fainting.

Hussein was becoming frantic. He had still not informed Muhad Bey of her fast and he spent hours by her side, pleading with her to just taste this morsel—did she want to die, away from home and unknown? Leita sat adamantly during these importunings. She had declared that she would eat when she had been allowed to see the Englishman, to tell him the truth of her condition, and not until. She thought Hussein was almost at the point of weakening but knew that he would not dare to contravene his master's orders. But tonight—tonight would see the end of it! She sat pensively, waiting for the uproar to cease. That would be the signal that Hussein had tasted and drunk the drugged nectar to prove to Yaquim that she wasn't the object of a plot.

It was dark now and the torches were lit. Leita waited and finally Yaquim pattered up to her and sat down.

"Hussein has gone back to his pavilion," she whispered sibilantly. "He hasn't yet partaken of the evening food. He will be asleep in no time. You must take the way through the side pavilion as I told you, and stay close to the wall. Don't forget to turn right at the third fountain."

There was no servant posted outside the second pavilion and Leita breathed more easily. Yaquim had seen to that, too, bless her! She skimmed along, staying in the shadow of the wall. When she stopped at the courtyard of the third fountain she heard a murmur of conversation. Her knees were trembling and cold perspiration bathed her face. She was weak beyond belief and she sank down onto the cool tiles, panting and trembling. She rested there a few moments, knowing she was in danger of being seen, but unable to rise. Finally she struggled upright and walked slowly, ducking into the shadows of the pillars. When she came to the inner courtyard she peeked around the corner.

Oh, thank God! There he was! She had never thought she would be glad to see that monster again but now she trembled with relief and tears spurted into her eyes.

They were sitting on cushions with bowls of hot food and plates of fruit spread out before them. Leita gathered up her courage and her strength and swept into the light, half-running toward the pair seated at the end of the courtyard.

Jack Hidel saw her and his eyes widened in surprise. He stood up. This was most gratifying! She had refused to see him, refused emphatically—and now here she was! He peered, anxious to see if she had fleshed out since he left her here.

Muhad Bey's deep-sunk eyes were dark upon Leita; his fingers holding a piece of mutton had stopped halfway to his mouth.

"I lost the baby!" Leita cried and pressed her hands to her bosom. Her heart was pounding so she could barely hear her own words. She spoke again and the words came out in a gasp. "I lost the baby! I had a miscarriage! You have to let me go now!"

Jack's pale blue eyes grew wider. "She is lying, isn't she?" He addressed Muhad Bey.

"Of course she is lying," Muhad Bey answered smoothly, but his eyes were grim.

"I am not lying. They won't tell you because he wants your money! They are keeping me prisoner. They wouldn't let me see you. I am here now because I crept out without anyone seeing me. I am not going to have your baby! You must believe me!"

Jack peered at her suspiciously. The torchlight flickered over her and he could see how pale and sunken her cheeks were. Could she be telling the truth? A bitter, raging disappointment welled up in him. It couldn't be! He must have that child!

'You lie!" he screamed. His voice rose higher. "You lie! It's a trick!"

Fadim entered, having heard the commotion. He looked questioningly at his father. Muhad Bey inclined his head slightly toward him, his eyes veiled.

"It is well you see through her tricks, M'sieur. She is a clever one." Muhad Bey spoke indifferently, then clapped his hands together. A manservant appeared. "This lady is to go back to the seraglio," Muhad Bey commanded. "She is disturbing us."

Fadim flinched as the servant took Leita's arm. She was helpless against his strength and collapsed to her knees.

"Send Hussein to me immediately," Muhad Bey whispered to the servant standing behind him.

Jack stood, his fists clenched at his sides. Leita called out to him. "You will see! You will have to believe the truth. No food has passed my mouth for eight days now. I said I would fast until I saw you to tell you the truth and they still refused!"

Leita pulled at her robe, unfastening it. The servant picked her up then, at a soundless command from Muhad Bey. She struggled, managing to bare her abdomen and screamed. "Look! Do I look as if I'm with child?"

The servant took long steps, carrying her out of the courtyard quickly. Fadim laced his fingers together and pulled on them nervously. Jack subsided, but still didn't sit down. None of them saw the dark-robed figure in the shadows of the pillared passage that led up one side of the courtyard.

Leita sagged wearily in the wiry arms of the slave. She had tried. And no matter how Muhad Bey lied, Jack could not be certain now. He would insist on seeing her—and one way or another he would finally

555

become convinced. But what if he didn't? Her blood chilled at the thought. He was half-mad, she knew. If he chose not to believe it, he wouldn't. He would leave her to rot there if he couldn't face the fact that she had told him the truth. She couldn't count on him at all. Oh, God! She was so tired!

Breve had removed his boots when he donned the black galabiah. The wall had been easy. It was after he was over that the test came. The robe and burnoose were both black, rendering him almost invisible in the shadows, and he was thankful for Tahir's presence of mind in procuring dark clothing. He had heard it all, having decided to reconnoiter in order to locate his antagonists before making for the seraglio. Now he moved noiselessly in the shadows in pursuit of the tall, sinewy figure carrying Leita.

He came up behind him in the arched passageway between two courtyards and when he struck it was with a silent force. The side of his powerful hand came down at the base of the skull and the man crumpled.

Leita had seen the dark-robed figure with arm upraised the instant before Breve struck. She gasped and then screamed in alarm as the man carrying her sank to the floor. She managed to get her feet under her and ran. Her fear was so intense that it gave her strength and she flew ahead, panting with fright. Her heart thudded into her throat when the arms grabbed her and one hand covered her mouth. She bit and fought, gurgling a scream under the hard palm that was suffocating her. She kicked and tried to free her pinned arms but the grip that held her felt like a vise of steel.

"Leita! Stop fighting me for God's sake!" The whisper in her ear froze her and the grip loosened. The man turned her and threw back the hood of his burnoose. She closed her eyes for a second. She must be dreaming! This couldn't be Breve. She blinked and felt the sting of tears. Then her knees gave way as she breathed his name and her cheek was against that hard shoulder. His mouth was warm in her hair and his arms clasped her so tightly she couldn't get her breath, but she didn't care. He was here! He had come for her and would take her away. How he had found her she couldn't dream—but he had! She sobbed and his lips found her mouth in a fierce, sweet kiss.

"And now, my darling, we have to get out of here," he whispered against her cheek.

"The only way out is by the front gate. There are no side gates," she whispered.

"Then it's over the wall," he said firmly. He picked her up and in a moment had set her on her feet beside the wall.

"If you can push that pot over I can stand . . ." He followed her pointed finger to a tall pot that held a small cypress tree.

He shoved at it, straining, and it moved. He gave another powerful shove and the heavy pot was against the wall. He lifted her and she teetered on the edge when his arms suddenly fell away from her. She looked around and drew in her breath in fright. The tall, wiry slave who had been carrying her was stealing toward them, and a long blade glinted in the moonlight. When Breve turned the slave ran, abandoning all efforts at stealth. Breve thrust his hand into his robe and drew out the derringer, flipping the safety off in the same moment. He couldn't fire yet—the distance was too great for accuracy and he could take no chances. The long blade of the dagger shone now, raised high in the hand of the slave who saw his chance for a great reward if he felled this interloper who had committed the unpardonable crime of making off with a woman of Muhad Bey's household. The slave's dark eyes glittered and he drew back his arm. The dagger curved in a perfect trajectory and hit the wall where Breve had stood only a second before. His shot rang out in the same second and the slave's arms spread as if he were bent on a great embrace. Breve fired again.

Leita looked on in horror as blood spurted out of the slave's chest. He began crumpling slowly when Breve looked up, alarm twisting his features.

Hoofbeats clattered in the road on the other side of the wall and a din of shouting and thunderous banging erupted in that instant. Breve paused for a second, then shook his head. No matter what was happening, they had to get over that wall. He jumped up and lifted Leita to the top, then scaled it himself easily, dropping down onto the ground outside.

Breve held out his arms and Leita jumped into them. When he caught her he chuckled aloud, and pressed her body tightly against his own. "Good for you, my love!" he whispered, then, holding her head against his shoulder he looked around. Torchlights flared among a dozen riders who were shouting and wheeling their mounts. Three of them were banging on the gates of Muhad Bey's house.

"Let us in. Our money's good! We have gold! Let us in!"

Two riderless horses were milling around in the melee, their reins held by men on horseback. Breve peered into the flaring light, then made a run into the throng and grasped the bridle of one of the horses. The man holding it relinquished it immediately and then tipped his hat.

What in hell was going on here? Breve thought as he led the horse quickly back to the shadow of the wall where Leita stood. Whatever it was, the timing couldn't be better. With all this shouting and pounding, the household of Muhad Bey would be very nicely diverted while they made their getaway. They must think it's a brothel, he chuckled to himself.

He leaped onto the horse and taking Leita's arms as she stepped into the stirrup he swung her up in front of him. Then a cry split the air—a shrill, piercing yell issuing from the throats of the drunken Europeans clattering about on their horses. He turned in amazement. Those weren't Europeans! That was a rebel yell! The same rebel yell that had carried countless Confederate troops into battle!

He took a second to sweep his gaze over the crowd of drunks. One of the men left off battering at the gate and yelling long enough to sweep his hat in Breve's direction. The light of the torch flared over Daniel O'Connell's features and Breve burst out in a mighty roar of laughter. How Daniel had gotten there he had no idea, but he knew now this was no crowd of drunks. It was Daniel and his friends, there to create a diversion while he went about the business of freeing Leita. God bless that ebullient Irishman!

Breve dug his stockinged heels into the horse's flanks and it burst into a gallop. One arm encircled Leita tightly and he was still chuckling when he felt her sag. He slowed the horse and looked down into her face. She breathed softly, eyes closed, their long lashes shadowing her pale cheeks. She had fainted.

My God, she is thin! he thought. Kidnapped, imprisoned, a miscarriage—and she said she hadn't eaten for eight days.

"No more, darling," he whispered, "no more travail for you. Your siege is over." And perhaps mine is too, he thought. We shall see.

Leita woke to thin, gray light. The ceiling was unfamiliar; there were figures painted on it, nude females with floating, gauzy drapery. The colors of the fresco were dim. Where am I? What is this place? she wondered. She moved her head on the pillow and an American voice broke the silence.

"I'll prop your pillows up, if I may." The man who spoke was gray-haired. He had shed his boots and his stockinged feet were propped on an ottoman.

Leita's perplexed gaze evidently amused him, for he chuckled. "I am Doctor Abernathy. That young man of yours had me rousted out in the middle of the night to look after you, and here I've slept. If that constitutes a scandal, so be it."

He was very short, with a rounded, almost babyish body. His gold watch chain dangled over the sheet as he bent over her, pushing the pillows into place and she smelled the pungent odor of cigars as he supported her shoulders so that she could sit up higher in the bed.

And she remembered now—if it wasn't a dream! Breve—Breve had appeared so magically in the courtyard, and in that floppy, black robe. He had shot a man, the man who threw the dagger at them. She closed her eyes, remembering the swift, sweet kiss and bliss melted through her. She breathed deeply, almost afraid to feel such happiness.

"I don't have to ask you how you feel. I can guess. I understand you've eaten nothing for over a week, and that on top of a difficult miscarriage. Is that correct?"

Leita nodded, a weak smile transfiguring her wan face.

"Well, we shall see the end to that now. I've run for a servant and you are going to have some hot gruel. It's very tasty and you needn't eat a great deal, just a little every two hours or so. I'll wait till later to examine you. Has the bleeding stopped completely?"

Doctor Abernathy's face was square with deep wrinkles running from nose to mouth and a large, gray mustache. His eyes were benign and sharply intelligent.

Leita smiled again. "Yes, the bleeding has stopped and I will be glad to eat. Everything is all right now, isn't it?"

"If by all right you mean that you have been delivered from that Moslem devil, yes—everything is all right. It remains to be seen how you have survived your ordeal. You have had quite an adventure, young lady." His own smile was benign. He had the look of a man who had seen a great deal and Leita warmed to him.

The gruel arrived. It was thin and sweetened with honey and after the first spoonful or two, which almost gagged her, Leita began to eat with relish and ended by scraping the bowl clean.

"Is there any more?"

Doctor Abernathy laughed outright. "There is, but no more now for you. We don't want to overload your stomach, you would end by losing it all. Here, try a few of these." He offered her a bowl heaped with the pale green grapes she had learned to love.

She nibbled at them. "Where is Mr. Pinchon?" she finally got the courage to ask. She had been too afraid that it had all been a dream.

"He is in the next suite. Sound asleep too, I should think. I imagine you will see him later this morning. I understand that your husband and brother are due to arrive soon, too—either today or tomorrow."

Leita drew in her breath. "Armand is coming here? Which brother? How did they know I was here?"

"I'll attempt to answer one question at a time. My mind moves rather laboriously, you see. As to the brother, I believe Mr. Pinchon mentioned the name of Eugene. Would that be correct?"

561

"Oh, yes!" Leita pictured Eugene's mobile face and happiness flowed through her in little, tingling currents.

"You've forgotten one question, Doctor Abernathy. How did they know I was here?"

"Ah, yes. I was avoiding that; it is rather mixed up in my mind. I believe Mr. Pinchon said, when he told me this tangled tale, that he wired your husband, the Count, and your brother the day after he arrived in Cairo. He had received letters from them, I believe that's how it went—they were forwarded here, telling him of your disappearance and since he saw you that first day, saw your abductor too, if I'm correct, he wired immediately that he had set about finding you."

Leita sat up, bewildered. "He, Mr. Pinchon, saw me the first day he was in Cairo? How on earth . . . I was locked up behind those walls from the time I arrived."

Doctor Abernathy appeared a trifle surprised. "I'm positive he said he glimpsed you in the bazaar, but didn't know it was you until later. He thought it was a lady who resembled you."

Of course, the day that Hussein had taken her to the goldsmith's. To think that Breve had been there, close enough to recognize her, and she hadn't seen him! Oh, when would he come in? She wanted nothing more than to throw her arms about those strong shoulders and never let go!

Contrary to Doctor Abernathy's assumption, Breve wasn't asleep in the next suite. He was walking through the cool grayness of the early dawn, taking long strides toward his objective, the Hotel Mamun. Tahir had appeared at the door of his suite at two A.M. with the news of what had occurred after Breve rode off with Leita.

The household had been in an uproar after the drunken Europeans had finally dispersed. Tahir regarded this as his crowning achievement! He had been

562

so fearful that Breve would be intercepted and killed unceremoniously that he hastened to the American Consulate and insisted that Daniel O'Connell be summoned. He had used Breve's name and Daniel appeared to hear the story of the dangerous venture his friend had embarked upon. Daniel dismissed him, after assuring him that he would be at Muhad Bey's house shortly. Then, and only then, had Tahir procured the galabiah and returned to Breve, saying nothing of what he had done. He was quite proud of his cleverness and Breve, amused and curious, as well as grateful, had asked how Tahir had known of his friendship with Daniel O'Connell.

"Oh, I followed you, too, M'sieur, once I had Mr. Beeron well-located. I had to inform myself about you, of course. It isn't everyone that promises to pay one thousand piastres and I had to make certain that you were not a thief."

This was said with such unabashed sincerity that Breve chuckled. "Well, thank God for your caution, Tahir."

Breve counted out the piastres onto a table. Tahir stared, overcome.

"I will have my own shop now, in the bazaar. I shall be a wealthy merchant and have at least three wives," he said dreamily.

"I hope you can postpone your plans for at least a day or two. I have further need of you, Tahir."

"What do you want of me now?" he asked eagerly. He had begun to like this huge foreigner. At least he hadn't tried to cheat him.

"Mr. Byron, that's what I need you for. He isn't out of the woods yet."

"Out of the woods?" Tahir repeated, thinking he had misunderstood.

Breve chuckled. "That means that I haven't gotten

him yet, but I intend to. He has to be taken back to France to stand trial. He committed a crime, a very serious crime, when he kidnapped the American lady."

"Kidnapped? What is kidnapped?" Tahir inquired, always ready to enlarge his vocabulary.

Breve pondered for a second. "He stole her."

"Without paying for her?" Tahir was only mildly horrified.

"No, you don't understand. We do not pay for women. He tricked her—stole her away and brought her here. Her husband has been looking for her, the police in Paris have searched everywhere. It is a very serious crime."

A light had broken on Tahir's face. "Oh, he stole her from her husband! That is very serious. He will be beheaded, of course, after they tear out his intestines."

Breve looked in the young man's face. Daniel's words came back to him. "The cultures are so far apart I wonder that we mix as well as we do with them."

"A tempting prospect, but Hidel will only stand trial and be put in prison," Breve explained.

Tahir shrugged. The Englishman's fate was immaterial to him—they could do what they liked, but it seemed a very gentle way to deal with him.

"He left the house of Muhad Bey very late and went back to his hotel," Tahir offered.

"Then he must know that Leita is gone," Breve speculated.

"They found a slave. He had been shot dead," Tahir said, with a sly, upward glance.

Breve's expression didn't change and Tahir shrugged. "It will not be reported. The police would ask many questions. My brother says that Muhad Bey put his household in great jeopardy when he took the foreign woman."

Breve snorted. He had plans of his own for Muhad

Bey, but they would have to wait. "Tahir, do you know when the first train leaves Cairo this morning?"

"There is a train to Alexandria at seven hours."

"That would be the one he would leave on. I want you to go back to the Hotel Mamun and stand watch. I will be there before six o'clock. Your Mr. Beeron probably thinks he is going to get away unscathed, but he has a surprise in store."

"How much will you pay now?" Tahir inquired and Breve laughed.

"The servant is worthy of his hire," he quoted. "I will pay twenty-five piastres, my boy, and a round two hundred when I have escorted Mr. Byron to the French Consul."

Tahir grinned and tightened his sash. "I go now." And he left the room at a trot.

Breve opened the door to Leita's room and stood watching her for a moment. The lamp threw a soft, gold light over the thin planes of her face but she breathed easily, one cheek on her palm, the absurdly dark hair spread out over her pillow. Doctor Abernathy was snoring softly, his feet propped up on the ottoman. Breve walked over and touched Leita's hair gently. Her eyelashes fluttered for a second and then stilled. The expression on his face was impenetrable, his eyes dark and intent and his mouth a hard line of resolve.

He turned and went back to his suite and lay down on the bed, fully clothed. He slept, but wakened easily before the first strip of saffron light marked the horizon. Rising, he splashed some tepid water on his face and took a coat from the armoire. He took the revolver from the inner pocket, broke it, examined the shells in the chamber and closed it again. He opened a drawer, reached under his shirts and withdrew a handful of shells. He dropped these into a side pocket, shrugged into the coat and left.

Chapter 34

A MIST HUNG OVER THE CITY AND COOL DAMP AIR SWIRLED around him. All was quiet in the pearly light of the pre-dawn hours as he walked along the thoroughfare and turned down the street that led to the Hotel Mamun. Tahir was perched on the wall opposite the hotel. Breve could see his galabiah shimmering white in the darkness. Breve approached and hoisted himself up onto the wall, his long legs dangling down.

"He has not come out," Tahir whispered.

"Too early yet, if that train is the way he intends to escape," Breve replied. "You better flop down and catch some sleep. We've got a good hour yet before he shows his nose."

"Then what do we do, M'sieur?" Tahir inquired, his eyes alight with excitement.

"I take him by the hand and lead him to the French Consul, who will send him back to France, under guard."

"And if he escapes?"

"He won't, but that's where you come in, Tahir. If he makes a break for it you head him off—block him any way you can, do you understand?"

"He is big man—not so big as you, but bigger than me."

"That's why you are going to carry this—as an emergency measure." Breve withdrew the little derringer from his belt and handed it to Tahir who handled it wonderingly.

"Did you ever shoot one?"

"No, never. But I have my knife. Better I use that," Tahir said regretfully.

"I think the gun will scare him more, and that should be all that is needed. I don't anticipate any difficulty, you see. You are just to be my backup. Here, I'll show you how it works." Breve demonstrated the safety catch and the trigger. "But wait until he is very close to you. It isn't accurate at long distances—too small. Then aim as you would if you were pointing your finger at him. He'll stop pretty quickly. If I read him right he's a monumental coward, and this is only if he makes a break for it before I get to him. He has seen me once, but he's going to be on the alert this morning and he might recognize me."

Tahir tucked the derringer into his sash and lay down atop the wall, pulling up the skirt of his galabiah and cushioning his head on it. In a minute or two he was fast asleep. Breve sat and watched the stars in the bowl of dark blue above the rooftops. They faded slowly and a glow of pink spread like dye through water up from the horizon. It wasn't long before the first eerie call of the muzzeins pierced the stillness and Tahir woke immediately. Jumping down from the wall he rubbed his eyes and prostrated himself several times, facing the pink glow in the east. A little later a water-carrier passed, the jug on his back clanking against the cups hanging on a leather thong. Breve bought water and he and Tahir drank. It was Nile water, not the water from the brackish wells, and it tasted sweet and cool. Cairo had stirred and the street-sleepers wakened. When the odor of coffee wafted toward them Tahir wrinkled his nose.

"There is coffee near here. I will get us some, yes?"

Breve checked his watch and nodded. "There's time."

He dropped a few coins into Tahir's brown hand and the boy took to his heels. He returned only minutes later with two cups in bronze holders. Breve sipped slowly; it was fragrant and strong. No one as yet had stirred from the hotel except the boab who was sweeping the flight of steps that led to the front doors.

Breve felt restive. The anger within him was not going to be assuaged by turning Jack Hidel over to the French Consul. His crimes were heinous; the thought that he might, by some technicality, elude the severe justice of the French courts gnawed at Breve. He jumped from the wall and paced back and forth restlessly. Tahir had run off to return the coffee cups and Breve looked up to see him running wildly toward him.

"He came out of the hotel, by the back way. I saw him, just as . . ."

Breve waited to hear no more but took off running. His boots clattered, a noise that would have gone unheard in the daytime clamor of the streets, but the sound of his running broke the silence now as he rounded the corner. Jack Hidel, a portmanteau in one hand turned to look behind him. His face was blank for a second, then his eyes widened.

"Stop!" Breve called. His deep voice booming out in the morning stillness, but Hidel was already running. His portmanteau fell, its contents spilling.

Tahir shucked his slippers and his bare feet pounded after Breve. Breve drew his pistol out, cocked it and aimed above Hidel's head. He fired, but at that moment Hidel turned into a narrow side street. They followed, just in time to see him turn again. And then they were in the labyrinth of twisting, winding, dark lanes that lay on the periphery of Cairo's poor quarter.

I have to keep him in sight, Breve thought. If I lose him here he could hide in any number of places and I'd never be able to find him. He ran on, with Tahir, lighter and fleeter of foot, gaining. Hidel disappeared around another turn. The mist still lay low here, the buildings so close together that the sun's rays wouldn't pierce the small space between them until almost noon. Breve bumped into a short man and wove around a black-robed woman. Tahir was standing peering down the little narrow lane ahead.

"There are two turnings off of this street. He turned before I saw him," Tahir panted.

"You take the one on the left. I'll take the next one," Breve shouted and ran to the curve where another narrow, dark little lane intersected with this one. Two children, a boy and his sister, the girl's face covered with a strip of cloth though her little stomach was bare, were running ahead of Breve. Breve ran the length of the lane, peering down dark alcoves and into shops— then came to a dead end!

He ran back and met Tahir who was leaping in and out of shops and residences indiscriminately. They searched together, then Tahir slowed and began questioning the shopkeepers and the few people in the street in rapid Arabic. To no avail—all disclaimed having seen a foreigner enter a shop, or they had just come into the street and had seen nothing at all.

Breve was breathing heavily. "My God, he couldn't have just gone up in smoke like a ginn!"

Tahir wiped his brow. "It is simple, of course. Someone is lying," he said matter-of-factly. "He has gone out the back door of one of these buildings and paid the dog to lie."

Breve's jaw clenched. "But which side of the street? We don't know which direction he took. . . . Well, that's simple enough. We'll split up. You go that direction and I'll go to the next street. If we haven't found him I'll meet you at the train station in an hour. That will still be before seven."

They parted quickly. Above them, his face pressed to the bars of a tiny window in the second story of the building that held a tobacco shop, Jack Hidel watched. He too was breathing heavily and perspiration poured down his neck, saturating his collar. He remembered the American, but not his name. What was he to do now? The fellow was hot after him! He would have to chance the train station anyway. He thought of the river, of hiring one of the fellucas. But it would be too slow in case he was pursued. No, he couldn't risk getting caught on one of those boats. He couldn't swim—he would have no retreat. Once the train left Cairo he would be safe. He frowned heavily and rubbed the clammy skin of his face. That fellow was an American, a friend of Darcy's—and he had known Leita! He must have. How did he come to be here? Was it he who had managed Leita's escape from Muhad Bey's last night? It was all too much to understand. His hopes were destroyed now, but if he could just get to Alexandria he could get a steamer there, get off in Italy and drop out of sight. Even if his uncle didn't send the promised annuity, he would be all right for money. Thank God he had always been frugal. Then too, his mother would send him money. He would have to confide in her to some extent, make up some story. No matter—she would pretend to believe whatever he told her. But for the present he had to get away from here—get out of Egypt.

Everything had gone so well, with Leita safe behind those walls and just a few months of waiting ahead. He had thought all danger was behind him; and then that horrible scene last night. Now he believed her, Muhad Bey had lied. He might have known he would, an Arab would do anything for money. He crept down the winding stairs a few minutes after Breve's broad back had disappeared in the mist–shrouded street. He stopped at the bottom and pulled some more money from his pocket and pressed it into the hand of the thin, large-eyed man who came into the dark hall. The fellow spoke only Arabic but Jack's handful of money, accompanied by the warning finger to his lips, had made his message clear when he rushed in to take refuge. The man had coolly denied seeing a foreigner when Tahir had questioned him, though Jack had just dashed through the green baize curtain and was tiptoeing his way up the tiny stairway.

Now Jack let himself out the front door of the shop. The back door he had investigated; it led onto a tiny square of rubbish-strewn dirt and a high wall which separated the shop from another. He lingered in the dark little doorway, making absolutely certain that his pursuer was gone. Then he sidled out, staying close to the sides of the buildings as he made his way along.

He considered hiring a donkey, then dismissed it. He would be too conspicuous in the street. He kept to the walkway, ever-watchful, and avoided the main thoroughfares, making his way toward the train station through narrow little side streets.

The square where the station was situated was set with palm trees and Jack approached it from the north, having detoured far out of the way. He stopped and narrowed his eyes, looking carefully over the scattered groups of people who milled around the square. The crowd was still sparse at this early hour. The slanting rays of the early sun had begun to burn off the mist and though it was still fairly cool, Jack's skin felt clammy and the palms of his hands were wet. His cheeks under the strain were pale and his eyes were bulging slightly. The fear that swept through him made his throat dry and he ventured a few steps from the corner and bought a raisin sherbet, drinking the spicy, sweet stuff greedily while his eyes swept the station square.

He saw no one resembling the tall American. Jack deliberated. He would wait here in the shadow of the buildings until just before the train left, then jump on as it moved out of the station. He settled back in the shadow of a doorway and tried to still his heavy breathing. It wouldn't do to be panicky; if he just kept his head he would soon be on his way.

Then his body went rigid. Surely not, it couldn't be! That tall figure darting through the traffic at the end of the square, was it the American? Jack squinted. The dust was rising already. He couldn't quite make out the silhouette that had alarmed him and now it had disappeared. He craned his neck, searching the crowd frantically, then took a hesitant step out of the shadows. He drew in his breath and jumped back into the doorway. The American was standing in the shadow of a palm tree at the end of the square. He had glimpsed him as he moved from one palm to another, quickly, but not so quickly that Jack hadn't identified his height and the width of his shoulders, though he couldn't discern his features at this distance.

Hidel groaned and mopped his face. That silly bitch was the cause of all this, he thought bitterly. And now his one avenue of escape was cut off. He couldn't pit himself against that ungainly brute. The whole thing was humiliating, and he was in danger, great danger! To

573

be sent back to France, manacled and accused of a crime! No one would understand his reasons. He hadn't harmed the girl, but his jeopardy would be no less for that. He had to get away, somehow. And then he bethought himself of the one other means possible of reaching Alexandria. It was a day's ride, but he could make it, with a change of horses!

He scuttled out of the doorway and ran up the thoroughfare. It was risky, but he was positive he had seen a stable along here. He stopped and asked a porter and received directions. Just a bit further on! He felt like shouting with relief!

Tahir was trotting down the middle of the street, his head turning from side to side as he watched every passer-by. He had traveled south, then cut back and now was nearing the station. He hadn't seen the Englishman, nor had anyone he questioned seen him. The fellow had disappeared like a ginn, as Mr. Pinchon said, but Tahir wasn't discouraged. He had come upon two of his friends and sent them scattering with the promise of many piastres if they found the Englishman.

He passed the high archway that led to the stables, searching the faces of the few Europeans who were out at this hour. Then his feet skidded in the dust of the road and he wheeled. He had glimpsed a figure in the shadow of the arch into the stables, saw it only in passing, almost without focusing, but now the possibility smote him. Of course the fellow might search out a horse. He decided to reconnoiter and have a word or two with the stableman, putting him on watch.

The gate was ajar when Tahir approached it carefully, listening to the conversation that came clearly from behind it.

"Three hundred piastres. A fine horse—good withers." The broken English of the stableman was followed by Jack's protest.

"Too much money. Two hundred piastres, and you must give me one that will carry me to Alexandria. I won't have one of your old nags."

"Two hundred and fifty piastres—no less," the stableman countered, preparing for his first battle of the day.

Tahir had already taken to his heels. He found Breve and after a few moments of whispering the two set off down another street. The horse Breve purchased was white, dappled with a little gray; it was fairly young and its mane was thick and flourishing. Afterward Breve and Tahir conferred, with Tahir drawing a diagram in the sand which Breve followed attentively. Then Breve cantered off on the horse, leaving Tahir, his white teeth bared in a grin, waving after him.

It's a good plan, Breve thought, as he made the turns Tahir had outlined in the dust. He was taking shortcuts, one after another, to reach the road to Alexandria well before Hidel could start out on it. Then he could ride back toward the city to meet him and cut him off. It would be on the open road this time, with no chance of Hidel's escaping. Now he concentrated his memory on Tahir's directions, which had been involved, but meant evading all the dead-end streets as well as the major thoroughfares between here and the open road.

It was a gathering of hovels that Breve wended his way through at the last before coming out onto the open road that led north to the capital city of Egypt. The road was far from empty. There were asses and mules, with their drivers urging them on, pedestrians, and other horsemen. The fellaheen labored already in the black dirt of the fields which sloped away on either side. Yellow-green shoots pushed up through the soil; the crops of beans and millet were burgeoning in September, Egypt's spring.

He was quite close to the city when he spotted Hidel

and spurred his horse to a gallop. The distance between them was dotted with travelers but Breve would have covered it quickly, giving Hidel no time to turn at the pace he was going, if it hadn't been for the wedding procession that emerged suddenly from a side road.

Hidel had squinted his eyes, staring ahead along the sunlit eighth of a mile that separated him from the white horse with its tall rider. It couldn't be the American, he thought wildly. Not coming from the north! He had been at the train station! It must be another European! But just a moment before the wedding procession cascaded into the road Jack uttered an oath. It was him, no doubt of it, and coming hell-bent! Breve's crinkly black hair and broad shoulders were illuminated unmistakably in that instant and Jack drew sharply at the reins. The horse gave a whinny as the bit pulled against its tongue and then it wheeled. Jack lashed it cruelly and bent low in the saddle as the horse struck out in a full gallop.

The drummers were guiding their colorfully bedecked donkeys full into the roadway, pounding exuberantly on their darabukkehs, the drums shaped like a huge, skin-covered goblet. Breve uttered a mighty oath and swerved his horse just in time to avoid colliding with the first donkey. The road was filled with the celebrants. Women in shades of rose and yellow, their yashmaks covering their faces up to the sparkling dark eyes, rode on donkeys with the specially built-up saddles that looked so precarious.

Breve looked to either side of the road. A wide, water-filled ditch ran along both edges. He could have jumped that but the dirt beyond would surely have thrown his horse. It was mire, soggy, wet mud that would have broken a leg as sure as the devil. And there was no getting through this milling crowd! They were bent on festivity and it was taken for granted that all passage would halt as they filed across. There were richly dressed children on small ponies and then a lumbering, languid camel bedecked with gold piastres. The bride rode atop the lugubrious beast, veiled and ornamented with a string of jewels across her forehead. Breve set his jaw and swore again. Hidel had seen him, he knew from the way he had turned and spurred his horse. Right now the bastard was covering precious ground—and would this goddamned circus never stop? Now there were two near-naked wrestlers, their bodies oiled and gleaming as they danced along, striking poses. The male dancer who followed them wore an embroidered jacket and his eyes were outlined vividly in kohl. A chain of gold discs hung down his back as he undulated and writhed, the muscles of his belly moving to the rhythms of the drums as if they had a life of their own. More drummers brought up the tail of the procession and when finally they joined the file Breve spurred his horse. The dust flew up from its hooves as Breve went flying down the road to the left of the wedding procession. It was the height of rudeness, to cover the group with dust, and they gazed after him in stricken surprise as the horse grew smaller in the distance.

He had lost sight of Hidel but after five minutes of hard riding saw him dimly ahead. And it was fortunate that he did, because Hidel reined his horse abruptly to the right and set off with the sun at his back.

Breve reached the spot where the main road inter-sected with the other, more narrow one and turned his horse onto it. He could see Jack far ahead and wondered where he would end up. Then he saw the looming shapes in the distance, purplish-gray and towering over the flat expanse of desert. This was the road to Gizeh and those were the pyramids. Hidel was a fool—thank God! He would have been better off to ride into the city. Breve almost relaxed. The fellow was as good as caught.

The sand was bathed in a clear yellow light with pools of violet shadows. The sphinx reared ahead, a gray pile reclining there in the desert with eagles wheeling and gliding around its giant, protruding ears. Breve barely glanced at it as his horse pelted past. The sphinx faced the sun that had traveled a quarter of the distance now toward its meridian and the reddish-gray stone above its staring eyes was white with bird droppings.

The mud-brick houses of Gizeh flew past in a blur. Hidel didn't stop, but rode on even faster. He was elated; he knew that once he reached the pyramids, with the head start he had, he would never be found. He had been here before, several times, and had been struck by the passageways into the three pyramids. The wild American would eventually go back into Cairo for reinforcements and then he would simply ride out and make it to Alexandria during the night. If his horse was taken, as it probably would be, he would buy one in Gizeh. The plan was foolproof.

Breve drew in his breath with awe as he came closer to the pyramids. Nothing had prepared him for their size. The first one, he knew, was the pyramid of Cheops. What appeared from a distance to be a smooth cone was actually rough stone. The blocks looked to be about three feet in height and they were a yellowish limestone. The top of the pyramid shone more whitely. It was still partially covered by a limestone casing of a lighter color. Hidel's figure and that of his horse were a black, swiftly moving silhouette in the distance and Breve speeded up.

Hidel turned his horse to the left when he drew close to the pyramid of Cheops. He was deep in its shadow and he rode even harder now, past the first corner and veered round to the north side. He pulled on the reins and jumped for it, all in the same moment, falling flat onto the hot sand. His eyes and mouth were filled with it, blinding and scalding. The long, chilly nights weren't long enough or cold enough to pull the heat from it. He leaped up, scratching wildly at his face and got a fingerhold on the top of the first block. He hoisted himself fairly easily to the top and only then did he take his handkerchief out and scrub at his sand-gritty eyes and mouth. It was like mud, mixed as it was with his perspiration, but never mind, he could see, and he had to hurry. He had almost fifty feet to climb and he must accomplish it swiftly.

He scrambled wildly, his long legs flailing as he struggled to reach the summit of each block. His chest ached now with a sharp, pulsating pain. He groaned, but didn't stop. It seemed an hour, with the sun beating down mercilessly now and his hands were bleeding from scraping the rough limestone. At the top of one block he wiped his forehead and left a scarlet trail of sticky blood.

Only three more of the vast chunks to scale! He could see the dark circle of the opening above and he threw every last ounce of his strength into pulling himself up, again and again, his muscles straining, the pain coursing through his chest and his watery blue eyes bulging with effort.

No one had ever really observed that Jack Hidel, despite his diffidence and timidity, his waspish pruderies and hypocrisy, was innately a fiercely aggressive man. He had conceived and brought off Leita's abduction with determination, as well as comparative ease. When it came to his own welfare his diffidence fell away and he was possessed of ferocity, a ferocity that had always been untouched by any misgivings about the well-being or needs of anyone but himself. Socially he was inept, but in the business of survival he was not to be bested. He was as single-minded as a wharf rat, fighting for the corner of a grain bag with teeth bared.

At last, he was there! Without pausing he threw himself into the dark opening on the wall of the pyramid, then dropped, panting and trembling. He didn't know whether the final steps of his ascent had been witnessed or not. He had been afraid to look down, but now he turned and peered out without exposing his head. Nothing! He hadn't been close enough behind him!

He looked at his horse which had wandered off several yards and allowed himself a grimace of satisfaction before he turned and began the descent down the smooth, even shaft.

He had come along this corridor before, with a guide. It was shaped like a large sewer and descended through the masonry down into the rocky soil where it ended in an unfinished, underground chamber. Further up, about two hundred feet from the entrance, a corridor branched off, ascending. This one led to the Queen's chamber if you took a turn to the left. It was a small, square room formed of granite blocks. He knew that there were two narrow shafts leading from the King's chamber to the exterior of the pyramid. Whether these were large enough to admit a man's body he didn't know. The corridor he was in now had been constructed to facilitate the sliding coffins. He inched ahead on his hands and knees. The blackness was so dense that he seemed to be in a vacuum. The gun that he had carried since the morning of his departure from the Gare de Lyon rested inside his belt, the metal warmed by his flesh.

Chapter 35

BREVE PULLED UP AS HE REACHED THE PYRAMID OF Cheops. The dark silhouette of horse and rider had disappeared! Hidel had ridden into the wide shadow cast by the towering pyramid and then simply disappeared. For Christ's sake, was the fellow going to play hide and seek? He probably was, Breve thought grimly, and wheeled his horse to the right. He rode around three sides of the pyramid before he spotted Hidel's horse. It took some little time to cover this distance. This one pyramid covered a space of thirteen acres.

Now Breve stared disbelievingly. Hidel's horse was riderless, its reins dragging in the sand. What kind of madness was this? There was no place to go—not even a tree to hide under. Only these towering edifices marked the desert floor.

Breve squinted around. The sunlight glared whitely over miles of sand and the looming silence of the four-thousand-year-old tombs. Breve blew out his breath in a long sigh, and then started violently at the sound of a giggle. He turned in his saddle and looked down.

There, in the shadows, were two little urchins, one evidently a girl, since she had a scrap of dingy cloth tied round her hips but her face covered up to her eyes by a long yashmak which swung down to her protruding brown stomach. The two children had a goatskin bag between them and a string of cups hung from the little boy's shoulder. He was probably eight years old, at the most, and the hank of hair that hung from the crown of his head was bound with red and gold thread.

Breve relaxed, slumping down into the sweat-dampened saddle. The giggle came again and the small girl pointed at Breve, chattering in Arabic to the boy. Breve grinned. They were like all the Egyptian children he had seen, friendly and inquisitive as kittens.

"What is in your bag?" he asked.

There was no answer but another giggle from the girl and a bright-eyed smile from the boy. Breve pointed to the goatskin bag and repeated the question.

The boy gazed at him, then burst out with the words "one piastre." He took a cup and pantomimed drinking.

Breve looked around sharply. There was not a trace of his quarry and Hidel hadn't had time to make it around the next pyramid, he was certain. He took a coin from his pocket and the boy, still grinning, removed the stopper from the neck of the bag, sloshed liquid into one of the cups and handed the cup to Breve.

Breve tasted it, wondering how many had drunk from this cup before him and if it was ever washed. The liquid was good, flavored with orange flowers and sugar. He drained it and signaled for another. These two had obviously come from the village to set up shop with their sherbet bag for whatever parties might come out to the pyramids today. He supposed they got a tidy little sum by their efforts; the price was four times what it had been in Cairo. He flipped them two extra coins and handed the cup down.

The little girl took it and wiped it out with the tail of her yashmak. Breve chuckled, then looked around again. Where in hell had that bastard gotten to? Struck by a thought he spoke to the children, indicating himself, then casting a hand around in a questioning gesture. The boy looked at his sister and they both giggled this time. The little girl looked up high on the wall of the pyramid and bent double in a gale of laughter. Breve shrugged. There was nothing to be gotten from this pair, that was evident! But his eye caught Hidel's horse and he decided to try again.

Pointing to the horse he then spread his hands wide and, putting his hands to his forehead, pantomimed a search.

The boy nodded his head, laughing all the while, and the little girl was convulsed with merriment. Deciding he had more to do than entertain these two, Breve started his horse off at a walk while he made up his mind what course to take. Hidel had to be somewhere in the periphery of this one pyramid. It was just possible he had scattered around to another side, eluding him in a macabre game of hide-and-seek. He would cover all four sides again at a fast trot; that would force him out into the open.

He heard the giggle again and looked down, surprised to see that the children were following him. They had propped the bag against the stones and were skipping along behind, their calloused little feet impervious to the hot sand. The girl ran alongside now, one arm stretched upward as she pointed to the pyramid wall. She was still laughing. Breve looked, but saw nothing, particularly nothing that would evoke any merriment. The boy ran ahead, his skinny brown legs flying over the sand, until he reached a point almost at the corner Breve was approaching. Then he too pointed upward. When Breve drew abreast of him the boy grabbed the bridle of the horse and settled himself, his feet wide apart and braced.

"I'm not getting off now," Breve said. Many Arab children followed a horseman, waiting for him to dismount so they could gain a few coins by waiting with the reins held tight in their sweaty brown hands.

The boy threw a puzzled glance at his sister. Then he pointed upward, vigorously waving his finger. The little girl scrambled acrobatically to the top of a stone and settled herself as if to wait.

Breve looked upward, shading his eyes from that sun. The boy was looking at him expectantly. Breve frowned—something was afoot here—and then his eyes fell on the small, black circle high on the face of the pyramid.

A cognitive shiver went down his spine. He remembered now reading of the shafts that led into these places. But it was a good fifty or sixty feet up. Could Hidel have climbed that? He realized in that moment that he could have!

Lowering his gaze, Breve entered into a drawn-out pantomime with the two urchins, involving climbing and another man. At the end of it he was satisfied that they had seen Hidel making the ascent. In fact, that had been the source of the little girl's amusement. They had followed him, assuming he was going to join his friend, looking forward to the spectacle of another strangely dressed person clambering up the side of the pyramid. Hidel was a clever devil, by God. That was why he had headed for Gizeh.

Breve leaped down from his horse and shucked his

jacket. He drew the pistol out of the breast pocket and stuck it behind him into his belt. He gave the boy a round handful of coins and signified that he wanted him to stay with his horse. The little girl watched with interested amusement as Breve scaled the first block, and then scrambled up onto her knees in order to view the rest of his ascent.

Breve grinned to himself. Those two were a pair of rabbit's feet; they were his luck for the day.

The blocks of limestone were hot to the touch and so rough that his palms were soon bleeding. It took a full ten minutes for him to climb the fifty feet up to the opening and he realized that Hidel could still have been on the face of the pyramid when he rounded the corner. He hadn't thought to look up, of course.

The coolness of the shaft when he entered it was a relief and he had gone several feet on his hands and knees before he heard a sudden fluttering that sounded like a hundred wings. The awakened bats fluttered and brushed over his back and head. He shuddered as the sounds of their tiny, squeaking cries filled the shaft. He kept his eyes closed, there was no need to see anyway, and tightened his lips as the velvety wings skimmed past his face. The floor of the tunnel was slippery with bat dung.

When he reached the shaft that turned off to the right he hesitated. God knows where it leads, but I'll take it and eliminate it if necessary. I can always come back and continue on this one. The air was cool and if it hadn't been for the horror of the bats he would have been supremely comfortable, if only for being out of the blinding sun.

Below, in the Queen's chamber, Jack Hidel raised up, listening. He had been leaning against the welcome

585

coolness of the granite stones. He carried tinder for his pipe, luckily, but saw no reason to use it now. His only problem would be thirst, and he would simply steel himself to wait through the day until sundown. Under cover of darkness he could get back down the wall of the pyramid. But now he heard a definite sound. It was far too early in the day for any guided parties. Close to sunset was considered the best time to view the splendors of the pyramids, then the trip back to Cairo could be made in the coolness of the early evening. There it was again! A scraping sound—and it came from the tunnel.

He crawled along the floor till he could feel the opening and listened. The bats were squeaking in a shrill little symphony. Someone was coming along that tunnel, and coming in silence. No conversation, as there would be if it were ordinary sightseers. And no glow from a light either. It couldn't possibly be the American. But it could be, he thought with a flash of alarm. The scraping sounds were drawing closer and he hunkered down, his eyes glittering in the dark like those of a cat. Then he crawled quickly into a far corner of the room and pressed himself against the wall. If he didn't have a light he couldn't see him. He would wait it out. But he pulled at the gun, drawing it from his belt. If worse came to worse it would be like shooting grouse, and he had always been better than good at that!

Breve reached the end of the tunnel and paused. The one thing he hadn't thought to carry was a torch of some kind. It was pitch black and he had no idea how steep a drop he had to the floor—or if there was a floor. But . . . the back of his neck was prickling in the old way. He had been ambushed more than once when he served in the cavalry. Each time he had felt the same

586

premonitory prickling and it had served him well. Hidel was here—he would bank on it—so there must be a floor. He forced his body to loosen in order to be relaxed when he fell, sat down on the edge of the opening and dropped. He almost chuckled aloud. It had only been a few feet! He drew out his revolver and threw off the safety. No point in being quiet now. If Hidel was in here he had heard him well ahead. Then he moved cautiously along the wall for a few paces. He stopped and waited several minutes, listening. He was positive he could hear breathing other than his own.

"Hidel, you may as well give yourself up." The echoes of his voice bounced back, the words resounding and then dying.

Jack Hidel was terrified, murderously terrified. The only retreat from the Queen's chamber was through the tunnel. Wait—let him speak again, no matter how the deep, thundering echoes frightened him. He could place him by his voice, but he wanted to be accurate. The echoes were misleading. Once he had killed him he could get out, and by the time his body was found he would be aboard ship. Let him speak again. His eyes bulged, straining to see into the darkness and his palm spurted sweat onto the butt of the pistol.

"Hidel, you may as well give yourself up now. The American Vice-Consul is on his way here. My Arab servant followed me and went back for help. You haven't much longer." Would that it were true, thought Breve, waiting for the answer.

Jack Hidel sweated this one out. He had seen Breve from that upper window speaking with an Arab. In fact, it had looked surprisingly like Tahir, but with the turbans they all looked alike from a distance. He chewed this over. It was possible, of course, that an Arab had been with the American on the road outside

587

Cairo. If his story was true, then it wasn't he that hadn't long, it was the American! He couldn't afford to delay now—he had to kill him. But he had to make him speak again. He had been so rattled by what the American said that he couldn't place his voice exactly.

He deliberated. . . . "What if I do come out?" he answered, his own voice ringing out harshly and bouncing back into the echoing darkness.

"I will take you to the French Consul. You will have to be . . ." The shot rang out and chipped the stone behind Breve's ear.

Breve threw himself onto the floor. The son of a bitch had a gun! And he had almost gotten him. He had been a damned, careless fool not to assume that he was armed. Breve waited till his breathing had quieted and while he waited he heard a tentative movement. It came from directly ahead—a small, sliding sound. Breve lay motionless and waited for the sound again. And Jack moved. He couldn't wait—he was crawling toward Breve.

"I didn't really think you would shoot at an unarmed man," Breve's voice echoed in the darkness.

Hidel caught his breath. He hadn't gotten him after all! But—he was unarmed. He had waited for a return shot and when none came he decided either that his own shot had gone home or the American didn't have a gun. His luck had held!

"I'm getting out of here—now! If you try to stop me it will be on your head," Jack's voice rang out triumphantly.

"You don't think I would let you get away scot-free . . ." Breve called out and then threw himself to one side in anticipation. And it happened! The cowardly bastard had leveled his gun and shot unerringly toward a man he thought to be unarmed. But Breve had watched carefully, waiting for the telltale flash. It had come from where he judged Hidel to be, directly across from him and a little to the left now.

Breve took aim in the dead, coal-black silence of the tomb and fired. The scream that came told him he had hit his mark. He shot again then, coolly and carefully.

"I realize how disappointed you must be to find that we are more evenly matched." He spoke through clenched teeth, but only silence answered. He could hear Hidel's rasping breath and he waited, waited several minutes while the rasping continued.

"I'm coming over to get you. I'm going to drag you out of here. If you're badly wounded I just might save your life, but I'll worry about that later," Breve called. There was no answer and Breve began crawling slowly in the direction of the breathing, his gun ready in his right hand.

Breve touched a leg with his left hand. The man didn't move. Breve sat back on his haunches and searched Hidel's pockets. He found the tinder and struck it. The flickering light showed Jack sprawled on the stone floor. The wound, the major wound was in his abdomen. Scarlet blood was pulsing out over his lower shirt front and there was another bullet wound in his right shoulder. His eyes were closed but his short, stiff lashes were fluttering.

I must have gotten him in an artery, Breve thought, looking at the blood gushing out and down onto Hidel's belt buckle. He tucked his gun back into his belt and took Hidel under the shoulders. He was heavy, a dead weight, as Breve dragged him toward the tunnel opening. Breve lifted him up and shoved him feet first into the down-slanting corridor, then climbed in himself and commenced to push and shove.

Hidel was groaning and barely conscious, but the descent was easy. It was on reaching the turnoff that things got difficult. Breve turned him into the ascending passageway, making several tries before his legs could be gotten straight into the opening. Then he crawled around him and with his hands in Hidel's armpits backed slowly and laboriously up the twenty feet or so till he reached the opening. Daylight and hot sun greeted him.

A cry came from below and Breve looked down to see small brown arms waving. He waved back and then began the struggle of getting Hidel out onto the ledge of stone. A full fifty feet of descent awaited him, with a wounded, semi-conscious man. He breathed deeply and jumped down to the next ledge. Reaching up, he grasped Hidel's arm and leg and pulled. The full weight of Hidel's body fell on him and Breve teetered precariously on the ledge for a long moment, then threw himself forward against the stone. More cautious now, he laid Hidel, who was moaning loudly, on the very edge before jumping down and pulling him after him.

The boy and girl watched, fascinated, as he made his way, block by block down the angled side of the pyramid with the inert body of the other man in his arms. When he jumped to the ground he stood weaving for a moment, panting from his exertions. The boy pulled at his trouser leg and held up a cup of the sweetened water. The boy's face was worried as he looked from Breve to the body of Hidel which still lay on the last ledge.

Breve sighed explosively and ran his hand over the boy's head. He drank from the cup and then pulled Hidel down and propped him against the stone. The boy had refilled the cup and handed it with both hands to Breve. His sister stood by watching as Breve pressed the cup to the lips of the bleeding man. There was no response. Breve wiped some of the fluid over Hidel's mouth and then Hidel swallowed once. Breve emptied his pocket of coins and held them out to the boy, who selected two. Breve shook his head and pushed the boy's palms together, then filled them with the coins.

He laid Hidel's body over his saddle and mounted the horse. The children stood watching after him as he started out, keeping the horse to a walk, down the road back to Cairo. Then they ran whooping back to the goatskin bag and dragged it behind them, shouting and laughing, exuberant over the pile of coins still clutched tightly in the boy's hand.

Chapter 36

Leita had slept and wakened again. When a servant entered, followed by two porters carrying a tub, Doctor Abernathy excused himself and Leita stepped into the tepid water gratefully. The servant swept Leita's hair to the top of her head, fixed it with an ivory comb and then began to wash her. The scent of musk rose in the room as Leita's body was oiled after the bath. The violet silk shirt and robe that Leita had worn when Breve carried her from the seraglio lay on the back of a chair. It had been washed and pressed and the rose and white striped trousers were clean and unwrinkled now. The servant dressed her and then brushed her hair, fixing the two locks that hung beside her cheeks in the prescribed fashion.

Leita felt stronger and was unaccountably hungry again. She waited impatiently while the servant fastened the ankle bracelets around her slender ankles. Where was Breve? Surely he was awake by now. She was sorely tempted to open the door that connected their rooms but decided against it. She had waited this long—a little longer could be borne. But not easily, she smiled to herself. Till her dying day she would never forget the sight of his face—had it only been last night? When he threw back the burnoose and she saw that it was Breve, his dark eyes glowing in the night and that wondrous smile! Her very knees grew weak at the thought of it. She looked in the mirror and felt disconsolate for a moment. The swarthy skin, that ludicrously black hair falling down over her shoulders; well, she would just have to wait for it to grow out. She examined her hands, still stained with henna despite the scrubbing she had given them. Actually it wasn't too unattractive on the nails. She peered down at her toes where the nails glowed a dusky red—pretty, really.

The porters re-entered and removed the tub and the servant came back with a tray. Heavenly! Boiled eggs and that clotted milk she had grown to like, with its faintly sour taste. She ate ravenously, drank the sweetened raisin-water and wiped up the last streak of egg with the flat bread.

She was sitting cross-legged on the floor beside the wide tray, just finishing, when the door opened and Armand entered with Eugene and Sir Charles behind him. Leita was transfixed for a moment, but Armand's eyes slid over her without recognition and looked past her to the empty bed. Eugene too only glanced at her.

"Where is your mistress?" Armand asked impatiently and Leita burst out laughing.

Armand's perplexed gaze rested on her and Eugene frowned, then gave a whoop and strode over and picked her up as if she had been a doll. He swung her around and hugged her and she choked on the mouthful of pastry she hadn't been able to swallow, then kissed his cheek as she squeezed her arms tightly about his neck.

Eugene set her down finally and burst out laughing too, wiping his handkerchief over his face. "Sticky—just like when you were little. Your kisses are sticky!"

Armand stood smiling and Leita ran into his arms. He held her close, patting her back as if she had been a lost child suddenly restored to him. She kissed him fervently, and then they all began to talk at once. Sir Charles took her hands in his, his sharp features aglow with pleasure, then abandoned ceremony and enveloped her in a hug which she returned in full measure. Questions poured out and Doctor Abernathy entered and officiated at the opening of the wine which he had ordered. Leita answered them all, radiant now.

"I think she will mend quickly," Doctor Abernathy assured Armand. "She sleeps well and she has begun to eat heartily and her system hasn't rejected the food as it sometimes does after a long fast. She went eight days without eating, you know."

"Why in the name of God didn't you eat? Do you mean that you were starved, too?" Eugene exploded.

Leita commenced an explanation which had to be abridged in order to go back to the beginning. The room fell silent as she told the story of her abduction. Armand and Eugene sat with grim faces as they listened to her tale of the train station and the ether-soaked handkerchief. Sir Charles paced the floor, muttering to himself and breaking off. When Leita told of her miscarriage Armand met Sir Charles's eyes.

"Thank God for that," Sir Charles said quietly.

Leita stopped and looked questioningly at Sir Charles.

"I will tell you the whole story at a later date, my dear, but suffice it to say that it is probable that any child fathered by that man would be blighted. That you were so ill is dreadful and frightening, but that you no longer carry Jack's child is one of providence's kinder blows."

Leita looked pensive for a moment, then went on. When she finished no one spoke for a few minutes. Then Eugene let out a fulsome sigh. "It's the second time Breve has rescued you. Thank God he was here."

"I understand that you and he were close friends back in America," Armand said gently.

Leita dropped her eyes. She had given so little thought to what exactly would happen now. It had been so intoxicating to be free—to know that Breve was here. But what now? What of Armand? And for that matter, what of Breve? He had rejected her before, time and again. Would he do the same thing now? Save her and go away?

Armand went on, seeming not to notice her silence. "Eugene has something he wants to tell you, something he feels you should know."

Sir Charles gave a discreet little cough and wandered over to the open door beside the balcony. Leita looked at them, a trifle perplexed. Something serious was being alluded to, touched on, in this moment, but she didn't know what it was. Doctor Abernathy felt the constraint and excused himself, closing the door softly behind him.

Armand continued then. "You know, of course, my dear, that our marriage, though it was a surprisingly great source of pleasure to me, was primarily because you were in dire need of protection at the time. Those circumstances have changed." Armand spoke softly, but his eyes as they met Leita's were clear and untroubled. "Whatever you desire, however you might wish to change your life now, will meet with no resistance from me. If you choose to go on as we began, so be it. I will be pleased. If you find that another future beckons you, I can only assure you that you will embark on it with the fullest of good wishes and love from me."

Tears stung Leita's eyes. She had known that Armand wasn't in love with her; she had diverted him, been a companionable friend to him, but she had never touched that deep pool of loss and sadness that lay within him. But what could she say to him now?

Eugene saved her. "I may as well tell her the other facts right now, since I've decided she's entitled to know."

Armand nodded and carried his wineglass out onto the balcony where he joined Sir Charles. Leita sat very still on the small chair. Eugene's face wore a solemn expression.

"Back when I visited Chicago last spring, Leita, Breve told me something one night—told me in confidence. I kept this confidence. I don't even think he would have told me then if he hadn't had quite a bit to drink—as we both had."

Leita smoothed her fingers nervously. What could be this serious?

Breve told me how his father died and some of the circumstances that led up to it. His mother, too, and those deaths have haunted him ever since. His feeling for you . . . well, he was convinced and had been since the beginning that it was inappropriate, impossible, really."

"But why?" Leita burst out. "He knew that I loved him!"

Eugene sighed. "Perhaps I'm not doing the right thing . . . but I decided in Paris that you should be able to judge for yourself, judge whether Breve's reluctance was well-founded. So, I'm going to break his confidence."

"I wish you would!" Leita declared fervently.

"Breve's father and mother fought bitterly, and in the end they both died because . . . well, primarily because Breve's father told him that Breve's grandmother had been a black woman."

Leita sat bolt upright. "How in the world did that happen?"

"I'll begin at the beginning," Eugene said earnestly, and he did, revealing what he knew from the journals of Breve's grandfather and father, right up to the day of Breve's father's death in the burning warehouse. He spared nothing. When he finished, Leita sat back, as limp and exhausted as he.

Her mind raced over the times that Breve had thrust her away, over the months in Indiana when he had ignored her so completely. So that was why! His father's Negro blood had not only destroyed his marriage but indirectly killed him and the wife he loved. Horrible! Horrible beyond words!

And Breve himself was one-quarter Negro. The man she loved, had loved forever it seemed, the man she wanted above all for her husband and the father of her children was, to all intents and purposes, a Negro.

Leita was a child of the South and the feelings that welled up in her now were those of a girl who had been raised with blacks, played with them, but knew in her bones that they were slaves.

She examined her feelings now—the slight, almost atavistic recoil she felt at the words. Black was black, and even one-fourth Negro was still Negro . . . anyone knew that. Breve's hair, of course, dark, almost blue-black, like a crow's wing . . . and wavy. The tan of his skin, dusky even in the winter. She swallowed. The idea smote her with such force that she reeled inwardly. And he had never told her—that had been his secret! Of course, he had anticipated her reaction. At that moment she was very glad that Eugene had been the one to present her with the truth.

The loud knock that sounded at the door just then made her jump from her chair. Eugene went to the door and when he opened it a tall, pink-cheeked man with sparkling blue eyes entered.

"Are you Miss Johnston?" he spoke directly to Leita. She nodded numbly.

The man turned to Eugene with a questioning look.

"I'm Miss Johnston's brother. Eugene Johnston at your service, sir."

Eugene extended his hand and Daniel O'Connell shook it vigorously. "I'm Daniel O'Connell. I'm the American Vice-Consul here and I thought I'd better come and tell you right away. I just received word that Breve Pinchon is at the police station, in the Cadi's office. He's been wounded, I understand, and he's brought back that Englishman. I'm on my way there now, but I heard that you had arrived too and I thought you might like to come along with me."

Eugene had already snatched his walking stick and Armand and Sir Charles were introduced quickly to the dark-haired young man.

"We'll be back as soon as we can," Eugene called back over his shoulder to Leita.

"Rest, and don't exert yourself, dear." Armand bent and brushed her cheek with a kiss in passing.

Leita sat, almost unseeing, staring at the wall opposite her. It was a long time before she rose, then she went to the pier glass and gazed at her reflection. She surveyed herself dispassionately, still numb with shock. She assessed her still-stained skin, the dull black hair. How superficial it all is, she thought . . . what ridiculous ideas that can prevent two people who love each other from being together! Breve has been fighting a meaningless ghost, where I'm concerned anyway.

She turned and ran toward the door. She opened it and trotted down the long stairway, holding her robe up with one hand. Through the lobby she ran out into the street. It took several long minutes to find a donkey driver who could understand her, but find one she did and urged him on with all speed. She was stared at, this unveiled woman; those that passed her assumed that she was a prostitute.

When the donkey halted in front of the glaringly white building Leita bade the driver to wait and ran up the shallow steps into the courtyard. Her ankle bracelets jingled as she ran, threading her way through the hundred or so cats that lay sprawled in the sun. The stray cats of Cairo came here to be fed daily; it was an old tradition and one of the functions of the Cadi. Leita looked around wildly. Several arched doorways punctuated the long, low building ahead of her. A man in uniform was crossing the courtyard, his ebony-handled flyswhisk tapping at his puttees.

"I am looking for the office of the Cadi," Leita cried.

"You have trouble, madame? Let me take you to the proper office."

"No, you don't understand. My brother and . . ." she hesitated, "and someone else are with the Cadi. I must go there now. They are expecting me," she lied determinedly.

He shrugged and ivory teeth gleamed below his thick mustache. "Very well. This way please."

Oh, let him not be badly wounded, she prayed silently. It had been her prayer during the agonizingly long donkey ride. Let him be all right and I will never ask anything of you again, she implored God.

The uniformed man tapped lightly at a closed door

and was answered with an Arabic growl. The door opened.

"This . . . woman says she is expected in your office," he began, then grabbed his fly-whisk which caught on Leita's robe as she sped past him.

The Cadi sat behind an ornate desk and Breve stood in front of it. His face was black with dust and grime and his shirt, arms and hands were reddish-brown with dried blood. He stared at Leita during the moment it took her to reach him. She threw her arms out, her own eyes wide with fear.

"Oh, my darling, are you badly hurt?"

Leita catapulted against his tall body and clenched her arms around him, gripping tightly as she burrowed her cheek in his chest. Breve's arms slid around her and his own cheek was buried in her hair.

Eugene had told him in a whispered aside, just a few minutes ago, that Leita knew his story now. "I took it on myself," he had whispered, half-apologetically. "I decided it was her right to know."

Now he whispered in her ear, "I'm not hurt at all," and felt her arms grip him tighter.

"Are you going to take me home?" she whispered, "and never leave me again?"

He felt the lump in his throat rise, but managed to speak through it. "I just might do that. I just might." But never was he more certain of anything in his life.

Epilogue

THE ENGINES OF THE STEAMSHIP CHUGGED IN AN EVEN rhythm as the boat pulled out of the harbor at Alexandria. The two slender shapes that rose into the sky were growing smaller by the moment. Cleopatra's obelisks were left behind, as was the famous lighthouse that had beckoned to Napoleon.

Breve drew Leita's cape more closely around her shoulders and kissed the top of her head tenderly as they stood watching the mauve shoreline recede in the distance.

"I never want to see Egypt again," Leita said firmly.

Breve chuckled. "But I've promised Armand that we will come back next year for the opening of the canal. Dan O'Connell, too. That's going to be a bang-up party, with the Empress coming on her own private yacht and every nabob in Europe here. Besides, it's a beautiful country."

"I suppose it is," Leita agreed dreamily. The sky above was a glittering cerulean blue and she remembered almost with nostalgia the beautiful minarets and dome-shaped mosques gleaming in the clear air.

"He'll be back in Paris now, locked up in jail, won't he?"

"In jail or under guard in a hospital. I'm still surprised that he lived, but it's just as well. Dying would have been too good for him. Devil's Island will be a whole lot better," Breve said grimly.

"Except they won't send him there. He didn't murder anyone," Leita objected.

"It wasn't for lack of trying. The devil is just lucky, that's all."

Leita pondered this, then a secret little smile curved her lips and she looked up into Breve's tanned face. "Not as lucky as I am," she whispered.

His eyes shone down on her tenderly and she snuggled closer to him, feeling the excitement of his long, muscular body against her.